Dragon Goddess

Complete Series

Copyright © 2022 by Sedona Ashe

Gobble Ink, LLC

Cover artwork by Manuela Serra

https://manuelaserradesign.com/

Interior formatting by Cauldron Press

www.cauldronpress.ca

WARNING POSSIBLE SPOILERS-
A SENSITIVITY NOTE FOR MY READERS

There are sections regarding loss of family, betrayal, battle and torture (although the latter comes late in the series). There is a scene where Tia is tricked during a "romantic" scene, but there are no forced "romantic" scenes in this book.

What will this book have? A heck of a lot of butt-kicking revenge! There are fight scenes with some violence. Oh! And did I mention sex? Several of the love making scenes in this book are probably best read when no one is looking over your shoulder... Tia's mates have great imaginations! *wink wink*

Thank you for reading!

DRAGON GODDESS

DRAGON GODDESS SERIES
BOOKS 1-3

SEDONA ASHE

CONTENTS

UNEXPECTED SHIFT
DRAGON GODDESS, BOOK 1

UNEXPECTED MATE
DRAGON GODDESS, BOOK 2

UNEXPECTED HEAT
DRAGON GODDESS, BOOK 3

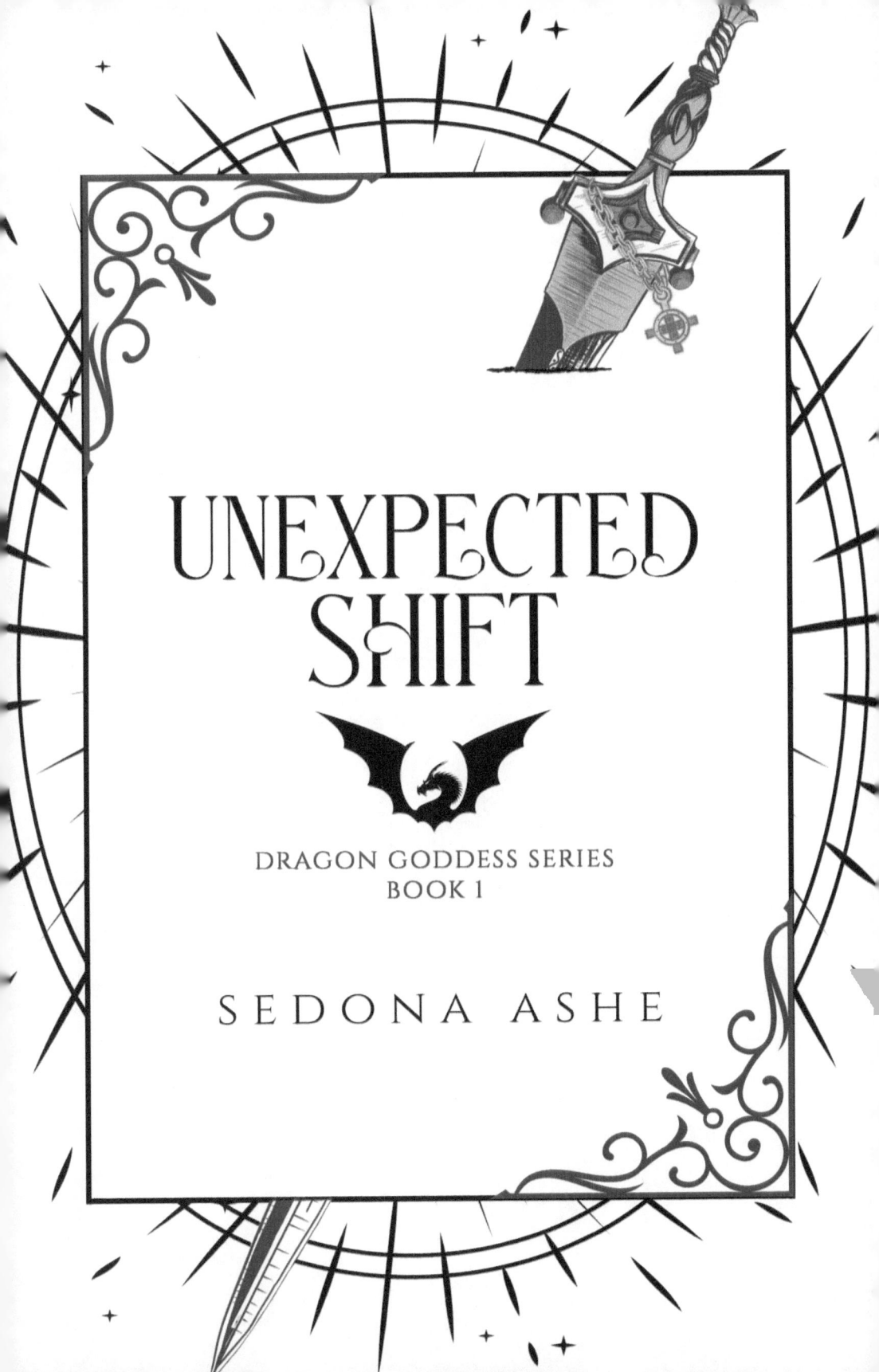

UNEXPECTED SHIFT

DRAGON GODDESS SERIES
BOOK 1

SEDONA ASHE

CHAPTER ONE

Tia

"Hurry Tiamat! You must crawl out through the tunnel and escape as quickly possible! Don't come back into the house! Remember that our love will always be with you. My precious daughter, you do not realize how special you are!" These were the last words I ever heard from my mother. She stroked her hand across my cheek before shoving me and my backpack down into the tunnel entrance. She then slammed the trapdoor shut above me, sending the tight space into pure darkness. Mere seconds later, a terrifying male voice filled the hushed, night air. "Where is it? I know it is here!" The rest of his words were too muffled to hear.

I sat shivering in the dark, staring up toward the floorboards. I was too shaken up to even move. What had just happened? I had been sleeping peacefully, only to be startled awake by my mom frantically shaking me and then dragging me out of bed. As she'd pulled me through the living room, I'd seen my dad stacking furniture to block all entries into our home. He'd stridden toward me, and, for a moment, he wrapped his arms around me and kissed my forehead. Mom had choked on a sob as she pushed me into the kitchen, before yanking free the trapdoor which was completely concealed among the beautiful wood planks of the floor.

I slowly began inching my way through the shaft that I knew would open in the hills behind our house. The tunnel was dim, and I was unable to stop the shivers that shook my body each time my palm squished into a substance I could not identify.

When I was young, my father had built the nearly mile long shaft, and I had thought it was glorious fun to take a light and explore the narrow passageway with him. Now those memories seemed so very far away.

As I crept along, I could hear muffled roaring echoing in the tunnel. It sounded like a horrific battle was coming from the house. The savage growls finally became quiet but were followed by the boom of two gunshots. I struggled to swallow my sobs as the tears started sliding down my cheeks, and my body trembled.

After two hours, I came to the end of the tunnel and dragged myself out and onto the ground, carefully breathing in and out in shaky breaths. I lay there on my back inhaling the sweet, smoky scent of scorching wood. The smell of fire had always been a comfort to me, but as I glanced back toward the house the blood in my veins turned to ice.

Flames were devouring my home, but before I could start to sob over losing my parents and the only home I had ever known, I realized that the fire was spreading into the forest and was burning quickly toward where I was hiding. I turned and snatched up the backpack my mom had given me and began running away from the hungry fire.

My family had always loved hiking, running, swimming and just about every other activity that involved building strength and spending time outdoors. We had spent weeks of my childhood camping in the woods. My dad had taught me to fish, and how to survive without modern conveniences.

My parents also taught me to fight and defend myself. I never understood why we had to live such a secretive life, or why I needed to know how to do things like throw knives, but my parents insisted I needed to be prepared. I wished I could talk to them and push them to explain things, because now I was scrambling through the burning forest, absolutely terrified, and without any idea of who might be after me.

I usually enjoyed running and could run for hours barely breaking a sweat, so spending the remaining four hours of the night racing down the mountain would have been a walk in the park. But with the aching heaviness in my mind weighing me down, it felt as though I were carrying a boulder while walking through sand.

I could hardly move one foot in front of the other by the

time I came to the old-fashioned looking town in the valley. I wasn't sure what had brought me here. Perhaps it just happened to be where I ended up after running for so long, but I didn't think so. Something in the fragments of my shattered heart had pulled me here, to this small town.

CHAPTER TWO

Luke

I woke up and stumbled into the kitchen. My chest was tight with worry, but I didn't understand the cause. My twin brother, Levi, was already sitting in the kitchen rubbing his palms through his short dark hair. We shared the same tall muscular frames, chocolate colored hair and vivid green eyes.

We also shared the role of Beta in the WaterStone pack and were darned good at our job. Very few wolves attempted to stir up trouble once they got a look at the size of our wolves. In most instances, a pack has only one Beta, but since we were twins, we could operate efficiently as a team without jealousy getting in the way. Personally, I thought it made us an even better team, and we had built a reputation of being a deadly duo.

"What woke you up Levi?" I asked while lowering myself into a chair.

"I'm not sure, bro. My wolf is pacing back and forth inside me and seems anxious to 'do' something," Levi replied, dropping his head down on the table with a dull thud.

"It is so odd. I'm feeling the same. You don't think something dangerous is about to happen to the pack, do you?" I rubbed a tanned hand down my face.

"No. I don't feel like that. It seems like a pull toward something or someone, but I can't seem to detect that person, so I don't believe it is a pack member."

"I say we shift and let our wolves run a bit, maybe that will settle them down," I stood and began taking off my clothes.

"Sounds like an excellent plan. This time you get to carry our bag with jeans though... I don't want a repeat of the last time we had to shift with no clothes around." We shivered in unison. I still remembered the guys' snickering, and the women's screeching (while also trying to sneak some not so discreet peeks).

"Ugh! Old Ms. Jenkins still winks at me when she sees me in the grocery store or pumping gas!" I couldn't hide the horror in my tone. I looked over and realized Levi's shoulders shook as he struggled not to laugh. "Jerk," I muttered.

We shifted and ran for several hours, but rather than settling our wolves, they became more anxious. Just as the sun rose over the mountain bathing our sleepy town in a beautiful pale pink light, we headed back toward the pack house; I sensed movement near the edge of the woods. Instantly, my hackles rose. Levi must have seen the movement as well because he nodded his head toward me, and then moved into position.

We prepared to circle for an attack in case this was a rogue. As we neared, the smell of ash and sweat filled my nose. I breathed in deeper, trying to see if I smelt the rotten scent of a rogue. Instead, a faint scent of caramel filled my nose. My wolf shoved forward in my mind, trying to take over full control. I pushed back and remained in control, but just barely.

Looking toward Levi, I could see his eyes flashing between his own green ones and the glowing orbs of his wolf. I slowly moved closer to the trespasser, with Levi mirroring my movements. I froze in my tracks as the intruder's face moved into the light. It was a female, maybe nineteen or twenty years old. She collapsed on her knees in the dirt and rested her head in her hands as she sobbed.

We remained motionless, uncertain what to do. My wolf pushed forward again, this time gaining more control. He whined softly, and slowly wagged his tail. The girl's head jerked in my direction, revealing the gleaming wet tracks her tears made through the grime on her face. As my eyes connected with her crystal blue ones, my wolf dropped to his belly and inched toward her with the words "must protect" echoing over and over in my mind. Glancing over, I saw that Levi's wolf was perfectly mirroring my own.

TIA

I remained motionless as the two giant wolves crawled toward me. I probably should have felt terror and tried to scream or something, but their green eyes glittered with intelligence, and the wind softly playing in their chocolate brown coats mesmerized me.

The wolves bumped up against my knees, raising their massive heads so I was staring directly into their faces. I felt my body move, but I wasn't in control. Gently, I put two fingers between the set of eyes on each of the identical wolves, and I felt my head tilt head back until I was staring at the sky. I was pretty sure I was going to be freaking out about this later. After all, no sane person would start touching two humongous wild wolves and then expose their neck to them. It felt like I was being guided by instinct.

The wolves moved forward and placed their heads on either side of my face and inhaled deeply behind my ears. In perfect harmony, they slid their snouts down my neck, pausing at the smooth skin above my collarbone. They stilled and then peered into my eyes, as if waiting on permission from me. I wasn't sure for what, but I felt myself nod.

I closed my eyes, the wolves took one final deep sniff, and then they bit down. Hard.

Rather than feeling pain, a sense of comfort and love overwhelmed me.

When I fled my home, and the fire, and later ran sobbing alone through the forest, I didn't think I would ever be able to feel safe again. Why was I feeling this way after being bitten by two giant wolves?

I must be going insane. I opened my eyes and was astonished at the soft buttery yellow glow enveloping us. Slight shock waves pulsed out from where we sat, and the ground trembled under us.

My eyes connected with the wolves once more, and an intense wave of energy came from me, slamming us to the ground, flattening grass, bending trees, and shaking houses in its wake. I lay panting on the earth as the power began to ebb from my body.

I was too exhausted to move, and I felt blackness taking over my vision. Right before passing out, I felt the two dark wolves crawl to either side of me and carefully shield my body.

I was safe.

CHAPTER THREE

Luke

I jolted awake to the sense of her distress and lumbered to my feet. I was still in my wolf form and the fur rose on the back of my neck. I felt her fear, and in response, I bared my elongated teeth, bracing to attack whoever had distressed the blue-eyed girl; this stranger that suddenly seemed like one of the most important people on earth to my wolf.

I glanced over at Levi on her other side. I could see his raised hackles and hear the low growl rumbling in his chest. The girl sat up, pulling her jacket tight around her, while darting her eyes this way and that, like a panicked rabbit ready to dart off at any moment.

Several concerned pack mates had us surrounded. Mitch,

a tall gangly man and a close friend, strode forward two steps and held out the clothing I had dropped when we found the girl.

My gaze locked on Levi and I silently communicated that he should change clothes while I remained on guard. With a jerk of his head, he walked into the woods. A few moments later, he came back, and I picked up my own clothes and went to dress.

As I rejoined the group, I spoke up, "So what's brought you and the others out to this part of our borders?"

Mitch looked uneasy. He scratched his head, "Um, well, we were kinda all awakened when something shook the house. It felt like an earthquake, but then we were shoved to the ground. It was so weird, man. It was like an invisible force was pressing us to the ground, and every time it seemed to ease up, another wave would pin us again. With the Alpha gone on business for the week, we hoped that you guys would know what happened."

Levi spoke up and explained our own experience, skipping the part about us "marking" her since we still hadn't figured out what on earth possessed us to do that. The jacket she had pulled around herself hid the bite marks from view, and hopefully that would give us time to figure out what was going on between us.

My wolf was repeating "protect" over and over in my head, instead of the usual "mate" or "mine" a wolf would claim upon meeting their fated mate. I wasn't sure why my wolf was in such a frenzy about her protection. Was this little female my mate? Maybe I could get some answers from him after I convinced my wolf that she was safe.

I rubbed my hand down my face. We needed to do some research on what was going on. The other wolves seemed bewildered as they eyed her with suspicion. I turned and awkwardly patted her shoulder. She peered up at me with her sad eyes, the tear tracks on her dirt covered face still clear.

I whispered, "I'm so sorry".

I couldn't help but wonder what she had been through, but it must have been terrible, judging from the anguish in her eyes. My wolf sensed her grief, and he whined in my head.

She burst into fresh tears and threw herself in my arms. Having so many people she didn't know surrounding her caused her more distress, and my wolf was ready to kill everyone around us. I hadn't struggled to control my wolf this much in years. It was time to take her home and give her a quiet place to rest. I scooped her up with ease while I mind linked with Levi and asked him to grab her backpack and follow me.

We were quite a distance from the pack house, but with the brisk pace I was moving, it didn't take us long to get back. I ignored the stares from the pack members sitting around watching TV and took her straight up the stairs to the connecting rooms that Levi and I shared. I still wasn't certain she was my mate, but I was sure my wolf was tied in some intimate way to her, and he wouldn't be happy putting her in the guest wing at the opposite side of the house.

The faster he calmed down and started talking to me, the

better. She didn't smell like a wolf, although she didn't smell human either. Levi had marked her as well, so did that mean she was both our mates? Or neither? I shared many things with Levi, but I hadn't thought I would share a mate.

I set her gently on the bed. When she fell asleep, I untied her military looking boots, and covered her with a thick blanket.

I will go talk to the pack and try to calm everyone down, Levi told me through the mind link. He tiptoed out of the room, shutting the door behind him with a soft click. A smile touched my lips. Levi was always trying to be the peacemaker. Neither of us had tempers, but he was a complete softy and always worried about others. Knowing that he had also marked her worried me. I knew how much he looked forward to the day he would have a mate to adore and spoil. I hoped that fate hadn't just taken that chance from him.

My wolf was still pacing back and forth in my mind. I turned to leave the room, and he surged forward, trying to force a shift. I pushed him back, gritting my teeth as I fought the transformation.

"Stay. Close. Please," he echoed in my head. My wolf had never been chatty, but right now he struggled to form single words.

I moved back to the bed, settling myself beside her. I lay on my back and listened to her breathe, the sound slowly calming my wolf. I turned to face her and was instantly hit with her caramel scent. The woodsy ash scent was still there and between the two, she smelled like toasted caramel.

Longing burned through me. Before I was able to stop myself, I had pulled her against me. She stiffened for a moment, and then relaxed against me with a sigh. What exactly was she? And what was she to me?

CHAPTER FOUR

Tia

I slowly opened my eyes and tried to figure out where I was and how in the world I'd gotten here. I was oh so warm, and the bed was softer than any I had slept on before. I went to shift the thick blankets off me, only to be stopped by an arm around my waist. I stilled as I realized my body was firmly pressed against someone's chest. His slow breathing ruffled my hair. My heart rate picked up. I took stock of my body. I wasn't injured, and I was fully clothed. I was safe. I felt protected, not trapped. My eyes fluttered closed as I relished the moment. They popped open again seconds later as a soft whine came from somewhere in the room. It took me a minute, but I finally spotted the large wolf sleeping on the floor. He twitched and whined in his sleep. It was like those cute videos of sleeping dogs that people were always posting online...except this was a wolf. A massive wolf. For a moment, I thought I was going to die of a heart attack. After all, it's not every day you see a wolf the size of a small horse inside a house.

Slowly, the events of last night came back to me and what had happened since meeting the two wolves earlier this morning. I faintly remembered being protected by the two identical chocolate wolves and then they'd turned into humans...wait...turned into humans? That was disturbing, but what was even more unsettling was the fact I wasn't as shocked by this. In my mind, this seemed normal, which was impossible because I didn't recall seeing a human turn into a giant wolf with huge teeth in my past.

The thought of my past sent a pang through me. My heart ached from the loss of my parents, and my body was exhausted from my escape through the woods. I wanted to hide in this room forever, but being a scared little girl, pampered and protected by two giant wolf-men, wasn't me. My parents had taught me to be a survivor. They worried the day might come when they wouldn't be there to protect me and had trained me hard to ensure I could watch my own back. But I could trust these two men. I didn't know why, but I knew it in the depths of my soul. I was not the weakling they probably believed me to be. Boy, oh boy, were they going to be in for a shock.

My stomach let out a ferocious growl, and I decided getting food was the first order of business. My gaze wandered around the room as I took in my surroundings. The furniture was roughhewn wood, and I wondered if the wolf-man had crafted them himself. There were two windows, both were partially open, and a gentle breeze moved the red plaid curtains. One wall had several framed portraits, and each showed the twins at different ages. My heart fluttered at how adorable they were.

I spotted a door that was partially open, revealing a small but tidy bathroom. Slowly rolling out of bed as quietly as I could, I reached for my backpack and tiptoed to the bathroom to change. Catching my reflection in the mirror, my mouth gaped open in horror. I looked like something a cat had caught, eaten, and then barfed back up. Okay, shower first, then breakfast.

I stepped into the warm spray of the shower and sighed. I stole some shampoo and soap, quickly scrubbing the dirt from my hair and skin. The soap smelled like the wolfy man who had been holding me this morning. I breathed the scent a little deeper and a little thrill went through me. Hm. Was it possible to be attached to someone you met only hours before?

I rinsed quickly and stepped from the shower. I decided on a pair of soft stonewashed blue jeans. I nearly cried when I realized my mom had packed several of my favorite type of t-shirts, the kind with funny sayings on the front.

It probably wouldn't be the best idea to wear "Cute but Psycho" while meeting a bunch of strangers for the first time; I put on a plain black t-shirt instead. I dug around in the back-pack and found several knives had been stashed inside as well. My mom must have had this bag prepared for an emergency.

I stuffed the t-shirts back into the bag making sure to cover the blades. I hurriedly rushed a brush through my long blonde hair.

Peeking out the door, I realized wolf-guy was still asleep and cautiously crept out into the hallway.

My goodness! The house was *huge*! I wandered around for what seemed like forever trying to find the kitchen (but was probably only about fifteen minutes in all actuality). Getting frustrated, I stopped and took a deep breath to calm myself. That was when the delicious scent of food hit me.

Following the smell, I found myself in the kitchen and dining area...did I mention the house was huge? The kitchen looked like it could take up nearly a full floor of a 'normal' house. It was like having a little café in your home. Tables were scattered around the room, with people sitting in groups chatting. How many people lived here?

As soon as I entered the room, everyone stopped talking and eyed me. I stood there, unsure of what to do, and eventually they went back to their dinner. I had missed out on lunch and slept most of the day.

A sweet looking older lady spotted my awkward self and bustled over. She handed me an empty plate and directed me over to a full buffet bar with so much food I thought my eyes would pop out of my head. I quickly filled my plate and found a quiet table in the corner. I focused on stuffing my face with the glorious mountain of food on my plate.

I was nearly halfway through my plate when the door banged open, and a flock of squawking crows came in. Okay, fine. They weren't crows. They only sounded like a loud flock of birds. These girls had the whole cliché 'cheerleader squad' vibe going on. They were around my age, so perhaps they were college cheerleaders? One girl was clearly the leader and as soon as she came in, she scanned the room to make sure every eye was on her in her tiny pink shorts, low-cut top, and wearing heels that were at least five inches tall. Impressive. I mean, the chick didn't teeter or wobble at all. I would never be caught in heels. Give me my military boots any day.

She made sure every male's eye was on her and then preened a bit. Having watched my fair share of movies, I had to swallow a laugh because they nailed the dramatic entrance. I chided myself for being so quick to judge. My mom had definitely taught me better.

I am sure they are delightful girls, I thought to myself.

I turned back to my food and stuck another spoonful of creamy mashed potatoes in my mouth, trying not to moan at the buttery perfection. I was engrossed in my food when a grating voice broke through my lusty haze.

"So, are you the little homeless loser the boys found on our land?"

Hmm. I guess this means they aren't nice girls. I didn't feel quite as bad for judging her earlier. I didn't respond, so she tried again. "I am glad they gave you a bath. At least you aren't completely repulsing to look at now."

I counted to ten and then tried to be polite like my mom always taught me. "Hi, I'm Tiamat, but you can call me Tia." I stood and stuck out my hand to shake.

She looked scornfully at my hand, raising a perfectly manicured eyebrow. "My name is Trixie, but you can call me Luna, since that is who I will be when the Alpha returns home and marks me tonight. He didn't want to do it before his trip out of town, so it wouldn't disrupt our bonding after the marking. I'm not sure he will have time to deal with a piece of trash like you for a few days, so I suggest you stay out of the way until he has time to send you packing."

Well, I guess being polite didn't always work. Sorry, mom. I still wasn't sure what the terms 'Alpha' and 'Luna' meant, but it sure as heck didn't feel right to say it to her. My insides squirmed just thinking about it.

"I have no plans to get in anyone's way, Trixie. A soon as I can figure out what is going on, I will be out of here." I said in a soft voice. I prepared to go back to eating and was totally not expecting the sudden yank on my hair that nearly toppled me out of my chair.

"I thought I told you to call me Luna, you little piece of trash!" she screeched.

I have been trained in many forms of martial arts and self-defense, which made the idea of being in a 'girl fight' down-right hilarious! I removed her hand and stood from my chair. Trixie must have spotted my smirk because she quickly threw out her hand to, what, slap me? I was used to punches, but a slap? This was getting funnier by the minute.

I spoke through my teeth, "Never try to touch me again."

Trixie's eyes grew wide, but then to not embarrass herself in front of her friends, she straightened her spine and growled out, "Or what? You think I'm afraid of a skinny stick like you? I bet your family didn't even want you, and that is why you were found all alone in the woods. Boo hoo." She burst into an evil little laugh, and the girls with her joined in.

This was funny right up until the part where she brought my family into it. Her words brought back fresh pain and anger - anger that was building inside, from my helplessness at defending my family and home, and at the cruel man who turned my world upside down, and now at the demented chick who stood in front of me.

My body grew warm from the rage. As my skin increased in temperature, the pendant around my neck felt like it was burning my skin. My anger had never heated my skin, and the little pendant - a gift from my parents - had never burned my skin in the past. If I hadn't been so focused on Trixie and her posse, I would have given more thought to this fresh development. But no. She couldn't resist insulting me a bit more.

"As soon as Alpha Cage comes home, he will throw you out like the garbage you are. But I can't allow you to disrespect me like this." She gave an evil smirk to her friends. "You will kiss my foot right now, and I won't make Cage kill you."

I thought the idea of calling someone 'Luna' was horrible. But the idea of kissing someone's foot...especially this witch's foot - well, that was the turning point where I couldn't control my rage. The burning sensation rushed through my entire body. A voice I didn't recognize came out of my mouth "I will not allow this insolence. On your knees now and I might show mercy."

Okay, I was freaking out a bit inside because I didn't think it was me who actually said those words, but not Trixie. She was either brave, stubborn, or plain old stupid (I am voting for the last one), because she stood up straighter, and lifted her freaking foot toward my face. She then tilted her head as a sign I should kiss it.

My skin began to glow a soft blue and the voice I didn't recognize spoke again, "On your knees!" A pulsing wave of power rolled from my body and the house shook. Several glasses and plates bounced off the tables and shattered on the floor.

Trixie tottered in her ridiculous stripper heels, but still didn't bow. Another wave of raw power pulsed from my body, this one stronger than the last. She fell to her knees along with her posse and everyone else in the room who had been watching our exchange.

Still refusing to submit, she tried to lift her hand and get back up. And that was the moment something inside me snapped. Power surged out of my body, rushing through the room. The chairs and tables toppled over, and cabinets emptied their contents. Everyone in the room was pushed to the floor.

The voice said, "I am Power. Do not underestimate me. Do not disrespect me."

I couldn't see anyone else's face, but I was definitely freaking out. The voice was coming from my mouth, but I wasn't the one speaking. I no longer had control of my body. A chocolate brown wolf dashed into the room, leaping over prone bodies and overturned furniture.

When he finally reached me, he put his muzzle in my hand. A little part of the chaos inside me calmed, but I was still unable to control my body. Tears welled in my eyes. I didn't want to hurt anyone, but I couldn't figure out a way to regain control of my limbs.

The back door of the kitchen slammed open, shattering the glass. The second chocolate haired guy with green eyes rushed in, followed by an enormous man. I only caught a quick glance of the man, before focusing back on the wolfy guy with the emerald eyes. He rushed to my side, shifting smoothly into his wolf, and placed his muzzle in my other hand. Slowly, my hands slid up to rest on top of their heads. The rage seeped out of me. My skin began to cool, and my pendant stopped searing my flesh.

The energy waves stopped, and people slowly lifted themselves from the ground. My skin was still glowing blue, but I was calmer. It was then I noticed the big man still standing by the door.

He was absolutely, mouth wateringly handsome.

Our gazes connected, and I froze.

CHAPTER FIVE

Cage

s I pulled into the driveway, I was both relieved to be home, and scared I would run into Trixie. Don't get me wrong, I didn't mind checking out that body (which was always on display for anyone to see), but I have always known that my mate was the only woman for me. While I've flirted from time to time, I've never had a girlfriend or had sex with a girl.

My guy friends always gave me a hard time; male wolves are extremely passionate and being alone is hard. Often, a wolf will never find his soulmate, and I could tell my friends fear I am going to be disappointed by never finding my other half.

Anyway, somehow that crazy Trixie chick got it in her

mind that she was going to be the new Luna, and I was too tired to deal with her drama.

After seeing the coast was clear, I got out and headed toward the house. I spotted one of the Beta twins coming back from the woods, and I waited for him to walk over and catch me up on pack news.

He asked politely about my trip to the council meeting and listened as I told him about their pressure for me to find a mate. Werewolves were dying out, and we needed to be reproducing to increase our numbers. I was from the oldest bloodline, which meant I had strong genes and my children would be formidable Alphas.

They had picked several "suitable" females with "worthy" bloodlines for me to choose a mate from, but I was stubbornly waiting for my true soul mate. Call me a ridiculous romantic, but my soul mate was supposed to be my other half and I didn't care if she is a powerful werewolf female or an everyday human.

Levi spoke up, startling me out of my thoughts, "We haven't had any rogue sightings, and everything was pretty normal while you were away, Alpha. But last night Luke and I were awakened, and something pulled at us. We searched the boarders and came across a girl."

I broke in, "Was she a human runaway?"

"She doesn't seem human, but she also doesn't smell wolf," he replied. "The strangest thing happened, though..."

Before he finished speaking, the house shook, and a pale blue light glowed in the windows. We stood dumbfounded for a minute, then surge after surge of power rattled the house and the grounds. I glanced over at Levi to see his eyes glazed over before he rushed off toward the kitchen door.

We entered the house and my head snapped toward the source of the energy. What I saw nearly brought me to my knees...and not from the power pulsing from her, but from her beauty. I have never seen a woman so perfect in all my life. She stood tall like a goddess of vengeance. My body responded to her even as I gazed around; all my pack members were lying on the ground, unable to lift their faces off the floor. I watched as Luke and Levi pressed in close on either side and her hands slowly sliding up their muzzles onto their heads. My eyes wandered up her body. She was taller than most of the pack females, but not as tall as the male wolves. Her body had curves in all the right places, even if she was a little on the thin side, and her gorgeous golden blonde hair moved as though a breeze was blowing through the room. The energy disappeared as abruptly as it started, and people were peeling themselves off the floor.

I met her eyes and my entire world stopped. She sucked in her breath and, after a moment, I took a couple of steps toward her. While I was focused on the girl, Trixie had apparently spotted me and brushed herself off. She edged closer to me until she was nearly pressing herself against me.

"Aww, Cage baby, I missed you so much. You came home just in time to stop this freak from bullying me." Her whiney voice grated my nerves.

Without even looking at her, I stepped around her and said absently, "It is Alpha to you. Don't call me Cage."

The gorgeous glowing girl was obviously in a daze, and I

gently reached out my hand to touch her cheek. They always say a tingle runs through your body when you meet your soulmate, but that is a total understatement. It was like being electrocuted, and the shocks were going through every vein and shooting to every part of my body. It was almost like it wanted to make sure I understood I belonged to my mate completely. As I leaned forward to kiss my mate's lips, Trixie jumped between us and grabbed my arm, jerking me to the side.

She screamed, "I am the Luna! You are supposed to mark me tonight. You can't kiss her. She isn't good enough for you."

I barely had a chance to blink before my true mate's eyes changed from sky blue to an electric blue. I was sure it was a trick of the light, but it appeared as if lightening flashed in their depths.

Her silky voice said "MINE," and she opened her mouth and blew.

The air moved through her lips gently, as though she was simply blowing out a single birthday candle, yet Trixie flew across the room and slammed against the wall. Several pack mates stepped forward, growling, ready to take down this threat to the pack. They believed my beautiful mate was a danger to them. Everything moved so fast that I didn't even have the chance to order them to stand down. My mate reached down and laid her hands on top of Levi and Luke's heads again. Their deep growls reverberated through the room, warning the pack to back off, but several of the braver guys stalked closer. The girl slid her hands forward until her fingers rested on their wolf foreheads. Her glow engulfed them, and their green eyes shifted, reflecting the electric blue color of her eyes. Everyone froze and turned toward me for guidance.

My mate remained focused on my eyes, and I couldn't stop myself, "I have searched for you so long, my Love."

Her eyes stopped flashing and the light surrounding the trio faded. She took in the room, her eyes widening at the damage. In a voice that sounded softer this time, she asked, "What happened?" and then collapsed.

As I caught her in my arms and clutched her against my chest, I took a deep sniff and only smelled toasted caramel. It was like Levi had said, there wasn't even the faintest scent of wolf. She was obviously not human either, though. No human was able to do the things we had just witnessed. Luke stepped up beside me and he appeared anxious, which was odd since nothing ever ruffled him.

"I don't think she knows anything about what she may be, Alpha," he said.

I believe he was worried I was going to throw her out.

"She is my mate, Luke."

I had finally found her. I whispered softly against her ear, "Nothing is going to take you from me."

CHAPTER SIX

Tia

I slowly rolled over and curled up tighter against the warm pillow on the bed...hold up! Bed? My eyes shot open. Yep, I was definitely back in a bed. This was turning into a habit. As my eyes focused, and my mind became less hazy, I realized two things: First, this was not the same bedroom as I woke up in last time, and second, it wasn't a pillow I was snuggling. My 'pillow' was the most attractive guy I had ever seen. Ok, to be honest, I had little to compare him to, other than guys on TV. While living in the woods, I did not meet many guys. This guy still had his eyes closed, and my insides were melting.

I went up on my knees and leaned in closer to study his face. I wasn't sure what made me do it, but I couldn't seem to control my hand as I reached out and caressed his stubble-covered cheek. At the exact moment my fingers touched his face, his eyes snapped open and his gaze locked with mine. A bolt of electricity shot through my body with so much force I tumbled backward off the bed. My fall was broken as I landed unceremoniously on a familiar mound of chocolate fur which promptly jumped up, rolling me off him and onto the floor with a thud. He growled, preparing for an ambush.

The yummy guy from the bed jumped up and began his own growling. *Hm.* It seemed he was a wolf too. I was finding I might have a thing for wolves. The chocolate wolf rolled me beneath him and remained in a protective stance over me. This infuriated the god moving toward us around the foot of the bed. Was that drool on my chin? I rubbed my face discreetly and decided I needed to do something before I was trapped in the midst of a brawl...*Although being caught between two hot, wolfy hunks...*Where had that thought come from? Thankfully, before things grew worse, my sarcasm came back from wherever it was hiding while playing the 'damsel-in-distress' the past day.

Rolling my eyes, I said in a bored tone, "Seriously girls, is it PMS time for both of you? Go take a Midol."

I twisted out from underneath the wolf and plopped back down on the bed where I crossed my legs and stared straight at the gorgeous hunk. "What's with trying to electrocute me?"

I tried to ignore the sharp snap of the wolf's head as he glanced between Mr. Hunk and me. Instead, I focused on the man in front of me and watched, fascinated as he ran his long, tanned fingers through his hair. He opened and closed his mouth a few times before he finally sighed, reached out, capturing my hand and tugging me to my feet.

"Let's go talk in my office. We both have an abundance of questions and it's time we sort out some details."

As we walked toward the door, I yanked my hand free of his; these people probably already saw me as weak. I struggled to ignore the coldness seeping into my body at the loss of contact between his skin and mine. Giving myself a mental shake, I breathed in and out and focused my mind like my dad had taught me. The twin wolves I could depend on, but I needed to remain on my toes and stay prepared for anything.

Deep in my soul, a sense of uneasiness was building. The evil that took my parents was still out there, and it was growing closer with every hour that ticked by.

UNKNOWN

"Master," Erik's voice broke through my thoughts. My right-hand man, at least for the moment, ambled into my office with his head bowed. I would have laughed at his obvious fear, but I was burning with rage over their failure within the last two days. A simple task was all I asked of them, gather the dragon pendant from the mountains. Sure, two formidable supernaturals protected it, but I had prepared my men, and the surprise attack had gone magnificently. How these idiots had pulled off the tough part of the mission (taking out two supernaturals), and yet failed to bring back the pendant was beyond comprehension or excuse. Which was why my previous right-hand man was in the dungeon, and my new one was all but crawling on his knees in my presence.

"Yes" I snapped, rousing myself from a line of thought which made me angrier by the minute.

"We have encountered signs a third person lived in the cabin we destroyed." He spoke in a rush, not thrilled to be giving me this information.

I leaned forward in my chair. "Our scouts never noticed a third supernatural presence in the area." My voice remained indifferent, but my men knew that was when they should fear me most.

Erik cowered, then straightened his spine, attempting to suppress his fear; it didn't work, the smell rolled off him in waves. "It was a young female, and she doesn't seem to be anything special, sir. Since we didn't find the necklace in the ruins, we assumed she somehow managed to escape with it."

"So, where is this girl?" I scarcely kept from flipping my desk and throttling the man. I desired that pendant. All my years of careful planning rode on me getting possession of that trinket.

"She proved to be challenging to track, but we believe she wandered into a small town several hours from where we attacked. A massive pack of werewolves run the township, and they are not particularly welcoming of strangers."

I leaned back in my chair and smirked.

"I have found you little girl. And now I am coming for what is mine."

CHAPTER SEVEN
Cage

I led the way toward my office while sending a mental message to all pack members to steer clear of my wing of the house. I knew this was going to be a highly interesting conversation.

I waved her into an armchair and closed the door behind us. Settling into my chair, I peered across the desk to find the spunky beauty had started a staring contest with me. She clearly expected me to start by answering her question. Not going to happen. Even though the mate bond was pulling at my insides, I had a pack to protect. After her little display of power downstairs, I was going to get my answers first.

I opened my mouth to speak and realized I didn't even know her name. "I suppose I should introduce myself. I am Cage, and I'm the Alpha of this pack-"

She interrupted me. "What does Alpha mean? And what do you mean by pack? Are you guys a gang?"

For a moment, I couldn't do anything but blink. Was she truly that clueless of shifter life? Or was this just an act? She had to be a supernatural to pull that stunt yesterday.

"A pack is a group of wolves: we are like a giant family. We stick close to each other for protection and support. It is in our very nature to crave companionship of our own kind, which is another reason for a pack. An Alpha is the leader or head of the pack. Almost like a king, boss, mayor, and father figure all rolled into one person. The Alpha keeps the pack running smoothly, helps to mediate quarrels within the ranks, and communicates with other packs. We are the WaterStone pack. We are one of the oldest packs in the world. Now, it's your turn. What is your name and how did you stumble into our territory?"

My heart softened at the sudden quiver of her lips, but I reminded myself that I needed to be firm for the security of my pack.

"My name is Tiamat - you can call me Tia, though. How I ended up here, well, that's harder to explain." She was quiet for a minute or two, unsure where to start. Dropping her shoulders and taking a deep breath, she poured out the story. She told me of her mother frantically waking her up, then of her escape from a home under attack, and finally of her fleeing through the woods with the fear of being burned alive pushing her forward, while her heart had ached with loss to the extent that she wanted to give up. When she finished, she sat peering out one of the wide full panel glass windows.

"I'm deeply sorry, Tia." I spoke gently.

If not for my werewolf hearing, I would have missed her soft reply. "It changes nothing though." A single tear slipped down her cheek.

Her intense grief filled the room. A loud banging on the office door made us both jump and before I could respond, Luke and Levi rushed in, grabbed her hands and started rubbing her back.

Before I could contain myself, a thundering growl ripped from my chest. All three of them turned towards me. They froze in shock and bewilderment. I knew it was uncalled for, but I couldn't push down the fury that smoldered in my chest seeing their hands on my mate. "What are you doing here? Didn't I tell everybody to stay away from this area of the house?"

"Alpha, we couldn't stop our wolves. They sensed her distress and wouldn't settle until seeing for themselves that she was alright." My Betas dropped their heads but continued to sneak glances at her.

I sagged into my armchair and stared at the three. "Her name is Tia." Waving my hand toward the twins, I spoke. "Tia, you already recognize these two. They are my Betas, Luke and Levi. Betas are second in authority to the Alpha. Now would someone please explain to me what is going on?" I exhaled and scrubbed my hand down my face. These two were acting like she was their mate. But that couldn't be true, could it?

Levi told me of what happened when they found Tia. When they spoke of the marking, my wolf nearly forced me to

43

shift on the spot. I wanted to rip something - or someone - to shreds.

"We don't know what is going on," Luke replied, speaking up for the first time "But I'm drawn to her. I must protect her."

Levi added, "Yeah, my wolf has been in a turmoil from the moment he sensed her. I don't know if we are mates because my wolf won't settle down enough to communicate with me. Right now, I desperately want her safe. We need to research if this has ever happened before and try to figure out what this connection means."

Hearing that, my wolf calmed. I didn't like the idea that she might be mated to my Betas and myself. That thought made me uneasy. I had never heard of any other form of markings besides the kind between mates. I still couldn't detect a wolf scent or, to be honest, any other supernatural scent on Tia. I was becoming increasingly concerned about the pack's safety. Was she bringing trouble to our doorstep?

"What is a mate?" Tia asked, looking up to meet my eyes.

I started to respond, but someone hammering on the door interrupted us again.

I gave a mental command to open the door, and John stepped into the room. John was one of my enforcers. He is rarely serious, and I am constantly dragging him out of messes when one of his practical jokes had backfired. I was dismayed to see that his face was utterly serious.

"Alpha, an intruder just strolled onto our territory. At first, we assumed he was a hiker or perhaps lost, but he has walked with purpose directly toward the pack house. He's nearly here." John reported all this in a rush. He kept stealing glances at the Beta twins and Tia.

"Is he wolf?" I asked.

"He doesn't give off the smell of wolf, although his scent differs from humans. It's strange. Almost as if his scent is a mixture of wolf, vampire, and perhaps something else."

"Allow him to approach, but assign a team to surround him, and another team to run the borders in case he has any followers planning to drop by later. Take the women and children to the safe house until he leaves." I dismissed John and stood, preparing for our unexpected and uninvited visitor. There were too many unknowns, and I would take every precaution possible until I figured out what the heck was going on.

I COULDN'T BELIEVE FINISHING A CONVERSATION HAD become nearly impossible. The WaterStone pack wasn't exactly welcoming to outsiders, which meant very few dared to breach our borders. I had to deal with this stranger immediately. I still needed to talk to Luke and Levi about why Tia hadn't been executed the moment they found her, or at least put in the holding cells until I returned. My wolf growled in my mind at the image of his mate restrained, and I agreed. But that didn't stop me from questioning why my Betas went against protocol for her.

I reached the front door just as the man was turning up the walkway toward the porch.

When he spotted me, he smiled and greeted me with, "Hello, Alpha."

Hm. Obviously, this guy is aware of supernaturals and made a trip here knowing full well the risks of trespassing on pack territory.

"And you are?" I asked, not even attempting to be civil. The sooner he was off my land, the better.

"I am Draven," he responded with a bow.

Was this guy from the Victorian era? Who bows these days? Other than vampires. They have impeccable manners until they get hungry and rip out your throat. I inhaled again. Although there was a faint vampire scent, it was mixed with several other odors. I had never smelled anyone quite like him. I remained silent with my arms across my chest.

He realized I wasn't in the mood to chat, and spoke again, "I understand that you have my niece here. I am ashamed that I hadn't visited them in years. I have been traveling for many years, and they moved to their mountain cottage to focus on their family and spending time together. When my brother died, I felt the pain in my heart and knew something was amiss. I came back as swiftly as possible and later tracked my niece through the woodlands to this location. Please tell me she is safe and unharmed."

His eyes appeared genuinely sorrowful. But something was off. Tia came out from behind Luke and Levi to stare at Draven.

She studied him carefully. "Why didn't my father or mother ever speak of you? If you are my family, they should have told me about you."

"I am so sorry, my dear." Striding forward he embraced her. She struggled for a minute, but he made shushing noises and rocked her. "I am hurting too. My brother and I constantly struggled to get along, and now I don't have the opportunity to make amends with him. I hope you will allow me to get to know you. We are all that remains of our family." She stilled and began to weep quietly. Draven looked over her head at me and then nodded his head toward the new pack members who had slipped into the room. "Would it be okay for me to take her to a private place in town to visit? I made reservations at a restaurant in the hopes she would allow me to explain more about me and our family."

My wolf was growling at the prospect of this man going anywhere with Tia. My human side thought he sounded sincere, and of course Tia would want to learn more about her family. Since she wasn't a pack member, it wasn't my right to tell her what she could or could not do.

Tia pulled free and peered around nervously. "Um, I'm not so sure. I'm exhausted and would rather stay here. You could come to the kitchen and speak with me?"

The twins suddenly turned wolf and shoved between Tia and Draven. They snapped at Draven, saliva dripping from their bared teeth. We all froze, shocked at their shift. I struggled to reach them with the mind link, but they were completely wolf, and either unwilling or unable to communicate. I mentally contacted several powerful guys from my security team, and they forcibly removed my Betas. I never thought I would witness anything like it. Luke and Levi were typically the last to shift during a chaotic situation, as they constantly worked to talk everyone out of a conflict.

Once they were out of hearing range, Draven spoke again. "If that would make you more comfortable, Niece, that would be fine with me. Although this discussion is better suited to a private setting." He emphasized the word 'private' with a sharp glance around the room, where more pack mates had come in to check out our unwanted guest.

Tia looked around the room, I saw the moment her eyes landed on the familiar figure of Trixie standing in the hallway with a sneer on her face. Tia came to some sort of decision and nodded her agreement to Draven, before slipping out of the room. She returned wearing a leather bomber jacket and a pair of boots. Draven called a driver and a black SUV pulled slowly to the front of the house.

Although I held no authority over her, my wolf pushed me to say, "Be back before dark."

Draven turned from climbing into the SUV and with a quick smile he responded, "You won't even miss her."

CHAPTER EIGHT

Tia

I slowly walked behind Draven to the glossy black SUV. I genuinely didn't want to go, but I needed to learn more about my parents and why they left the city to raise me in the middle of nowhere.

I clambered into the backseat and Draven directed his driver to drive into town. I couldn't stop myself from peering out the back window toward the pack house. Cage remained on the porch with a perturbed expression on his face.

We rode in silence for several miles and as we neared town, the driver slowed, and a man opened the rear door and climbed in beside me. *Hold up.* My stomach knotted. Something wasn't right here.

"Did anyone follow us, Scott?" Draven spoke up for the first time since leaving the pack's mansion.

I peeked over at the massive man he called Scott. His black hair was greasy and scruffy facial hair covered his face. Not in the sexy five o'clock shadow sort of way, but in the 'I haven't bathed in days' sort of way. A narrow scar split his left eyebrow, and a long twisted scar ran the length of his jawline on the right side. I bet he had spent time in prison at some point.

"What are you gawking at, princess?" He leered at me. Menace radiated from him.

"Scott, leave the girl alone and answer my question," Draven barked.

"We ain't got no one following," Scott snarled.

"Who taught you English? Hillbillies?" I asked with a snicker. Normally I'm very nice, but this guy had been nasty from the second he got into the vehicle, and it rubbed me the wrong way.

Faster than I could blink, he reached out his hand and slapped me. He slapped me! This wasn't a chick slap either. This was the type of slap that made my neck snap, and my eyes burn with tears from the sharp sting. *Oh. No. He. Did. Not.* He didn't even have time to smirk; I punched him so hard his nose made a loud crack.

Before we launched into a full-blown fight, Draven broke in by pulling handcuffs from his pocket. I found that odd. Why would he bother picking Scott up if he planned to cuff him? Scott reached out, snatched the cuffs, and brought the first one down on my wrist. That was the moment I recognized I was knee deep in crap and needed to get out of the car. Now.

I struggled, but in the confines of the SUV, there wasn't much I could do. He snapped the other cuff on my wrist in seconds. Scott shoved me in my seat, smiling a cruel smile, undoubtedly assuming he had won.

"What is going on, Draven? Why are you allowing this? What would Dad think if he knew?" I resolved to not cry or show any weakness. When Draven had showed up, I had hoped I was going to have family, and someone to share the grief with.

Draven laughed. It was not a pleasant sound. Even Scott stiffened next to me. "My dear, you are not my niece. I only met your parents once before they went into hiding with something that should be mine. I spent centuries tracking them. They not only managed to erase any signs they existed but also kept you a secret. Now shut up and sit tight until we arrive back at my grounds." With that he dismissed me and turned up the classical music that was playing in the car.

The driver rolled up a window partition dividing the front of the vehicle from the back, leaving me cuffed and alone with the burly thug.

I was too trusting and eager to learn of my parents, and had crashed right into the trap Draven set for me. I cursed myself. My parents had given me years of strenuous training, and I'd blown it the first time I needed to use those skills. Although, perhaps if they had been honest and warned me about Draven, I would have been better prepared.

I sat back against the seat, struggling to concentrate. With my hands cuffed behind my back, I couldn't win a fight in the constraints of the car. I had left all my knives in my backpack in the pack house, except for a small blade in my boot. I could use my speed and comfort in forests to my advantage, but I needed to get out of this vehicle first. If I leaned forward and made a visible move to open the door, Scott would stop me. But if Scott threw me...

"The big bad man was soooo afwaid of a wittle girl that he put cuffs on her to stop a scarwy fight." I taunted him in a tone usually reserved for babies.

He growled but didn't move. *Darn it, I thought for sure that would rile him up.*

"Is the lap dog cranky from being on a short leash today?" I cooed and watched as his fists tightened and a muscle in his jaw ticked. Almost there...

"Aww, Draven didn't give you a doggie treat for your hard work today, huh? No wonder you are so grumpy," I said, scooting toward him on the seat.

Bang! The speed at which he seized my jacket front and flung me back against the door shocked me, even though I was expecting it. The back of my head smashed into the window with so much force it surprised me the glass didn't shatter. I made a mental note not to underestimate him again.

As soon as my back struck the door, I pulled my hands up and slid the chain around the door handle and yanked. Thankfully, the door wasn't locked, and it lacked the child safety lock feature that would have made opening the door from the inside impossible. The idiots underestimated me as well. That made me grin.

When the door opened, I rolled backwards out of the car. That stunt hurt. Springing backwards out of a moving vehicle isn't something I would recommend. I dashed for the woods. I had mere seconds to escape before Scott alerted the other two and came after me himself.

Although I got my cuffed hands in front of me, running through the woods at top speed without full use of my hands to move branches out of the way, or to balance myself was not a wise plan.

I paused, closing my eyes for a moment to clear my mind as my dad trained me. I needed to think as the predator, not as the prey. After a few deep breaths, my eyes opened wide and my vision completely transformed. My father used to tease me about this, saying that I must be part reptilian with heat seeking vision. I don't know if he was telling the truth or joking, but I didn't care. I sensed my captors in the woods and knew I didn't have a hope of outrunning them.

I raced toward the nearest tree, lightly running up the side to do a back flip and threw my legs over the branch, hanging upside down like a bat. I did a stomach crunch and drew myself up into a somewhat stable standing position before crouching and jumping to the next branch. I did this until I sat about thirty feet off the ground.

I prayed that they would run right by the tree, believing it impossible I could have gotten off the ground with my hands behind my back. I watched silently, scarcely breathing as I focused on the sounds of the forest.

At first, the three men passed under the tree in their haste, but in minutes they circled back toward me. Scott was either a werewolf, or they had traded him in for a werewolf while out of sight. A giant burly red wolf came back, his nose to the ground and following my scent straight toward the tree I hid in.

He looked up with creepy glowing eyes. The wolf's scars were in nearly the same places as Scott's had been on his human face. I guess that would explain the super speed and growling in the car.

He let loose an ear-piercing howl, and then almost salivated while glaring at me, like I was a sirloin steak he wanted to devour. Draven walked to the base of the tree and motioned for Scott to back off while peering up at me.

"My dear, although I applaud your acrobatic skills, it will take a lot more than a quick run and scaling a tree to elude me. I am not mortal, and you are utterly unprepared to challenge me." His tone was low and filled with a cold fury. I shuddered.

"Scott, if you don't mind," Draven stepped back and gestured toward the base of the tree. Wolfy barked, backed a few feet away, and ran full speed into the tree. It shook, and the sound of splintering wood filled the air. I barely managed to balance myself on the limb.

I was so stupid, thinking climbing a tree would help, but really, what other choice did I have? And how was I supposed to know that Scott was a werewolf? Another slam to the tree and it sat at an angle. With the third blow to the trunk, I hurtled toward the ground where I smashed into the dirt. *Hard.* My vision went dark.

I roused to icy water on my face. I choked and struggled to take in a breath. Instead of air, water flowed into my lungs. Opening my eyes, I realized I was underwater. Hadn't these nut-bags ever heard of simply splashing water in a person's face to wake them up? Why dunk me completely? I thrashed against whoever held me.

I was wrenched up, and Draven's silky voice rang in my ears. "Ah, so the princess has awakened from her beauty sleep."

I choked and gagged as I worked to get the water out of my lungs "What the heck do you want with me?"

I coughed. My head throbbed, no doubt from impact with the window and the fall from the tree. And now my chest burned from the near drowning. I had a feeling I was going to die if Scott and Draven had anything to say about it. They certainly weren't concerned about my well-being.

Sneaking a glimpse around, I realized the driver of the SUV was missing, and Scott had shifted back to his human form. His hand was fisted so tight in my hair that my scalp burned. I tried to assess the situation. I still wore my boots and clothes, my hands remained cuffed and in front of my body, and I had been dragged to a nearby stream or lake, where I was now being forcibly dunked beneath the frigid water.

"I demand what has always been meant for me." Draven came so close his breath blew on my face. It was the strangest smell, almost sweet but with an underlying stench of decay, like when someone tries to hide the odor of cigarette or garlic on their breath by eating a mint. The scent becomes faint, but it's still there if you get close enough.

I opened my mouth to reply when pain shot through my head. It sizzled like electricity and left static in its place. I thought I heard a voice in the static.

"Brat. Pendant. Always mine."

I cried out, "What are you doing to my mind?"

Draven cocked his head to the side and studied me. "You have already stolen some energy from the dragon pendant. It is mine. When you give it to me, the power will be mine! Where have you hidden it?"

Once again, the electricity exploded through my skull and in the static, more words reverberated in my brain. "Then the girl must die."

Okay, I may not be a rocket scientist, but I was fairly confident that voice belonged to Draven, and his plan sucked. Especially, if that girl happened to be me. I needed to get away. I could worry about why I heard his thoughts in my mind later.

"Not a freaking chance, creep. I have no idea what you are talking about, but you are not getting anything from me."

I realized he must be speaking about the necklace my mom gave to me as a child, and the one which I wore at that very moment. But since my shirt hid it from view, I didn't feel the need to let him know it was mere inches from his greedy face. He really wasn't pretty enough to be this stupid. He should have checked around my neck first. *Duh.*

Before I caught my breath, Scott shoved me under the water again. He kept me down until stars flashed before my eyes and my lungs burned like they were filled with alcohol.

I was tugged back above the water, to hear Draven say, "Where is it?"

When I refused to answer, I was shoved under the water again. They repeated the process over and over until my body began shaking uncontrollably, and my mind had trouble focusing.

"You brat," Draven screeched. Although the repeated dunking was doing nothing to crack me, it had clearly made a dent in his patience. And boy, red did not look good on him. *Maybe he should let Scott baptize him next.* I snickered in my head over my own stupid joke. Hey, at least I would die with my sense of humor intact.

"The pendant was always supposed to be mine. After I confronted your parents, they retreated into hiding with it. Apparently, that is when they had you, their precious little offspring. They were only custodians of the dragon pendant, and when The One arrived, they had to hand it over. I am The One. It is my destiny. Yet, they refused to give it to me. They were selfish and went rogue to keep it for themselves. I spent years of my life trying to find them, and their assassination went off without so much as a hitch. But then I find out that, somehow, they helped you escape before my men attacked. My restraint is at an end little girl. Now tell me where you have hidden it."

My brain snapped back to attention. Rage boiled up from deep inside me. *He killed my parents.* Now, I wanted to fight. I needed to live, if only to watch him die. He continued ranting, and I struggled to process what he was saying through the roaring in my ears.

"That pendant holds the strength of the dragon. The one who wears it will gain the powers of the ancients. Nothing will be able to stop The One."

Honestly, I couldn't care less about the supposed powers

of the necklace, but I was angrier than I had ever been in my life. Electricity zipped through my body, and all my nerve endings hummed.

My mind must have been losing it because I swore a voice in my mind said, 'He *will* pay.' The tone was savage and sounded nothing like me.

Once more, Scott dunked me, but this time I was ready to fight. I would beat this dog-breathed dirtbag. As he shoved me under, I snapped the handcuff chain in two as if it had been made of string.

With my hands free, I pulled the blade from my boot and waited for him to drag me up. As soon as he did, I instantly struck out and embedded the knife in the artery on the inside of Scott's arm, the one he was using to grip my hair. He howled in pain and went down as blood began flowing from the wound at an astonishing rate.

His curses filled the air, and he moaned something about silver. *Hmm, how interesting.* So those TV shows about werewolves got the part about silver bothering werewolves correct. Who would have guessed?

All this took place in a matter of seconds. Turning, I locked my gaze on Draven. Something in my eyes must have freaked him out because he took a couple of faltering steps back. But then his rage and greed overruled his good judgement and he charged at me.

I let out a roar. *Oh, snap!* The sound was so terrifying it made my skin prickle and made the somewhat sane part of me freak out a little.

I didn't dwell on that because the bloodlust still controlled my body. On instinct, I raised my arms, and a spray of water shot fifteen feet into the air behind me. *Holy guacamole, I'm a water bender!*

Draven came to a halt and stared at the water that now appeared as substantial as any brick wall. He shrieked, "You thief! Give me the power that belongs to me."

I didn't wait. I hurled the wall of water at his body, flinging him backward as though he weighed nothing more than a ragdoll. He attempted to stand back up, but I raised my arms again making the water once again rush forward and hammer his body. We repeated this several more times until he collapsed onto the ground covered in mud. I let my arms drop to my sides and sauntered toward him.

When I stood over him, my mouth opened and the voice I didn't recognize as my own (aka the scary voice) spoke. "You will pay for the misery you have caused my family. You are not The One. You are nothing. You can't even comprehend that kind of power." The air hummed and crackled with electricity.

A whistling noise behind me caught my attention, and I turned just as a knife penetrated my side under my rib cage. Apparently, during the unfolding drama, the driver had snuck back with two other guys. They all looked like they belonged to the mafia. Scott remained motionless on the ground.

The rational part of me knew I should have been paralyzed with fear, but I heard myself laugh.

"You think you scare me, boys?" I raised one palm and sent a blast of water toward the SUV driver, filling his lungs until he passed out. In a single swift movement, I pulled the knife out of my side and sent it singing through the air and into the second guy's throat. Not to brag, but knives are kinda my thing. SUV dude really shouldn't have put one within my grasp. I clicked my tongue in amusement at their stupidity.

The third guy fancied himself some sort of ninja and snuck up behind me. I swung around, tsking behind my teeth as I stared him straight in the eyes before blowing lightly in his face. He went sailing backward and smashed into a tree. I genuinely hoped I never got a cold with this new power, or I'd have to watch out who I sneezed at.

My energy began declining, and my limbs quivered with fatigue. My shirt and pants stuck to me from the blood draining from my side. I needed to make my exit. I turned to end things with Draven, but he had slipped away while I dealt with the three ding-dongs. Carved on the tree were the words, 'It is mine'.

There was no way I could hunt him down and fight with my injuries. I spun and took off running into the woods, heading back toward the pack house. I believed I was several miles from the pack borders and didn't know if I had the strength to make it so far in my condition. A wave of dizziness made me stumble, and the forest in front of me swirled.

I am going to feel lousy tomorrow, was my last thought before my vision faded to black and the ground rushed up to meet me.

CHAPTER NINE
Cage

The unsettled feeling in the pit of my stomach rose as I watched the vehicle drive away. Draven's last words sent a glacial chill up my spine even though he had spoken them with a friendly smile.

Sighing, and hoping I hadn't made a decision I would grow to regret, I made my way toward the basement level where the Betas had been confined.

I could still hear their wolves, but they had simmered down to pitiful whines rather than the howling of savage beasts.

As I strode through the kitchen toward the staircase, I was suddenly attacked from behind. I reached behind me, gripping the individual by their throat and smashing them against the wall. My anger simmered to frustration as I recognized the face belonging to one particularly dense she-wolf. My irritation intensified as soon as she opened her mouth.

"I should have realized you would enjoy it rough," she purred while licking her lip. Instead of it looking sexy, she looked like she was licking off a milk mustache.

I nearly laughed in her face, and my wolf was so appalled by her that he scrambled backward in my mind until I could nearly imagine his butt hitting the back of my skull as he sought desperately to un-see her attempt at seduction.

I worked to set aside my feelings of annoyance that she wouldn't take the hint at my straight up refusal. But I was still her Alpha, and I wanted to be a good one.

"Trixie, I can't understand why you are still trying to force this relationship between us. You need to be out searching for your mate. He will cherish you better than any other person in the world is able-"

She cut me off with a whine, "Aww, Cagie baby, you are the only wolf that's meant for me. The entire pack knows we are practically engaged. You just need to make it official."

I gawked at her, utterly flabbergasted. I sighed, closed my eyes and pinched the bridge of my nose. "Trixie, now is not the time. We will settle this once and for all tomorrow." And with that, I eased her out of my way and followed the pitiful whines coming from the basement. Thankfully, I heard Trixie's heels click-clacking in the opposite direction.

I wasn't prepared to find the twins still in wolf form, laying on the floor like whipped puppies. They both turned their eyes to meet mine, but neither of them moved their bodies or even lifted their heads. I exhaled loudly and sat down on the bare floor.

It had been several years since I had been down to this room. The house has been in my family for generations. The basement was originally used to hold rogue wolves, or anyone perceived as a threat to the security of the pack.

Over the years, we had grown powerful enough to deter most intruders by sheer reputation alone, so we'd converted the basement to a game room. Since it was soundproof, my mom had pushed my dad into creating a sort of hang out place where the young, male wolves could be rambunctious without damaging her lovely kitchen, sitting room, or her eardrums. I had a lot of wonderful memories centered around this room.

Shaking my head to get my focus back on the issue at hand, I glanced back at Luke and Levi. They were still observing me.

"Shift." Neither wolf made to move. "Shift!" I growled and pushed slightly with my Alpha tone. At that, both wolves growled, but moments later the noise of snapping of bones filled the area. I tossed two of the throw blankets off a couch toward them. They covered themselves but refused to make eye contact.

"Care to explain that display upstairs?"

We went on in silence for several minutes, and I thought they weren't going to answer me. How had one human girl caused a rift in our pack bond so quickly?

"I wish I could explain it," Luke answered, the puzzlement clear in his voice. "All I know is that we were on patrol in case of a threat to the pack from the visitor. Suddenly, I was overcome with the sense that she was seriously freaked out about the dude and my wolf lost it."

"Does this have something to do with your weird connection to her?" I grit my teeth. I hated the idea of these guys having any sort of connection to *my* mate, and at the moment, their connection seemed quite a bit stronger than my own. My wolf growled.

"Yeah. I'm pretty sure it does," Luke responded.

"Are you still picking up emotions from her?"

Levi spoke up for the first time, "I dunno. It's hard to sift through the emotions from our wolves and what might be coming from her. Right now, I feel apprehension. Are we sure the guy is who he claims?"

I started to answer but stopped myself. My wolf was unsettled by Draven, yet it was as if he exuded some type of reassuring energy that had made us all second guess our instincts. I thought about everything Draven had said, a chill race down my spine.

He never said her name. Not once.

If he genuinely was her uncle, he would have at least known her name. As I came to that horrifying conclusion, the twins simultaneously groaned, shifted into their wolves, and tore up the stairs.

Fear encircled my heart. Had I just lost the most important thing in my world before she even knew what she meant to me? I roused myself from my pity party to find my wolf had forced a shift and taken off hot on the heels of Luke and Levi. I put down my mental barrier and concentrated on the shimmering silver strands of the pack bond, which lead from my wolf to theirs and allowed us to communicate even while in wolf form.

"What happened? Is she okay?" I demanded the instant our invisible connection snapped into place.

Levi spoke up first, "She is injured. I don't know how severely, but she must still be okay because all I am getting now is intense rage."

"Are we going to be able to locate them? He didn't mention where they were going." My tension continued building. Whoever touched her was going to die.

"Yes, locating her is not a problem. Our link to her makes her shine like a flare. The closer we are to her, the stronger our connection. She is calling to our wolves." Luke had a hint of wonder in his tone.

Once again, envy flashed through me at their closeness to my mate. What was going on between them? What was she? Definitely not human. Was she masking an inner wolf? Thoughts swirled round and round in my head as we raced across pack lands. The Betas grew more anxious as each mile passed. I focused on speeding up so that I could reach my little mate sooner.

A deafening roar filled the air, sending terrified birds shrieking and flitting from their roost in the trees. I nearly tripped as I realized the sound must have come from the twin wolves howling at the same time. I watched horrified as their bodies bulked up right in front of my eyes. The twins were already huge wolves, but now they were a foot taller, and their muscles had swelled so much that I marveled their skin didn't shred. In my mind, I overheard words that sent a devastating crack through my heart.

"Pain. Despair. Dying. Dying. They are murdering her."

Luke and Levi jumped forward with a velocity I didn't believe was possible, and although I was one of the most powerful Alpha's in the world, I fell behind. I willed my wolf to run harder, but he seemed to be in a state of complete shock. I pushed to catch up with the twins, but barely managed to keep them in my sight.

The ground trembled and shifted. More birds took flight, attempting to escape. A pulse of power so intense it created a blue hue as it flowed across the ground rushed toward me before it slammed into my body. It knocked my feet from under me, and I hit the ground with bone crunching force. It felt like a giant hand was slapping me about and trying to crush me. I lurched to my feet and picked my pace back up, but I didn't get far before another wash of energy rolled into me. This happened five times, each time stronger than the last.

As I searched for the twins, who I could only barely make out in the distance, I saw they were affected by the energy as well. They looked like creatures that had fallen into a vat of toxic waste. Their entire bodies shone with that eerie blue color that was around Tia the first time I saw her. This meant she was still alive, right? This was some side effect of her freaky bond with Luke and Levi. The shadowy forest vibrated with electricity. We were close. Even without being bonded, I could sense my mate was nearby.

The otherworldly light and energy suddenly clicked off as

if someone had flipped a light switch. All was silent for several moments and then I heard the Beta's howl of triumph at finding her, but it immediately turned to roars of outrage. I knew, even before seeing her crumpled on the ground, that she was badly hurt. The coppery scent of blood filled the air. So much blood. My wolf froze in my mind. Then, with a fury and force I didn't realize he had, he charged forward and smashed into the pair of massive wolves standing over her broken body. I couldn't have apologized even if I had wanted to because my wolf had seized complete control. The sight of his mate, battered, soaking wet, covered in lacerations, and with blood spilling from a hole in her side, was more than he could handle. Why would someone do this to her? How could I have failed her?

My wolf spoke in a chillingly calm voice in my head, "You failed our mate. I tried to warn you, but you have become tame with human ways. Until my mate is safe, you will not have control. I will protect my mate."

I struggled to shove him back and regain control, but my wolf had driven me into the area of my mind normally reserved for him. I've never been known for my overwhelming kindness, but with my wolf in control, the world was about to meet a beast I had worked hard to keep suppressed.

Chapter Ten

Cage

My wolf was barely holding himself back from being completely animalistic. Since we share both mind and body, he knew all about the customs and knowledge of the current human world. Usually, he just didn't care. He had shifted us back but had remained in command of our human body.

We watched the young female doctor examine Tia. I wished she had more experience, but with our pack's chief doctor being injured and in the clinic himself, it couldn't be helped. Well, it could've been helped if my wolf hadn't gone nuts at the sight of another man touching his mate and hurled the exceptional man through a wall. After finding her in the woods, the twins had surged into action. Luke had shifted back to his human form, scooped her up in his arms, and taken off at a blurring speed toward the pack house. Levi had remained in his wolf form to run alongside and watch for any assailants. My wolf had been livid at them for handling his mate. He hurtled forward to snatch her away from Luke, but to his utter horror, for the first time in his life, my wolf had found he was outmatched. He'd struggled to stay close enough to Luke's running figure to keep him in sight.

The doctor finished hooking up an IV and scribbled down all of Tia's vital signs before turning to talk to me.

"She is stable, but she should've woken up by now. I suspect she exhausted herself both mentally and physically, and her body forced a complete shut-down to heal." Her tone was compassionate, but wary. I couldn't fault her for her fear since we had just thrown her colleague and mentor through a brick wall.

"You mean like werewolves do? When their wolves shut down to mend? But she isn't a wolf." My wolf spoke the questions that were racing through my mind. The doctor flinched at the harsh sound of my wolf's voice.

"Alpha, she is not a wolf. But her blood shares some similarities with ours. She is a supernatural, and if I were to speculate, a shifter. But she's not werewolf."

My wolf nodded his head to dismiss her and then closed the door so fast it locked the twins out of the room. We watched our mate breathe in and out, accompanied by beeps from the monitors. The doctor must have changed her out of her clothes and into the open-sided hospital gown. She had bandages across her head, a smaller one on her cheek, and a large patch on her side. Seeing how fragile she appeared, my wolf grew more outraged. His thoughts became more animal, and I could only pick up on his emotions, not actual words. I felt his remorse for failing her, his rage toward the men who did this, and the last - which alarmed me most - his anger toward me for holding him back from marking her the moment he'd laid eyes on her. My wolf stilled before he dashed forward and started sniffing her neck.

"No, no, no," I yelled over and over in our mind. I struggled to take back control of our body.

My wolf fought back and remained in command. "Our mate will wear our mark and be bound to us. She will share some of our Alpha strength and will be able to reach us with the mind-link when she is in trouble before she is nearly killed," he snapped, growling at me in my head.

With that, he directed his attention back on her neck, grunting when he sniffed where one of the Betas had marked her. As he reached a spot of delicate skin on her neck that hadn't been marked, a tidal wave of desire shot through our body. My cock twitched in my pants. I had never known desire like this in my life. Our mate was so perfect. She was ours. With that, I watched with equal parts relief and dismay as he bit down hard on her neck, leaving his Alpha mark.

Neither of us expected to be hurled back against the wall as rolling waves of shimmering blue light flowed down her frame. The area around our bite glowed brilliantly, and a pattern formed out of it. It was as if a tattoo was being created out of sheer light. The elegant lines slid down her neck from the imprint, connecting with the Beta's marks, before they continued down her arms. From the smoldering heat radiating from the bed, I would bet those lines were being traced down her back as well. When the dancing light reached her wounds, it grew more intense and pulsed. We were completely captivated, watching as pure energy wrapped her body in an almost loving caress.

The monitors in the room began making all sorts of screeching noises, and her eyes fluttered open wide. She must have spotted the light because she raised her head and peered down at her arms. With a shocked gasp, she scrambled out of bed, holding her arms out in front of her in fear. She followed the lacey swirls of light up her arms and then down her sides. When her gaze landed on the bandage covering her side, from what we believed was a knife wound, she ripped off the bandage. I stared in wonder at the flawless skin she uncovered. There was not a single hint of a blade wound, no pink scar, not even a paper cut. It was completely healed. Slowly, she lifted her gaze and saw the mirror that was against the back of the door, and stepped toward it in a dreamlike trance. The mirror was a couple of feet from where I stood, still propped against the wall where I had been tossed by her power. As she neared me, I realized that what had appeared to be a random pattern of lace-like lines, were scales, like the pattern found on a serpent.

I was a paranormal, so weird stuff shouldn't bother me, right? Wrong. This was so far outside the realm of what I considered normal, it wasn't even funny. As she inhaled, I quickly refocused my attention on her face which was reflected in the mirror. Her beautiful eyes were blazing blue and glittering, just like the tattoos the sapphire light had created.

Oh crap.

Tia's fingers settled on the bite mark my wolf had left. Her voice rang out clear as a bell in the room, and each word had a strange echo to it as though someone else was speaking them at the same time. But that wasn't what had us pressing against the wall. It was the ferocity with which she said, "You. Marked. *Me?*"

Who had explained to her what marking meant? I wondered if I would get that answer before she killed us? It was evident that that was her intention as she raised her palm, sending a swirl of energy crashing into us and pinning us against the wall.

And why the devil was my wolf nearly purring in satisfaction at how sexy our mate looked?

CHAPTER ELEVEN

Tia

"Wha... how do you know about mates?"

I would have laughed at the big bad Alpha stuttering, but as his words sunk in, I froze in confusion. How did I know? Hearing a soft snickering, I immediately dropped into a fighting stance and glanced around the room.

"What's wrong, Tia?" Cage asked cautiously.

"Shh. I heard something that sounded like a person snickering." I began checking each corner of the room.

After not finding anyone, I stood still and rubbed the back of my neck.

"I could have sworn-" I began speaking, only to be cut off with a loud, "BOO!"

I'm ashamed to admit I vaulted onto the bed and let out a

girly screech rivaling any preteen girl at a Bieber concert.

With a concerned expression, Cage struggled with whether to step closer or back away.

"Who said that?" My heart hammered as my eyes scanned the room again.

"Come on, cupcake. You are acting a bit dense."

Staring at Cage, I realized he didn't hear the voice, so it must be...

"In your head? Very good. Who's a smart girl? Tia's a smart girl," the silken voice in my head teased.

"Who are you? Am I crazy?" I must be losing my marbles. I was trying to communicate with a voice in my head.

Listen closely. I'm your conscience. I'm here to guide you into making good decisions. She giggled. *Just kidding. I'm your inner beast, and I prefer to make entertaining and, occasionally, illegal decisions.*

"Am I supposed to believe that? Inner beast? That's the best you can come up with?" I snorted at my brain's weirdness.

Yes, your inner beast. More specifically, a dragoness. There is a lot more you will need to learn, but frankly, you are too freaked out right now to take in everything. I will explain more in time. Your parents and Draven are tied up in this as well. Again, we will deal with that later. Right now, I need to finish explaining what marking means. You kinda went hysterical on his butt before I was finished.

Every supernatural is granted a soulmate. This is the individual who should love you so much they will constantly watch your back. They help keep your life in balance, which helps maintain your mental health and happiness. This person is destined for you and when they are gone, there is not another being on earth who is created for you in the same way. Your soulmate is like the puzzle piece meant to complete you.

This pertains to all supers, but your situation is unique. You are extraordinarily powerful, and you have some say so over whom you wish your mate, or mates, to be. If you were wolf, or one of the blood driven, then the bite this Alpha just gave you would have bound you two together, and you would have had no choice. Your thoughts and his would have become interwoven, and you would have gone into heat with the need to finish tying you two together for the rest of eternity.

But you, cupcake, are incredibly special, and these rules don't apply to you. You not only have to accept the bond, but you have to bite back. Meaning ten Alphas could mark you, and they would all be bound to you. They are stuck with you until you either mark them back, or your mating circle is complete.

This means you cannot be forced into choosing him, but since he marked you, he has bound himself to you. Someone is not going to be pleased. Her voice echoed, and her laughter reverberated in my head at the image of Cage's frustrated wolf.

I didn't know Cage well enough to decide if I wanted to be bound to him forever. I tried to absorb all the information she had just dumped on me, when suddenly everything clicked.

"Are you telling me that had I not been special, I would have been joined to him permanently? With no way out? Like married?"

Yep, pretty much. Such a naughty wolf. She sounded more amused than angry about this. *Darling, with time, you will learn we are something the earth hasn't seen in centuries. Men are going to want you, crave to claim you. That is one of the reasons we were given the ability to choose whether to bond. We don't have to worry about being marked as a play for power, rather than for love. It isn't all bad though. Basically, we are going to have horny guys lining up to please us. And boy, it has been way too long since I experienced-*

I tuned her out in my head. I needed to deal with this situation, not imagine what dirty things a werewolf mate might be eager and able to do to me. *Ugh.* Now I was thinking about sex. Although my body twinged with desire (thanks, stupid traitorous vagina), Cage had betrayed my trust. The thought of all the things that would have been stolen from me, without so much as asking my opinion, wasn't going to fly with me. Perhaps this was okay with werewolf females. Perhaps it was even expected in a pack. But this wasn't cool with me. I pivoted to face Cage where he had been gradually inching from the wall toward me.

Whatever he saw in my eyes must have intimidated the almighty Alpha wolf, because he let out a whimper and slunk back against the wall. Grief seared my chest. I was finally grasping the notion of soulmates, and the gift they should be, but mine had basically forced his claim on me. How could he? My soul cried out for comfort. As my fury and despair increased, the air crackled. It became harder to breathe. I would have gone into a full-blown panic attack had the door not crashed in, giving way to my brown-haired... What?

Friends? Rescuers? Acquaintances? Mates? Son of a monkey! Were they my soulmates?

Blood Guards. Although we could claim them as our mates. Just imagine. Twin hunks who are used to working together. She cackled.

Had I been in a steadier state of mind, I would have pursued the whole Blood Guard thing, but I was so relieved to see the twins. All I could do was throw myself at them and cry. They must have picked up on my emotions like they had back in Cage's office because Luke, who was in wolf form, started sniffing, searching for an injury or threat. Levi was in human form and held me tightly, his growls vibrating his chest. I immediately calmed under their touch.

I pulled myself together and then stiffened as Luke brushed my hair away from my face, which was wet and sticky from tears. He was going to see the mark Cage had left on my neck, and that was going to go down like a box of rocks. A roar burst from his chest as he grabbed Cage by the throat and slammed him into the wall, causing the wall to crack. Cage is a massive dude, and my mouth dropped open in shock at Luke's brute strength.

"You marked her while she was unconscious? How dare you." He ground out the words through clenched teeth.

"She is my mate, and I will protect her. It is my duty, and a decision only for me to make." Cage struggled in Luke's unwavering grasp.

It was then I noticed Cage's eyes were not his natural color. They were a glowing green, practically neon. His eyes snapped up to meet mine, and I felt a sharp pain in my head.

His eyes narrowed, and he finally shoved Luke off him and stalked toward me. Levi circled my body and kept his eyes fastened on Cage. No, this wasn't Cage. This was Cage's wolf. I watched him suspiciously and flinched as his palm pushed my hair back from where it had once again hid his mark.

"I don't understand. Why can't I read your thoughts? The mark is here, and it appears to be a successful bonding. I can sense your emotions better than before, but I can't read your mind. A female can't resist their mate once she has been claimed. Even if you were annoyed, you should be trying to mount me, or at least touch me." He tilted his head like a bewildered puppy, and if I hadn't been furious about him marking me without asking, I would have found it adorable. But I was still angry and heartsick, so I flipped my long hair back to where it covered his mark and straightened my shoulders.

He rumbled, "Don't cover your mark. Please." Cage was studying the mark with a perplexed expression.

How dare he ask anything of me. He certainly hadn't asked before attempting to bind us together for life. My rage had reached a boiling point, and I couldn't stop myself from saying, "Your mark was successful. Successful in binding you to me." I explained as I slipped on a pair of jeans someone had laid out for me.

All three sets of eyes jerked up to see if I was serious. I shrugged and searched around the room until I spotted a hoodie. I picked it up and sniffed; it smelled like Levi. My heart fluttered at his familiar scent.

"Turn around," I ordered and nearly burst out laughing at

how quick a blush covered all three faces. They spun around so fast they nearly lost their balance. I slipped off the gown, if you can call a scrap of material with two huge slits in it a gown. I pulled the large hoodie over my head.

"Finished." I walked over to the mirror I had looked in earlier. Dark circles under my eyes, a bite mark on my neck, and skin so pale I should have been a vampire, or I guess it's Blood Driven, according to my inner beast. I couldn't help but snort at the reminder of what the voice called herself. It sounded like a women's ad for a razor or mascara.

I strolled across the shattered door, pausing for a moment to figure out which direction the pack house was in. The three guys stumbled out behind me. They were still letting out little growls as they followed me.

There was a pounding in my ears. It felt like something inside of me was pressing against my skin to get out. Maybe I just needed to eat something. I made a beeline for the kitchen door. I sensed the big, bad Alpha was about to question me again, so I flung open the door and scurried in.

If only I had known what waited for me inside, I would have ordered pizza and stayed in the hospital bed... then again, maybe I wouldn't have. I was done putting up with crap.

"Who marked you, freak? I feel sorry for whoever is stuck with you."

I couldn't help the smirk spreading across my face.

My inner beast uncoiled with a chuckle, and I knew she was coming out to play.

CHAPTER TWELVE

Tia

I felt warmth flow from my center through my body. The heat spread up my throat and my face flushed. What in the world was happening? Glancing to the left, I spotted my reflection in the glass of a grandfather clock.

My tattoos were showing again, the blue scales shimmering on my skin. When I looked at my eyes, I stopped breathing. There was that eerie glowing blue, but in the middle of the iris, they flashed like lightening. *Great. I just keep getting weirder.*

I snapped out of my daze when I realized my body was moving on its own. My hands shot out to my side, my arm outstretched, and then pointed straight at Trixie.

Oh darn. This was some kind of creepy, demon possession-level crap.

Internally, I was freaking out. A snake formed from water, rushed from the direction of the kitchen, and soaked her to the bone. Her mascara ran, and her hair dripped on the floor. Before she had a chance to open her mouth, my left hand twirled in a circle and the door shot open, allowing a blast of air to blow in and dance around Trixie.

When the gust died down, she stood turning a darkening shade of crimson, while her two look-a-like friends became pale and swung their wide eyes to stare at me. Trixie looked like the Bride of Frankenstein with her hair sticking straight up at odd angles and her mascara dried in streaks both above and below her eyes.

I don't think anybody else had caught her new look though, because everyone was gawking at me, awestruck. I chortled in my mind at Trixie's makeover. I wasn't nearly as disturbed about the whole possession thing anymore.

With a graceful sexiness I knew I didn't own, my body sauntered toward the little witch. Obviously, having every unmated wolf in the area drooling at my feet made Trixie a little unhappy. I'm sure her fury had absolutely nothing to do with the makeover I had given her. Nope, nothing at all.

I smirked.

She stamped her foot. No joke. The chick stomped like she was a five-year-old, and shrieked, "You will not treat me like this. You are a homeless nobody; even our Omega has a higher position in the pack than you."

My eyes slowly rose to study at her as one of my eyebrows arched. I had been trying to do the cool eyebrow thing for years. Son of a gun, I wasn't the one controlling my body; I was simply watching a movie starring a super-cool version of myself. I was loving it.

A velvety voice filled the silence, "I walked into this room, and you immediately insulted me. I will give you to the count of three to apologize. One..."

Everyone in the room bowed to the voice I instantly identified as my beast. It was alluring yet commanding at the same time. I wouldn't have been surprised to find the males on their knees from the power, but still crawling toward the sound at the same time. *Heck, yeah! Tia 2.0 is in the house.* If I had control of my body, I would have fist pumped the air.

I guess jealousy was really messing with Trixie's common sense. She crossed her arms under her breasts, giving us all an eye full, and huffed.

"Two." My inner beast drew the word out while staring at Trixie, "Girl, you should start talking before I give you the scare of your life."

At this point, I felt a tiny seed of respect for Trixie, because she was either incredibly brave, or unbelievably stupid.

Trixie popped her hip out and declared, "Bring it, Hobo."

"Three." Beasty (yeah, I'm totally rolling with that nickname) sauntered out the front door.

Lo and behold, guess who followed us out within seconds? Trixie! Man, that girl must have a death wish.

"You do not walk away from me, you little freak!" she shouted.

My body quivered. Electricity vibrated in my rib cage. I struggled to pull this strange feeling back into my center. I had a feeling if it flowed to my limbs, we were all going to be terrified. While I was busy fighting this internal battle, Trixie just couldn't shut up. Did she eat a lot of paint chips growing up?

"I see you shaking. You talk big, but we all know you are a little coward," Trixie taunted.

My inner beast moved inside me, and the tingles spread out a little farther.

"Come on, Tia. Stop resisting me. It's time." Her tone was gentle, but firm.

"No, no. I don't even know what is happening." I was more than a little alarmed. I was downright terrified of what was about to go down unless I found a way to stop it.

Tia, this is normal. It is time for you to embrace our power. It is nothing to dread. We won't hurt Trixie. Too much. She finished with a chuckle that made me nervous, but her other words had reassured me a bit. At least one of us knew what was going on.

"Little orphaned freak. Your parents probably died from the embarrassment of having a kid like you," sneered Trixie.

A pang hit my heart, and my anger blazed. And that was just enough to make me lose focus. The energy that I had been hanging onto for dear life escaped my grasp. The tingles rushed from my ribcage to the tips of my fingers and toes. Peace enveloped me in a hug. It was the happiest I had felt since losing my parents.

I was forced back to reality by Trixie. She walked over to me and raised her hand to slap me. What was it with her and slapping? Before her palm could strike my face, my hand caught her wrist. I peered at her palm for a minute like it was a foreign body I had never seen before. My reflexes had always been fast, but never this quick.

"Does the wee little pup want to play?" I felt the beast inside shift.

Close your eyes and relax. I will help you with the transition, Beasty coached.

I did as she requested. My body hummed and tingles traveled through my frame. It was over in moments.

I opened my eyes to find the world was clearer. Details were so sharp that I could cut myself on them. It altered my hearing too. I tuned in and heard a bee a mile away. I felt emotions rolling off the people crowded around us. And then I heard Trixie's heartbeat and realized I was still grasping her wrist inches from my face.

With the sultry voice I now realized belonged to me, I whispered, "Are you scared yet?"

She snatched her hand away while snarling, "Never, freak."

She shifted into her she-wolf. If I were a male wolf, I would have found her dove-grey coat beautiful. She was athletic and elegant. If I batted for the other team, I would have been chasing her tail. Literally.

A wave of agony flooded through my body and I bent at the waist, trying to ease the stabbing pain. When it finally eased, I uncurled my frame, only to find I was now a foot taller.

But did the weirdness stop there? *Nope.* My fingertips burned, and I was stunned when I glanced down to discover my fingers were slightly longer. Not in a creepy monster-looking way, but in an elegant model sort of way. The nails were iridescent mother-of-pearl and so sharp they probably needed to be registered as lethal weapons. These were going to be awesome next time I had to get all stabby on someone.

My ears distracted me when they began tingling. I reached up to rub them and choked. They had shifted as well. My ears came to a point and were about three inches longer than they had been moments before. I had fairy ears?

Beasty snorted, *They are dragon ears, Boo.* Alrighty then.

I looked to the grey wolf examining me with wary eyes. "Do you still want a piece of me, pup?"

And to her credit, while everyone else backed away in fear, Trixie growled and darted toward me, flashing her teeth. As she lunged for my throat, I crouched and whirled around, my hair fanning out around me. I heard her pained whimper. My hair had evidently changed, and it was sharp, slicing her like a knife.

She immediately spun around and darted back, trying to trap my leg in her jaws. I easily sidestepped the bite and rounded, kicking out with my opposite leg. She sailed ten feet back and struck a tree. Apparently, my new form never missed leg day at the gym. I grinned.

She winced as she stood but suddenly straightened her spine and began circling me, licking her fangs like she was starved. Periodically, she leapt forward while snapping, and I swung out with a punch or a swift kick.

After being somersaulted through the air and into a tree several more times and being sliced with my nails and hair, she gathered her strength for a final attack. In a last-ditch attempt to take me down, she launched herself into the air, aiming for my neck. She was in a frenzy of rage at not even being able to put a scratch on me.

I was growing tired of the game, ready to see her submit so we could finally end this. I surged forward to meet her body and grabbed her throat. My momentum propelled us several feet through the air where I landed with one knee bent and my left hand touching the dirt, while my right hand slammed her into the earth hard enough to send a spiderweb of cracks through the ground. Yep, I was pretty certain I was a super-hero now.

"You will submit. This conflict was over before it started, and I have no wish to cause you permanent injury or death. You will heal from these scratches and fractured bones, but you must surrender now."

She set her jaw and deliberately made sure her tail was straight out, rather than tucking in submission. I had remained calm and in control of my anger, but now it bubbled up inside me. I don't enjoy fighting. I had just shifted into a new form, and I was beyond exhausted. This was a waste of time and energy.

I stared deep into her eyes and spoke, my voice resonating with authority, "Submit. Now."

My tone left no room for argument, and at least her wolf recognized this. The bloody and dirt covered grey wolf tucked her tail in and curled into a ball. Satisfied, I stood, brushing the dirt from my hands. I took in all the pale faces around me. The entire pack had witnessed the fight, and now nearly two hundred wolves watched me.

"I am Tiamat. The Dragoness of the Sea."

A searing pain ripped through my back. It was so unexpected. I arched and screamed. Wings burst through my skin and tore through the hoodie. I stared at the enormous wings. That was the moment I freaked out. I bent my body and flung myself up, spinning into the air and away from the horrified faces of the werewolves below me.

Chapter Thirteen

Cage

After watching Tia swirl up into the sky and disappear, the entire pack continued to stare up. No one could believe what they had just witnessed. Hearing whines, I glanced over to see Levi and Luke in wolf form pacing back and forth. Their anxiety swept through the pack bond. I started moving toward them. I couldn't be near my mate. I got some weird comfort in being close to them. And that was doubtless because of the blood bond they shared with her.

Before I had taken more than half a dozen steps, a shriek of pure fury halted me. I turned around to see Trixie stomping her foot and ranting about the winged monster. Looking around, I realized the pack was now staring in open-mouthed horror at her. Obviously, they, like myself, couldn't comprehend how an average female wolf would continue to be contemptuous toward such a powerful creature. Trixie's wolf had submitted, acknowledging that she didn't have a chance against a shifter like Tia. But the human part of Trixie didn't appear to be smart enough to understand exactly how foolish her actions were. I prepared to reprimand her but decided that Tia was more than capable of showing her authority and her absolute right to lead this pack at my side. I resolved to let Trixie either learn or dig her own grave.

Turning back toward the twins, I saw they had shifted to their human forms and were sitting on the grass, a glazed over expression on their faces. With a start, I realized my wolf had withdrawn back into my mind, giving up most of the control. He remained beyond confused at why his mate wasn't fully bound to him, and why she hadn't submitted to his claim. He admired her display of strength but was conflicted as well. His she-wolf was to be protected; she was not meant to fight. I'm not certain he liked that he was beneath her in power. My skull reverberated with his growl at my last assessment.

"Is she okay?" I demanded when I stopped a few feet in front of them.

Neither moved for a moment, and then Luke slowly angled his body toward me with troubled eyes; "She is nearby. I can feel her exhaustion and bewilderment. I just don't know precisely where she is. When she becomes one with her beast, it seems she can choose what to share with us through the bond."

"Did you realize she was a dragon?"

Levi answered this time, "No. But I'm betting this is the reason they kidnapped her."

I thought about that for several minutes. "I disagree. If they knew she was physically this powerful, they would have immediately sedated and, likely, caged her. I think we did get a few more pieces to the puzzle though."

I watched as the members of the pack slowly broke out of their befuddled state and dusted themselves off, finally returning to what they had been doing before the fight. Levi, Luke, and I remained sitting in the same spot, staring at the skies, and hoping to catch any trace of Tia's return.

TIA

I flew at a pace so swift everything around me was a blur. The wind whipped my hair around me, and I enjoyed feeling the power of my wings as they moved. Eventually, the exhaustion from the day caught up with me and I drifted closer and closer to the treetops, before finally spotting a creek. I dropped smoothly to the ground and touched down with a grace I knew came from 'Beasty'.

I closed my eyes and kneeled by the creek to drink heavily from my cupped palms. When I finished drinking, I kept my eyes squeezed shut as I splashed water on my face. I couldn't find the courage to look at my reflection. Would I see a monster?

I continued to sit and focus on breathing for what seemed like a lifetime before finally cracking my eyes open and taking the smallest peek at my image. The first thing I noticed was my glowing blue eyes. I was almost getting used to them now.

Then I saw my hair. It tumbled around my face, and it was such a pale blonde that it was almost white. The individual strands were iridescent, lightly reflecting hints of pale lilac, gold, and pink. As I turned my head, I realized my skin shimmered as I moved.

Before I even had time to process my sparkly new skin, my twitchy and very pointy ears caught my attention. I couldn't stop my gasp.

Good grief. Beasty had lied. I was a flipping fairy. I wouldn't be surprised if I started leaving a trail of glitter everywhere.

Beasty growled out dragon, but I heard the amusement in her tone.

Who cares?? Fairy, dragon, pixie.... all were imaginary.

Ugh. Don't talk about pixies. They are such miserable little creatures. Beasty shuddered.

I huffed in irritation only to end with a yelp as my wings fluttered behind me. How could I have overlooked them? Who gets wings and forgets about them? I gave myself a mental face slap.

Gathering my determination, I leaned further over the creek, squinting at my body. Levi's hoodie was virtually shredded. It now ended right above my belly button, exposing skin on my breast and abdomen. Skin which shimmered.

Faint scale looking marks ran down along my torso and neck. The marks matched my tattoos, which glowed in my human form, but now it was like someone had brushed them on using pearl paint.

What was I? A five-year-old girl's pretty princess painting project? I had never seen that much sparkle and shimmer in my life. This was a lot to take in for a girl that loved her worn military boots and leather bomber jacket.

"Breathtakingly beautiful." A deep voice whispered from behind me.

I let out a shriek and tumbled face forward toward the creek, stopping only when my hands touched it. Instead of plunging into the frigid water, the water beneath me had become as solid as glass. I was temporarily distracted.

"If I had a breath that could be taken."

And I remembered what had sent me tumbling toward the water. I screamed, clutching my heart, which was fighting to tear through my ribcage. I peered into the gathering twilight to locate the voice.

Slowly, the silhouette of a figure stepped out from the shelter of the forest surrounding the stream. *Sweet, powdered-sugar brownies!* The shape turned into a guy so hot he should be on the cover of magazines.

"Yes, you are absolutely exquisite. In fact, you look good enough to eat." The man grinned, and slid his tongue over his teeth, revealing two pearly white, and very pointy fangs.

Scrambling backwards and off the solid slab of water, I was transfixed. *I should run. Yeah. Definitely.* Still smiling, he took a step toward me and made a low hiss.

I was positive I would have yelled in terror, had Beasty not distracted me.

Meow, she purred.

You freak, I cried in my head. *He's about to devour us.*

We can only hope. Beasty giggled. Yes, she actually giggled. I was about to be eaten, and where was my butt-kicking inner beast? Off acting like a horny teenager.

I focused on my soon-to-be murderer and watched as his cerulean eyes changed to an ominous maroon. If he bit my neck, he was going to have to suck really hard to pull the blood back up from where it had now drained from my head down to my toes. I squeezed my eyes closed so I wouldn't see his teeth coming.

I felt his skin brush mine as he lifted my hair away from my neck. I still couldn't fathom why Beasty wasn't going all ninja on his butt like she did on Trixie. I waited for the bite. And waited... and waited. After the crazy roller coaster of a day, I was ready to get this over with.

"Seriously, just do it," I gritted out. I heard a strangling noise. Opening my eyes, I glared at the stranger bent over with his elbows on his knees. Laughing his super shapely butt off. He was laughing.

"You should have seen your face," he chortled. "*Just do it,*" he said, mimicking me. He was laughing so hard that he would have passed out had he actually needed to breathe.

"Oh, that's it!" I was going to whoop his butt with or without Beasty's help. Standing up, I strode over to him and stuck my finger in his face. The dork only laughed harder.

I screamed, and then one of my wings swung around and whacked him upside his head.

"Ouch!" He grabbed his head, but still kept chuckling.

My other wing swung around and smacked him again. This time he crouched down, attempting to evade my wings. Man, who knew these things were so helpful? I smirked.

Tall, mysterious, and handsome was still kneeling in the dirt. He stared up at me with 'puppy eyes' and whimpered, "Please don't beat me. I'll behave."

And with that, we both cracked up laughing. I laughed like a deranged person. All my emotions from the last few days washed over me and I let it all out. I laughed until I sobbed. My cries turned to hiccups.

Finally, there was nothing left. I rolled unto my side so I could study the goofy guy. He was holding my hand and stroking the back of it with his thumb while regarding me with worry and curiosity.

"So, you aren't going to eat me?" I asked.

"Not a chance. I'm vegetarian." He spoke with an absolutely straight face.

We looked at each other before bursting into giggles, although more softly this time.

"I could drink your blood, but I prefer to buy my blood in bottles and enjoy them chilled."

I didn't even know that was an option. I had so many things to learn about supernatural creatures.

"Who are you running from?" His tone was soothing.

"What makes you think I am running?"

"Hmmm. Let's see. You are wearing a shirt that has been ripped to shreds. You are in the middle of a national park with no trace of a tent or supplies. You also just had a near emotional breakdown. I think it's clear you aren't here on vacation."

I exhaled. How much should I tell him? Why did I feel like I could trust him? A complete stranger. I guess laughter could bring two people together. Or maybe I was simply desperate for someone to talk to.

I told him everything. My middle of the night run through the burning forest, the twins finding me, my kidnapping, the werewolf Alpha creating a bond that didn't completely work, annoying Trixie, my transformation, and then my mind-numbing flight which had landed me by the creek.

He didn't say a word the entire time. He only listened. When I finished, we were both silent for several minutes. Finally, he broke the silence. "So now what? Will you go back?"

"I don't know. I need time to think things through. I already miss Levi and Luke. And there is some sort of tie to Cage."

"Do you want to come home with me? It's nothing fancy, but you can have some quiet time, and it's safe."

I rolled to my back and stared up at the night sky. The stars were glittering, and the moon was nearly full. A wolf howled in the distance, and another wolf answered. It was an eerie sound that made my skin prickle. It was hauntingly beautiful.

Next to me, my new friend shifted and sat up, "You better decide quick, chica, because those are your friends, and they are coming for you."

My heart skipped an excited couple of beats at the

thought of seeing them. The fact that they were coming for me meant my transformation hadn't disgusted them. But I still needed time to process everything. I didn't want to go back to all the stares at the pack house yet.

"Let's go," I replied. He stood up in a single swift movement. He thrust out a hand and pulled me to my feet.

He continued clasping my hand and said, "Don't let go."

I was about to ask why, but I was quickly sucked into a dark vortex. The earth spun wildly. Just as abruptly, my feet connected with a hard surface. I stood swaying like a newborn deer against my murderer-now-turned-bff.

"Holy crap. What was that?" I closed my eyes, waiting for the churning to stop, and struggling not to barf all over him.

"Teleporting," he declared in a chirpy tone.

"Why didn't you warn me?" I demanded.

"Because this is so much more entertaining," he said with a grin. He spun around and strolled out of the room. I followed him through the passage into an utterly gorgeous marble hallway. The domed ceilings were covered in gold fabric, and the floors were white marble with golden strands running through them.

"I thought you said your house was nothing fancy?" I growled in a stage whisper, as though we were robbers that had broken into the house.

"Once again, your reactions are way too much fun." He chuckled.

As we rounded the corner into another elegant room, I caught sight of a figure coming down an imposing staircase. As our gazes locked, energy snapped out from me and crackled through the room. Beasty sighed, and her contentment hummed inside me.

The newcomer moved down the stairs at the speed of light. I was wrapped in his embrace in mere seconds, and he was giving me the kiss of a lifetime. He kissed me as though he was a dying man, and I was the only thing keeping him alive.

What truly astonished me wasn't the panty drenching kiss. It was the fact that my wings, which evidently have a mind of their own, circled around our bodies, creating a warm cocoon. It made the embrace even more intimate and intense.

His only reaction was to deepen the kiss and pull me tighter against him.

CHAPTER FOURTEEN

Tia

T he kiss was sheer torture and pure bliss at the same time. Emotions slammed into my body with a force that was almost painful. Shock, lust, confusion, and desire set every nerve ending humming. How on earth was it possible for me to worry about what was happening, but also feel as if I had come home?

My core began tightening, and my hunger increased. My nipples became two aching peaks, and the friction as they rubbed against the hard ridges of his chest had me moaning. It took every fiber of willpower I possessed not to climb this man like a tree.

I think he might have been a mind reader because his palms glided down my sides and over the rounded curve of my butt. He lifted my body, allowing my long legs to wrap around his impeccable torso. And boy, did I wrap them. I clung to him like a spider monkey.

His hands explored my body. When his knuckles brushed against the inside of my wing, I gasped from the sensation. I nearly orgasmed on the spot. Who knew having my wings petted would be such a turn on? He stilled, deciding if I had gasped from pain or desire.

I stunned myself by growling against his stubble covered jaw and dragging myself tighter against his magnificent body. His bulging hardness bumped against my bottom. It was straining against his slacks. Although we were both fully dressed, I couldn't stop myself from aligning our bodies until the heat radiating from his cock seared through the layers of clothing, making me tremble with need.

Reaching out, he gently stroked his fingertips down my wing. Oh, goddess! I was going to come just from his touch. The kiss had already made me wet, but now I was drenched. My core tightened and I ground down harder against his erection, seeking relief.

One of his hands snaked into my hair, intensifying our kiss, while the other ran across the remains of my hoodie, halting right under my breast to circle his thumb across my swollen nipple.

My skin burned hotter, and I was reasonably sure I was being set on fire from the inside out. Before I could spontaneously combust, I was forced out of my lust-induced haze by the sound of someone gagging.

I peeked over the shoulder of this sex-dream guy come to life to find my friend - I'm using that term loosely since he had just interrupted one of the best moments of my life - grasping his throat and rolling around on the marbled floor in feigned agony.

"Ugh. My eyes! My innocent eyes! I'm melting..." He choked out while performing an extraordinarily theatrical death.

The handsome hunk, still holding me against him snorted in disdain. "Innocent? You haven't been innocent in roughly a century. And we are Blood Driven, not witches, so you wouldn't melt. You would disintegrate into dust. And right now, that wouldn't upset me the slightest."

I had never been so mortified in my life. You would think I was a cat in heat with the way I had just jumped this complete stranger in front of another guy I barely knew. Even after being brought back to my senses, I was reluctant to unwrap myself from this mysterious man who had just rocked my entire world with a kiss. I prayed the earth would just open and swallow me whole. When nothing happened, I sighed and slid down his body to stand up. My wing, still with a mind of its own, reached out and slapped the overly dramatic guy for interrupting us.

"Ow," he whined.

"Dork," I shot back, sticking out my tongue.

Mr. Sexy Pants gently turned me back toward him. He tenderly brushed a lock of blonde hair from my face before whispering, "Tu ești sufletul meu pereche."

He stared at me with an expression of wonder. I could tell the words were significant, and the language was beautiful, but I couldn't figure out a word he had said.

He must have noticed my confusion. "It is Romanian, meaning you are my soulmate. I have waited for you for over a century. The longer a Blood Driven lives, the more his world dims. The colors, our sense of taste, and our emotions all fade. Our heart beats slower and slower with each passing century until it eventually ceases to beat, and we turn into the living dead. But if we find our suflet pereche, it halts the process. You are what completes me. In a sense, you make me alive again."

My hand rested on his broad chest, his heartbeat steady against my palm. It was not as strong as mine, but it was definitely there.

"But I feel your heart. You aren't dead," I protested.

"I am not dead like most of the vampires in modern stories and television." He paused, deciding how to phrase the rest of what he wished to say. "I am from an original line of Blood Driven. I was born, not made. My father found his soulmate before his heart stopped beating. My mother, also Blood Driven, was only a few decades old when my father found her, and her body could still carry a baby. I was born much the same way as a mortal child."

"So, all of your kind are born?" I questioned.

"No, but that discussion can wait for another day."

"Is a suflet pereche," I grimaced as I mangled the pronunciation, "similar to the soulmates in the werewolf world?"

"Yes, very similar. Except that a werewolf can choose to reject the bond, and mate with a wolf other than their soulmate. Yes, a Driven can have a relationship with partners other than their suflet pereche, or soulmate, but it will not keep their heart beating. For me, there will only ever be you." With those words, he leaned in and placed a tender kiss on my nose.

I couldn't stop the dopey grin on my face. Come on. Admit it. It was adorable.

A voice I was beginning to be less fond of spoke up behind me, "I thought it was customary to at least learn a girl's name before you slobber all over her."

"Oh yes. Because we all know that you have never woken up beside a girl and didn't know her name." Hunky spoke with a tone that dripped sarcasm.

Mouth-wateringly handsome, and he spoke my language? The language of sarcasm? I was done for. I was ready to rip off his clothes and lick him all over. What? Don't judge me. Haven't you ever heard of 'I licked it, so it's mine'?

Yes, excellent plan. Let's get right on that! Beasty purred.

Focusing back on the two men, I couldn't stop my laugh. They scowled as they glared at each other.

Breaking up their staring competition, I cut in, "Okay, so what are your names?"

Gently stroking my cheek with his finger, Hunky said, "My name is Mithraheal, and it is a distinct pleasure to meet you. Something I am confident will continue to bring even more pleasure."

I shivered. *Somebody call the fire station because it is getting H-O-T in here!*

The guy from the woods burst out laughing. He rolled his eyes. "And I am Damien, and we are the Conlier brothers." He flung out his arms as if he was a side show circus performer. I half expected the circus theme song "Entry of the Gladiators" to start playing in the background.

"Wait, what?" I sputtered in shock. "You two are brothers? Other than the whole hotter-than-anything-else-walking-on-two-legs thing, you two look nothing a like."

Damien spoke up, "Well, see, after my parents had him, they figured they knew what their mistakes were and could make a more perfect version. Ta Da! Say hello to the perfect Conlier!"

Mithraheal ran his hand through his stylishly long hair, chuckling softly. It was clear he was used to his younger brother's ridiculous antics and had a genuine affection for Damien.

Meeting my eyes, he asked, "What is your name, gorgeous?"

"Tiamat, but call me Tia."

Damien laughed so hard he snorted, "Fitting. So very fitting!"

I lifted my eyebrow at him.

He continued, "In Babylonian mythology, Tiamat was the personification of the sea, sometimes appearing as an enormous dragon." He looked me up and down. "You don't plan to get any bigger, right? Cause I rather like our roof. If you plan to go full dragon, we need to get you outside."

My mouth hung open, and I looked at Mithraheal. He answered my unspoken question. "My brother has picked up several odd hobbies over the decades, one of which is studying the meaning behind names."

I turned back to Damien and snapped, "I already told you, I never planned to sprout wings, or get freakin' fairy ears in the first place! I'm still weirded out by my reflection!"

His face softened up, and he looked at me with compassion.

I sighed. "Although Beasty, I mean my inner voice, said something about me being the Dragoness of the Sea after our transformation. Honestly, I am not sure about a lot of things at the moment."

Obviously, trying to distract me from the topic at hand and realizing I was utterly exhausted, he reached for my hand, "Come on Tia. You look exhausted. Let's tuck you into bed."

Before our hands connected, Mithraheal pulled me roughly against his chest and hissed at his brother, "Mine."

Startled, I jerked my eyes up to his face to find his pupils had shifted to slits resembling a serpent. His golden-brown irises were slowly trickling into crimson.

"Come on, bro. She's tired. We need to let her sleep."

Mithraheal's grip loosened, and he appeared to be listening. But Damien just had to open his big mouth again. "She's been through so much in the last few days. Even now she has a furious werewolf mate tracking her. The last thing she needs is another overprotective super trying to stake his claim right now."

Mithraheal let out something between a growl and a hiss. He lifted me up in his arms bridal style, easily maneuvering my wings, and teleported me out of the room. When I felt our bodies materializing and the vortex stopped whirling, I cracked open one eye to peek around. I was in yet another elegant room.

This time, the ceiling was all gold on the edges, but in the center, it had a recessed circle painted to look like the glittering night sky. The bed that sat right in the middle of the floor was massive.

Incredibly colored silks draped on the canopy and over the bed. There was a marble walkway leading to the bed, and on either side were pools designed to look like ponds. The pools looked deep enough to swim in. A thick plush carpet was also in the middle of the marble floor that the bed sat on. Looking to the right, I caught sight of a doorway leading into the bathroom.

I am so going to kill Damien when I saw him again. Nothing fancy, my butt. This was the type of house a god or goddess would own.

Sweeping me up the marble walkway, he lightly tossed me onto the bed. I let out an "Oomph." But before I could ask what he thought he was doing, he had scooted in bed beside me and pulled me against him again. His eyes were closed, and the muscle in his jaw was clenched and unclenched.

I attempted to wiggle free, but he held me tighter and spoke in a strained voice, "Please Tia, let me hold you. I need to listen to your heart and know you are next to me. I am trying my best to stay calm, but I just found you. My heart feels like it is going to shatter into a million pieces at the thought of losing you. You have my word I will do nothing more than hold you." His eyes were still closed, and I watched as a tear slid out of one corner.

How could I say no? And why deny him something that my own heart so desperately wanted as well? I turned over completely to face him. I snuggled up tighter against his body until there was no space between us and gently draped my wing over him.

Beasty whispered in my head, "He belongs to us."

I already had strong feelings for him, and the thought of belonging to someone sent a contented thrill through my body. In the last few days, my life had been full of so many ups and downs, and I was beyond emotionally exhausted.

I still had a connection with Cage, even if he was impulsive and pushy. Thinking of Luke and Levi, I felt their marks on my neck burn. I missed them. I wondered where the wolves were. Were they worried? Angry? And what was Mithraheal going to think of them?

With a heavy heart, I finally drifted off to sleep.

CHAPTER FIFTEEN
Cage

Where is she? My Betas and I had sat on the ground for roughly an hour before the twins growled in unison, shifted into their wolves, and sprinted off.

Knowing that when they were focused on Tia, I would have a tough time keeping up, I immediately shifted, not caring as my clothes ripped to shreds and rushed after them. Calling out to them through our pack link, I demanded to know if she was injured.

Luke replied in a clipped tone, "No, she's not in pain. But she is alarmed, and I feel her fear."

Those words pushed me to run harder. Had Draven come back to take her from me? He better not so much as lay a finger on her or I would-

The twins howled again, and I caught the worried glance they gave each other.

"What? What happened now?" I growled into the link.

Why couldn't my bite mark have worked like it was supposed to? I should have been able to sense her emotions and hear her thoughts. Instead, I had to rely on my Betas to tell me of *my* mate's feelings.

Levi's voice was a murmur in my mind, "She is petrified. I think her life is at stake. She is not fighting and angry. Instead, she is accepting. She is beyond exhausted."

I howled out my pain. I couldn't lose her. Not after I just found her. Sure, it was a little bizarre that my mate looked like a dragon, but I was sure I would grow used to it. She wouldn't need to shift. Once our mating bond was completed, I would keep her guarded. Even as I thought of her in dragon form, I could imagine my Tia's beautiful human form inside.

After running for nearly two hours, I inhaled her scent. We broke into the clearing ready for battle, but it was eerily silent. There were no traces of a conflict, and no odor of blood. It was totally empty. I sat down on my haunches and peered around with glazed eyes. She was gone.

The twins circled around the clearing and then sniffed the edge of the woods surrounding the stream. With a jolt, I felt their absolute panic in my mind. Snapping my head in their direction, they met my eyes. A single word traveled through the mind-link.

Conlier.

My heart stalled.

My breathing ceased.

My entire body hit the dirt in horror. Of all the things on earth that could have snatched my mate, why did it have to be the Conlier brothers? They were nasty Blood Driven creatures. They weren't regular Blood Driven. No; they were rulers of the entire race of Blood Driven.

Mithraheal was the older of the two. He had the reputation of being intense and ruling with an iron fist. He was a good king, but he led by instilling fear of his power. Mithraheal had yet to find his other half, and the whole supernatural world was trembling in dread of the day his heart stopped beating. He would quite literally be heartless, and, in such a forceful leader, that would mean an abundance of problems for all supernaturals.

There wasn't a whole lot more known in the supernatural world about his brother Damien. He had mingled with other supernaturals over the decades, but he was said to be ruthless. He did whatever he wanted, seldom considering the consequences.

The brothers weren't considered kind men. I couldn't understand why one of them would even bother to talk to Tia, let alone take her somewhere. They rarely bothered to acknowledge anyone other than Blood Driven.

But what had me truly alarmed was that if they decided they wanted to keep Tia, it would take nothing less than a full-blown war to get her back.

MITHRAHEAL

I had finally calmed myself by listening to her breathing as it slowly evened out. Her heart thumped steadily as I held her in my arms. She slept deeply, but I could tell she was troubled and not completely at peace. Something inside me shattered when I thought of anything causing her pain or sadness. I planned to spend the rest of my life, which was pretty much forever, making her life full of love and happiness. I would spend eternity doing everything in my power to make her laugh and her eyes sparkly with joy.

Wow. Love certainly turned you into a total sap, a voice in my head said.

Damien! What have I told you about reading my mind? It's rude and obnoxious.

Fine, fine. I was going to tell you what she had been thinking as she went to sleep, but I will just pretend to forget it.

Sighing out loud, I laid my arm over my eyes. I wanted to know. Badly. But it wasn't fair to Tia. She had the right to tell me things when she felt comfortable sharing with me.

Damien must still have been reading my mind because he spoke up quietly, *You love her. I never thought I would see the man of ice love someone.*

She is now my reason for existing. The single most impor-tant thing on earth.

Then we need to find out more about what she is. From what I discovered when I was reading her mind and the things she told me in the woods, I believe she is part of something that will shake the world. And, unfortunately, she is already being hunted down for it.

I couldn't help the hiss that escaped. No one would ever touch her again.

No. One. Ever.

Tia must have sensed my anger, because she cuddled closer to my chest and her wing gently pulled me closer to her. She mumbled, still deep in sleep. I smiled. She was trying to comfort me.

I agree, bro. But we need to figure out what, or who, we are dealing with. I'm sure we can easily defeat her enemies. We just need to find the rock they are hiding under. I have a friend we can visit tomorrow who I believe can tell us more about who she is and what we are dealing with. And maybe help answer some of her own questions.

I thought for a few minutes. *Yes, we will leave as soon as she awakens.*

CHAPTER SIXTEEN

Tia

I rolled over in bed and stretched like a feline. That was the best night's sleep I'd had since... well, I didn't think I had ever slept so well. Touching the cool place beside me, I realized Mithraheal had been up for quite a while.

A smile formed on my lips as I thought about him. He was absolute eye-candy, and he was also so unbelievably sweet. The fact he wasn't creeped out at all by my shifted self was a relief, it was as if seeing a half-dragon and half-human girl was an everyday occurrence. Although maybe it was just me who needed time to get used to my new appearance.

I thought about his smiling bronze eyes, and how they went soft when he looked at me. I remembered how wonderful his arms felt when he held me and kissed me. I would give anything to be pressing my lips against him right now. I imagined feeling his slow, soothing heartbeat against my palms, and the firmness of his lips against mine.

Holy cannoli. My imagination had gotten pretty dang vivid. It seemed incredibly real. His heated breath moved against my lips; his hands glided up my back leaving my skin tingling. I opened my eyes to break the trance I was in before it went further, only to find my lips pressed up against his.

Before I could express my shock, Mithraheal let out a yelp and pushed back from me, sending me tumbling off his lap. I landed on my backside with a thump. As suddenly as I had been tossed off his lap, I found myself gathered back in his arms while his hands checked me all over for injuries. He moved so fast, I worried I might have whiplash.

This time, it was me who let out a surprised screech when his hands drifted across my derriere. I smacked his hands away. "How did you sneak in here so quietly? I didn't even hear you coming. You nearly gave me a heart attack."

He erupted into a deep, rumbling laugh that curled my toes. "Look around, Tia."

"Why would- " I peered around and realized I was in an office. I was no longer in the silk-covered bed. "How in the world did I end up in here?" I squeaked.

"I was hoping you could tell me. I was sitting here replying to some emails, and the next thing I know you are straddling my lap and kissing me. Not that I minded in the least." He leaned forward and nipped my bottom lip.

I was apparently easily distracted. I giggled and gave a playful growl when he drew away.

The office door swung open so hard it crashed against the wall. "She's gone. I went up to offer her breakfast like you suggested and the room was empty. Obviously, no one has broken in or we would have sensed them, but where could she..."

Damien trailed off as he belatedly realized I was sitting on Mithraheal's lap with his arms wrapped around me.

"How did you get in here?" Damien demanded.

And that, my friend, is the million-dollar question.

I leaned forward and confided, "I'm a ninja." I couldn't hold back the laughter at the scowl Damien gave me.

"Love, what did you do when you woke up?" Mithraheal questioned while brushing my wild tangle of hair from my face.

"I stretched, and then I started thinking about you." I blushed. There was no way on earth I wanted to confess I had been fantasizing about us making out.

"So basically, you were dreaming about locking lips with my bro and voilà, you were magically in the office?" Leave it to Damien to make me blush even harder.

"How intriguing! You can teleport, Dragostea mea!"

Mithraheal believed this was a remarkable development. I wasn't too sure. What if I started randomly appearing and disappearing? What if I were to pop up somewhere at an unquestionably bad time, like in the middle of the field during a soccer game right as the guy is kicking the final goal, or a bank in the middle of a robbery? What if I started thinking about kissing Mithraheal and appeared while he was taking a shower, running his long fingers through his wet hair, while the spray slid down his sexy toned chest, heading down toward...

I was abruptly brought back to reality by Damien's laugh. He laughed so hard tears started rolling down his face. I spun back to Mithraheal just in time to catch the harsh expression he threw at his brother, before he hurriedly replaced it with a smile for me. "What's gotten into him?" I inquired.

"He's insane," Mithraheal grumbled.

Out of breath but still chuckling, Damien reached out and grabbed my hand. "Let's feed you some breakfast, lizard girl."

"Lizard girl? That's the best you could come up with?" I snorted.

"I'm going through some different options to see what works." He gave me a lopsided grin.

"Damien, after she has eaten, see that she finds our room again. She will need time to prepare for our trip."

I had done enough running around lately. I was ready to slip into some sweatpants, park my backside on a comfy couch, and binge watch some TV. This better be worth it. "Trip? Where are we going?"

"To get answers, grasshopper. To get answers." And with that vague answer, Damien led me out of the room and toward the kitchen.

I filled up on prepackaged breakfast pastries and orange juice. Seriously, who would have guessed these two vampires would be so obsessed with breakfast pastries? They had boxes of every flavor lining their shelves.

Afterwards, we made our way back to the bedroom that I assumed belonged to Mithraheal. The trip from the kitchen to the room took several minutes. This place was a freaking mansion. We passed room after room. Why did they have so much space for just the two of them?

The walls were a warm brown color with a purple undertone, and exquisite paintings were hung every few feet in huge ornate gold frames. Some were of people, some were more modern abstracts, while others were stunning landscapes from all around the world.

"Here we go," Damien said as he pulled me into the room. "The tub is that way, and you will find towels and soap on the sink." He bowed with a ridiculous little flourish and turned to go.

I caught his wrist. "Um, do you think there is anything around here I could borrow to wear?" I made a motion with my hand to indicate my ripped and filthy clothes. I couldn't believe Mithraheal let me sleep in his bed in these.

He slapped his forehead. "Of course. There are new clothes in the wardrobe. Mithraheal sent for clothes last night. Hopefully, something in there will work."

"Thanks," I replied, embarrassed. I was not used to being pampered. My parents loved me and took care of my needs, but I did my fair share of the work around the cottage to help. Freeloading was not my thing.

He waved his hand, brushing me off, and with a wink he closed the door.

I stepped into the bathroom and was blown away by the luxuriousness of it all. Everything was over the top. The towels were lush, the marble floor was heated, the glass shower was the size of a bedroom, and the tub was spacious enough to swim in. Turning to the mirror, I started removing my clothes. Although I wasn't shocked by my appearance, I wasn't exactly getting used to it either.

We are beautiful, Beasty said.

I jumped. "You haven't been very chatty this morning."

I have just been enjoying being in our mate's home.

I smiled. I was glad to know she was feeling content.

After taking my shower and blow drying my hair, I went to put on some makeup but stopped with a laugh. When your skin shimmers like you were dusted in glitter, how in the world are you supposed to find the correct shade of foundation? I settled for clear lip gloss and went to open the wardrobe.

A little sticky note was stuck on the outside. I beamed as I read the note: *I didn't know what you preferred, so I had them send several styles. Love, M.*

Opening the closet, I choked at all the clothes. Every style under the sun had to be in there; boho chic, goth, rock star, girly pink, western wear, dignified businesswoman. Did he buy an entire clothing store? I was one hundred per cent overwhelmed by so many choices.

I finally put on a pair of light blue jeans that had a softness that only came from wearing them for years, or a monstrous price tag. I slipped on a pair of black thigh-high boots. It took a bit of searching, but I eventually spotted a backless white cotton top. I was relieved I wouldn't have to cut holes in any of the beautiful shirts to create a spot for my wings. I wondered if I would ever be back in human form, or if this was permanent.

I slid the blouse over my head and then tucked my wings tight against my back. I spied a long velvet jewelry box on the bed. A note had been left on it as well, letting me know it was from Mithraheal.

I wasn't much of a jewelry girl, but I was a curious one. I opened the box and let out a delighted scream. Inside were two gorgeous knives. Their handles had been hand-carved and depicted two dragons in remarkable detail. I picked them up, testing the weight in my palms. They were perfectly balanced.

Tears clouded my eyes at the thoughtfulness of his gift. He had known me less than twenty-four hours, but already knew that the way to my heart wasn't with expensive jewelry, but with shiny, stabby knives. I couldn't wait to hug him, so I squeezed my eyes shut and imagined being in his arms.

I was sucked into the swirling vortex. Moments later my vision cleared, and I was standing in front of him. I whooped in triumph and flung myself into his arms. He hadn't been prepared for my sudden arrival and staggered back a few steps into the wall. I pinned him against the wall between my hands and grinned like a lunatic into his bewildered face. I was so happy.

"Munchkin, I am rather fond of you, but if you so much as move those knives another inch toward my brother, I will rip your heart out." Damien's normally playful tone was filled with ice, and his deadly intent was unmistakable.

I was so confused. What had happened? I would never hurt Mithraheal.

"It's okay, Damien. She doesn't mean me harm." Mithraheal spoke in a steady, soothing voice.

"From where I am standing, she just popped into the room yelling, fully armed, charged you, and then pinned you against the wall."

I glanced back toward the wall where I had Mithraheal pinned. I held a knife in each fist, on either side of his face. Okay, so it did look like I was attacking him. See? My new ability was a disastrous idea.

I eased away and dropped my head. "I'm sorry. I found the knives you left for me, and I had never been given such an incredible gift. I just couldn't wait to thank you. I didn't realize how it would appear."

Bending slightly, I slid the blades inside the boots. He must have had the boots custom made as well, because they had sheaths inside that fit the blades perfectly.

"Sweetheart don't be sorry." He dragged me into his embrace. His chest shook as he laughed. "Dragostea mea, my life has been boring for over a century. You waltzed into my life and in one morning you have managed to create more excitement than the last several decades combined. And if I had known how happy those blades were going to make you, I would have bought you an entire armory."

Damien had relaxed back against the wall but eyed me carefully. "I think it might be a little weird for someone to get so overjoyed over knives. We haven't been surprised by anyone for an extremely long time, and she managed to get the drop on us twice-"

He was cut off as my knife embedded itself in the wall

between his legs, mere inches from his giggle berries. "Three times," I corrected with smug satisfaction.

He clutched his man-junk and screamed like a schoolgirl. I just rolled my eyes and strode over to retrieve my blade. You wouldn't think his voice could get that high, since my knife hadn't so much as nicked him.

Mithraheal laughed so hard he had to wipe tears from his eyes.

Damien watched his brother laughing, his eyes softening. It was clear they shared an intense bond.

"All right, we need to get a move on before munchkin gets all stabby again." Damien winked at me as he snatched a package of sugary breakfast snacks. "For the road."

"You aren't eating them in my car." Mithraheal smacked him upside the head.

I followed them into the garage as they continued to bicker. Car after beautiful car filled the garage. I didn't know much about cars, but these looked like the variety that only serious collectors owned. Mithraheal motioned for me to get into the front seat of a sleek black SUV with dark tinted windows. Did all supers own black SUVs?

They eventually stopped quarreling, leaving behind the pastries, and we were finally on the highway. I spoke up. "Now, will you tell me where we are going?"

Damien replied in a petulant tone, apparently still sulking over his snack. "To see Ernie, an ancient one."

I couldn't help it. I started to chuckle. "Ernie?"

"Erechtheus is his actual name. But I call him Ernie since

it annoys him." He turned from staring out the window and tossed me a mischievous grin.

Mithraheal rolled his eyes before filling in the blanks, "Erechtheus has been around for a long time. We believe him to be immortal, but since no one is altogether certain what kind of supernatural he is, we do not know if it is true. Damien made friends with him a century ago. He knows more about the supernatural world than any other being living on earth. We hope he can give us answers about what you are. Perhaps then we will know why you have been targeted by Draven."

"So, you don't know exactly what I am?" I couldn't believe it. He had not blinked an eye at my odd appearance, and Damien hadn't seemed shocked in the woods either.

Damien spoke up from the backseat, "Nope! You are one odd little creature!"

Mithraheal gave him a look that would have made anybody else tremble in fear. "My love, we know you are a dragon, but we didn't know that dragons were real. Bedtime stories have been told about dragon shifters since the beginning of time, but everyone believed they were only myths. Your kind is a fantasy that does not exist."

I snorted, "Says the guy who hisses and has pointy fangs."

"Burn." Damien snickered.

We settled into a comfortable silence, and I watched the scenery pass. Four hours later, we finally pulled up outside a remarkably ordinary looking place. It was a little yellow house with an adorable white picket fence in the middle of nowhere. There were no other homes or buildings. Yeah, this wasn't weird at all.

"Why didn't we just teleport here?" I inquired, stretching my sore muscles. My wings ached from being crammed into the vehicle for that long. Buckling a seatbelt around wings was awkward and uncomfortable, even in the spacious interior of the SUV. I would have liked the ability to shift between forms like my werewolves. Thinking of them sent a brief pang of sadness through me.

"Because Ernie said he is too old to be getting surprised by me popping in unannounced. He said he would refuse to talk to me the next time I did it." Damien pouted, and I laughed.

The door swung open, and a hunched over man tottered out. "Well, are you all just going to stand there yacking, or would you like to come in? I ain't a young man. I could die before you guys get in here."

He ushered us into the house. After we were seated, he offered us all a drink. Mithraheal and I accepted the glasses of sunshine yellow lemonade he offered, but Damien declined. He kept muttering under his breath. Something about the last drink Ernie gave him making him pee blue for a week. I hid my smile behind my glass at the thought of Ernie pranking Damien.

Ernie stared at me in silence for several minutes before finally speaking up and giving me a pleased smile. "I did not think I would ever have the pleasure of seeing another drakon. You are absolutely splendid, young lady."

Mithraheal let out a low hiss and drew me closer. Possessive, much? Turning my attention back to Ernie I asked, "So I am a dragon, or a 'drakon'? Are they the same thing?"

He nodded. "They are the same. Every language possesses

its own word for dragon. In my tongue, you would be a 'drace-na', a female dragoness. I had thought the royal dragons were lost when I heard that Draco and his mate were attacked and killed in their home a few days ago. The attackers burned everything to the ground."

I sat in shock, letting it all sink in. My dad was a dragon. How could I not have realized? Why didn't he tell me? Tears burned my eyes.

Mithraheal must have seen I was incapable of forming questions, so he spoke up. "That was her father. She is a royal dragon? Are there other types of dragons?"

"I never knew he had a daughter. Absolutely incredible! That would explain why he disappeared. To care for his family and hide her from the world. It is true that dragons hoard their riches and defend them passionately. She would have been his most prized treasure. As his offspring, she is a royal. His death is a terrible loss to this world. Draco was not one to confide in others, but I regarded him as my friend. They are dragons with capabilities beyond your wildest imagination, possessing more power than any other supernatural species. Tragically, this led to them being hunted.

"Dragons are peaceful, and preserved harmony between the different groups by having respect for the pure-hearted leaders and instilling fear in the hearts of the greedy. If a supernatural species attempted to cheat or start a war with another species, the royals would step in and end it swiftly. This kept peace among the species for centuries.

"Eventually, evil spread and corrupted more of the earth and its leaders. These cruel leaders gathered to hunt the royals, and by eliminating them, there were no longer any obstacles in their way. Wars between species began.

"Your father was the last of the royals. He lost his siblings and the entirety of his family. It shattered him. He couldn't bear anymore loss, and so he took his mate and disappeared.

"After that, dragons became nothing more than fictional stories. As for other dragons, I have heard there may be two or three left on earth. They all have powers and each control a single element. But their power pales compared to the power of the drakena sitting with us now."

My mind was spiraling out of control. Grief over my loss, and what my dad had lost, overwhelmed me. I realized I had been holding my breath and slowly breathed out. "Is that why Draven is after me?"

The noise of a glass shattering had all our heads snapping in Ernie's direction. "That son of a viper! He is evil and full of venom."

Clearly there was no love lost between Ernie and Draven.

"I am confused though. He thinks that the power is in my necklace." I absentmindedly rubbed the pendant between my fingers.

Ernie laughed out loud at that. "Your father was a sly man. Centuries after he went into hiding, when dragons were nothing more than myths to most, he became worried that someone might start researching those tales and begin searching for him.

"He remained friends with a few ancient ones whom he trusted, and I suppose he must have feared it might be leaked that he was still alive. So, he made up that story in case he was ever captured. His captor would believe that true dragons didn't exist; it was simply power held in the pendant. That would give him the element of surprise to free himself. I thought it was the stupidest thing I had ever heard. Who would be idiotic enough to believe some trinket held nearly unlimited power? But it seems your father was wise as ever." Ernie's eyes grew tender, and I knew he was remembering my father.

My heart shattered all over again. The only reason my dad wouldn't have survived that attack was if he was defending my mom, which gave me time to escape. My eyes dimmed with tears.

There were so many changes in my life, and all of them were happening too fast. I was basically tossed into this insane world full of fantasy creatures I hadn't even realized existed. I needed my parents. I desperately needed to talk with them, I wanted them to help me sort out the chaotic mess my life had turned into.

I was falling in love with Mithraheal. And what about the strange pull toward Cage? My mind then drifted to my Blood Guards Luke and Levi. With each passing hour, my separation from them made our bond ache. I missed them. I wished I could bury my fists and face in their plush wolf coats.

That sounded ridiculous. Maybe because, in my mind, they were oversized dogs in their wolfy forms. Everybody knows that stroking your hands through a dog's coat is the most calming thing on earth.

As I thought about Luke and Levi's chocolate brown coats, I realized my palms were literally running through

Luke's fur. Shut the front door. How did that happen? I glanced around, but instead of teleporting myself to them, I had brought them to me.

Luke was in wolf form in front of me, while Levi stood with his hand on Cage's shoulder where he had apparently been explaining something right before I somehow teleported them here. Luke licked my cheek in glee, toppling me onto the floor. Levi remained standing, gazing around the room in shock.

The silence that had encompassed the room was broken as Cage's eyes landed on me, and he bolted forward, growling, "Mate."

An ear-splitting hiss followed, and my eyes shot to Mithraheal, who was about to murder someone if his expression was anything to go by.

And that is when the poop hit the fan.

CHAPTER SEVENTEEN

Tia

Cage rushed toward me. Before he reached me, a giant blur moved across the room and smashed into him. They went hurtling through the wall and out into the garden.

With my heart in my throat, I jumped to my feet and sprinted outside. Mithraheal had Cage pinned in the dirt, and although Cage was marginally larger, he could not escape Mithraheal's steely grip on his neck.

"She is not your mate, pup," Mithraheal hissed. His deadly calm voice sent a shiver down my spine.

How was I both horrified and turned on at the same time? I needed therapy as soon as this was over. Are there therapists for supers? I mean, if the therapist didn't know about our existence, they might decide to just admit me to a mental ward, right?

Cage's vicious growls brought my focus back to the dispute at hand.

"Stop. Let him up, Mithraheal!" I was honestly concerned about what might happen to Cage.

Cage grunted and attempted to kick Mithraheal, but the latter simply swatted it away like was nothing more than a pesky mosquito.

Levi took several strides forward, undoubtedly planning to help his Alpha, but Damien let out an ominous chuckle from where he remained propped against the wall. "Do not even think about it."

Levi stopped moving but fixed his eyes on Damien, a threatening growl rumbling from his rib cage.

"Mithraheal, please don't injure him. Come on. Let's talk this through guys." I struggled to reason with the stubborn men in my life. Mithraheal gazed at me for a minute and began easing his grasp.

Cage's ego was bruised, so naturally this was an excellent opportunity to open his big mouth. "Yeah. You better back away before I show you what's what," he snarled.

And it was on all over again.

They moved so incredibly fast it was impossible to keep my eyes on them let alone see who had the upper hand. Luke remained at my side and leaned against me as I unconsciously brushed my fingers through his fur. I sensed Damien shift from his position. I glanced over to find his head tilted. He kept looking back and forth between Luke and me curiously.

"What?" I challenged. Couldn't he see that the fight of the century was taking place in front of us? Shouldn't he do something?

"You're petting him, and he is allowing it." He said it as a statement, but it sounded more like a question.

"Yeah, so?"

"Werewolves dislike being touched while they are in wolf form. They barely tolerate it from their own mates. Wolves only allow other wolves to touch them, yet he is standing there nearly purring while his Alpha is being whipped into a meringue right in front of him."

I didn't have time to process the importance of what he was saying, because the two brawling blurs nearly collided with me. They would have sent me flying had Luke not leaped in front of me and taken the brunt of the impact. That was enough.

I stared at the snarling men in a heap and begged, "Please, guys. Stop this nonsense. For me?"

I held my breath and waited, wondering what would happen. Luke whined and limped back to my side, apparently a little tender from the blow he had taken. Mithraheal stood and brushed dust off his trousers, still managing to look like he had just stepped off the glossy cover of a magazine. He bent and reached out his hand to help Cage up in a visible attempt at a truce. Cage glared at Mithraheal, before ignoring the hand and standing up on his own.

As they walked toward me, Cage said under his breath, "She is mine."

Mithraheal's headed snapped in his direction and he

hissed loudly, "You are sorely mistaken. She is mine. Do not test me again, mutt."

Cage did the absolute worst thing he could have done and brought up the one thing I had been hoping he wouldn't. "I marked her."

"How dare you?" Mithraheal leaped at Cage's throat.

Normally, it's pretty tough to get me riled and even more difficult to make me angry. But the way these two men tossed each other around, each claiming that I was *his* infuriated me. I did have a soft spot for Cage, and I was falling for Mithraheal, but it was *I* who decided who to love, who to claim as mine. I was not a piece of property that would belong to anyone, unless that's what I chose.

Or maybe you want both, Beasty smirked, but I sensed her annoyance as well.

"Uh, guys..."

I heard Damien speaking, but it sounded distorted, like I was hearing him while underwater. "Tia, calm down. It's okay. Don't get upset, Tiny." He was speaking to me like I was a toddler who needed to be pacified. I felt another wave of anger roll through my body.

Hearing a whimper, I looked down to meet Luke's anxious, wolfy eyes. I slid my palm up his neck, and then down his head until my fingers rested between his eyes, just like the night they found me. Immediately his eyes jerked to mine, and they gleamed. The eerie cerulean blue light streamed out of my body to envelop us.

Heck yeah. Let's remind these boys who they are messing

with. Beasty chuckled, and I could practically hear her cracking her knuckles at the prospect of getting to play.

Looking at Luke, I whispered, "Watch my back."

Stepping forward, I lifted my hands like a mother who was being driven nuts by her kids. "I said *stop.*" And when my dragoness voice commanded something, you had no choice but to stand still and listen.

Cage looked at me. I saw fear as he remembered what transpired the last time I got ticked off. Mithraheal, however, hadn't had the chance to experience what it was like when Beasty and I joined together for play time. No fear appeared on his face, merely pure adoration.

Behind me, Damien whooped. "Whoa. My BFF is just so freaking cool."

I couldn't help but roll my eyes at him, and Beasty snickered in my head.

Bringing my fists down, a tidal wave of energy rushed out from me, flattening all the garden plants, an apple tree, and the perfect little picket fence. It also shoved the stupid guys flat on their butts. Pointing my left finger at Mithraheal, and my right finger at Cage, I gradually raised them off the ground using my mind. I continued lifting them until both men floating in thin air.

I spoke again, although this time I used a seductive tone. "While I am flattered you both want me, you two are quarreling over me as if I am a possession to own. That's disturbing. I will determine who I wish to spend eternity with. That is a decision that I alone will make. I have had enough violence to last me for the rest of my life, and I am certain that more bloodshed is brewing on the horizon with Draven. I am here to learn about what I am, so that I can prepare myself."

Mithraheal continued to stare at me with sheer wonder.

Cage was less charmed by my display of power. He spoke up, attempting to placate me. "Tia, please. You don't need to do this. I know you are powerful. I have witnessed it before. You don't have to fret about the approaching battle. I will protect you. My pack will defend you. As my mate, you don't have to worry. Just set us down so we can talk."

As he spoke, I hadn't noticed my hands had wavered, and their feet were nearly back to touching the ground.

"There. See? That's a good girl. Set us down and calm yourself so you can shift back to the beautiful girl I fell in love with."

I felt an intense pain inside me and recognized that the hurt came from Beasty. What had upset her? Was it that he thought we were going to hurt them? Or that he didn't believe we could protect ourselves and defend those around us?

As quickly as my anger had appeared, it evaporated. I was beyond tired. My energy level dropped, and the power that had been dancing around us vanished. I dropped my two would be mates to the ground with a hard thud. I slumped to the ground and dropped my head into my hands.

No one moved for several moments until a voice broke in. A voice that belonged to someone I had completely forgotten was here.

"You are The One. The time is here."

I slowly raised my head and found Ernie, who was sitting in the corner of his porch, casually rocking in his armchair, as though we hadn't just torn out a wall in his home and destroyed his lovely garden. I watched as he rose and ambled toward me. Luke stepped in front of me protectively and growled.

"Hush, pup," Ernie chided before turning to study my eyes. "It is all up to you," he whispered.

"What is? What are you talking about, Ernie?"

The look in his eyes told me I wasn't going to like the answer.

"You will determine whether this is the end of the world, or a new beginning."

I passed out.

I ROUSED TO THE SOUNDS OF HISSING AND GROWLING. I instantly opened my eyes, worried that the guys had started arguing again while I was out of it. I discovered only one pair of eyes peering back at me. Ernie's.

Looking around, I realized we were alone in his house. Looking through the new window the guys had made in his wall, I saw the vampire brothers, an angry Alpha wolf, and my two protectors, all pacing back and forth. Damien just winked and blew me a kiss. Weirdo.

I watched in bewilderment, wondering why they were out there when it was clear they wanted badly to be inside.

Ernie answered my unspoken question. "I have a bit of magic, precious one." He chortled at my perplexed expression. "It is a force field. They can't break through it. I needed to talk with you, and I didn't want to be interrupted by their squabbling. We have but a short time left to speak."

"Why only a short time? What is going on?"

"Evil approaches, precious one. You need to retreat and hide until you are prepared for war."

"Why do you keep calling me precious one?" This day just kept getting weirder and weirder. Or more accurately, my life kept getting weirder and weirder.

"I already knew you were a royal dragon. But after witnessing the incredible display of your power, I now realize that you are the dragon that was spoken of in prophecy.

"Many years ago, supernatural beings existed peacefully with humans. But as time went on, a few power-hungry supers tried to enslave humanity. The rest of the supers fought against them to try to restore harmony.

"But by the time they destroyed the evil ones, humanity was terrified and untrusting of all supers. A few cruel human leaders took advantage of this and drove the humans to seek out and murder the supers one by one. The few that survived went into hiding.

"Once the supernaturals no longer mingled with the humans on a routine basis, or protected them from disasters, the evil humans turned their brutal soldiers onto their own kind.

"Bloody wars broke out and humanity was near annihilation. But a few forgiving supernaturals stepped out of the shadows and aided. Once again, evil was destroyed and supernaturals melted back into the shadows. And now, very few humans know of our existence.

"Unfortunately, all the violence and bloodshed had awakened a sinister and exceedingly powerful evil. After centuries of existing without a physical body, that evil is hunting for a host body. The only thing that will be able to hold back his power and keep the world balanced is the Dragon Heart."

"I thought you said the necklace was just a diversion?" I interrupted.

"I am not speaking of your pendant. I am talking about your literal heart. It was foretold by an ancient one after those terrible wars, that when the darkness is unleashed, the precious one who carries the Dragon Heart will fight. She alone will determine if the entire world becomes slaves to the evil, or if the evil will be destroyed so the supernaturals and humans can start anew with mutual respect."

I couldn't form words to ask what I needed to know, but he seemed to read my mind. "You are the one that was prophesied. You are the one who carries the Dragon Heart, not as a necklace, but in your chest."

"H...how? Are...you...sure?" I was quivering. This was too much to take in.

"Surely you can see your energy surrounding you. All dragons have some energy to use, but not even the royal dragons had energy so powerful and pure that it can be seen. When you put your fingers between the wolf's eyes and he glowed, I understood. Only the chosen mate of a dragon can share their energy. Since I don't see your mark on his neck, that must mean he is a Blood Guard. And if I am not mistaken, you have bound two, correct?"

"Yes," I whispered, still working to take in all he was

saying. I sat there stupidly, staring at my fists. It felt like an enormous weight was crushing the life out of me. How was I supposed to bring balance back to the world? How was I expected to beat Draven, when frankly he scared the life out of me?

"Tiamat. Do not be frightened. You must be wise and cautious. Harboring fear will make you second guess yourself, and that could cost lives. You are strong. Look outside." He waved his hand toward the men who were anxiously gazing at the house.

"These men would all die for you. The Blood Guard wolves have bound themselves to you, and that means they cannot have a soulmate bond with any other wolf. You do not have to take them as soulmates, but I wanted you to know the reality.

"The Alpha and Blood Driven are both fighting over the chance to be your mate. I understand you know little of these men, but both are noteworthy among their kind. They are impressive, as you will learn with time.

"However, you will need to claim at least one soulmate, and soon. Not only will your beloved share some of your power, which will give him an added measure of safety, but when you complete the bond, it will also enhance your own strength. It will take everything you have to defeat what is coming.

"In the past, a strong drakena would often take more than one mate. As the most powerful drakena to exist, you may find it crucial to take several mates. You cannot fight this evil on your own. And when your entire power is freed, you will need help to control it."

I gazed outside at the two guys who both insisted that I was his, and the twins who had shown me such trust and devotion. As if I didn't have enough to worry about, now I had to determine who to bind myself to for the rest of our lives.

The prospect of taking more than one mate absolutely petrified me. How could I handle several mates? Especially, if they couldn't be in the same room without arguing? Tears pricked the back of my eyes. I never asked for any of this. I hadn't even believed in supernatural beings a week ago.

Ernie patted my shoulder. Hooking his finger under my chin, he turned my head toward him. "I am sorry, precious one. It is unfair, but nothing will alter the prophecy. You need to find safety immediately so that you can train and prepare for what is coming. I am well known in the supernatural world, and I am sure spies have already reported your visit."

I lurched to my feet. I wasn't ready to face Draven. Not today. Maybe never.

"One last thing, Tia." I spun to face him again. "I wish to teach you how to shift back into your human body, so you can hide more efficiently."

I nodded my head and waited for his instructions.

"Close your eyes. You need to connect with your inner dragon. You cannot shift back unless she allows it. If she agrees, all you must do is to visualize your human form."

Closing my eyes, I called to Beasty. Normally, she was a spitfire, but she seemed subdued somehow. She quietly nodded her head before receding into the shadows of my mind. I envisioned my human body. Instantly, tingles spread across my limbs.

I opened my eyes and was both relieved and a little sad to see my normal sun-kissed skin again. I peered behind me and felt a pang when I realized my wings had vanished.

"Goodbye. I hope to meet you again one day, little lady. We have more to discuss regarding who I sense inside you." Ernie led me to the demolished wall and brought down the shield.

The guys must have noticed my solemn expression because they quietly followed me to the vehicle. Kind-hearted Ernie must keep extra clothes on hand for rowdy shifters, as both Cage and Levi were now clothed. Mithraheal and Cage sandwiched me between them in the backseat. Damien opened the rear of the SUV and Luke hopped in, still in his wolf form.

Damien motioned for Levi to take shotgun, before sliding into the driver's seat. They must have calmed down enough to have discussed a plan while Ernie was talking with me, because Damien began driving without being given directions.

My eyes became heavy, and I let my head drop onto Mithraheal's shoulder. Before the darkness of sleep completely sucked me in, I heard him murmur against my hair, "I should have known your human form would be beautiful, just as your dragon form is stunning."

I felt Beasty do a little happy dance at hearing his compliment. I smiled as I let sleep take me.

Chapter Eighteen

Tia

"Dragostea mea, wake up. We have nearly arrived." Mithraheal slid his finger across my cheek.

I yawned. "You keep calling me that name. What does it mean?"

Leaning forward, he nipped my lower lip. "It means my love in Romanian, my mother tongue."

I smiled against his lips and kissed him back. Pulling away, I stretched my sore muscles and leaned over him to peer out the window. Trees surrounded us, and a picturesque little log cabin came into view. After parking, we all piled out of the SUV. The tension in the vehicle was nearly palpable, which made me relieved I had snoozed through most of the awkward ride.

I squealed as someone swept me up in their arms. My

heart did a crazy little flip when I realized it was Mithraheal. Looking over his shoulder, I saw Cage dragging his feet and growling low, all while staring stakes through Mithraheal's back.

Damien was behind Cage, alternating between making silly girlish faces, and then grumpy caveman faces. He was clearly poking fun at Cage's mood swings. I couldn't help the giggle that escaped, which made them both to glance up.

Cage's eyes lit up when he noticed me peeking at him. "Hello, Tia. I've missed you," he said gently.

"Uh, hi." I stammered and blushed. A part of me had missed him, but another part hadn't. I still felt a tug toward him. I was struggling to handle my emotions from him forcing the mark on me. I sighed before angling my body back toward the cabin.

Searching my mind, I looked for Beasty. *Heya... Beasty? You there?*

Where else would I be? she countered sarcastically.

I got straight to the point. *What did I miss when I fell asleep in the car? Where are we? And are Cage and Mithraheal going to be staying under the same roof?*

Well, if you hadn't been so lazy and slept the entire six-hour road trip, you would know all those answers, she grumbled back.

Seriously, this chick - er, dragon - needed to get some beauty sleep.

You realize I can hear your thoughts, right? Beasty snapped.

I chuckled, then pretended to be fascinated by the sky when Mithraheal watched me curiously.

Fine. The guys decided they needed to bring you to a private location to keep you away from Draven. They are hoping to give you a chance to train and get accustomed to being a dragon. And yes, they somehow believe they can live under the same roof and not murder each other. Which I highly doubt.

This made me snort. I had to avoid eye contact again when Mithraheal's eyes flashed back to my face. These guys were stupid. Had anyone bothered to ask me about my fighting skills? Nope.

They just assumed that I was a typical female and couldn't protect myself. They were going to be in for the shock of their lives. My annoyance changed to delight. This was going to be entertaining. I snuggled back against Mithraheal's chest with an evil grin.

The trip had taken all afternoon, and the last few hours before bedtime were beyond boring. Cage, Mithraheal, and Damien all had business to take care of, and they were fixated on their laptops. Levi and Luke were doing regular perimeter checks to check for intruders.

I wandered around flopping down on the various sofas and armchairs until I found one that was just right. After wasting three hours staring at the ceiling, I warmed a microwave dinner, and headed to bed. Damien had informed me that my training was beginning in the morning, and I wanted to be in tip-top shape.

I was going to spank these arrogant guys, and I didn't mean in the fun, sexy way either.

BANG, BANG, BANG!

I tried to jump up, but my legs were wrapped up in the blanket, and I flew off the bed and slammed onto the floor. I hit with a thud and let out a moan. Damien cackled like a crazy old witch from the doorway where he was holding the metal pie pan he had been smacking with a metal serving spoon.

"Are you insane?" I demanded. Who in their right mind wakes people up like that? Definitely not a normal human being. Then again, he wasn't exactly normal and, technically, he wasn't a human either. Ugh. "A gentleman would come over and help me, instead of laughing his butt off."

"Lady bug, I never claimed to be a gentleman," he chirped.

Seriously, I thought Blood Driven were supposed to sleep all day. Why does this one have to be so danged cheerful? I glowered at him from my position on the floor.

"Put these on and be downstairs in ten minutes to start your training." He tossed a shirt and a pair of tight black biker shorts on the bed, then flounced - yes, he actually flounced - down the hallway.

"Fart knocker," I mumbled into the floorboards.

"Heard that," he shouted back and started banging his pie pan again.

I untangled myself from the blanket, grabbed the clothes, and marched to the bathroom to get ready to face the day. I slid on the shorts, then unfolded the t-shirt, reading the words on the front. I let out a frustrated groan. Who thought this was funny? Never mind, I knew exactly who bought me this shirt. And I also realized he must die. Okay, not really die, but he would definitely pay.

I finished dressing and pulled my long hair up in a sleek ponytail before heading downstairs. When I strolled into the kitchen, the five guys looked first at my glowering face, and then their eyes slid down to my shirt. Every single guy burst out laughing. And I don't mean soft snickers, but huge guffaws that reverberated through the room.

Levi and Damien fell off their stools and onto the kitchen floor where they continued to howl in glee. I swear Mithraheal was wiping tears from his eyes. Even Cage was shaking with laughter.

I stuck my nose up and marched right through the kitchen and out the back door.

Where had Damien found a shirt that had the words 'Dragon in Training', above a little dragon lifting weights? Childish vampire. I smiled. Let them have their fun.

They followed me outside. I smirked as I looked at each of their faces and found condescending expressions. It was obvious they thought I was hopeless without summoning my dragon powers.

I motioned first to Levi. He walked toward me, and I could hear both Cage and Mithraheal tell him to be gentle.

Ha. That would just make it all the more fun for me. I'd planned to go easy on them, but all bets were off now.

I remained perfectly still until he finally ran toward me. I ran a few steps in his direction and at the last second, I flipped over his back while putting my hands together as if I were playing volleyball. I slammed my combined fist into the back of his head. He went down like a box of rocks.

He wasn't permanently damaged - the dude is a werewolf after all - but it was hard enough to knock him out for a few minutes. I turned back to the boys with a sassy grin and girly flip of my hair. Turning, I motioned for Luke. He looked bewildered about what had just happened.

Damien leaned toward him and whispered, "Lucky hit."

Luke eyed me carefully. He circled and did a couple of fake lunges in my direction. I pretended to be bored and picked at my fingernails. I ended his indecision by running toward him. But instead of attacking him head on as he expected, I grabbed his arm as I ran by him, and used it to swing myself backwards, throwing my legs around his neck.

My weight threw him off balance and as he toppled onto his stomach. I whacked his head, effectively knocking him out. I sat on his back with my legs around his neck, doing an exaggerated fake yawn before stretching like a cat and getting to my feet.

Beasty's loud, sexy laugh rang out in my head.

I motioned to Damien. "You. Here. Now." I swayed from side to side and dropped into my best ninja fighting position, one arm extended in front of me and the other behind me. I jerked my hand twice in the universal sign to bring it.

Instead of looking nervous, he sauntered right up to me. "Just because you took down two dogs without breaking a sweat, don't think that taking down my kind is going to be as easy. We are quite skilled at fighting. Humans and were-wolves don't pose a challenge for us."

The dork was full of his ego.

I closed my eyes and curved my lips into a sugary sweet smile. When I opened my eyes, they glowed the color of sapphire. Hesitation flickered in his eyes, and I chose that moment to let my wings rip through my shirt and stretch behind me. I let the light travel across my body, completely transforming me back into my dragon form. I could barely contain my laughter when actual fear skittered across his face.

I leaned forward and in my sultry, shifter voice I purred, "But don't you remember? You *wanted* to train a dragon."

I finished by gently running my beautiful razor-sharp nail down his cheek.

"It was... was a... joke," he stammered.

I looked at Mithraheal. He had a broad grin on his face. When he caught my eye, he sent a sexy wink that nearly melted my panties.

Cage had a disgruntled look on his face. *What's got his tail in a knot?*

Damien edged away from me, holding up his hands in a defensive gesture. I licked my lips and took several steps towards him, swaying my hips seductively. I really didn't know what magic happened when Beasty and I joined, but me likey!

He stopped moving backwards and stared at me, mesmerized. I smiled and fluttered my lashes before swinging one of my wings around and smacking him on the back of the head, successfully knocking him out.

I threw my hands up in the air shouting, "And another score for the dragon girl." I wiggled my butt and shimmied in a weird victory dance.

Mithraheal's deep laughter filled the air. I ran toward him and Cage, throwing up my palms to high five them. Mithraheal immediately put up his palm and smacked my hand, but Cage stood still, watching me. A brief flash of pain shot through me, and Beasty flinched.

"Baby, time to change back now," he urged me, his voice thick with emotion.

I came to a halt in front of him. He avoided making eye contact with me. I stared at him, confused, until it slowly dawned on me that what I was hearing in his voice was disgust. He didn't like me in my dragon form. He only liked my human side. He didn't like Beasty. Beasty let out a choked sob in my mind.

Now I understood why I kept feeling pain, and why she kept retreating in my mind.

She knew.

She'd picked up on the little things that he had said, and probably things he had failed to say.

"You don't like me." I expected my voice to be hysterical, broken, or angry, but it was completely flat.

"I love you." His expression was pained. "I love the *real* you! The beautiful human that you have been all your life."

I stared at him. As the weight of his words settled, it was as though I had been sucker punched. I struggled to breathe.

"But you are my mate. Or one of them. You said so yourself. You even marked me. How could you not love me?" This time I couldn't hide the anguish in my voice. My heart had bonded more quickly to Mithraheal, but the soulmate bond still pulled me toward Cage as well.

"Change back, love. We can talk this through. There is no need for you to be a shifter. I will protect you. Our pack will protect you. You won't ever have a reason to shift. Everything will be fine-"

I wasn't sure what else he was going to say because he was cut off by Luke and Levi growling loudly in unison. They had come to and had moved to stand against my back. They were offering me support, and the heat radiating from their bodies was comforting.

Levi ground out between his teeth, "That was cruel, Cage. You have been a shifter your entire life. You know the relief you feel when you shift and join forms with your wolf. You would deny her of that for eternity?"

Cage spoke up quickly. "Of course not. I can set aside a few hours of gym time each week for her to shift and release energy. It can be done, so that she has complete privacy, and we won't need to worry about pack members becoming fearful of their Luna."

He had clearly thought this through carefully. He had claimed me without taking my thoughts into account, and now he was planning my future without discussing it with me?

Beasty disappeared back into the recesses of my mind. Her hurt and betrayal ripped through me. My body shifted back to my human form without me consciously thinking about. The shift was effortless and happened in the blink of an eye.

As soon as I was fully human, a slight smile appeared on Cage's face.

He thought I had shifted back for him?

I slapped him. Hard.

His neck snapped to the side. He slowly turned back to look at my face, and I glared at him through the tears blurring my vision. How could he? A mate was supposed to accept you for who or what you were. It shouldn't matter if I was a human or supernatural. And I wasn't just a human. I was a dragon. Horrific pain radiated through my body. I clutched at my chest and tumbled to my knees.

What's happening, Beasty? Why does this hurt so much? I cried out to her in my mind.

It's because he has rejected you. He didn't reject your human form, only your shifter side. He has felt this way since the first day but now that you have realized it, and we have acknowledged that rejection, you are feeling the effects of a rejected mate bond. Her voice shook as she spoke.

My mighty inner dragon was in pain too.

Mithraheal picked me up gently in his arms. He must have used his vampire speed because seconds later, I was being lowered onto a fluffy down comforter. Sitting next to me, he tenderly brushed my blonde hair away from my tear-stained cheeks.

The bed sank lower and creaked in protest as Luke, in his

massive wolf form, jumped up beside me. Soft fur rubbed against my skin as he cuddled close to me, trying to comfort me. A huffing sound had me glancing toward the edge of the bed. Levi's wolf head was resting on the bed, giving me the most pitiful expression.

A little of the excruciating pain in my chest eased knowing they were here for me, no matter what form my body took. The tie that pulled me toward Mithraheal grew stronger, as my energy swirled through the connection. He was mine.

Burying my face in Luke's coat, and reaching out to stroke Levi's head, a new sensation danced through our bond, a feeling that sent butterflies fluttering around in my stomach and caused certain parts of my body to clench in desire. It made me wish they were cuddling me in their human forms. And just like that, my hands were stroking their hard muscled chests, instead of plush wolf coats.

CHAPTER NINETEEN

Tia

The next week was pretty calm. I continued training each day with Luke, Levi, and Damien. They had yet to even come close to beating me, but the practice was giving me a chance to study how supernaturals fight. I hoped that would give me an edge when I had to face Draven.

Mithraheal still declined to train with me. I think he was afraid of injuring me. As if he could. Cage was completely avoiding me and staying locked in the office.

Sighing, I rolled to my stomach and gazed down at the brilliant water in front of me. We had completed training for the day, so I was relaxing beside the little stream that was within view of the cabin. Being near water filled me with such a sense of tranquility.

The guys were extremely bossy about me staying where they could see me at all times and honestly, I just wanted a bit of quiet time alone. I closed my eyes and listened as the water gurgled over the rocks. I let my hand slip into the water, delighting in the coolness as it flowed between my fingers.

Sighing, I decided to go ahead and let Luke know I was aware he was spying on me. "Are you going to come sit and talk, or just lurk in the shadows like some creepy stalker?"

He let out a huff of air. "We won't ever be able to sneak up on you, will we?"

"Nope." I drawled the word out and popped the p.

We remained in silence for several minutes before he began speaking. "Cage isn't a bad guy, Tia. I realize he's come off as a jerk, but I want to explain where he is coming from."

My throat had already clogged with emotion, so I merely nodded my head for him to go on.

"Cage has dreamed of his soulmate since we were all pups still using puppy training pads."

A giggle escaped me at that mental image.

Luke smiled and continued. "As kids he was teased because he was so obsessed with finding the she-wolf who would belong to him. Not because he wished to control her, or treat her as a possession, but because he wanted to cherish her. In the werewolf world, females are considered weaker." He hesitated, seeing my expression. "Let me finish before you interrupt, Tia. The females are okay with it. Our males are the protectors. The females enjoy being pampered. It is simply the way things have always been. But going back to Cage's story. We were all eager for the day we would discover our mates, but Cage talked about it constantly.

"He didn't have the most stable family environment growing up, and I think he looked forward to creating his own little family. That hope is what pulled him through the dark days. He cares for you. He could never force himself to fully reject you, his wolf wouldn't allow it. But you aren't the one his human side spent years building daydreams around."

Tears blurred my vision. I was sad for Cage. "But I didn't ask for this, Luke. I didn't get a choice in being a dragon. No one asked if I wished to fulfill some ancient prophecy."

"I realize that. We all do. I am just trying to help you understand Cage better. Cage had imagined he would meet a perfect little she-wolf who had been dreaming of meeting her other half for her entire life as well. She would be sweet and gentle.

"They would bond, and he would mark her immediately, which is typical among werewolves. He would sweep her off her feet, carry her to his home and give her everything her heart desired. She would cook and clean, and they would start a family.

"He would protect her from outside stresses and threats. She would be free to shift, but purely to run and play, never needing to fight.

"You are the opposite of what he imagined. You are independent and speak your mind. You never even knew about soulmates, much less spent years fantasizing about meeting yours. Tia, you have the capability to choose your mate; you aren't bound only to one wolf like a normal she-wolf is.

"You have the choice to claim multiple mates, if you desire. You are far more powerful than all of us. You are destined to battle, not only for your life, but for the entire world. Simply put, you don't need him."

I was speechless. I stared unseeing at the stream as tears streaked down my face. I did understand him a little better. We were from different worlds.

Meeting both Cage and Mithraheal had shown me the pull of a soulmate, and what an extraordinary bond they shared. I wished Cage could have met the mate he dreamed of, and a small part of me wished I had been that person. Luke was mistaken. I needed him, but not if he couldn't accept all of me.

"Regardless of what he had wished and waited for, he does love you, Tia. His wolf is constantly pressuring him to get closer to you. He feels you belong to him. Cage needs to sort through his feelings.

"He is acting like a fool, and I don't think he realizes he may drive you away completely while he is struggling to let go of his fantasy." And with that he stood quietly, brushed off his slacks and melted back into the shadows of the forest.

I sat in the same spot until the sun traveled across the sky and disappeared behind the trees. I rose, dragging my feet toward the cabin.

As I came near it, I noticed all the guys were standing on the porch, sharing heated words. I scanned each of their faces, but only Luke made eye contact with me. The look he threw me was miserable.

"What's going on?" I inquired.

Cage turned to face me. "I'm taking off, love."

I couldn't stop the gasp that slipped from my lips. He was leaving me?

"Shh. I need to check on the pack. I have responsibilities, and I need to select and train a new Beta."

Startled, I looked first to Luke then Levi. "But you two are the Betas."

"No, we have resigned. Our duty is to you above all else. We can't properly safeguard the pack since we will always protect you first," Levi answered.

"Goodbye Tia. It will be okay." Cage gently pressed a kiss to my forehead, and I watched as his eye color flashed. It was clear he was struggling to maintain control of his wolf.

"Bye," I choked out. "I'm sorry."

Giving me a sad smile, he turned and strode away. I stared after him. I was sorry that I wasn't what he wanted; I was sorry that my first mate didn't want me. Thanks to Luke, I understood him better, but that didn't change the fact that as a fated mate, he should have loved me for who I was. But he was so fixated on his idea of the perfect mate, he couldn't love all of me.

I think we all knew he may never come back, and I wasn't certain I wanted to see him again. The guys pressed closer, attempting to comfort me. Turning toward them, I spoke without making eye contact with any of them, "I need to be alone. Please."

I trudged toward the trees, heading to the rocky cliff that

overlooked the valley. I quickly scaled the rock face without breaking a sweat. I lay down and wished for peace to engulf me, as it usually did when I visited this spot, but nothing happened.

A chaos of emotions roiled in me. I knew my heart was already binding itself to Mithraheal, and the bond between Luke and Levi was evolving as well. But sadness over Cage's leaving still weighed me down. What was wrong with me? How could I be drawn toward someone who rejected part of my very being?

It isn't your fault, Beasty whispered. *This is why you were given the ability to choose your mate. So you will be able to have a mate that is thoroughly in love with you, not specific aspects of you. Not for the power they will obtain by mating with you. Not because they just have to because of the fates. But because they absolutely adore you, both as a human and a powerful dragon.*

"But why-"

I didn't get to complete the sentence before I felt a hard impact on the back of my skull.

And as the blackness swallowed me, I finally got what I wanted... peace.

I WAS SLEEPING SO GOOD. I FELT AS THOUGH I WAS LIGHT as a feather! I giggled in my sleep.

Wake up! Beasty hissed.

"Five more minutes," I groaned.

Tia. We are in trouble. Open your eyes.

Ugh. Seriously? Ms. Cranky Pants needed to take a nap. I slowly cracked open an eye, but the light immediately sent a stabbing pain through my skull.

"Ow," I grunted.

You were hit, and your head is going to hurt. But that is the least of our worries right now. Beasty's tone filled me with apprehension. Beasty was always so confident. Now she sounded stressed.

What's wrong, Beasty? What happened?

They knocked you out and kidnapped you. Draven's men had been staking out the cabin, and when they finally got the chance to snatch you, they did. From what I've heard while you were out cold, Draven is on his way here now. He plans to take the dragon pendant from you. They have used dark magic to hide this place. We won't be able to teleport through the barrier.

Well, that is pretty stupid. The necklace has no power.

He doesn't know that, and at this moment, that will be our best chance at survival.

Once again, I cracked my eyes open. Beasty surged forward to take over part of my body, and my eyes turned to slits as my vision shifted. My gaze darted around the area as I took in my surroundings. They had chained me to a block wall in what appeared to be a warehouse. Barrels of aging scotch were stored along the walls. Since I was unfamiliar with the area, this information didn't help me figure out how far I was from the cabin I was staying in.

A guy was slumped over a table in one corner of the warehouse, sleeping. I couldn't see anyone else in the building.

Turning back to the space immediately around me, I tried pulling my hands free of the handcuffs. No luck. I couldn't sit down properly as they had the chains holding my arms up slightly. I had only three feet on each chain to move around marginally.

I decided to conserve my energy until Draven made his appearance.

Six hours later, I finally heard a car crunching over the gravel outside, then I recognized his voice. It was about dang time. My arms were completely numb from being held up for so long.

I listened to Draven as he yelled at his men. Well, didn't someone sound happy? That lightened my sour mood a bit. Honestly, leaving me waiting was possibly the worst thing the moron could have done. My fear had changed to rage, and I was so hungry. I was barely holding back my dragon form. I wanted to shift and demand respect. Whoa. Where had that come from? This girl was getting hangry.

"Well, well, well. I see we were able to tame the little beast," Draven mocked.

I simply raised an eyebrow at his choice of words. He had no idea what he had chained in his warehouse. I smirked.

His lips twisted into a cruel smile as he slid his finger

down my neck. *Ew!* This guy was probably like a hundred years old. I gagged.

And exactly how old do you think Mithraheal is? Beasty howled in amusement.

Not the time, Beasty. Kinda busy with the creepy-old-power-stealing dude right now, I muttered to her.

"I would remove your finger before I bite it off, which I really don't want to do, since who knows where it has been," I ground out through gritted teeth.

He didn't bother to reply as his gaze dropped to the dragon heart pendant peeking out from my partially unbuttoned shirt. I wasn't going to just hand it over, so I sprung back hitting the wall, then used the shackles to lift myself up. Flinging out both legs, I smashed his skull between my boots. As he doubled over in agony from the ringing in his ears, I quickly kicked, slamming it into his abdomen. That blow effectively knocked him on his backside. I grinned widely.

Sadly, all my awesomeness was spoiled when I felt a prick in my thigh. I glanced down to find a green dart was sticking out of my dirt-stained pants. I looked up to where Draven's second-in-command was holding a dart gun.

I started feeling tipsy and struggled to remain upright. Draven stood up with some help (big baby), then walked toward me. Beasty snickered when she noticed how cautiously he was approaching us. Even with me being shot with sedatives, he was apprehensive.

"Oh, the evil man is frightened of a little girl?" I wanted it to come out like a taunt, but it was more slurred than I've liked.

He ripped my shirt open and tore my necklace off. I didn't move, as I was still battling the effects of the tranquilizer. I refused to pass out.

Then Draven did the freakiest thing. He held the pendant in the air and yelled, "The day has arrived! Bow and worship me!" He finished with the super cliché black-and-white cartoon villain's evil laugh.

Come on. Who actually does that? In kids' cartoons, sure. But in real life?

I couldn't help it. I burst out laughing. I laughed until my sides ached. I rubbed at the tears running down my face. "Dude. That was the funniest crap I've ever witnessed. How am I supposed to take you seriously?"

Okay, so the last part was dumb to say out loud; a fact I understood after the knife pierced my leg. He was horrible at villain banter, but his aim with knives was no laughing matter. Hissing in pain, I glowered at him.

"Will it be difficult to take me seriously when I rule all the governments on earth? How about when I start killing off supernaturals? I think I will start with your mates. What? You didn't think I knew about them? Such a busy, busy girl. Of course, from what my spies tell me, your werewolf is acting like a, how should I put it? Ah yes. After leaving you behind, sobbing your heart out, he went home and is now acting like a dog."

I tried to ignore the twinge of grief from his words. He was lying. He had to be. A mate being unfaithful was unheard of. Cage had said he just needed time to think.

Confusion must have crossed my face because with a

sharp glance to one of his minions, Draven was suddenly holding a stack of papers. He flicked his wrist, and they fluttered onto the dirty stones at my feet.

Looking down, my heart split in two. Cage was in every photo with a dainty brown-haired woman. Through the tears in my eyes, I could see that she was his perfect Luna. She looked like a 1950s housewife; delicate and proper. He was holding her hand, opening car doors...and kissing her.

Cage had betrayed me. He was wooing his fantasy girl while his mate, the one he had attempted to claim by force, was shackled and drugged. I felt something in my heart snap, like a rubber band breaking. I didn't need Beasty to tell me I had just severed the soulmate bond completely.

I wanted to sink to my knees and scream from the pain, but I couldn't show any weakness. I held back my tears, refusing to let Draven see me break down. I lifted my head to find him looking at his palms and arms, perplexed. He was wearing the pendant, but just like I'd expected, nothing happened.

Because the dragon's heart was inside me.

I stared coldly at him.

"I don't understand. I'm wearing it." Turning to me, he shouted, "How do you activate it? I'm the owner of the Dragon Heart, and its powers belong to me."

I spat at him. I owed him nothing. Ice poured through my veins, and my human emotions began to slip away.

He screeched, "I am going to kill you and all the other low life supers who refuse to acknowledge my authority, Starting with your parasitic Blood Driven mate. I don't care if he is the ruler of his kind. He will surrender, or he will die."

I felt something exploded inside me. Mithraheal was my bonded. Forever. Draven would not lay a freaking hand on what was mine. No one touches a dragon's mate.

I roared in fury!

Draven stumbled away from me with horror stamped on his face.

I tracked his every movement, letting my eyes shift to my dragon's eyes for the second time that day. I saw his fear. I let the shift take over my body, but I forced it to be slow so he could watch everything. My ears elongated, my skin shimmered, my scales glowed, and my hair slowly faded from blond to a pale opalescent.

With no effort at all, I pulled the chains holding me from the wall. The ground rumbled under my feet as I walked toward him. The stink of his fear permeated the area, and I licked my lips. He stumbled back in terror.

"I am the owner of the Dragon Heart." I let my wings rip from my back, and my fingernails lengthened into claws. "Since you seem to be fond of horribly, cliché villain lines, I'm going to use one of my own, Draven." I ran my fingernail down his cheek, leaving behind a trail of blood that he didn't appear to notice, "You will rue the day you messed with me and what is mine."

I spun and breathed fire at the leftover scotch kegs, watching with fascination as they exploded into flames one right after the other. The whole warehouse lit up with intense blue and crimson fire, and pieces of flaming wood fell like glittering rain. I took one last look at Draven's awestruck face before spiraling into the sky. My insides were still filled with ice, and my emotions were nowhere to be found. I realized I wasn't human at that moment. We were Dragon, and we had zeroed in on our mate like a homing beacon.

I hoped he was ready for our arrival.

CHAPTER TWENTY

Tia

I had never felt so alive. I was repeatedly astounded by how enhanced senses became when I shifted. None of my previous shifts compared with this one, though. In the past, I had still felt like my human side held more authority. This time, my human side had been put in a corner for a timeout.

I had no control over my body; I was simply along for the ride. I trusted Beasty, so I wasn't worried for my safety. Although I felt a spasm of apprehension for my mate, and for anyone who tried to come between us.

She could have teleported after we destroyed the warehouse, but I felt she needed to fly and taste freedom. Since we were traveling at a speed that I suspected was only 'dragonly' possible, I wasn't shocked to see the cabin come into view rather quickly. I was, however, surprised at the entrance Beasty made. She headed straight for the grand floor-to-ceiling glass windows. At the last minute, she thrust her wings in front of our face as we made impact with the window. The sound of the shattering glass was deafening to my sensitive hearing.

Looking around, the twins were frozen in place on the couch, Damien was in a fighting stance a few feet from us, and my drool-worthy mate was standing by the fireplace on the far side of the room.

They all shared the same horrified expressions. I could only imagine the image we made. Glass fell around us while blue light from my scales reflected on the glass shards, creating a glittering confetti effect.

Beasty breathed deeply, inhaling in our mate's spicy scent. But rather than soothing the animalistic side, it seemed to cause a frenzy in the dragon.

"Mate," she growled.

She lunged for Mithraheal. Damien's brotherly instinct must have overridden his survival one because he flung himself at us, blocking our view of Mithraheal. With a roar, Beasty smacked him with our wing and followed up by breathing out a flood of intense blue flames.

The tiny part of me that was still human was relieved when my protectors jumped between him and my flames as Damien slammed into the wall. It appeared they were unaffected by my flames.

Damien pulled himself from the floor, and I sensed the air

shifting as he moved behind me. Who needs eyes in the back of their head when the air can tell you what is going on?

Levi grabbed his arm and rumbled, "Don't move, don't even blink."

"What is going on?" Damien asked, but thankfully didn't move.

"She is an animal, not human. Something happened. Her dragon is in control and craves her mate. You're lucky she didn't kill you when you jumped in her path the first time. Her dragon must have a soft spot for you. But her patience is gone; she won't hesitate to kill you if you try again. So, don't freaking move." Luke explained all this without even twitching a muscle in his face, not wanting to risk triggering Beasty's wrath.

Beasty seemed to take in Luke and Levi for the first time since our grand entrance. She purred.

"Mates. Mine. Soon." Her words reverberated in my brain.

After deciding they weren't going to interrupt again, we swung back to Mithraheal. His expression hadn't faltered; and he hadn't moved. When our eyes met, I realized instantly what was about to happen, what my dragon was about to do. I wished I could talk to him first, to know he wanted this as much as Beasty and I wanted it.

Then I heard his soft whisper, "I love you."

And with that, my Dragon lurched forward with a moan, and plunged her teeth into his neck.

THE MOMENT MY TEETH SANK INTO HIS FLESH, I FELT MY power surging into him. With a loud groan, Mithraheal leaned down, running his fangs down my skin, and bit just above my left breast. The power flowed between both of us now.

In my mind, I could see a golden rope tying his soul to mine. He would be eternally mine. My eyes watered, realizing that I would never be alone again. I belonged. I felt Mithraheal gently suck, his fangs still in my skin.

I let out a muffled moan against his neck, not yet able to convince Beasty to pull back enough to remove my teeth from his skin. With each gentle tug of my blood through his bite, my skin heated until I felt like I was on fire. My body trembled with a need I hadn't experienced before.

I finally managed to extract my teeth and choked in a lungful of air. I whimpered as he withdrew his fangs from my skin. I wanted his fangs to remain in me permanently. I craved; I didn't even know precisely what I wanted at that moment.

Sensing my need, or perhaps responding to his own desire, Mithraheal lowered his head even further and left a trail of kisses down my breast. When he came to my areola, he gently slid his fangs along the hypersensitive skin before sucking my aching nipple into his mouth.

Never had I experienced something so mind blowing; I nearly collapsed on the floor as my knees gave out. Mithraheal held me up with ease and teleported us to his bedroom before lowering me onto the bed.

As he drew away from me, I tried to desperately grasp onto him. I didn't want him to leave me. Beasty and I were battling for control.

"Be still, dragostea mea. I will not leave you," he soothed.

I realized he was removing his clothing. I should have turned my head away. I should have at least blushed. I had never seen a man naked, let alone one that was sculpted like a Greek god. But I couldn't look anywhere but at him. I drank in the sight of him. I am pretty certain I drooled a little. He was mine. Every single inch belonged to me, and I wanted to worship it.

Looking up from unbuttoning his slacks, I heard his words in my mind.

No. I will be worshipping you.

Shocked, I realized he had been reading my thoughts. I blushed at the thought that he knew how inexperienced I was. I dropped my gaze. I heard his pants hit the floor and then the bed dipped as he slid beside me. His palm caressed my jaw as he turned my face to look into my eyes.

"You are the most precious person in the world to me. Being able to share your first moments of passion is the greatest gift you could have given me."

When his lips found mine, I kissed him with a hunger of a woman possessed. I felt his hands glide down my body, and he gently removed the tattered remains of my clothes. Pulling me against his warm, taut skin, he intensified the kiss.

The full skin-to-skin contact was unlike anything I had experienced before, better than anything I could have imagined. Sensing my need for more, he pushed his thigh between my legs, forcing them apart. My slick folds now pressed tightly against him.

A burning began deep in my core, a demand for something that I didn't understand. I had to do something to relieve this smoldering fire. I needed friction. I moved against the rock-hard muscles of his thigh and gasped at how incredible it felt. Taking advantage of my gasp, Mithraheal delved his tongue into my mouth, and it danced against mine.

Sensation overwhelmed me and I ground my clit against his leg harder, desiring more. I was going to burn alive from these overwhelming feelings. He didn't push me but let me slowly explore these unfamiliar sensations - and this new intimacy - at my own pace. I began a steady rocking motion against him and felt myself flying higher and higher.

Something coiled deep in my pelvis and I desperately sought release. Moving his mouth from mine, Mithraheal again trailed kisses down my neck and my breast. With one palm, he cupped and squeezed my breast. When he sucked my nipple into his mouth and swirled his tongue around the hardened peak, I screamed out.

I was going to pass out if I didn't find release. His hand drifted from my hip and up my leg until it settled against the apex of my thighs. He hesitated for a moment before slipping a finger inside my soaking wet slit. I moaned at the invasion, and stars bursting behind my eyes.

"Please," I pleaded. I wasn't even sure I knew what I was asking for. He flicked his finger against the little pleasure center inside me, and I came undone. I screamed my release.

I'd been flying high while my climax built, and now I felt

like I was plummeting back to earth. Mithraheal stroked loving hands down my torso.

As my glazed over vision cleared, I realized what I had done. I had humped him like I was a dog in heat. I angled my head, so I didn't have to see his expression.

His voice was soft in my head, "Look at me, my darling."

I shook my head. I wanted the earth to open and swallow me whole. He spoke in my head again.

Watching you come was the most magnificent thing I have ever seen. Use me. Make me yours. Take what you need from me. There is no shame in your need, and it gives me pleasure to take care of all your desires.

I still couldn't bring myself to meet his gaze. I felt the sincerity and love in his voice. Then I felt his hands move down my body.

My core immediately tightened again as desire built. Once wasn't enough. I wanted more, much more. I couldn't stop my hands from running down his chiseled chest and then lower. As my fingertips brushed his manhood, he moaned.

Slowly, I ran my hand down the length of him, and my mouth became as dry as the desert. I had zero experience, but I was pretty sure he was much bigger than a man was supposed to be. How on earth was that going to fit inside me? Maybe I should have checked his size for compatibility before marking him as my mate for life.

In my brain, Beasty roared with laughter.

Personally, I found this alarming, not a laughing matter. Mithraheal let out a cough that sounded suspiciously like a laugh, and my eyes jumped to his to glare at him.

Quit worrying, little dragon. You were created for me, and we will fit together perfectly.

I was about to argue with him, but he flipped me onto my back and shifted his body over mine. He kissed me with a passion that stole my breath. In his fervent kisses, I felt the pent-up love and desire he'd held within himself for decades, or perhaps centuries.

He needed me just as much as I needed him.

I relaxed and kissed him back. I stroked my hands over his back, gently digging my nails in just enough to leave marks, but not enough to break the skin. I wanted him to feel my love for him. His hand burrowed into my hair, deepening the kiss while I wrapped my legs around his waist, dragging his body against my own.

I couldn't stop the moan that escaped at the sensation. He was right; we fit together. I wished we could melt completely into each other. His erection bumped against my entrance, and I froze.

It was so hot, it felt like a branding iron was searing my wet center. I started to panic, but the need that ripped through me quickly banished my nerves. Just the thought of his heated erection sliding inside me sent another wave of desire shuddering through my body.

His hard member pressed hard against my folds, not pushing himself in, just pressing against me. Mithraheal had stopped moving and held me, obviously giving me time to sort through the jumbled mess of desire and panic in my head. I moved my hips slightly and even just feeling his erection against my slick clit made me pant. This was what I wanted. And I wanted it NOW.

"I'm ready. Please Mithraheal, I need you in ways I don't even understand." I couldn't have hidden my neediness if I had tried.

"I love you," he said against my mouth. He shifted, lining himself up with my throbbing slit, and gradually pushed until the head of his erection slid through my entrance. I gasped from the slight spasm of discomfort, and because I had never imagined it would feel this extraordinary.

With infinite control, he slid a little more of him inside me, stopping inch by inch, giving me time to adjust to his size. His face was pained with concentration. Obviously, he was struggling to keep control and be gentle with me. I felt him press hard against the barrier within me.

"No matter how gentle I am, this is going to hurt. The first time always does." His tone was miserable at the thought of hurting me.

I was panting hard. I was working to adjust to his size, but as he continued to fill my soaked channel, a tightening in my lower abdomen was building and it was nearly painful at this point.

"Just do it fast," I ground out through my clenched teeth.

With a bit of vampiric speed, he slid back out and then slammed inside me hard and fast, burying himself completely.

I shrieked. I knew it hurt when you lost your virginity, but dang. I seriously think people underplayed how much it hurts.

Mithraheal remained motionless, allowing me to breathe

through the pain. As the pain ebbed, desire filled my belly again; I wanted him to...

Mithraheal let out a feral sounding growl. My eyes snapped up to meet his, and the look was that of a starved predator.

"Uh, Mithraheal. You okay? You are looking a bit intense right now," I giggled nervously. I also didn't want to admit that the glow in his eyes and that deep growl that had vibrated through my body had sent molten liquid to my core. I wasn't sure what had changed, though. How had he gone from tender man to Blood Driven in two seconds flat? And then a smell tickled my nose. Blood. My blood.

Not just any blood, doll. Virgin blood. The virgin blood of his beloved. Beasty sounded downright giddy.

What exactly does that mean for me? I asked, watching Mithraheal's eyes track every movement in my face. His nostrils flared as he inhaled the scent of my blood deeper into his lungs. Blood Driven didn't even need to breathe, and yet here he was inhaling deeply.

It means, buckle up, buttercup! We are about to have the type of sex people would literally die for. She cackled in glee.

She barely finished before Mithraheal had me in his arms. He flashed across the room and slammed my backside against the wall before driving himself deep inside me in one hard stroke. I gasped as fireworks exploded behind my eyes.

He pumped into me at a speed so fast, my body hummed. I felt my orgasm building but before I could reach the climax, he flashed us across the room again and had me pressed into the headboard.

I had no idea why he was flashing us about the room, but my body sure didn't seem to mind. My need had grown into a painful lead weight in my stomach. He was slamming his cock deep with every thrust, the feral look in his eyes watching me as though he couldn't decide if he wanted sex or a snack. I honestly didn't care at that point; I was too far gone.

My vision blurred and my climax built until it ripped through my body. I screamed his name as electric shocks felt like they were frying every nerve ending in my body. I was still reeling when he flashed again, and I found myself face down on the edge of the bed.

He was behind me, pumping his engorged cock back into my silky folds all in one swift movement. I just had an earth-shattering orgasm, but this new position and the mind-blowing speed at which he moved had my body tightening again.

I was pretty sure I was going to die if I orgasmed again. He slammed deep into me... and I decided this wasn't a bad way to go.

Over and over, he pulled out and then buried himself to the hilt. The pace was frenzied, and we were slippery with sweat. He moved his hand around my hip, sliding one down to where we were joined. His pace never faltered as his finger expertly found my clit.

That put me over the edge. As my next orgasm built, I screamed, "Bite me!"

Without hesitation, he wrapped his other arm around me and yanked my body nearly flush against his. I turned my head toward him, and he sank his teeth into my throat. The moment he sucked, I was pushed over the edge and rode wave after wave of pleasure.

I felt him slam into me twice more before he stilled, a growl vibrating into my throat from where his fangs remained embedded. I felt his erection pulsing inside me as he found his own release.

I was nothing more than a limp noodle at this point. As he pulled his fangs from me, I collapsed onto the bed. Even my mind was a puddle of hazy mush.

I knew it was going to be good, but HO-LY cow. That boy is sinfully good. We definitely know how to pick 'em. Let's do it again. Beasty prattled on and on, making all sorts of dirty plans in my mind.

I couldn't keep up and tuned her out. I was face-down on the bed and decided I should just close my eyes and take a little nap. Yeah, that sounded nice.

Seconds later, I was being cradled like a child against Mithraheal's chest.

"I'm so sorry. I never meant to lose control like that. It has been decades since my vampire nature broke through my control. I wanted our first time to be special. The smell of your blood just sent me over the edge. Are you hurt? Did I take too much blood? Please talk to me." His voice broke as his fingers gently touched where his fangs had just been.

I was too stunned by his outburst to even attempt to string words together. I watched as a tear escaped and rolled down his cheek. What on earth was wrong with him?

"Why are you crying? Did you hurt yourself? You made my first time better than I even thought possible. Beasty is busy trying to figure out ways to keep you trapped in this room, having sex for the rest of your life. I'm fine. Actually, I am better than fine and could totally die happy right now." I let out a contented sigh.

The relief on his face was adorable.

"Next time, I will make sure it is sweet and gentle, and everything you deserve, dragostea mea."

In my head, Beasty let out an annoyed huff. *He better not. He has set a pretty high bar, no going back now.*

Before I could decide whether to grouch at her response or ignore her and focus on Mithraheal, I felt her stiffen with apprehension. Alarm bells rang in my head.

"We have to go!" I shouted as I rolled off the bed and made a dash for some clothing. It seemed Mithraheal had hoped we would share a room at some point, and he had items he thought I might need laid out neatly on the dresser top.

I hurriedly wiggled into some jeans and threw a shirt over my head while he did the same. I grabbed a pair of combat boots and yanked them on while I rushed toward the door. Without questioning my sanity, Mithraheal followed right on my heels.

As we tumbled out the door and into the fresh air, I darted my gaze around the clearing. I felt a sense of relief when I spotted the twins and Damian lounging near a water hose watching me warily. What was wrong with them? *Weirdos.*

"We have to go now. Do you guys have a safe place where we can teleport?"

The guys just continued to stare at me in dumbfounded silence.

"They are almost here!" I screamed.

"Who are they?" Damien asked cautiously.

I opened my mouth to answer, but the sound of helicopters in the distance caught everyone's attention. A large dust cloud floated up from the ground only a few miles from the cabin, and it was getting nearer by the second.

Without another word, Mithraheal grabbed me, while Damien grabbed Levi and Luke by their shoulders, and right before we popped into the vortex, I saw the cabin we had been in just moments before exploding into a fiery inferno.

Then everything went black.

I don't think I would ever get used to the spinning vortex of teleporting. I bent over and braced myself on my knees as a wave of nausea rolled over me.

"Are you okay, love?" Mithraheal asked as he rubbed my back in gentle circles.

"I'm feeling better," I responded and slowly straightened.

Levi and Luke were a few feet away, looking a bit green. I don't think wolves enjoyed teleporting at all.

"How did you know we needed to leave, and they were coming?" Damien watched me curiously.

"My dragon became aware, and I heard alarms in my head. I knew danger was coming. Not exactly what type of danger, just that we needed to get out of there." I peered around but didn't recognize our surroundings.

"We are in a different part of the mountains, several hours from the cabin," Mithraheal responded to my unasked question.

It was a beautiful area. Trees surrounded us. Looking down, I could see a beautiful lake. I had never seen a mountain lake before, and it took my breath away.

Luke and Levi came to either side of me and squeezed in close, resting their nose against my neck and breathing in deeply.

"We were so worried - not knowing where Draven had taken you, or what was happening to you. Don't scare us like that again!" Levi spoke muffled against my neck. He pressed his lips against my skin, sending delicious shivers down my body.

I reached out to touch them, trying to reassure them I was okay. I never made promises I wasn't sure I could keep, and Draven wasn't finished with me. Far from it.

"Okay, but can we just skip to the part where you came flying through the window like something out of a movie? I mean, it was totally cool, but you had me so freaked out. I thought you were going to eat Mithraheal. And instead, you just wanted to *eat* him." Damien finished speaking and waggled his eyebrows at me.

I groaned.

Mithraheal rubbed a hand down his face.

My mind drifted back to those moments we had together in bed, and I blushed as I thought about what we had been doing when we got interrupted. Damien must have seen my blush because he winked.

"Come on. Let's get everyone settled in." Damien headed toward another cabin.

Luke reached for my hand and we followed Damien up a small path to a beautiful cabin.

I really hoped that we wouldn't accidently set this one on fire.

Sigh.

CHAPTER TWENTY-ONE

Tia

We spent the next few days with everyone anxious and on edge. While flipping through channels, trying to find something to take our minds off our current situation, Damien had found a news report showing the charred remains of the house. They were calling it a gas explosion. Yeah, right. In the background of some of the video footage, we saw military jeeps and guys in military gear. The news hadn't commented on why they were there, but we knew they had been the ones to come after us and bomb the house. Why on earth was the military interested in me, though? Did Draven have ties to the military? If he had a connection, then we had to assume he was going to locate us again fairly quickly.

"We need to come up with a plan," I stated quietly. "If

this is Draven's doing, he will not stop coming after me. We don't have the manpower to fight the military. We are going to have to find a way to take him down when he isn't surrounded by hired guns."

Just the mere thought of having to take someone's life made me sick. But knowing he tried to end the lives of those I loved lit a fire in me. He had to pay. He had to be stopped before he managed to hurt one of us.

I slowly rose to my feet and headed down the hall and into the bedroom. I couldn't bear to watch any more of the news footage. I just wanted to hide from the world.

The bedroom in this house was beautiful. The furniture was made from a dark wood. The bed itself was a monstrosity and easily the largest bed I had ever seen. It was so massive it would have filled the entire living room of the home I had grown up in. It had four large pillars, each with an intricate design carved into it. A pile of fluffy pillows made it look like a cloud.

One wall of the room was all glass, and it gave a panoramic view of the lake and mountains surrounding it. The sun was setting, and the sky had turned rich golds, pinks, and purples which reflected on the lake's glass-like surface.

I stood still in front of the window. Slowly, the tension drained from my body as I soaked in the beauty of the scene in front of me.

I was so focused on the lake, that I didn't hear the door open or the soft sound of footsteps. I jumped when warm arms wrap themselves around my middle. I let out a gasp, spinning around and coming face to face with Luke's concerned blue eyes.

"I didn't mean to scare you. I just wanted to check and make sure you were okay. I could feel your distress through our bond," he said.

I threw my arms around his neck, pulling him closer. A little piece in my heart shifted and fell into place. This was right. He was mine. His arms tightened, and he lowered his head until his warm breath moved through my hair.

Beasty, who had been quiet since escaping the last disaster, stirred in my mind. *He loves us,* she whispered.

I felt it through the bond. I could also feel the desire building as well.

What about Levi? I asked Beasty. *And what about Mithraheal? How can I want more than one person so badly?* The thought of them being hurt was devastating.

You are thinking like a human, she scoffed. *We are different. Dragons are unbelievably powerful, but they have hunted us since the beginning of our time on earth. Our women are vulnerable while pregnant, and children are easy for those hunting us to capture and kill.*

Our species adapted to this by creating a strong mating circle. Usually, a female dragon will have two mates. This means that while one mate hunts, or works, or must be away from the nest, the other mate can stay to guard the pregnant mate or children.

Occasionally, there have been female dragons that took three mates, but those cases have been rare and the dragoness was quite powerful. What you are feeling isn't wrong. This is the way of the dragons. This is how we survived for so many centuries.

I understood what she was saying, but I still struggled to absorb the information. *You are saying that I should take these men as my mates? All three?* I asked her.

Darling, there has never been a dragon or dragoness like us. It will not be just these three. There will be more capable mates drawn to us. And you will be drawn to some of them and will claim them as yours. You can choose to ignore the pull toward other mates if you wish, but you also need to remember that we are more powerful than any dragons that have come before.

Our offspring may be what saves our entire species. We will save the world. Even with all our power, we cannot do all this alone. You need to get this into your stubborn head now and stop thinking like a human.

I felt like the wind had been knocked from my lungs. Not only was I going to have this crazy need to bond with Mithraheal, Levi, and Luke, but I was most likely going to have more mates? Would they leave me when they found out? Were they going to be okay raising each other's kids, assuming I ever had children?

My knees went slack. I would have sunk to the floor if Luke hadn't tightened his grip, holding me against him and keeping me upright. I was held so tightly against Luke that I could feel his every muscle. Heat radiated off his body, even through our clothes.

Beasty must have been done trying to explain things to me and convince me I had nothing to feel bad about, because she surged forward. My markings glowed as desire burned through my body.

I pulled back from Luke so that I could see his face. Desire shimmered in his eyes. He reached up and pulled his face toward me. I stopped when our lips were mere centimeters from each other.

"Luke, are you sure?" My voice quavered, and I tried to steady my voice as I continued, "The others..."

"I don't care. I have known from the moment I saw you I would forever be tied to you. I have watched your strength grow and have fallen in love with your sense of humor. I don't care if I have to share you with the others, as long as I get to have you too." Luke finished by pressing his lips to mine.

The kiss set my entire body on fire, and I gasped against his lips. He used that opening to slip his tongue inside my mouth, and the kiss became so hot that my insides melted, and wetness drenched my panties. I needed more. Now.

He must have sensed my growing need because his hands slid to the front of my jeans and unbuttoned them before gently slipping them down my hips. My panties quickly followed the same path. As he unbuttoned the comfy flannel shirt I was wearing, I slid my hands to the stretchy band of his low riding sweatpants. With a couple of quick tugs, they hit the floor.

Apparently, the man liked going commando because there was nothing under those pants. He let go of me for a moment to lift his shirt over his head. Stepping forward, he pushed me back into the glass of the windows.

Although the sun had set, there was enough light to show

the fierce desire on his face while lights and shadows played on his body.

I couldn't help but admire the muscles, nor could I stop my gaze from following the trail of hair that led down his lower abs. He had very little body hair, which was surprising. I mean, you would think werewolves would be a little extra hairy, right?

Before I could drink in more of his body, he lifted me, and I immediately wrapped my legs around him. He began kissing up the side of my neck and then across my check until he found my lips again. Our kiss this time was much more frantic. I was sure I would die if it stopped.

My stomach was clenching and unclenching, my desire so strong that it hurt. His hot skin pressed against my core and I ground against his hard, flat stomach. As I moved, his erection poked my rear. We were both burning with need.

"Please," I whimpered, wanting him to ease the ache.

I barely got the word out before Luke loosened his grip and thrust his cock deep inside me with one hard stroke. I let out a sound between a gasp and a groan. I was so full. It was equal parts pain and pleasure.

He remained still, giving me time to adjust to his size, while pinning me between his body and the glass and keeping me speared on his throbbing erection. Slowly, he kissed my lips and the last bits of pain disappeared as my desire washed over me in a tidal wave. I tried to move against his body, seeking relief to the building pressure in my core, but it wasn't enough.

"Luke," I growled in frustration.

He must have realized I was ready because he slid out and then slid back in, the head of his erection rubbing my clit just right. Over and over, he did this at an achingly slow pace that was creating a frenzy in me. I could feel my wetness coating my inner thighs.

I growled again and bit his chest. When my teeth nicked his skin, the last bit of his composure broke. This time when he pulled out, he thrust into me with a force that smacked me into the glass.

Before I could even gasp, he had already pulled out and was thrusting in again. He drove himself into me, faster and harder with each stroke. I stretched and burned and became increasingly wet with each thrust.

"I'm going to come," I panted.

"Yes. Come. For. Me." He slammed his cock into me with each word.

The orgasm hit me, my vision going black. As I screamed out his name, my teeth elongated into my dragon's teeth. I sank them deep into his chest above his heart. He shoved into me once more, grinding hard against me. He roared his release and then sank his teeth into my neck. The moment his teeth broke my skin, I came again, clinging to him as the pleasure washed over me.

We stood there panting hard. My legs were still around his waist, and he still held me pinned against the glass. He gripped me tighter and walked over to the bed where he sat down with me straddling his lap and him still deep inside me. We held each other for several long minutes, trying to catch our breaths, and relishing the closeness.

I noticed a bit of blood drip from the bite I left on his chest and leaned over and licked it off. His body shuddered and his erection twitched inside me. My eyes widened.

"I am going to need a few minutes before I am ready for round two," he replied with a smirk.

"Don't worry, brother. I will happily take her off your lap and entertain her until then," a new voice said. I shivered as his hands moved under the bra we hadn't bothered to remove, to pinch my nipples. I turned to find Levi had slipped into the room unnoticed.

My shock must have shown because he leaned forward to nuzzle my face and whispered, "I could feel everything through the bond. It was pure torture, and one of the most amazing experiences of my life. Please tell me you want me too."

The insecure look on his face told me he worried I would tell him no, and that he would be on the outside of this bond forever.

"Oh, Levi," I breathed. I turned, wrapped my arms around his neck, and pressed my mouth against his.

Luke lifted me off him and shifted me so that I was straddling the fully clothed Levi. Levi pulled me tighter against his chest and unclasped my bra. Once that was removed, his hands continued to explore my body, smiling against my lips each time he caused me to gasp.

I heard shuffling behind me, and Luke's arms snaked around my waist, pulling me further back onto the bed. His back was propped against the headboard, and he pulled me toward him until I was flat on my back on the bed with my side touching him.

Levi was quick to shed his clothes and crawl across the bed. He gently lowered his body until he was covering me completely with his massive muscular frame.

I had barely recovered from the mind-numbing sex with Luke, yet my stomach clenched as I looked into the eyes of my Levi. I liked how that sounded. My Levi.

His hands slid up and down my body as though he was trying to memorize every curve. He bent his head, sucked my nipple into his mouth, and desire ripped through me. It felt like an electric current had gone straight from my breast to my core.

I wouldn't have thought it was possible to become even wetter, but holy cow! I was going to soak the bed at this rate.

His fiery mouth continued to suck my nipple. I was so caught up in that sensation, I hadn't noticed his hand had found a new area to explore. I nearly came the moment his finger slid into my silky folds. His fingers gently brushed around the edges and teased just inside the depths. I tried to push against his hand to find some relief, but he continued his teasing.

"Please," I begged.

"Please, what?" he said as he licked across my chest and sucked at my other breast.

I mumbled incoherent nonsense as I tried to squirm under him. I needed more. The tightening in my stomach was growing by the second. His amused laugh vibrated through me, but he took mercy. The fingers that had been feather light suddenly thrust deep into me. At the same moment, he gently bit my nipple.

I sucked in air from the sudden explosion of pleasure, and before I sucked in my next breath, he began moving his finger in and out of me with a steady rhythm. He applied just the right amount of pressure as he fingered my pleasure center, and the need in me grew with each stroke.

He must have heard my breathing change because he increased his speed until I was seeing fireworks. My body began moving on its own to find the relief I craved. Suddenly, his mouth disappeared from my breast. A moment later, his mouth pressed against my slick folds. The sucking and warmth from his tongue added to the faster movement of his fingers to push me over the edge, and I cried out as waves of pleasure washed over me.

Afterwards, I lay there trembling as I watched him lick his lips and move back up my body with a predatory gleam in his eye. His eyes glowed, showing that his wolf was very close to the surface.

Luke must have gotten up from the bed and lit some candles, bathing the room in a soft warm glow.

The bed shifted as Luke climbed back onto it to resume his position near me. He still didn't touch me, he simply observed us.

My gaze shifted back to Levi, who had positioned himself over my body again. He seemed to be waiting for a signal from me.

"Show me how much you want me," I whispered.

He didn't break eye contact as he lined himself up with

my throbbing entrance. I could see the glistening bead on the tip of his erection. I wanted to lick it, to taste him. He was so engorged; the veins were clearly visible. He wanted me, and I loved that.

I thought he would sink into me hard and fast like his brother, but with incredible slowness he pressed his girth into me inch by inch. It was deliciously painful. I wanted him in me more than anything else at that moment, but there was a sweetness to his movement I wanted to savor.

This was the first time I was feeling his cock fill me up, and I wanted to remember this moment. I went from being full, to my walls burning from the size of him. Just when I thought I couldn't possibly take any more without ripping in two, he stopped. I breathed a little sigh of relief that he fit.

With equal slowness, he began the tortuously slow movement of sliding back out until the head rubbed against my clit. I immediately ached for that fullness again, and he slid slowly back inside me. My core dripped and my walls quivered as his cock massaged every inch. He repeated this incredible torture and the knot inside me tightened more.

"You love my brother's cock, don't you?" Luke's words startled me.

I had been so caught up in the moment with Levi that I had forgotten we weren't alone. I glanced up to where Luke's head rested against the headboard and saw him watching us intently with glowing eyes. My eyes tracked down his body and stopped as I came to his groin.

Since he was sitting up, and I was flat on my back, my head brushed against his large thigh. Mere inches past that was his massive erection. He certainly hadn't needed much time to be ready to go again.

He had his fist wrapped around his thick cock and was sliding it up and down at the same pace his brother was moving in and out of me. Not only did he not mind sharing, he also enjoyed watching. This turned me on even more, and a flush of feverish need prickled my skin.

"Are you going to answer me?" Luke said, snapping me out of the trance the movement of his hand on his erection had caused. "I asked if you love my brother's thick cock."

"Yesss," I moaned out.

"Do you want him to slow down?"

"No!" I growled.

"Would you like him to move faster?" Luke continued stroking himself as he teased me.

"Yes!" My eyes focused back on Levi's face, and I saw he was overcome with need as well.

"Please, Levi. I need you. Now."

He slid out one last time and then slammed back into me, pulling out and slamming home again before I even took a breath. The coil inside of me tightened until it was almost painful. Need clouded my brain and I could think of nothing but the sensation of Levi's cock inside me.

Sweat had broken out on my body as I dug my nails into Levi's back and held on. The pleasure and pain mixed, and I neared my release, but it was just out of reach. Suddenly, Luke's hands slid between our bodies and cupped my aching breasts. He massaged them gently and then just when I thought I couldn't take anymore, he roughly pinched my nipples.

I came so hard I thought my body had shattered. I screamed Levi's name as my body shuddered and trembled. My back arched and as I snapped against him again, I sunk my elongated teeth into his chest. I marked him right above his heart, exactly where I had marked his brother. He thrust into me one final time and bellowed his release, before dropping his head and sinking his teeth into my neck, marking me as his.

The moment his teeth broke my skin, it was as though the bond between the three of us snapped into place. Luke and Levi's features sharpened, shifting to show the wolf beneath their skin. My own body shimmered and shifted slightly as Beasty pressed hard against my skin.

The sudden wave of need and pleasure hit us with a force that was nearly painful. I thought my body was spent and I wasn't likely to be walking anytime soon. But when that force hit us, it was as though I hadn't had an orgasm at all.

The force hit again, and the need in me built at an unbelievable speed. It must have been doing the same to the twins because Levi suddenly jerked, flipped me onto my hands and knees, and plunged into me again. His erection felt even larger and just as hard as it had been before he emptied himself inside me.

Luke was rubbing up and down his erection at a frantic pace, and there was a need in his eyes that made him look like he was in pain. I scooted toward him and swirled my tongue around the head of his erection. He groaned.

Maybe I was crazy, but it seemed thicker and longer than it had been just moments before. I wrapped my hand around his cock, my fingers not able to fully circle his girth. I slid his erection into my mouth and the muscles in his thighs quivered. I guided him in and out of my mouth faster, taking him as deep as I could.

The force of need and pleasure slammed into us again and our pace became frenzied. Levi was slamming into me so hard that his balls smacked my butt. Luke was bent over, kissing me as though his next breath depended on it. The invisible force hit us one last time, and we all reached our climax at the same moment.

Levi and Luke bit their marks on either side of my neck. Levi slammed into me a final time and I felt him jerking inside me. Warm cream filled my mouth as Luke came. I moaned as pure primal pleasure shattered my body.

A loud *pop* sounded in the room. The force that had vibrated in the air surrounding us disappeared with a blink, leaving us to collapse in a heap, utterly exhausted.

CHAPTER TWENTY-TWO

Tia

The following morning, I woke up feeling cozy and warm. On one side of me, Levi was sprawled with his leg draped over my body, and on the other side, a monstrous wolf lay pressed against my back. I was always obsessed with fuzzy blankets but having your own very soft wolf to cuddle was the best thing ever.

I rolled over and pressed my face into his fur, breathing in deeply. His fur smelled of woods and smoke and reminded me of evenings spent around a campfire with my family.

I slid out from under Levi's leg and rose hastily, so I could escape to the bathroom before the boys woke. As soon as I stood up, my legs wobbled, and I hit the floor.

Evidently, I had been loved so thoroughly the night before, I couldn't even stand. I sat there for a second until another realization struck me. I stunk and was a sticky mess. Still attempting to not wake the guys, I went into stealth mode and crawled to the bathroom.

I nearly made it to the door when I heard a snicker. I swung my head around to find Levi propped up on his elbow looking sexier than any guy should be allowed, and he was watching my progress with a smirk. Luke's huge wolf was sitting up, following my movements as well.

"Any particular reason you are crawling to the bathroom, gorgeous?" Levi inquired.

Not wishing to fuel his ego, I shrugged nonchalantly. "I was impressed by the softness of the carpet and wanted to admire it."

Luke's wolf let out a huffing sound that made me think he was laughing at my predicament.

I narrowed my eyes at him.

"Are you sure it wasn't because we not only blew your mind last night, but we also gave you the best work out of your life?"

I ignored him and glanced back toward the bathroom, struggling to decide if it would hurt my pride more to crawl the last few feet, or try to stand and risk wobbling or hitting my backside again.

Before I could decide, Luke's wolf had bounced off the bed and pranced over to me. He nuzzled my hair before he pressed his snout against the bite mark on my neck and inhaled deeply. I reached out and stroked his fur with my fingertips, enjoying this bonding time with his wolf.

Finally, his huge wolf head drew back, and he began

licking my face with joyful abandon. I could barely catch my breath from laughter and tried to cover my face. When that didn't work, I attempted to push myself to my feet so I could escape to the bathroom.

I had nearly managed a standing position when a hand smacked my rear and swept me off my feet. Startled, I let out a yelp. Levi chuckled as he carried me into the bathroom. He seated me on the sink, which elicited a squeal when the cold of the marble touched my bare bum.

He kneeled and began to run a steamy hot bath in what looked almost like a swimming pool. Was this place built for giants? First, a bed the size of two California Kings put together, and now a tub that was nearly big enough to swim in.

"I could have run my own bath water. You are going to end up spoiling me," I spoke from my perch. I did like being independent, but I was also enjoying watching his tight butt as he leaned down to test the water temperature and adjust the faucets.

He must have been satisfied with the bath because he turned and came to stand in front of me. "Darling, you better get used to it. I will spend the rest of my life trying to show you just how much I adore you."

He scooped me up and gently lowered my body into the warm water. It felt so incredible that I couldn't stop the moan that escaped my lips.

Levi froze. "On that note, I am going to give you some privacy and go take a shower down the hall. A very cold shower."

He left the room, and I closed my eyes. I let myself sink a little lower in the tub, sighing in absolute bliss. I thought back over the previous night and still couldn't quite believe what had happened. My cheeks heated with embarrassment while my heart did some weird fluttering in my chest. But I realized at that moment, I was truly happy.

My heart still ached at the loss of my parents and the sting of Cage's betrayal. I had a psycho killer trying to capture me to use me in some type of power play. Beasty had introduced herself and turned me into a freaking dragon. And oh, yeah, I had claimed not one, but three mates.

The girl who had never even kissed a boy suddenly had three life mates. At that last thought, my heart gave a pang. What was Mithraheal going to think of me after last night? I'm sure with his vampire hearing he knew exactly what was going on.

While he wasn't bound to the twins, he was still going to be sharing the rest of his life with them as well. I didn't know if I could survive him rejecting me. I needed to talk with him. Not just about mates, but about what Draven had said about him. Was Mithraheal some type of leader?

A wet nose pressed against my face, and I opened my eyes to find Luke's wolf head laying on the side of the tub, watching me closely. When our eyes connected, his tail thumped the floor, and he whined. I hadn't even realized that he had stayed in the room after Levi left.

I pressed my forehead to his. "Everything is happening so fast. A part of me wishes I could just hide in this tub forever."

Leaning back against the tub, I tried to pull myself

together again. Luke lowered his massive head until his nose touched the water, I wasn't sure what he was going to do, but when he blew bubbles out his nose, I couldn't stop the giggle that escaped.

He took this as encouragement and blew some more, his tail creating a breeze in the room from how hard he was wagging it. Seeing a werewolf, the size of a small horse, acting like a silly puppy was such a weird contrast, and it totally made me love him more.

I burst out laughing and tried shoving his head out of the tub, but he stuck his face further in the water. He flicked his muzzle toward me, creating a splash that soaked the part of my hair that was still dry and drenched the wall behind me.

Blinking the water from my eyes, I laughed harder and surprised him by grabbing him around the neck and pulling him further into the water. He lifted his head up and I was reminded of his strength as I was nearly jerked from the tub altogether. I let go and laughed again as the water splashed around me.

Luke did a weird bouncy dance around the tub, barking and nipping at me, before jumping into the tub right beside me. At this point, I had tears running down my cheeks from laughter at his antics. I threw my arms around him. I needed him. Not just in the bedroom, not just as my protector, but I needed his companionship.

I never had to be lonely again. No matter what was coming our way, I knew I wouldn't face it alone. The guys loved me, no matter what freaky power my body unleashed or what I shifted into. I belonged to them.

It was time to plan. I was tired of running, and if I wanted a home with my guys, I needed to take the fight to Draven and finish this. With that thought, I reached for the orange scented shampoo and quickly washed and rinsed my hair.

Luke still sat next to me in the tub. Apparently, his wolf enjoyed a hot bath too. Before he could react, I poured some shampoo on his head and lathered it up until he was covered in white foam. His eyes watched me, and it was clear he wasn't amused.

There was a soft knock on the door before it slid open and Mithraheal came into view. I wasn't sure what he expected to find but from the shocked look on his face, it was not a girl happily sculpting a white soapy lion mane on a werewolf. He stood there without saying a word then burst into a laugh so sexy it sent heat racing straight to my lady bits.

He finally composed himself enough to get out, "We have visitors. They are asking for you." Then he closed the door. I thought I heard him say the word 'whipped' as his footsteps retreated from the room, but I wasn't sure.

I looked back at Luke, who was glaring at me through slit eyes. I was definitely going to pay for this later, but it was oh so worth it. Hopping from the tub, I realized the heat had done wonders for my sore muscles. Grabbing a thick fluffy towel, I dried myself off. Finishing, I looked toward the tub as Luke came up from under the water.

He had managed to get all the shampoo out and leaped from the tub. I had only a moment to see the twinkle in his eye before he shook his fur dry. When he stopped, the only some-what dry thing in the room was him! I was dripping wet again.

One minute, I was staring at the smug wolf in front of me and moments later Luke's smirking face was looking down at me. He stepped closer, pressing our naked bodies together, causing little goosebumps to travel down my skin. His hand moved under my jaw, lifting my lips to meet his.

Right as his lips touched mine, he whispered, "You better hurry beautiful, you have people waiting and you're still soaking wet." Chuckling, he moved around me, pinching my butt as he left the room.

Jerk. He knew he was leaving me panting for more.

Beasty stretched and purred in my mind. "Did you catch a look at his-"

"Hush up!" I grumbled at her.

Of course, I had stolen a peek, but I wasn't going to tell her horny self that.

I quickly dried off again and hurried to throw on some clothes. I wasn't sure who was visiting, but I really wanted to know how they had found us. Were we that easy to find?

CHAPTER TWENTY-THREE

Tia

I sauntered into a room pulsating with tension. Mithraheal, Damien, Levi, and Luke lounged in chairs nearing the hallway to the bedroom, clearly prepared to block anyone who tried to get to me. Their protectiveness warmed my heart. Although I couldn't help but smirk knowing when I shifted, I wasn't someone you wanted to mess with.

I quickly examined the three visitors who were standing stiffly just a few feet inside the front door. They were dressed all in black with a goth vibe going on. Each man had a sword strapped to his back and several blades strapped to their thighs.

Beasty moved in my mind, and some of my power rippled

through the area before jerking back into me. Huh. Well, that was new.

I was studying their power. I wanted to see what we might be dealing with, Beasty said in response to my bewilderment.

And what did we find out?

They're wizards, and exceptionally powerful ones. They would be entertaining to fight.

Of course, it was all about fighting or sex with her.

It can also be fun to do both... at the same time, she confided.

Inwardly, I rolled my eyes.

I plopped down on the big beanbag in the middle of the room and waved for them to take seats. "You might as well sit down. You came here for a reason, and you aren't leaving until I get some answers."

They exchanged sharp looks. It was obvious, after seeing me, they didn't consider me much of a threat. Good. I wanted them to let their guards down.

"We have come to offer assistance," one of the guys spoke.

I waited, but he said nothing more. I had arrangements to make and evil villains to track down, so he needed to get on with it or get out.

"I don't have time to do this dance, so let me blunt. You are three of the strongest wizards living. You have somehow tracked me, and I want to know how. You offer your help, but if we are going to be working together, then you need to start talking. Why should I trust that you are truly here to aid me?"

I sensed my boys shift in their seats when I mentioned

wizards, but they stayed quiet, leaving me in control of the conversation. I loved knowing they were confident in me.

The three strangers exchanged glances in silent communication, and apparently came to some type of agreement because their bodies relaxed onto the chairs. The guy I assumed was the leader spoke again.

"I am Gregor, and these are my brothers Hans and Lars. Yes, we are wizards. We have actually been trying to locate you. When you were being held captive by Draven, we were working on an escape plan, but you managed to handle that with no help."

I couldn't stop the self-satisfied grin curving my lips. I had managed just fine, and carried out a fabulous, fiery exit rivaling any Hollywood action movie.

Gregor nodded at me with a smile before continuing, "We have been trying to track your magic since then. It's roughly like tracking footprints, but we were following your unique magical signature. Unfortunately for us, you are not like most supernaturals, and you don't leak magic.

"Our team has been teleporting to various areas around the US over and over, hoping you would release some magic while one of us was nearby. We aren't sure what happened, but last night an immense wave of magic slammed into all the magic users within a hundred-mile radius of this cabin. The power didn't feel exactly like your signature we had been pursuing, but since none of us had felt energy like that, well, ever, we thought it might have been you.

"We then traced it back to this location. Were we right, it

was you? The power was incredible." He leaned forward eagerly, and it was obvious he was hoping I would elaborate on precisely what I had done to cause the magical wave.

I felt the tips of my ears turning crimson. Behind me, I was pretty sure I heard a snicker from one of my mates.

"Uh, yeah. That was me. Just trying something new," I squeaked out.

Damien snorted a laugh, which he tried to cover with a coughing fit.

I was going to kill him later. Top of my to-do list - Kill Damien. Slowly.

Sensing he wasn't going to get more of an explanation, Gregor continued, "We know about Draven's obsession with the Dragon Heart. After you proved the power wasn't in the pendant and made your escape, we thought he would let it go. He has always been power hungry, spending most of his life searching for ways to increase his abilities.

"Until we learned of your kidnapping, we hadn't realized he was prepared to destroy others in his pursuit.

"The council has consistently turned a blind eye when he bent the law a bit. Now they realize he needs to be brought down. We believe he has found a way to manipulate his powers to have people drop their guards and trust him more easily. We think he has been using that on the council as well.

"His intentions aren't to help wizards and other supernaturals, but rather to enhance his power to a level where he can take control, and no one will be strong enough to stop him. If you plan to take him down, we are ready to pledge our assistance as allies.

"We have a team of fifteen with varying skills ready to join you as well. We want to end Draven before he hurts anyone else. We also propose a peace treaty with you. Our council would like to have you as an ally, rather than an enemy."

The three men each crossed one arm across their chests and kneeled in front of me. I sat, absorbing this information. So, Draven was also a wizard. I already knew he was insane, but I also knew I couldn't take on his brainwashed followers and whatever military guys he had bought. At least I couldn't do it alone. But with a small team of highly trained supers, we could take him out swiftly and quietly.

I smiled as hope built in my chest. We could do this. Then, I could spend my life with my soulmates. No more running. I rose to my feet and heard my boys do the same behind me.

Beasty pressed forward and a tingle fluttered across my skin as a partial shift took over. My eyes and markings began to glow brilliantly, and my voice changed as I spoke.

"We accept your offer. Let's kick some butt."

Seriously? We did that display of power, and the best you can come up with is kick some butt? I don't know why I even bother with you. I felt her rolling her eyes in my head.

Hey! It wasn't like you came up with some outstanding movie line! I retorted.

The guys regarded me with weird expressions. I really needed to stop making faces when talking to the crazy drag-oness in my brain.

"Call your team. Damien, will you go pick up some pizza,

please? After we eat, we can sit down and form a plan. The sooner we get this over with, the better."

I turned and looked at each of my guys. Damien stuck his tongue out at me before grabbing his car keys and heading out to pick up the pizza. Levi and Luke both wore proud expressions. I sensed their wolves were on edge and antsy for the upcoming battle.

I locked eyes with Mithraheal, half afraid I would see his feelings had changed after what happened last night. He looked back at me and his presence brushed my mind with the tenderness of a lover.

"Stop your fretting, sweetheart. Nothing has changed between us. My love for you will not change. Although, if you take more mates, we are going to need a bigger bed."

More mates? Was he crazy? I hadn't planned to claim the three I had now. I was finished. No more, not a chance.

In my mind, I heard Beasty snicker. Then she spoke with a serious tone I hadn't ever heard from her, *Remember how I told you a dragoness will take mates according to their power? Honey, not even you understand the power sealed inside you. You have barely scratched the surface of your potential. We are dragon, but you are so much more.*

You are Tiamat, the Dragon Goddess of Babylon. History tells of our past life, but those myths have been twisted. We have been reborn to set matters right. Every kingdom on earth would be trembling if they had an inkling of who you were.

Evil has contaminated the rulers, both in the human and supernatural communities. The world is about to change. You are going to bring that transformation.

My limbs trembled as her words sank in.

Beasty, I can't do this. Where do I even start?

I would start by buying a bigger bed, little goddess, she said, licking her lips.

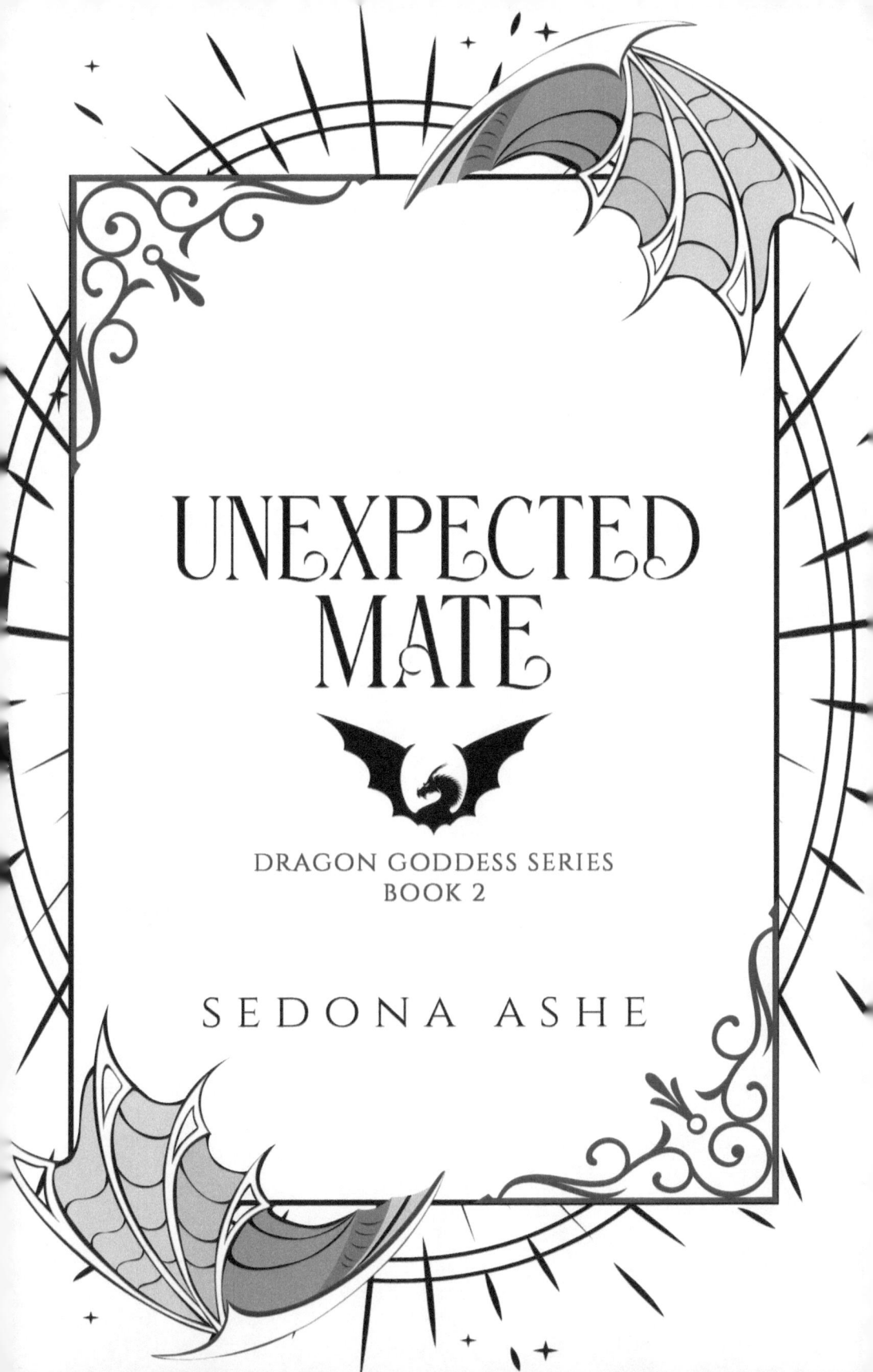

UNEXPECTED MATE

DRAGON GODDESS SERIES
BOOK 2

SEDONA ASHE

CHAPTER ONE

Tia

The scent of blood was thick in the smoky haze of the battleground. Casualties of both sides lay broken on the ground, their lives over far too soon—all because of Draven's greed. This battle had been fast yet devastating. Incredibly, my team had managed to take out half of Draven's men, even though they were drastically outnumbered.

Levi and Luke's wolves lunged and snapped at the men who were circled around them. Patches of their beautiful furs were missing and charred. Levi's twisted back leg dangled uselessly, and the skin that hung open at Luke's throat revealed the mangled muscles beneath. Could his wolf heal that? Would he be able to speak? Would he be able to join the wolves as they howled their beautiful, melancholy song to the full moon? I *furiously blinked back tears as I turned to search out my other mates scattered through the extensive clearing.*

Mithraheal stood on a heap of corpses. His eyes were feral and blood red. Long white fangs dripped blood as he dropped into a combat stance, clearly preparing for a last assault. His enraged hiss sent chills over my body. I knew that few who heard that sound survived to describe it. But even this powerful vampire showed signs of struggling after the savage battle, his speed barely better than that of a mortal. Dark blood seeped from lacerations that should have already healed. How had they weakened such a strong blood driven?

Damien stood back-to-back with another man, blades drawn and pointed at the men raising their weapons. His clothes hung in shreds, his skin oozed maroon blood. A dagger was embedded in his leg, another in his back at the base of his spine, and a third in his chest mere inches from his heart. It was clear he had defended the nameless man as best he was capable during the vicious attack.

I tried to catch a better view of the guy, but his face was obscured. Yet even without seeing his features, I knew. This was my fourth mate, and Damien had tried to protect him. My unknown mate's arm hung limp at his side. An inch-wide gash traveled from his scalp to his jawbone, the skin gaping in some sections, the bone and cartilage beneath visible like some type of macabre Halloween makeup. Blood flowed in a continuous stream down his leg from a brutal knife wound on his thigh.

The few wizards from my unit that remained standing were in far worse shape than my guys. As the mercenaries closed in on them, they couldn't even find the strength to lift their weapons or teleport themselves elsewhere.

I wanted to stand and rush forward to protect my men. I begged my exhausted power to return and give me a final surge of energy to end this before more good men lost their lives. It made no difference. My body was desperately trying to repair the damage I had suffered, but the internal trauma was extensive. They had shattered my ribs with the savage punches I hadn't dodged fast enough. A piece of rib had pierced my right lung, leaving me struggling to draw in a breath. My beautiful wing lay broken across the ground beside me, rather than tight against my back like the other. The unnatural angle twisted my stomach and compelled me to look away.

In choked anguish I watched the mercenaries prepare to slaughter the last of my team, and my mates. I had failed them.

Ear-piercing screams roused me from my tumultuous sleep. My throat was raw, my vocal cords burning like I had swallowed acid. I realized with a start that it was me who was screaming. My wild blonde hair clung to my tear-soaked face. The sheets tangled around me, soaked with my sweat, and I desperately struggled to free myself from them. The memory of my nightmare came rushing back, bringing with it the feelings of absolute terror and bone crushing sorrow.

I needed air, but the harder I tried to draw in a breath, the tighter my lungs seized. They refused to expand. The burning in my chest became unbearable as my heart rate climbed, the muscles jerking hard with each beat.

"Shh. It was just a dream, you're safe."

Levi's voice washed over me with compassion. As Mithraheal finished untangling my body from the sheets that had threatened to strangle me, I sucked in lungfuls of air. Strong arms wrapped around me, pulling me into the safety of Levi's embrace. I pressed myself against him. My skin was still tacky from my tears and perspiration, and I felt our skin stick together ... something I would have found hilarious if I hadn't found such comfort in the feel of his skin pressed so tightly against my own.

He was alive. It was just a stupid dream created by my stressed out mind. The gruesome scenes from the nightmare continued their cruel playback over and over. Great wracking sobs shook my torso, clattering my teeth together. Too much anguish, too much pain. I couldn't lose my mates.

Mithraheal moved in closer until his body pressed against my back, his arms encircling us, sandwiching me between him and Levi. An unusual gesture of affection since my men rarely touched each other. His cool skin against my feverishly hot skin was like paradise on earth, and my heart slowed its out-of-control rhythm.

I choked on a sob when I felt a warm, wet lick on my thigh. The weight of Luke's massive wolf head quickly followed as he nudged his way into the embrace and dropped his head against my abdomen. When his silky fur brushed against my skin I tried not to picture the horrific images of his beautiful coat matted in blood. He whimpered, the sound powerful enough to vibrate my insides. I slipped my hand to his nape and plunged my fingers deep into his thick fur. I clutched him so tightly I worried I might hurt him, but my fingers refused to uncurl.

I never wanted them to move. I never wanted them to leave. They must have sensed this because once my breathing and heart rate were normal, and my sobs had turned into hiccups, Levi scooted us off the bed. Mithraheal quickly ripped off the sweat-saturated sheets that smelled of my terror. Moving with his vampire speed, he spread a large blanket across the mattress. Apparently no one wanted to waste time remaking the bed. Levi laid down in the middle of the bed on his back, gently stretching me out on top of him and never breaking our skin to skin contact.

The bed creaked and groaned as Luke's wolf jumped up. He promptly moved to Levi's side, squeezing in tight so my body was pressed against as much of him as possible. I threaded my arm around his neck, trying to hug him to me as my fingers stroked his fur.

Mithraheal's face flashed in front of my own. He hadn't even made a sound as he joined us in the bed. His fingertips were featherlight as they moved the hair from my face. The movement of his fingers tracing every curve of my face was tender instead of sensual. Slowly, he captured my lips with his own. The kiss was soft and sweet; a gentle reminder of his love. To my shock, he settled next to Levi, close enough that his arm could snake around my body. They surrounded me with their reassuring touch as I sank back into sleep.

I forced the awful nightmare from my head, determined to not think of it again.

Chapter Two

Tia

"**W**hat do you mean they're bringing more wizards here? Why didn't they ask us about it first?"

I was not at all pleased with this news. Over the last two months, we had settled into an odd, but comfortable, routine. We spent our mornings training, and I had quickly earned the respect of my mates with the skills my father had drilled into me. We spent our afternoons researching Draven and everything we could on all his known allies.

The wizards had moved into the lower portion of the cabin. I loved this place and didn't want to move from it until it was time to launch our attack. The sprawling cabin was split level, giving the wizards their own bathrooms and kitchen, whilst allowing us the ability to lock them out of our living areas. I was thankful for their help against our common enemy, but I still wasn't sure who I could trust.

"I wish they would have spoken with us first, but I am also relieved to have additional allies join us. This will not be easy to pull off, and I want you as safe as possible."

As he spoke, Luke's tanned arms slid around my waist, pulling me against him. I buried my face in his shirt and breathed in his woody scent. The tight knot of anxiety coiled in my chest eased. I relaxed into his embrace and let out a sigh. Well, it was supposed to be a sigh, but instead a purr came out. I purred... like I was a freaking cat.

"Did you just purr?" Luke's tone was incredulous.

"I absolutely did not." I could handle glowing tattoos and wings popping out of my back, but I refused to accept purring.

You definitely purred. Beasty snickered.

"Aw! You are the cutest kitty cat!" Luke began stroking my hair as though he was petting a fluffy Persian cat.

I huffed my annoyance and pushed away from him, which only caused him to laugh harder.

"Is the angry little kitty going to hiss at me now?"

I stiffened my shoulders at his teasing, realizing moments later that I probably looked like an angry cat with its hair raised on end. Beasty laughed even harder at my expense.

I was a terrifying fire-breathing dragon. I absolutely *did not* purr.

Lifting my chin, I turned and walked out of the room and outside into the brilliant sunshine. Luke's laughter rang through the air as I shut the door behind me. Would I ever admit that I had purred? Not a chance. Happiness surged in my chest at the joyful sound, and my lips stretched into a smile as I walked around the side of the cabin and down to the lower entrance. Things had been rough recently, and my guys had all grown tense. Seeing the stress disappear from Luke's face while he laughed, albeit at my expense, was totally worth my embarrassment.

You could always purr more often for them. Beasty's voice cut through my thoughts. *There are many amazing studies about the health benefits of adopting a cat as your pet—*

I shoved her still-laughing self into a dark corner in my mind. I needed to deal with the wizards, and I couldn't have her sidetracking me. They had been invited into our home, and we had allowed them to bring their team. We had all gotten along well, and I even found myself enjoying their company. However, I hadn't agreed to having additional strangers brought into my home, and I didn't appreciate not being consulted.

I yanked open the glass patio doors and stepped into the make-shift command station they had set up. Either a state-of-the-art computer or a hulking stack of paper covered every table and flat surface in the room. The whirring of computer fans and the clicking of keyboard keys filled the room. I glanced around, attempting to focus my eyes in the sudden darkness.

"Where is Gregor?" I spoke with authority. Gone was the scared girl I became after my parents' murder. I was back for good, baby!

I had stumbled from one life-shattering event to the next,

without so much as a moment to breathe or adjust to each revelation. Thankfully, the past few weeks had given me time to process my sorrow and confusion. I also had a decent mental grip on my new reality of supernaturals, mate bonds, and prophecies. With practice, I had mastered shifting between forms with ease, and I was learning to incorporate my new dragon talents into my fighting. My father would be proud.

For the time being, this cabin was my nest, and I would defend it. No one entered a dragon's nest, or touched what a dragon treasured, without having their butts handed to them. Warm heat trickled through my chest as my irritation grew, my dragon fire restless and ready to turn any threat to ash.

Gregor came around the corner and into the room, stopping abruptly when he spotted me standing there with literal smoke coming out of my nose.

"Why was I not informed you were bringing more wizards to my home?" I asked.

"It's only two more wizards!" he insisted, sounding somewhat panicked. "We didn't think it mattered enough to bother you with the details. You see, we've had issues trying to gain access to the computers in Draven's main company—the one he uses as a front for his illegal business deals. If we could get access, we could gain vital details which would help us take him and his allies down. We called the council for assistance, and they're sending us their tech genius, along with his handler."

Gregor speech raced as he rushed to get out his explanation. And a small part of me felt bad for making him so nervous. We had grown friendly, and I liked his team. Damien and my three mates all seemed to enjoy their company, especially when took guard shifts alongside the wizards to keep watch on our nest night and day. Draven had been very quiet, but we would not allow him to catch us off guard again.

I closed my eyes and breathed in slowly, pulling the heat back to my center and slowly extinguishing the fire.

"I'm sorry, Gregor," I said. "I appreciate everything your team is doing. I'm just a little on edge and don't enjoy surprises right now."

"I apologize for not informing you of the issue and the new arrivals," Gregor replied. "The male coming is a nadir, with incredible skill in creating and hacking technology. Whilst this talent has given him a higher position than most nadirs within the community, as he still remains a nadir, it didn't even occur to me that his presence would be worth bringing to your attention. I will not make that mistake again."

"A nadir?" I asked in confusion. I had not heard this term before.

"IN THE WIZARD COMMUNITY, ALL MALES ARE BORN WITH magic, but their level of magical ability can vary greatly," Gregor explained. "In the case of my team, it consists of those who possess an amount of magic much larger than the general wizard population. There are a small number of wizards born without magic, or with such a scant amount of magic that we don't even call them wizards. They are 'nadirs'. These males do not attend our schools, nor do they attend meetings held by the council. Nadirs are sent to non-supernatural schools and colleges, and then allowed to work the more menial jobs that require no magic within our community."

I barely kept my mouth from dropping open. While his tone held no disdain toward the non-magic males, it was clear that they had no respect within their own community. They were essentially rejects. Before I could even string together words to form a sentence, Gregor spoke again.

"The nadir I spoke of will arrive this evening. I'll send someone to alert you immediately. You can come and meet him and his handler to ensure you're comfortable hosting them under your roof."

Gregor gave me a stiff half bow, and I was so dumb-founded I could do nothing more than nod my head before turning and leaving the darkened room.

I strode back to my porch and sat heavily on the porch swing. The wood groaned, and the chains squeaked as I began rocking. I had spent several hours each evening studying supernaturals and their different cultures. It had been a defi-nite struggle to not judge all the strange laws through a human lens. Some of their customs were downright creepy.

I had discovered that many supers held disdain for other supers. They avoided spending any significant amount of time with each other. The elaborate balls and high court meetings were the only occasions all the supers came together, and that happened only three or four times each year.

While it made me uncomfortable knowing how the supers regarded each other, it was heartbreaking to think of them treating others in their own communities with that same disdain. You were judged based on your level of magic, not by who you were as a person, or even by your intelligence. The nadir had their entire lives dictated for them by 'superior' wizards. I wished that it could be changed, but supernaturals lived very long lives and were dead-set in their old ways. Change only happened at a snail's pace.

One day, little dragon.

A sigh escaped me as Beasty's words echoed in my mind. I hoped she was right, because I wanted so badly to bring that change to the antiquated paranormal world.

CHAPTER THREE

Tia

I tossed and turned most of the night. As faint morning light crept into the room, I opened my eyes. They felt as if someone had poured sand into them. Normally, being snuggled between two of my mates ensured a peaceful night's sleep, but my anger towards the wizards had my mind spinning far into the night.

Mithraheal's arm wrapped around me, drawing me into his body. Levi scooted in tighter on my opposite side and let out a contented humming in his sleep. I loved these men so much. Luke, Levi and Mithraheal had fallen into a comfortable camaraderie over the past few weeks. They had adjusted to the idea of my having several mates much quicker than even I had adjusted.

Every evening, I would find two of them sitting on my bed

ready to sandwich me in-between them for the night, while my third mate guarded our home. I never knew which two would be waiting for me, and couldn't figure out how they made that decision, but it was a relief that they got along with each other.

"Dragostea mea, why are you flopping around in the bed like a fish out of water?" Mithraheal groaned into the curve of my neck.

"I'm anxious about today," I whispered. "The wizards have been a tremendous help in planning our attack, but they make me uncomfortable. I don't feel as though I can fully trust them."

"Is it their beliefs that make you feel this way?" Mithraheal asked. When I nodded, he continued: "It is important to remember that many of their customs are long-standing and the newer generations often don't even think to question those long-held opinions. I agree with you that their treatment of the nadir is cruel, but there are many other vampires who would take no issue with it. Vampires can be cruel too. They often kill the weak among our kind. This reckless regard for a life is one of the reasons I challenged my father for the throne."

I drew imaginary circles up and down his muscled arm as I listened. I shuddered as I remembered the bits and pieces that he and Damien had told me about the challenge—a bloody battle where the two royal vampires attempted to kill each other, the winning vampire receiving the throne. The winner was declared only after he "killed" his opponent. It wasn't a permanent death; vampires were the hardest to kill among the paranormal species, and aside from having their heart crushed, whilst their head was simultaneously ripped from their shoulders, there was no way to for them to die. They were dang near invincible.

The thought of Mithraheal going through the physical pain of the battle, as well as the emotional pain of fighting his father, sent a pang through my heart. Mithraheal hadn't wanted to rule, but as the blood driven had grown more and more powerful, his father had begun to rule with more cruelty. He ruled without mercy, whilst turning a blind eye to the illegal activities of his friends. The blood driven had become restless and a war amongst their kind had been looming on the horizon.

Mithraheal had challenged his father for the throne to restore balance. After his victory, he had immediately gone to work, trying to right the wrongs that had people been subjected to. It had taken many decades, but eventually his father had apologized to the blood driven for his behavior, and for allowing power to blind him to their needs. Mithraheal's parents now spent their time traveling the world, enjoying freedom from the duties of reigning royalty. Duties that weighed heavily on my handsome vampire mate.

Damien and Mithraheal teleported back and forth from our hideout in the woods to their palace on a daily basis. Until we were able to determine if Draven had followers among the blood driven, we didn't feel it was safe to make it known exactly where I was living. I also worried that innocent lives would be lost if I moved into the castle and Draven attacked. It was better to wait until the threat was gone; then we could sort out more permanent living arrangements.

The warm morning sun had now filled my room and I knew it was time to get up and prepare myself for the day. Closing my eyes, I teleported myself to the bathroom. You can call me lazy, but I viewed this as a way of continuing to improve my skills. Okay, fine. It is lazy, but also extremely convenient.

I rushed through my morning routine, slipping on a worn pair of jeans and a backless red shirt. Mithraheal had replaced most of the shirts in my wardrobe with backless tops, which pleased Beasty immensely. We were both still hurt over Cage's rejection, and it was nice to have little reminders that our other mates loved us no matter which form we took.

After slipping on a pair of black riding boots and strapping on my beautiful daggers, I teleported myself directly into Luke's lap. He barely even started, quickly setting down his mug of coffee before wrapping his arms around me. He had shadows under his green eyes, no doubt from staying up to guard the cabin the night before.

"You are going to give me a heart attack one of these days." His words held amusement as he leaned forward and captured my lips with his own.

I laughed against his mouth, knowing that my men had grown used to me randomly popping in on them throughout the day. Sure, Levi had screamed the first several times I had done it to him, but now he only jerked in shock when I suddenly appeared in front of him.

Luke nipped at my bottom lip, and I parted my lips, allowing him to deepen our kiss. As his tongue danced across mine, I tasted the toasted caramel flavors of his coffee. My heart lurched and danced to a rhythm only I could hear. I scooted tighter against him as I straddled his lap. One of his hands sunk deep into my hair, while the other slid under my shirt. I gasped as his fingers caressed my breast.

I felt his smirk against my lips; he was teasing me. Jerk. Two could play at this game! I ground myself against the bulge that had grown harder beneath me. He inhaled a ragged breath. I began a slow rhythmic rocking, keeping a slow and unhurried pace. His groan quickly turned into a growl and his hands moved to grip my hips. He pressed me down tighter against his erection, causing heat to rush to my core. Our kissing had gone from playful to frantic in mere seconds, something that often happened with all my mates.

As his lips slid down my neck and his hands fumbled to unbutton my jeans, I tilted my head back and groaned. I stiffened. Luke sat back and then burst into a throaty laugh.

"You purred!"

"I did not!"

His booming laughter filled the kitchen. Indignant, I hopped off his lap with as much grace as I could manage, ignoring the protests from my throbbing lady bits that begged me to ride him like a carnival ride. Goddesses do not purr. I sniffed and turned to leave.

Luke caught my hand and brought it to his lips. "I love you... Kitty."

His eyes twinkled and his lips twitched as he attempted to hide his amusement. I opened my mouth to respond with something I hoped would be witty but stopped as my ears popped. I had come to recognize this as a sign that a supernatural was about to arrive via teleportation magic. Apparently this was a dragon ability, as other paranormal species couldn't sense when someone was about to teleport themselves to a nearby location. We were keeping that nifty little talent a secret for the time being.

"Someone's just arrived. I need to go see who." I leaned forward, giving Luke a swift kiss before moving out the door and toward the wizards' command area.

Beasty stirred in my mind, stretching languidly as she focused on our surroundings. She hated waking up early, and for a second I wondered what had woken the sleeping dragon. A tingle rushed through my body and my tattoos began to glow. Hmm ... this was a new reaction.

I sent my magic out to seek a threat, but I found none. It did, however, find the new arrival, and I felt the magic as it twisted around him like a cat before returning to me. Good grief! I was a dragon, not a house cat! What was wrong with me?

As my magic merged with me again, a new emotion over-whelmed me. Anticipation. I barely kept myself from running to the room that held the new arrival. My back itched as my wings tried to burst free, my gums ached as my fangs burned to be released, and my ears twitched. I didn't want to alarm everyone in the room by bursting in mid-shift, so I strained to maintain control and keep a mostly human form.

First impressions were important, especially when meeting your newest mate for the first time.

CHAPTER FOUR

Mithraheal

I jerked awake as Tia's wild emotions consumed me. On the far side of the bed, Levi sat up abruptly and his gaze darted around the room, clearly searching for our little mate. Without thinking, I lunged forward and grabbed his shoulder, teleporting us directly to her side. Materializing into a room full of supers was something we avoided; it was risky since we could not prepare for an attack. But at that moment, I didn't care about anything except being at Tia's side, even if it meant getting a knife in my back from an enemy.

The moment we appeared in the room, Levi shifted smoothly into his wolf. He flanked her left side, while I stepped to her right. My eyes slid around the room, assessing the number of wizards and any potential dangers. I recognized five of the wizards as the men I had spent many hours with over the past few weeks, sometimes guarding and other times relaxing on the porches. Tension eased from my body. Tia was safe from these men.

I turned toward Tia and immediately took in her expression. I had seen that expression before, on the day we first met when Damien had teleported her into our mansion. She had her hands clasped tightly in front of her, and I noticed the trembling that she was desperately trying to hide. Her beautiful eyes were glowing blue, as if holding fire in their depths, while the light in her tattoos ebbed and flowed in a hypnotic dance.

Her emotions continued to wash through my mind; anxiety, excitement, apprehension and desire all fought to surge forward. Her spine straightened ever so slightly and I couldn't help but smile. My mate was experiencing a tumult of emotions, but she was determined to appear confident in front of these men.

I wanted to continue to observe my gorgeous dragon, but curiosity got the best of me. Glancing across the room, I studied the man that was Tia's newest mate. I prayed he would be worthy of her. She hid her pain, but I was well aware she still felt the pain of Cage's rejection. I had seen her puffy red eyes after one of her long showers. She thought she was hiding her pain from us, but we all felt it through our bond.

There were times when her thoughts flittered through my head, and it was clear that she was still going over the "what ifs?" in her mind. What if she had shown him more love?

What if she had accepted their bond the moment he marked her? What if she had begged him to stay?

She worried that maybe they hadn't even had a chance to bond because of Draven's kidnapping, and the emotional state that she had been in after her parents' murder. Levi, Luke and I had all tried to tell her that Cage could have stayed. He wasn't forced to leave. He had made that choice. She was born to fulfill a prophecy, to change the world. Cage didn't want a warrior; he wanted a soft mate to keep tucked away safety, and that was a role Tia couldn't fill, no matter how much she desired it.

Now she was meeting her fourth mate, and her insecurities were rising to the surface. *This man better not hurt my beloved, or I will be tempted to make him disappear from the face of the earth.* I was fairly confident Tia wouldn't approve of me murdering people on her behalf.

The man had obviously been speaking with Gregor, his handler standing a few steps behind him. I didn't recognize either of them. Since I had always preferred to stay among my own kind, this was unsurprising. My gaze traveled over his light brown hair tied neatly at the nape of his neck. His face was clean shaven and his dark eyes were filled with wonder as he gazed at Tia. His expression was unguarded, allowing his emotions to be seen, which was unusual as very few supers would allow their faces to be so easily read.

I couldn't stop myself from using telepathy, even though I knew Tia would not be pleased if she ever found out. I listened to his thoughts.

Is she the dragon shifter? No one mentioned how beautiful she is, how she draws you to her.

I smirked. He didn't yet realize what he felt was the pull of the mate bond.

Oh no. She's getting closer to me, what should I say? No one mentioned how blue her eyes are... are her ears wiggling? How is she so adorable?

I wanted to laugh at his consternation, but held it in. The poor guy was rambling in his head, clearly nervous. He still had no idea he was Tia's mate. He wanted to impress her; he wanted her to notice him. Thankfully Gregor stepped towards Tia, holding out his hand in greeting.

"Welcome, Tia! You are just in time to meet the new arrivals. This is Leo, the nadir I was telling you about yesterday."

He motioned casually toward Leo before continuing: "And this is his handler, Elani. As nadirs cannot teleport or use magic, the few who are employed by the council are given a handler to guide them in our world and ensure the council's needs are properly met."

Tia's eyes narrowed slightly as she took in the woman standing against the wall behind Leo. It was obvious that she had only had eyes for Leo and hadn't noticed Elani's presence in the room. Little was known about dragon females but, based on the tendrils of her magic that were swirling around the room, I thought it was safe to assume they weren't fond of having other females in their nest.

To Elani's credit, she didn't seem phased by Tia's magic as it circled around her like a lion stalking its prey. Pushing herself off the wall, she stepped towards Tia and stretched out her hand in greeting.

"It's wonderful to meet the dragoness that has caused such a stir among the wizards."

Tia accepted the offered hand and gave it a firm shake. "I didn't expect to meet a female wizard."

Elani let out a throaty laugh as she moved to Leo's side. "Very few people have the opportunity to meet a female wizard. We are rare among our kind, as most of our females are born without magic. Our females are typically nadir, like this nerd." She punched Leo's shoulder as she finished speaking.

My mate had gone from irritated to angry in mere moments. Her control slipped and her adorable ears lengthened to the pointed tips she insisted belonged on a fairy. I was proud to see that she was still controlling the rest of her shift, a skill we had been drilling in hard these past weeks. We wanted her to be able to maintain whichever form benefited her most in any given situation, rather than letting her emotions control her shifts.

Neither Gregor nor Elani had noticed Tia's slip, but Leo was staring at her ears with a mix of curiosity and admiration. Our beautiful mate completely enchanted him. He stepped forward as if he were in a trance. Tia held her breath as he approached. With one hand he unconsciously pushed his glasses back up his nose, while he reached out with his other hand and gently stroked the length of her ear.

Tia shivered at his tentative touch, but otherwise, she remained motionless. His fingers continued to trace the delicate curve of her ear, and he leaned forward to get a closer look. His body blocked the wizard's view of Tia. His face was so close to Tia that she had to be feeling his warm breath against her skin. Indeed, she seemed unable to remain still any longer.

I watched as she ever so slightly leaned forward and pressed her lips against the corner of his mouth. He was startled out of his fixation on her ears but didn't jerk away. Instead, he turned his head and pressed his lips firmly against her own. I knew I should look away, but I kept watching the scene in front of me like some type of creepy stalker.

An adorable blush crept across Tia's cheeks, and she leaned back from Leo. He wasn't ready for their first kiss to end, and instead he captured her bottom lip between his teeth and nipped her gently. I couldn't stop a chuckle from escaping. It seemed that the nerd might not be as inexperienced as I had thought. There was no denying he felt the pull of the mate bond.

My laugh brought them both back to the present, and Leo quickly dropped his hand and took a step back. Desire and disappointment flooded my mind as Tia struggled to regain her composure.

"Hello, I'm Tia." Her voice was low and raspy, and it sent a wave of desire through my body.

"I'm Leo."

Elani laughed from behind him. "Yes, we already told her that. How can you be so smart, and yet a complete idiot sometimes? This is why nadirs are meant to work within the community, not be paraded around in front of outsiders."

A growl rumbled Tia's chest, and I didn't miss the look of surprise that flitted across Leo's face at her reaction.

"We won't take up anymore of your time, Tia," said Gregor, stepping forward. "Our team has the computer set up and ready for you to begin working, Leo." Gregor took Leo by the arm and, after a nod to us, guided him toward the corner where his workstation had been set up.

Leo threw a longing look back over his shoulder and then allowed himself to be led away. I tucked Tia's hand into the crook of my arm and began walking her toward the glass doors of the patio, Levi following behind us, guarding our backs.

As we stepped into the sun, we both looked once more in Leo's direction. My eyes must have been playing a trick on me, because I swore he winked at us. This was quite an interesting development!

CHAPTER FIVE

Tia

I watched as Damien ran at me using his vampire speed. I smirked. When we had first begun training, I had found his speed unnerving and had struggled to track his movements. As he ran at me now, I realized that his supernatural speed was as easy to follow as that of a human. The long hours of intense training had paid off. With each passing day my fighting reflexes became faster and smoother. I regularly alternated which form I fought in, and with each shift my dragon gifted talents grew stronger.

The biggest surprise had been the melding between my human and dragon forms. While there was an obvious visible difference between them, I had realized my human form had begun to access my dragon talents with more ease. I had also noticed that Beasty was quiet and slept within the recesses of my mind with increased frequency. I had grown so used to her witty commentary inside my head, and her silence worried me.

There is no need to worry, sweet cheeks. Everything is as it should be.

Her words were meant to reassure me, but her tone sounded exhausted.

Deal with that idiot who thinks he is about to sneak-attack you and let me nap in peace! What does a goddess have to do to get some sleep around here?

She moved back into the dark corners in my mind, and I reluctantly turned my attention to Damien. He had been tele-porting from spot to spot, trying to confuse me, but this was child's play for me now. I knew that Levi was also slowly stalking me from behind. He was quiet, but his movements had set off the magical trip-wires I had erected around myself. This was another nifty trick my dragon power had given me: undetectable magic. If I used only the faintest amount of magic, I could keep the energy level low enough that it was invisible to those around me. My mates were unaware of this recent development, and I was enjoying their constant efforts to catch me off guard.

As Damien teleported a few feet in front of me and lunged, I felt Levi leap for my back. In one smooth motion, I leapt forward and ducked, causing Levi's wolf to go sailing over my shoulder. Just as he passed over me, I released control and allowed my wings to burst free. Throwing out my right wing, I knocked Levi and threw him off balance, sending him tumbling into the dirt. At the same time, I used my left wing to smack the back of Damien's head. He also fell face-first into the dirt. I sprang forward, landed on his back, and grabbed him in a choke hold. Laughing like a maniac, I ground my knuckles into the top of his head and messed up his hair.

Not wanting to be left out, Levi bounded toward me, his tail wagging so hard that the dirt billowed around us. He barked twice, then pushed his muzzle into my face, licking me with abandon.

"Ack! That's so gross!" I rubbed at my face, trying to remove his doggy drool. He chuffed (his version of a wolf laugh) and continued to lick my hands and whatever bits of my skin he could find between my fingers.

I sunk my fingers into the thick, soft fur around his neck and flipped onto his back. Levi yipped while playfully attempting to buck me off.

"I hate to break up this weird, yet strangely adorable scene, but Leo has finished collecting the necessary information from Draven's hard drive," said Mithraheal, appearing before us. "It's time to sit down and finalize our plan of attack."

Mithraheal's words sent ice shooting through me, and my stomach dropped. I wanted this to be over, but another part of me hated the thought of my men going into battle with me. I knew I wouldn't be able to bear losing a mate and wished there was a way I could take Draven down alone. The intel we gathered had made it clear I would need help.

My skills had grown, and I was no longer the girl he had met only a few short months ago, but I couldn't take on an experienced wizard and his closest followers at the same time.

I sighed and slowly got to my feet. "Let's get this over with," I said. "I'm ready to put this evil behind us so we can focus on building our lives together."

I strode toward the large outdoor deck where I could see the wizards spreading out papers and tablets. As we drew near, I spotted Leo. He was sitting to one side of the sprawling table. Gregor and his team didn't acknowledge his presence as they talked and joked among themselves. He might as well have been invisible. Annoyance stirred my dragon fire, and it bubbled up in my chest like lava.

Leo's gaze locked with mine as he slid his glasses back up his nose, a habit I found completely endearing. His smile was shy, but it caused the heat inside me to burn hotter. Only this time, the flames were from desire, not anger. He dropped his eyes back to the tablet he held in his hands.

I blinked away the tears that burned in my eyes. We had sneaked small touches and discreet smiles, but a personal conversation was near impossible with Elani lurking near him constantly. I craved my mate. The strain of controlling my dragon's instincts was exhausting. There had to be a way to be with Leo alone; I needed to explain the mate pull. I had to maintain control long enough to give him time to decide if he wished to be a dragon's mate.

I sat down in the chair opposite Leo, biting back a growl as Elani casually laid her hand on his shoulder and idly stroked it as she listened to Gregor begin the briefing. The cool metal armrest creaked as it bent beneath my punishing grip. Something bumped my leg, distracting me from my growing ire as I watched another female touching my mate with familiarity.

Leo's leg bumped me again and then pressed tight against my calf.

With this simple touch, my anger melted away, and peace washed through me. I wiggled my butt in a weird happy dance. He had felt the mate pull and wanted to comfort me. Hope rose up, telling me that he would want me as his mate. I moved forward and trapped his lower leg between both of mine. His quick intake of breath made me smile. My new mate was ridiculously sweet.

Luke's overly loud throat clearing pulled my focus back to the discussion going on around me, and away from flirting with Leo.

I leaned forward. It was time to plan the last details of our attack. Draven was going down, and then I could spend hours working up a sweat with my mates—in bed, not on the fighting mats. Sneaking one last look at Leo's face, I saw that his eyes smoldered with promises of things to come. Things I didn't want to wait any longer for.

Just go ahead and jump his bones. Claim him as ours. It's clear he desires us.

Beasty's encouragement had me sliding to the edge of my seat, and I nearly launched myself into Leo's lap. But it wasn't time; I wanted to do this correctly. And right now, that meant I needed to give my full attention to planning the showdown with Draven.

Soon, I promised my inner horn-dog.

CHAPTER SIX

Levi

I smiled as I watched Tia lean over the table, her cute little forehead scrunched up and the tip of her tongue caught between her teeth. She was completely focused as she studied the maps of Draven's base.

"So, there's only one entrance to his inner office?" she asked. "He's going to have tightened security near that corridor, not to mention the cameras tracking anything that dares move."

"Yes, although I'll hack the cameras," Leo replied. "Anyone monitoring those cameras will believe they're watching a live feed, but they'll actually be watching a video loop of the guards." I barely held back a laugh at the ridiculous lovesick look on Leo's face as he spoke to Tia. They were acting like they were in middle school, and I wouldn't have been shocked to see Tia pass him a note with the little boxes where he could mark if he liked her or not. I rolled my eyes at the thought and my wolf let out a snort.

Why does our mate delay? She knows he is intended to be in our circle - best to mark him and begin building the bond.

Wolves could be so primal, their animal sides strong. Human logic rarely made sense to a wolf, although in this case, I had to agree with him. Leo was clearly smitten, and Tia was fighting her dragon nature as the urge to bond with him grew increasingly harder for her to resist. She had already spoken to Luke, Mithraheal, and I about Leo joining our circle, and we had made it very clear that we were all in favor.

We had each spent time talking with Leo, as well as observing him from a distance. He was quiet and spent most of his time focused on his computer. The other wizards rarely noticed him unless they needed help with their own computers or had another target for him to hack. Yet he didn't seem to notice their dismissive and indifferent attitudes toward him. He worked hard and absorbed himself in his mission.

It was fascinating that a male with no magic had been selected by fate to be a dragon mate. I didn't care if he was human or a super, I just wondered at fate's logic. It was believed that fate only chose the strongest of the supernaturals to be dragon mates. Dragons were rare and had been hunted to near extinction. Mates were needed to guard the female during her pregnancies and to help guard the offspring. I didn't believe that fate made mistakes; Leo was meant to bond with Tia and that was all that mattered.

The morning after Tia bonded with my brother and myself, she had come out of that bedroom stronger. She had sashayed into the room of waiting wizards with the grace of a queen. I had known she was strong, but her confidence had washed over us as her magic probed the room and I had fallen in love all over again. She grew stronger with each day that passed. We feared for her safety in the upcoming confrontation with Draven, but it was clear she was focused and ready.

"I will take Mithraheal with me to Draven's office," Tia began. "Luke and Levi will shift and take out the guards. Your men can assist them and watch out for any reinforcements that may arrive. Thanks to Leo, we know Draven's holding a meeting with the leaders in his organization on Tuesday afternoon, two days from today. We will attack that morning. After Draven is taken down, we need to cut off any outside communications to ensure no one warns the visiting leaders. Once inside the building, we will release gas through the vents to knock them out with a minimum of bloodshed. These men will be powerful, but you must remember that they do not possess the same skills as Draven. This will not be easy, but we will be victorious. Evil will not win."

Several of the wizards, along with Luke and Damien, whistled and stomped their boots. Her call to war excited our bloodlust. Draven was trying to destroy the balance among supernaturals, and he could not be allowed to continue.

"Your plan is strong, Dragoness!" cried Gregor. "We will proudly follow you into battle! However, I wish to join you and Mithraheal into Draven's office. I may be of assistance if he tries to use his magic. The three of us will be a formidable force."

Gregor's words were heartfelt, and he bowed his head after presenting his request. I focused on Tia's face and watched as indecision danced across it for a brief moment.

"I will welcome you at my side," she said.

Her voice had changed; it reverberated with raw power, her energy pulsed around us. Several wizards looked to the ground, unable to maintain eye contact, even at such a small display of her dragon gifts.

I stood, stepping to her side, and watched as Damien, Luke, and Mithraheal did the same. The wizards bent down on one knee, pressing their fists against their hearts in the sign of allegiance.

"Thank you," Tia whispered.

Her words were soft, but they were sincere. She turned and walked away, heading back toward our level of the cabin. We shook hands and slaps on the backs with the wizards, before going in search of our little mate.

"I can't believe I'm going to say this," said Damien, "because we all know the last thing I need is to have to listen to another person getting their freak on in that bedroom, but Tia would be stronger if she bonded with the nerd. She's already a force to be reckoned with, but if fate has brought her another mate, it will only strengthen her. I know she's worried about him accepting such a permanent bond without having the chance to know her, but we all know the kid is head-over-heels in love with her."

Damien was right. I wished Tia and Leo could have the

luxury of dating, but right now, I just wanted to take every precaution to keep her safe. I rubbed my aching head.

"We've already told her it was fine with us!" Luke added. "We've encouraged her to move forward, or at the very least to have an actual conversation with him."

"I think she's been wanting a moment away from the other wizards to speak with him," said Mithraheal. "Elani is close to him all the time, and it sets Tia on edge. She doesn't want to risk Elani overhearing such a personal conversation."

I mulled over Mithraheal's words. I turned toward him and asked: "Can you teleport him to our room tonight after everyone turns in for the night?"

"Yes, I will bring him," Mithraheal replied. "It's late, the wizards will prepare for bed soon. Get our mate comfortable. I will bring him shortly, prepare Tia." He disappeared before anyone could respond.

"I'll take guard duty tonight," said Damien. "Your circle needs to be together." His tone was serious, a stark contrast to his usual playfulness.

Luke and I headed into the house, following the delicious scent of our mate. She lay stretched out across the bed, her long blonde hair damp from showering. I felt my rod stand to attention, and my mouth dried as I took in what she was wearing. Our sexy little mate had grabbed one of the sheer robes that Mithraheal had purchased for her. As she moved, her skin shimmered through the gauzy blue fabric and I realized she had partially shifted. Her adorable ears twitched and her glowing blue eyes danced.

Luke groaned, a sound filled with pain and desire. It was

clear what Tia had planned for our evening. I sucked in a deep breath and regretted it instantly. The heady scent of her desire rushed into my lungs. Her dragon nature had been pushing her to claim Leo, and the longer she resisted, the stronger the drive became. We happily did what we could to ease the drive, but it was becoming a struggle, even with three male mates.

She slid toward us on the bed, her gown falling to the side, giving me a teasing glimpse of the bare skin at the apex of her thighs.

I growled, my erection straining against my pants. I forgot everything around us and prepared to pounce on my temptress of a mate.

At that moment Mithraheal popped into the room, his hand on Leo's shoulder.

"What the—" Mithraheal started, his mouth hanging open. "I know I told you to prepare her for his arrival, but this was not what I meant!"

Tia didn't seem to hear Mithraheal, her eyes focused on Leo. I couldn't look away from the vision of perfection she made on our monstrosity of a bed.

"Mine."

Her vocal cords sounded rough, and her tone promised mind-blowing sex. She eyed him like a predator sizing up their prey. Her tattoos glowed, and when she licked her lips, I caught sight of her fangs.

Oh crap.

CHAPTER SEVEN

Tia

I watched desire fill Levi's face as he entered our bedroom, and Luke's expression mirrored his brother's. I felt my lips curve into a wicked smile. They were mere moments away from ripping this silly little robe off my body when I realized that someone was teleporting into our room. My body was already on edge from my continued refusal to claim Leo, but the knowledge that someone was teleporting into my personal chambers made adrenaline pump through my veins. It created a dangerous combination of desire and the need to defend my nest. If it was Mithraheal, I would likely rip his perfectly tailored suit off the moment he materialized. If it was an intruder, he would be on the ground taking a long nap before he had the chance to speak.

It was worse. Mithraheal appeared, his hand gripping

Leo's shoulder. At the sight of my four unearthly beautiful mates, in my bedroom, with no outsiders, I could barely take in a breath. Passionate desire spread like a wildfire inside me; my body burned and I struggled to think. I wanted to touch these men, to feel their hands and lips press against my skin.

I looked back at Leo and felt myself moving toward him on the bed. His pupils dilated and his breathing was as ragged as my own. He wanted me. The restraints I had wrapped around my dragon to delay claiming him snapped. He was mine, and I was his. Fate had made it so. The blue gown clung to my skin as a fine sheen of perspiration slicked my shimmering body. My fangs dropped, and the need inside me beat out a chaotic rhythm worthy of a rock concert.

"Mine." I wouldn't be able to stop myself this time.

Shock registered on Leo's face as he realized I was speaking to him. I rose from the bed and made my way over to him. The shock disappeared, only to be replaced by a look of longing. His eyes had always held a depth of sadness that called to my soul, but his look of longing to be accepted and loved, that was so obvious now, nearly broke me. By delaying the claim in order to give him time, had I just prolonged his pain and added more hurt?

I pressed my body against his, relishing the feel of his heat radiating into my skin. Sliding my hands around his neck, I sunk my fingers into his thick hair. Moving to my tiptoes, I pressed my lips to the corner of his mouth, giving him a chance to turn his head away if he didn't want this. Instead, he moved his hands to my waist, I assumed to pull me tighter against him, but instead he paused for a moment as he realized his hands had slid under the partially open robe. He was touching my burning bare skin.

I moaned at the pleasure of the simple touch, and that was all the encouragement he needed. His hands slid confidently under the robe and his palms flattened against my back. His arms were like steel bars as they tightened, forcing us even closer. The rough material of his jeans and shirt created friction against my flushed skin, and another wave of heat went straight to the aching apex of my thighs.

Turning his head, he deepened the kiss, his tongue delving into my mouth to dance against my tongue. His palms slid up my back until they were on my sides, and his thumbs brushed the sides of my breasts. Goosebumps pebbled my skin, and I nearly wept at the sensations overwhelming every part of me.

"Mine," I whispered against his lips, although this time it sounded almost like a question, rather than the assertive statement it had been before.

"Yours." He spoke softly, but with confidence.

My dragon nature was ready to bite him and make him mine on the spot, but my human side still needed reassurance.

"Are you sure?" I asked. "I am dangerous, Leo. This claim is forever. Dragons are difficult to live with."

He pulled his lips away from where he had been sucking and kissing his way up my neck. His joyful laughter filled the room, startling everyone.

"Darling, I would follow you off the side of a volcano if you asked it of me," he replied. "I was a little slow in realizing that we were fated mates; after all, it isn't something that happens very often to wizards, let alone a nadir. But I was already in love with you before I figured out what was causing the pull. It is a great honor to be taken as a mate, and to be a dragon's mate is a rare gift. I am not powerful. I am not worthy to be claimed by you. It would be wise for you to reject this bond and find a more powerful mate for your circle who can protect you and your nest."

I choked out a pained cry. He was not rejecting me because he didn't want me; he wanted me protected and didn't believe he was good enough to be a dragon's mate. I had observed him and knew he wasn't simply smart. The man was a genius. He had not crumbled under the cool treatment of the wizards, instead he worked hard. He was a powerful man in his own right, whether or not he possessed magic.

Tears slid down my face as I cried. He deserved so much and had received so very little in his life. A gasp escaped me as I was suddenly lifted off my feet and cradled against him like a doll before moving to sit on the end of the bed.

"Don't cry, I understand the struggle you must be going through," Leo whispered gently. "Your heart says to claim me, but your mind knows I am not a wise choice as a dragon's mate. I will leave soon, and the pull will ease for you, but please don't let my last private moments with you be filled with tears." His thumb wiped at the tears still staining my face.

I heard Luke mumble, "What an idiot." Levi and Mithraheal snorted their agreement.

"Leo, stop," I said through my tears. "I'm crying because you are incredible, and you don't see it. I wanted to claim you from the moment you arrived. I fought the urge to claim you, only because I wanted to allow you the time to decide if this bond was what you wanted: instead it has made you believe that I had second thoughts. You are mine, and unless you do not want me, I wish to claim you. Now."

He was motionless, his body as stiff as a statue as he studied my face. As I waited for his answer, his hard erection pressed against my butt; the heat felt good as it burned against my skin. I bit my lip to stifle a moan while my control began slipping.

"If you do not want to be claimed, you need to leave immediately. I'm not going to be able to maintain my hold on my dragon nature much longer." I spoke my words through clenched teeth. Leo had no more than a minute before the last chains of my control snapped.

"Darling, I am never leaving," he said. "You are mine, forever."

Relief flooded me, and I turned to straddle him. We kissed as though our very lives depended on it and only stopped when we desperately needed to take in air.

"As sensual and enjoyable as this has been to watch, I believe this is where we will excuse ourselves and give you two privacy to form the bond."

I turned around to face my three bonded, now straddling Leo in reverse, and took in their uneven breathing. All three had dilated pupils, but while the twins' eyes glowed an other-worldly green, Mithraheal's were blood red. My vampire stood stiff as a soldier at attention, but my naughty twins were less self-conscious. They continued slowly stroking their hardened erections, the shape clearly visible through their low slung jogging pants.

"No."

Leo's single word was sharp, and we all turned to look at him.

"I am a nadir," he said. "I've been overlooked, often even ignored among my kind. They have always seen me as nothing within the community; not worth a second glance, born to work without complaint, in order to make lives easier for the special ones gifted with magic. You have all gone out of your way to include me in conversations, to acknowledge me. These are small things to you, but everything to me. Working in your home is the first time I have been treated with respect, as an equal. Are you guys truly okay with having me in Tia's circle?"

Without hesitation, my bonded spoke their agreement, and from behind me I could feel the remaining tension drain from Leo's taut body.

"Then I wish for you all to remain present while Tia and I claim each other, as long as she is comfortable with that," Leo added. "I am tired of being invisible."

His words were barely above a whisper as he finished. Tears pricked my eyes for a moment. I looked at each of my bonded to ensure they were okay with this; Mithraheal and Luke nodded, but Levi gave me a devilish wink. I had learned all my bonded enjoyed watching. Kinky freaks.

"If that is your wish, I am happy to have them stay."

The second those words left my lips, Leo's hands gripped my hips and ground me down against his burning member. I moaned, arching my back into him. His warm mouth settled on my shoulder and he sucked gently as he rolled his hips against my throbbing center. I felt his teeth graze my skin. I was burning alive, slick with the need that had now soaked his pants where he was grinding against my sensitive folds.

Through lust-clouded vision, I watched as my men removed their shirts and spread around the room, relaxing in chairs or on the floor, unabashedly stroking themselves as they watched Leo explore my body. It was going to be a very, very long night. I nearly startled when Beasty spoke up.

Now this is what I'm talking about! Let's do some squat thrusts in this incredible cucumber patch!

CHAPTER EIGHT

Tia

I felt Leo stiffen, and then the room turned to chaos as my men roared in laughter. Beasty had spoken directly into the mental link, and my men clearly loved the visual her idiotic comment had created. I rolled my eyes in irritation at the immaturity of it all.

"Did I just hear you in my mind?" Leo whispered, his warmth breath tickling my neck and sending a shiver down my body.

How had he heard Beasty? I knew the wizards could communicate telepathically, but he didn't possess magic.

"That wasn't me, it was Beasty; my always horny, and often embarrassing inner dragon. I don't know why you could hear her. Are you telepathic?"

My vampire and wolves wiped tears from their eyes as

they struggled to regain their composure, a random snicker escaping periodically.

"No, I'm not," Leo said. "I've never heard another person in my head. Do you think this is because we're mates? It would be a thrill to be able to speak with you telepathically, I have never had the chance to experience magic like this."

Less talking - let's get on with making some magic.

I snorted, and began to get off Leo's lap, assuming that he wanted to talk. I gasped when he grabbed my hips and yanked me back down into his lap.

"I agree with Beasty," he said, "we can discuss things for the rest of our lives. Now is not the time."

His fingertips gently stroked up my arms, finally stopping to knead my shoulder muscles. Tension drained from my body and I moaned. The room became silent as my bonded realized that things had grown serious again, and lust-filled eyes met my own.

I attempted to turn and face Leo, but he held me firmly in place, exploring my body and allowing the others to watch my reaction. The featherlight touch of my robe sliding over my shoulders to pool at my waist sent another shiver through my body, my sensitive skin begging to be touched. My naked breasts were on display for the three gorgeous men lounging around the room in front of me, my nipples becoming hard little peaks in the cool air.

Leo's hands massaged my back as his mouth licked and kissed my skin, as though he was savoring the taste. His lips began exploring my neck in the same way, sliding my hair across my back and out of the way. Another wave of intense need burned through me as he kissed behind my ear and nipped my neck. His teeth nibbled my earlobe, followed quickly by his hot tongue tracing and delving into my ear. I thought I would climax that very moment. I felt my entrance grow wetter, and I longed for him to take me.

I realized that each of my mates were quite different, especially in the bedroom. Leo was in no hurry; rather than claiming me hard and fast, he was going to take his time and make love to me as he memorized every curve of my body. I only hoped I could hang onto control and not force a quick, and likely rough, climax to our first time together.

I needed more; I ached to be touched. Moving my hands up, I squeezed my breasts. Leo's hand quickly grabbed my hands and brought them down to my lap. I growled in protest, but that changed to a groan as his hands teased along my ribs before cupping my breasts. His tongue continued to trace an elaborate design along my neck and ear, while his hands gently stroked my breasts, his thumbs brushing the hardened peaks.

"Leo," I breathed out, my voice husky as he continued to stimulate me past what I had thought possible.

"Hmm?" The sound was muffled as he began kissing my shoulders.

"I love you."

He stilled. My lust-filled brain worried that I had messed up by expressing my feelings so soon, but seconds later I felt something cool and wet run down my back. I realized it was a tear. Leo's tear.

"I do not think words exist to describe my feelings for you," he murmured. "I love you too."

The three mates in front of me wore similar expressions of love, and at this moment, my world was absolutely perfect.

Leo's hands moved from my breasts to my thighs, gently tickling his fingertips across the iridescent skin. With aching slowness, he moved up my inner thighs toward my most sensitive area. I wanted to push forward into his hand or grind down on his lap to relieve some of the building pressure. My body trembled as I forced myself to remain still.

When his finger traced along my folds, as though he was tracing the edge of a flower petal, I thought I would cry from the need that threatened to explode within me at any moment. I sat shaking on his lap as his fingers continued their exploration at a languid pace. Desire burned within me, turning my blood to lava and twisting my insides into a knot. My body needed release, but I wanted to treasure these first moments.

I whimpered as a single finger delved slowly into me. Stars danced against my closed eyelids as he moved the single digit in and out, brushing against my most sensitive spot. With effort I cracked open my heavy-lidded eyes and saw the twins and Mithraheal watching through bedroom eyes as well. I realized I must make quite the sight; my naked breasts on display, the gown pooled at my waist and flowing to the ground on either side of me, my legs slightly spread giving them an embarrassingly clear view of what Leo's fingers were doing.

I should have felt shy, perhaps closed my legs. My mates

and I shared a sex life that made me blush every time I thought about it, but this was the first time I had been put on display in front of them. They were watching another man tease me, make love to me, and instead of feeling shame, it was turning me on even more.

Mithraheal had taken off his belt and unbuttoned his pants, no doubt to ease the pressure from his arousal. His eyes were the color of fresh blood as he stared back at me.

Levi and Luke sat in opposite corners of the room, their movements mirroring each other unconsciously. Both men had slid a hand under the band of their pants, and it was obvious they were stroking down the length of their shafts. The motion was steady and unhurried; they were clearly enjoying the show.

With each deliciously slow stroke of his finger, I felt myself grow slicker, my insides coiling tight. I tried to rock my hips against his finger, but his other hand clamped down on my hip for a moment, holding me still. I needed something; the growing need was going to drive me insane!

As I opened my mouth to suck in another ragged breath, his hand disappeared from my hip to slip his finger between my parted lips. For a moment I was tempted to bite down, but as I felt the fingers of his other hand moving in and out of my lower set of lips, instinct kicked in and I sucked instead.

His breathing hitched behind me, so I sucked harder, swirling my tongue around his finger, letting him imagine all the things I would do if he would just let me get up and undress him. A second finger joined his first, stretching my wet folds, his fingers moving a little faster now. Yes. This was what I wanted! Gently scrapping my teeth along the finger still in my mouth, I began moving it in and out of my mouth. His forehead fell against my shoulder as he groaned.

The pace suddenly changed and his fingers began moving in and out of me with the same speed I had watched them fly across a keyboard. With each stroke, he rubbed against the hidden spot and forced the coil inside of me to tighten like a constrictor around its prey. A little sob escaped around the finger in my mouth as my release neared. This wasn't enough, I needed more.

Forgetting about my fangs, I accidentally nicked his finger as I sucked him harder. It wasn't a deep wound, but the coppery tang of his blood still filled my mouth. I fought to hang onto my control as my dragon surged forward; the blood setting off every primal instinct. All that I could think was that this man was mine, and yet he remained unclaimed.

His mouth pressed against me, his breath stirring the fine hairs at the nape of my neck sending chills traveling my body. I couldn't help myself, I ground my hips against him as his fingers continued to pump in and out of me.

Through the haze of my desire, I saw the twins had slid their pants off their hips, their erections stiff and long. They mesmerized me for a moment as I watched them stroke and squeeze themselves. Neither man had noticed the other; both were focused solely on me.

My climax came, and I screamed Leo's name in absolute ecstasy. My body trembled as I fell back against him, panting. Gently he cradled me against his chest before moving me up the bed and resting my head on the cloud filled pillows. For a few minutes he lay beside me, simply stroking the hair away from my face and memorizing every detail of it. Smiling, I traced his face with my fingers.

"Are you ready for us to claim each other?" His voice wavered, giving away the fact that he was worried I would change my mind.

Instead of answering him, I began unbuttoning his shirt, ready to be rid of any barriers between us. His smile was breathtaking, and he shoved my hands aside so he could strip as quickly as possible, earning a laugh from me over his sudden eagerness.

He jumped back onto the bed, bouncing me as his weight slammed into the mattress. Capturing my lips with his own, he kissed me with a thoroughness that curled my toes. His hands untied the string that was barely holding my flimsy gown around my hips, and then we were both bare in front of each other.

I drank in every inch of him. He was lean, not skinny, but also not as heavily muscled as my wolves. It was clear he was in shape; perhaps a swimmer, or maybe a runner. His skin was a creamy color rather than tanned; it was clear he spent most of his time in front of a computer rather than outside. His erection was rigid, and warmth flooded my belly again. He may not be as big as certain other mates, but he was beautiful. Perfect.

I reached down and hesitantly wrapped my fingers around his rigid member. His breath came out in a hiss, and his erection jerked hard in my hand. Feeling encouraged, I moved my thumb over the tip, the digit becoming wet as it slid through the evidence of his desire. Leo's body trembled.

"I need to tell you something," he gasped.

I froze, my eyes snapping up to his face.

"Among the wizards, nadir are not guaranteed to become a mate," he continued. "Most remain unmarried, which the wizards prefer, as they do not want to risk diluting bloodlines and weakening the magic. A few will marry other nadir, although receiving permission from the council to approve these marriages is nearly impossible. However, it is acceptable for a family to take in an adult nadir, if a female member has taken an interest in a particular nadir. The females are careful to not produce offspring with the nadir; he is but a plaything. Life as a nadir can be very lonely, so most nadir will jump at the opportunity to join a family, even in the knowledge that they will never truly be accepted as a part of the family."

"How can the council be so cruel?" I asked in astonishment. I had grown to respect the wizards under my roof. Their honor was of supreme importance to them, and I knew they were strong allies in the upcoming attack. However, I couldn't understand their indifference toward members of their community.

"They don't see it as cruelty, none of the community views it that way," Leo explained. "It's been this way for so long, for so many centuries, that no one even thinks of questioning it. But that's not what I wanted to tell you. Nadirs are seen as those who provide within the community. We provide services, food, hard labor, and in many situations, relief from sexual tension. We can say no, but it is frowned upon. I have had things requested of me many times, private things, and I have always refused. The council has allowed my continued refusal because of my skills with tech. They would rather I focus on work for them, than assist another wizard with their personal needs."

My horror must have shown on my face, because he stopped speaking, and pressed his lips against mine. It proved to be a handy distraction, and I quickly forgot what we had been discussing. He reluctantly pulled away.

"I need to finish, but I will make it quick," he said.

"I want to finish too, and I don't care if it is slow or fast!" I tried to pull his head back down so we could continue our kiss... and other things.

Leo barked out a laugh, confusing me.

"I meant I needed to finish explaining something," he said with a smile. "You are quite a little minx! As I said before, I refused the requests. The council didn't force the issue. I focused on my work. So... I haven't ever been with a woman. This will be my first time."

His cheeks flushed red at his confession, and I fought the desire to cover his adorable face with kisses.

"You will be my first, and my only, forever."

My heart swelled with love toward this gentle genius of a guy.

"I love you, Leo." The words didn't seem to be enough in that moment, but it was all that came out.

He pulled me into his arms, and our lips melded together. I loved the feeling his skin pressed firmly against the length of my body for the first time. Nothing between us. Our hands began feverishly touching and exploring each other's bodies. As my hand found his erection, he groaned into my mouth. I let my hand glide lower until I held his testicles in my hand, I gently massaged him, feeling the skin tighten under my attention.

"Darling, I will not last long if you keep touching me." His voice was rough, as though he had swallowed gravel.

I wrapped my arms around his neck, threw a leg over his hip, and then rolled, pulling him on top of me. He used his arms to lift some of his weight off my body and stared down into my eyes. I could see the reflection of my glowing blue irises in his own eyes.

"Please. Claim me." I couldn't hide the desperation in my voice.

He shifted, lining himself up at my slick entrance, and then thrusted inside me with one smooth stroke.

I moaned as my walls stretched to accommodate him. He trembled as he sunk so deep he could go no further. Inch by inch, he slid out of me, before thrusting back into my hot channel. His rhythm was excruciatingly slow and yet steady, each stroke fanning the flames of need inside me.

In and out.

In and out.

Sweet, buttered biscuits. This man was going to drive me insane.

He shifted inside me, and I jerked as his erection rubbed my most sensitive spot. He repeated the movement, obviously studying my reaction. I moaned.

He smiled and began his steady rhythm again, burying

himself deep with each stroke. I clung to him as he took us closer and closer to that precipice. His paced suddenly changed, his breathing labored. The quickened pace rushed me toward the edge, and as his burning member thrust in deep again, I screamed out my release and sank my fangs into his neck.

I wasn't a vampire, but as wave after wave of my climax washed over me, I couldn't stop myself from sucking, my fangs still embedded deep in his neck. As the copper taste filled my mouth, Beasty stirred in my mind, silent but intrigued.

With three hard thrusts, Leo found his own release and stilled inside me. He leaned down and pressed his lips to my ear, the same one he had lavished such attention on.

"Mine," he whispered.

Reluctantly pulling my fangs from his neck, and licking the two tiny holes, I responded: "Mine."

Glowing light swirled around our bodies and danced around the dimly-lit room. It circled my mates, brilliant gold strands of light tying us all together. I had never witnessed anything so beautiful in my life. It wasn't the mind blowing release of power that happened after the twins and I claimed each other, but it was equally special, and I was convinced that this was something that few ever experienced.

Leo rolled to his side and pulled me against him. Mithra-heal appeared suddenly beside the bed and pressed himself against my other side, sandwiching me between them. Luke crawled onto the end of the bed, slipping a hand under my calves and resting his head against them, his rough beard tickling my sensitive skin.

Levi looked at the bed. The men had an agreement that, while they loved each other as brothers, they had no desire to touch each other beyond a fist pump or a slap on the back. Mischief sparkled in Levi's eyes, and moments later a chocolate wolf stood where he had been standing. With a playful bark, he leaped up on the bed and settled himself on top of the pillows, tucking his muzzle against my head. I laughed as he licked my face before closing his eyes.

The next two days were going to be some of the hardest of my life, but for tonight, I was going to forget all my worries and treasure this perfect moment in time.

CHAPTER NINE
Mithraheal

I sipped my tea, enjoying the quiet of the morning and the time with my family. Watching Leo turn from the shy young man I had come to know, into a man that gave orders to our feisty mate. I could not deny that watching him pleasure her, while she was bare and on display in front of us, was the hottest thing I had ever witnessed in my exceedingly long life.

Leo fit into our family like a missing piece to a puzzle. He had a gentleness to him that a blood driven or werewolf simply couldn't possess. Even now as she sat on the couch, leaning into Luke's side, Leo had propped her feet in his lap and was absently massaging them as he studied something on his tablet. Levi had shifted to his wolf and was lying on the floor beside the couch. I stifled a laugh as I watched him swish his tail, smacking Tia in the face, and then repeat it again as soon as she went back to eating, earning a frustrated growl from her. He would definitely pay for that the next time they sparred. Only Damien was missing; he was enjoying some sleep after taking the night shift.

Turning my attention back to Leo, I studied him carefully, feeling as though I was missing something. There was something different about him and I couldn't put my finger on it. I had noticed that his scent had changed slightly after the claiming, but that had also happened with the rest of us.

I heard a door click in the lower level of the house, and then two sets of footsteps making their way around the house toward the front door. Ah, yes. Our first morning as a family was about to come to an abrupt end. Sighing, I set my cup into the saucer and stood to brush the invisible crumbs from my neatly-pressed slacks.

I opened the door before Gregor had the chance to knock, stepping aside to allow him and Elani entry into our living room. I knew that the wolves and Tia had heard them coming as well, but they hadn't moved; they were acting as if this was any other morning, not the morning after we'd kidnapped a nadir.

Gregor and Elani froze, taking in the sweet domestic scene in front of them. Leo was so focused on whatever he was reading that he only looked up at the sound of my voice as I invited our guests to sit. His face paled, and I noticed the tablet shaking for a moment before he steadied his hand.

"We came to ask if you had seen our nadir," said Gregor. "His quarters were empty this morning. His glass were laying haphazardly on the bed, and we were concerned about what could've caused him to leave them in such a rush."

Leo's face bore a look of confusion as he processed Gregor's words. He reached up to feel for his glasses, as if to confirm that they were gone. I hadn't noticed the missing glasses either. This morning he had moved about the room, helped prepare breakfast and read on his tablet with no signs of struggling to see. Interesting. Leo looked back toward the tablet and moved it closer to his face, then further away, his face changing from confusion to disbelief.

My love, do you know anything about this? I asked Tia as I watched a faint smile dance around her mouth.

There are things I am learning and so much I still don't understand, but yes, there are things I can share with my mates. This is a gift to him from my dragon.

My mate continued to amaze me with the abilities she possessed. Over the last few weeks, her skills had grown and new talents had manifested. She had taken each one in stride. I worried if she was pushing herself too hard; just the thought of her burning out terrified me.

Leo's excited whoop filled the quiet room, causing everyone to jump.

"I've spent my life looking at everything through a blur!" he cried. "Even with my glasses, everything remained slightly fuzzy. I can see the wings of that tiny fly on Mithraheal's teacup!"

As his happiness bubbled over, he reached over, sinking his hand into Tia's golden waves and pulling her to him as their lips met in an enthusiastic kiss. Luke laughed, and Levi let out a joyous bark while his wagging tail thudded against the wooden floor.

"What is *that!*" Elani's tone was shrill and demanding. Rising quickly to her feet, she sprung toward the kissing couple. Levi's demeanor changed from happy pup to werewolf fast enough to cause whiplash. His body blocked her advancement, while a vicious growl rattled through the room. Elani was so focused on whatever had caught her attention that she didn't even realize the danger she was in, until Gregor rushed forward and hauled her backward.

"Do *not* move a muscle." Gregor's voice was commanding and low. "That is a werewolf protecting its mate, his instincts are more animal than human at the moment. What were you thinking?"

"Didn't you notice her ear and neck?" Elani answered, her eyes focused warily on Levi. "She has the mark of being bonded to a wizard; a mark that wasn't there yesterday. I wished to inspect it, to determine its authenticity, to see which of the bloodlines created it. If she has been secretly meeting with other wizards, we should know. I'm not eager to follow a deceiver into battle." Venom laced her words.

Jealousy. She is so full of jealousy that it's eating her from the inside out. Damien's amused voice echoed in my mind, and moments later he was sitting sprawled on one of the oversized bean bags clutching something in his hands. Was that... popcorn?

He tossed a butter-covered piece into the air, catching it in his mouth and giving me a wink. Wasn't he supposed to be sleeping?

I smell drama, and there is no way I am missing my new favorite show!

I rolled my eyes. What a cad.

Luke shifted on the couch until he was pressed against Tia's back. He carefully brushed every silky strand of her hair away, revealing the delicate curve of her neck and the adorable, pointed tips of her ears. A collective gasp went through the room at the sight. Unbelievably intricate lines wove and swirled up Tia's neck, the design continuing on to her ear. As with her light tattoos, these also glowed from within, but with varying shades of gold instead of blue.

I moved closer, tracing the lines on her ear as I studied them. Leo leaned forward to inspect it as well.

"It's from last night, from my kiss." He was whispering, but in the quiet of the room, his words may as well have been a shout.

"You marked her?" Elani was outraged. "You have refused *my* advances, but you marked *this* female? She isn't a wizard, and you are a nadir! The council indulged your reluctance, but that will end when they hear of this!"

To be honest, I had expected Tia to fling her across the room, set her on fire, or suddenly develop a new talent that involved making people disappear. Instead, she ignored Elani and scooted onto Leo's lap.

"You marked me?" Tia said, smiling at Leo. "I didn't know that was possible! What does it look like?"

Leo melted at her eager expression and quickly picked up his tablet, turning on the selfie camera mode and handing it to her so she could use it as a mirror. She made little sounds of excitement. shifting the angle of the tablet to see the whole design.

"It's incredible! It's the most beautiful piece of artwork I have ever seen! You traced this with your tongue last night, didn't you?"

Tia blushed, and to my astonishment, the colors in Leo's mark began to change as well.

"Yes, although I didn't believe it would work, since I am a nadir," Leo explained. "This mark is made from ancient magic, a magic thought to be long extinct from earth. Legend claims that when pure blood wizards found their soulmate, they had the ability to channel their love into a design through a kiss as they bonded. It is said that male wizards would often work on that piece of art for decades, as they waited to find their soulmate. I had thought it was just a story told to children, but I loved the idea. I secretly worked on my own design, hoping to kiss it onto my soulmate's skin one day. It was a far-fetched dream, but it made life more bearable to believe that it could happen. I traced it with my lips and tongue last night, knowing it would never show on your skin. At least in my heart I would know that my dream had come true."

Crystal tears made glimmering paths down Tia's face, and I watched, mesmerized, as the tattoo shifted in color yet again.

"That's just not possible," said Gregor. "There hasn't been a wizard mark since those stories of old. Our females wear jewelry to signify their relationship status, much like human females. It is believed that the legends are mere stories, or that the bloodlines are no longer pure enough to create such magic between soulmates. You are a nadir, a talented man with skills beyond compare on a computer, but you hold no magic."

Tia faced Gregor. She was still sitting on Leo's lap, her back pressed firmly against his chest. Leo's arms circled her waist and his chin rested on her shoulder. The colors shifted again; this time it seemed to pulsate.

"It's a mood ring!" Damien cackled and spilled some of his popcorn.

Everyone stared at him, waiting for him to explain his random comment.

"Oh, for the love of a hellhound!" he cried. "The mark that Leo apparently (ew) licked all over her neck"—he shuddered dramatically—"keeps changing colors. It swirled one color when she was confused. It changed when Elani started ranting. The color morphed again when she got all lovey-dovey with Leo, and when Gregor insulted Leo, it shifted again. It doesn't take a rocket scientist to figure out that her mood is changing the colors." Turning toward the wizards, he added, "I would probably watch what you two say right now, because I have $100 that says she is getting really ticked off. You do not want to poke a sleeping dragon. Actually, I take that back. Go ahead and say whatever pops into your head! It's been really boring around here lately."

He finished and leaned forward eagerly, obviously wishing things would get more exciting.

His wish was granted.

CHAPTER TEN

Leo

I was shocked at how quickly Damien had picked up on the link between Tia's emotions and the mark. That was another part of the old legends that were believed to be fiction. I didn't understand his warning, or the mischievous glint in his eyes as he told Elani and Gregor to disregard it. As it was, I didn't have to wait long to find out his reasoning.

"Nadir, report to your quarters immediately!" Elani demanded. "I will be speaking to the council about your behavior." Her tone was patronizing, as though she was speaking to a toddler.

The nadir training urged me to drop my eyes and follow the orders of my handler, but things had changed. I was part of a circle; this was my home for as long as Tia resided here, and no other woman would order me out of it. Ignoring Elani, I nuzzled Tia's neck, kissing the mark that I had practiced in my long hours alone. I squeezed my arms around her playfully, earning a squeal as she wiggled. Her hair tickled my face, and I laughed. I finally straightened my spine and turned to look Elani in the eye.

"I respect your position in our community, and time permitting, I will continue to work on cases for the council, if they wish it," I said. "However, I am no longer a nadir. I am a human, and now a bonded mate with a circle. I will no longer be ordered around simply because I was born without magic."

Those were words I had dreamed of being able to speak someday. I deserved to be treated with the same respect that was given to others, regardless of magic. A weight rolled off my shoulders, and I felt several inches taller. Elani had never been able to handle being told "no" and this time wasn't any different.

"You do not have the right to say no!" she cried. "As your handler, I am responsible for ensuring that you remain in line, and refrain from doing anything stupid that would bring shame upon the wizard community. Return to your quarters immediately and await my return."

I had nothing more to say to her, so I remained quiet. Tia was frozen in my lap, her eyes unblinking as she stared at Elani. A tingling spread through my fingers, and for a moment I wondered if they had fallen asleep as they rested on her waist. The tingling spread up my arms, before moving to the tops of my thighs, until my body tingled everywhere it was touching Tia. I had listened to others describe how magic "felt" and their excitement as it moved about them, but it was something I hadn't experienced as a nadir. The air began to vibrate around Tia. I felt that this was what it must be like in the moments before you are struck by lightning.

"Little dragon," said Luke, "focus on your breathing." His words were reassuring, and it seemed that they were working, until he said the two words that every man, of every species, in every galaxy, knew he shouldn't say to an angry woman. "Calm yourself."

Damien cackled in glee, sounding like a two hundred-year-old witch that had just found the secret to eternal beauty. Mithraheal, always so proper, groaned and slumped into a chair, wrinkling his immaculate suit. Levi gave Luke a disgusted look, before dropping to the floor and covering his snout and eyes with his massive paws. Gregor took a few cautious steps backwards, taking a position closer to the door.

They left me holding what might as well have been an atomic bomb on my lap.

Please tell me that the mutt did not just tell us to be calm? We should neuter him, we could just keep the other twin for the baby making! Why didn't he tell the chick with a stick up her butt to be calm? She's the one that barged into our nest, the one that's trying to take our newly-bonded mate away from us. We cannot let her have him! He's adorable, and the things he can do with his tongue—

The word vomit ended abruptly, and I assumed that Tia had somehow silenced her dragon. I glanced at the other men and knew instantly that they had heard the same thing as me. Damien howled with laughter, Mithraheal looked perplexed,

Luke looked green, and Levi's glee at the mention of babies rolled off him in waves, even in wolf form.

Overwhelming happiness warmed my chest, filling every cold, lonely spot in my soul. I had a family, a home, and I was going to cherish every ridiculously insane minute of belonging to a dragoness. Laughter spilled from my lips. I laughed until tears streamed down my face and my sides ached. I laughed until every bit of hurt and sadness I had endured was swept away.

Tia turned herself on my lap so she was facing me, her eyes lighting up as I struggled to regain my composure. Her hands slipped around my neck, her laughter escaping to join my own. I loved this woman, and I wanted to show her just how much I did. I stood quickly, grabbing her plump bum to keep her from slipping. She quickly wrapped those beautiful long legs around my waist and pulled herself tightly against me. I felt my body react instantly and my breathing hitched; I could live for centuries and I doubt I would ever grow tired of feeling her pressed against me.

As I moved to leave the room, we neared the spot Elani stood. Tia's back was to her, so she did not see the look that passed across my handler's face. Elani's hand shot out and grabbed my arm to halt me.

"Remove your hand from my mate. Now." It was not a request, it was an order, and Tia's voice reverberated as though two people spoke instead of one.

Elani removed her hand but refused to stand aside. "By wizard law, he is a nadir and I am his handle," she said. "That makes him my property. This will not change, unless the council sees fit to reassign him, which is unlikely as I have already submitted the papers to gain ownership of him. He has refused in the past, and the council has allowed his tantrums, only because they believed he shouldn't have his attention divided. However, I have it in writing that, after this final hack, he is going to see to my needs as a reward for my outstanding performance as his handler. Thanks to my diligence, he has assisted the council on many challenging cases, and they are pleased. The date of his new assignment, focused on me, is today. So unless you would like to start an interspecies war, I suggest you remove your horny self from my nadir."

Elani finished by pulling out stationary that I was very familiar with. It carried the seal of the council and was signed by each member. It was all true. I had deluded myself into believing the council would not force something on a nadir; that we had some rights within the community, even if we did not have respect. The wind was knocked out of me. This type of decree was official; the council rarely revoked such things, and I couldn't allow my mate to bring another battle to her door.

A sharp snap like the cracking of a whip spilt the air as my mate's wings sprang free. One wing smacked the paper from Elani's hand, wrenching a pained yelp from my handler as she clutched her smarting hand to her chest.

Sliding down my body to stand on her own feet, Tia faced Elani. "Elani, I would like to introduce you to my bonded mate, Leo," she said. "If you, or the council, have business with him, you are welcome in our home to discuss whether he wishes to take on the case. He will choose what he wishes to work on, so I suggest the council treat him with respect if they wish him to consider any of their requests. My mates are not to be disrespected in my nest. This is the one and *only* time I will give you a warning. In the future, your behavior will result in your being banned permanently. I understand that some traditions are old and long-standing within supernatural communities, but the treatment of those that have been labeled as 'nadir' is horrifying and unacceptable. They are tricked into believing they are free, while in reality, they are servants, even slaves."

Elani opened her mouth to argue, but Tia waved her hand in a casual gesture. Elani's mouth continued to attempt to form words, but no sound came out. She clutched at her throat in panic.

"Calm your tits, it's not permanent," Tia said with a sigh. "I simply wish to finish without interruption. My mates and I will head into battle soon and I have much better things to do with my time right now. You will deliver a message to the council for me. Tell them that the treatment of those they label 'nadir' ends today. They are free to make their own decisions regarding careers, families, studies, and traveling. Contracts cannot be made regarding them without their willing consent. They deserve to be treated as valuable members of the wizard community, and if that is not possible, then I welcome them to join me. I am goddess Tiamat, dragoness of the sea! I am here to balance our world. If I do not receive word from the council before we leave on our mission, giving their express agreement to these terms, I will assume that we are no longer allies."

Tia moved into my arms, her wings enveloping me in her warmth. I wanted to study her wings, to touch them and observe them in motion, but for now, I enjoyed my mate's embrace.

"One last thing," she added. "Leo is mine, and I am his. Forget any thoughts of trying to lay claim to him. Touch him again, and you will die."

She waved her hand once more and Elani vanished instantly. Tia climbed back up my body like a lizard, her lush lips touching mine in a feather light brush. My hands moved to explore her body, feeling my own body began to burn with the desire to bury myself deep inside her. I tripped as I made a dash for the bedroom, swallowing her giggle as my mouth covered hers.

"Goddess," interrupted Gregor, "with permission, may I ask what happened to Elani?"

I slowed just for a moment at Gregor's question. I was curious too, but I was more worried about stripping my gorgeous little mate.

Tia reluctantly pulled back from our kiss and peered around my arm to find Gregor kneeling with his head bowed. "Don't worry, Gregor, she is fine. I sent her to the council chambers, and she will find her voice has returned. No hard feelings, okay?"

She had gone from a demanding avenging goddess to the girl you share beers with while watching sports. It was such a crazy switch of roles, but she remained in control at all times. My skin was tingling and my nerves felt raw, both of which I chalked up to the dragoness currently trying to unbutton my shirt. I had a feeling that we had only scratched the surface when it came to the secrets and power this little queen possessed.

Chapter Eleven

Tia

I strapped my weapon harness around my chest and quickly settled my swords in their sheaths against my back. The harness was butter-soft leather and had been hand-crafted to fit my body perfectly. It allowed my wings to move freely, while also positioning my swords in a way that kept me from slicing them accidentally. Mithraheal had gifted it to me, and while I scolded him about spoiling me, it had thrilled me.

Bending down, I slipped my twin knives into the hidden sheaths inside my boots. Outside, my face showed calm confidence, but a tumultuous storm whirled inside me. We had planned this attack down to the last detail; we had practiced our movements until they flowed like water without conscious thought. I had enjoyed private moments with each of my mates, and my bonds had never felt so strong.

The pressure building in my ears distracted me from my inner turmoil.

"Wizards incoming!" I yelled. My mates looked up from strapping on their own weapons and I nearly fainted on the spot. How did I get so lucky? Each man was jaw dropping in his own way, and all were shining examples of powerful warriors. It was rare to see Mithraheal out of a suit, and the sight of him clad in expensive leather that clung to his skin in all the right ways had me wishing for one more hour alone with him.

The cool mountain breeze swirled around us and I rubbed my arms, more out of habit than actually being cold. It was quite a handy perk to have dragon fire warming you from the inside out.

Gregor popped into the yard first, followed quickly by the wizards we had come to know well during the planning of our attack. We had spent many hours researching Draven's business dealings, all of us horrified at how low he was willing to go to secure alliances and power.

The things being done behind closed doors, the lives being ruined by his smuggled shipments, the sudden disappearances of those who crossed him; all had sent me rushing to the bathroom several times to empty my stomach. I had watched these wizards' reactions too, when they thought no one was looking. They had been just as outraged; their hands had shaken and their jaws clenched. I could not understand their customs regarding the nadir, but I also knew they were not all heartless.

My spine stiffened as the last wizard popped in—Elani. It surprised me that she was willing to face me again so soon. I crossed my arms across my chest, my eyes narrowing and mouth tightening as Gregor walked toward me. We would take Draven down this morning, with or without the help of the wizards.

Gregor stopped in front of me, then he dropped to one knee and bowed his head. Soft thuds sounded around me as one by one every wizard in the yard dropped to one knee. They were back-lit by the gorgeous pinks and golds of the sunrise, the sun slowly making its climb above the mountain range. It was surreal, and to be honest, it totally freaked me out. This was not the quiet life I had always believed I would live. The prophecy had ensured I couldn't have that life; at least not until things had been set right.

Whine about it all you want, but you were born for more. Today is just the beginning.

Beasty and her sucky pep talks, just what a girl wanted while she waited to find out if she had started a war with the wizards, shortly before she had to leave to take out a murdering piece of dog crap who was determined to take power that did not belong to him in order to take over the world like an old-school cartoon villain. How was this my life now?

"The council spent many long hours last night discussing your requirements for our continued alliance," said Gregor. "Our elders were given the chance to view nadir customs through an outsider's eyes; something that hadn't been done in centuries. Overwhelming disgust and sorrow plagues them now. The council wishes to thank you for risking so much to help members of the wizard community. All contracts regarding the nadir will be reviewed, and they will have the option to renegotiate or cancel those agreements. At this moment, the council is working to ensure that fair housing, career, and study options are made available. An apology to the nadir is being aired in the community as we speak. It will take some time, but the changes are already in motion."

Gregor stood and turned toward Leo, whose gentle eyes shimmered with unshed tears. Gregor crossed his arm across his chest, his fist pressed against his heart.

"The council, the wizards present, and I myself, all wish to apologize for our behavior toward you. Your skills have been an incredible asset within our community, and yet you never received acknowledgement of that fact. The disrespect with which you have been treated, intentionally or unintentionally, was unacceptable. Our council is grateful for your offer to work on cases for them in the future. If you chose to accept, they will pay handsomely for your skills and time. The marking between you and Tia was a shock to the council; they are confused by it. Bonds to mates outside of the wizard community are always discussed with the council first and only completed once they receive approval. This applies to all wizards. Scholars are researching the mating mark you left on Tia's neck, and the council wishes to have the pleasure of you and your mate's company once they have information to share. At this time, the contract with Elani is void."

Leo stood still, at a loss for words. Cool relief flowed across my frayed nerves, and hope soared in my heart. Things were changing.

Elani stepped forward, keeping her head bowed. "Leo and Tia, I am sorry for my behavior and blatant disrespect of the mate bond in your home," she said. "I wish you both happiness."

"We are proud to call your circle our allies," added Gregor, "and we are ready to follow you into battle."

My stomach turned at the word "battle", my almost forgotten nightmare flashing through my mind. No, it wouldn't be anything like that bloody scene created by an anguished mind. This was a stealth mission; no muss, no fuss. Raw fear began to tighten a fist around my heart, and a tsunami of anxiety threatened to drown me beneath it.

You are the dragoness of the sea - a tsunami could not kill you. Focus on now, worry will have you second guessing your every action and that could be deadly.

Dang. When had Beasty gone from crazy nymphomaniac to wise sensei?

Hardy, har, har. Her tone dripped with sarcasm, and I smiled.

I stepped forward with my arm outstretched. Gregor met me and we clasped our forearms together, prepared to fight side by side. Slowly, each wizard rose from their kneeling position and stepped forward to offer their arm, and each time I clasped it tightly against my own. Elani also stepped forward; her arm shook a little as she held it out. Without hesitation, I extended my arm and clasped hers just as firmly as I had with the men.

"I know you will find the happiness that I have found with Leo, and it will be more than you hoped for," I said.

Her eyes met mine, and for the first time that morning she smiled back at me.

"I know I will," she replied. "I just hope I don't have to wait forever. Our species live an awful long time!" Her lilting laughter broke the lingering tension between us, and I couldn't resist laughing with her. It was so true; my Mithra-heal had waited many human lifetimes for his soulmate, me. I caught his eye and blew him a kiss. The elegant king of the blood driven lifted his hand, pretending to catch my kiss, and then pressed it to his lips.

My anxiety became joy, and hope fluttered inside me. Running, I threw myself onto Luke's back. In a swift motion, I freed my sword and lifted it into the air screaming: "Forward into battle, my noble stead!"

My playful moment with my mate was taken far too seriously by the wizards and my ears rang with the whistles of swords slicing the air as they were quickly drawn. Luke and Levi threw back their heads and released an eerie howl that echoed in the lush valley below. The wizards joined with their own battle cry. It was a sound the raised the hair on my arms; one that movie producers could never reproduce.

My noble stead took off, ready for battle, and I whooped as I bounced on his back... all the way to the sleek black SUV.

Chapter Twelve

Tia

A bead of sweat ran down the length of my spine. It was only mid-morning, but the sun was already beating down on the earth mercilessly. Deep breath in, deep breath out. I worked to steady my frantic heart, which was currently attempting to slam out of my chest. Within hours, I would be at home with my mates, snuggling and eating pizza.

Let's bring the house down, so we can get back to our house and go down!

I choked on my own spit. Mithraheal let out an unmanly squeak next to me, and I knew Beasty had once again sent her thoughts into the bond for all my boys to hear.

It gives them a reason to hurry this up, she whispered

conspiratorially, while still projecting her every word in the bond.

I wanted to scold her, but frankly, I had missed her ridiculous remarks the past few weeks and it was a relief to have her nonsense cut through the tension.

Aw! I love you too, Teacup!

Okay, I was going back to ignoring her. I closed my eyes, allowing my magic to sweep across the ground unseen. I had discovered that my dragon magic differed greatly from other magic, meaning Draven wouldn't be able to detect it as I sent out subtle tendrils.

With my eyes closed, I mapped out everyone's location; my dragon giving me a rough grid-line guide of the area surrounding me, and energy signatures for the living things nearby. Each of the men were in position, simply waiting for my cue to move on the building and guards. Focusing on the members of my team, I spoke directly into their minds.

It's time. Stick to the plan and don't take unnecessary risks. Move. Now!

I ducked out from the thick hedges that had hidden me. I grabbed Gregor's arm and, using my dragon strength and speed, I flashed to the building, hauling the wizard with me with Mithraheal right on my heels. We were careful to stay out of the cameras' line of sight as we moved swiftly down the side of the wall.

I touched Levi's and Luke's minds to check their progress. They had taken down the guards with ease, and their wolves were nearly salivating to have more of a challenge. I moved to Leo, butterflies fluttering in my stomach at the intimacy of touching minds with my new mate. My life had been utter chaos, and I was nearly desperate to have time alone with each of my mates to learn more about them. Leo and I had spent less than seventy-two hours together and had only exchanged broken bits of conversation before that. The soulmate, or fated mate, bond was incredible, allowing me to feel closer to these men than I had felt to anyone in my life. They were literally a piece of my soul. But now, I wanted to know them, not just their bodies.

Leo's mind brushed against mine, much like how his hand brushed my hair away from face. I startled, not realizing he had the ability to physically react in the bond. We had so much to learn about our abilities as mates.

Reassuring myself that Damien had gotten him safely settled into the guardroom, and that he was now typing away with a ferocious speed, I checked in on the wizards. This neat trick was possible because I had clasped arms with them only hours before; it was a newer ability and I had yet to figure out the specifics of how it worked.

They were all uninjured, and in position. I lingered for a moment in Elani's mind.

She was whispering furiously to Lars: "Can you believe that? It isn't fair!"

He whispered back: "Now's not the time, Elani. You are out of line."

"I'm out of line?" she hissed.

"It'll be over soon. We have all worked for this day, let's finish this mission so we can return home. I miss my own bed."

"It better be."

It seems I was not the only one eager to have this day over. Everyone was sick of the chronic stress and grueling training.

We made our way in through a side door, the guard absent thanks to my wolves. Moving deeper into the depths of the building, I focused on one thing and one thing only. Stopping Draven before he destroyed more lives.

The dark hallway stretched in front of us, seeming to have no end. The utter stillness in the air was unnerving. There was no way he could've known we were coming, could he? My magic slithered under the crack in the door and tested the room. Draven was sitting at his desk. I carefully unsheathed my knives, finding strength in their familiar weight. Glancing to Mithraheal and Gregor, I waited for their nod before twisting the knob and throwing the door open. I spun to the side quickly out of the way of a possible attack. But none came.

I have watched plenty of action movies, and I spend most of my time screaming at the scream at them to stop talking and just take down the villain. I wouldn't make that mistake. In the blink of an eye, I sent my beautiful blades singing through the air to embed with a sickening thud into Draven's chest. He moved at the last second, my blades just barely missing their intended lethal target.

He screamed in pain, but remained sitting at his desk, looking for all the world like he had been waiting on a business appointment. I had learned enough about him to know he had developed powerful skills with magic and couldn't understand why he wasn't wrapping it around himself now or using it to make an escape.

"You are a little ahead of schedule," he said. "I'm impressed, little dragon."

I said nothing, drawing my swords and dropping into a fighting stance.

"No matter, everyone's waiting. Let's go."

The room shifted, the floor beneath me rocking. I didn't even have a chance to teleport us out of there as the oxygen was sucked out of the room and we were plunged into a vortex. I don't know how long we were in that churning black hole before it sent us smashing into hard earth. Icy pain shot through my body, my bones groaning from the force of the impact.

Moaning in pain, I rolled onto my hands and knees, the world around me still spinning like I was on a carnival ride. My stomach lurched and then emptied its contents, leaving me panting and dry heaving.

Get up. Get up now! Beasty roared in my head.

I staggered to my feet, pulling my magic to me in an effort to heal some of my injuries. My ankle gave out under my weight, my teeth sinking into my lip to muffle my scream. I remained standing, but the grinding of my bones against each other had my stomach twisting again.

You will heal. Suck it up. If you don't focus, you'll be dead and your injuries will not matter!

I searched the clearing, studying my surroundings and trying to form a new strategy. My mates and the wizards were all struggling to their feet, some obviously dealing with broken bones, but at least none were dead. We were in a field: sparse green shrubs dotted the area, clinging to the cracked red dirt.

As my gaze darted around, I noticed the shadows. No, wait. Those weren't shadows; those were men, heavily armed men, and they were surrounding us.

"To steal a phrase from the current generation, how dope is this?" Draven threw out his hands, motioning toward my confused team and his men standing to attention. I said nothing, letting him continue to gloat while I attempted to figure out a plan to get my team out of here. I wanted to teleport them to safety, but I knew I didn't yet have the strength to move so many at once. If they began disappearing, Draven would notice and no doubt order the others to be attacked. *Think, Tia, think.*

"I knew you would come from me," Draven began. "You are smart, so it was inevitable. I too have spent the last months honing my skills, in preparation for your arrival. Today's display required me to reserve my magic until it was time; transporting everyone here was no easy task. It's also taking an incredible amount of power to maintain the spell that has nulled your wizards' magic. You see, I've been planning this moment carefully, and now you will accept my terms—or watch everyone in this clearing die."

Anger burned white hot inside me. How could we have prepared so hard for this, only to have the tables turned so suddenly? My dragon side had grown more powerful, and yet I felt powerless facing Draven. The answer hit me like a physical blow and I began searching each face of my team, looking for the traitor that had been leaking our plans.

"You can keep searching, but truth be told, I don't even know who it is," Draven said, as if reading my mind. "The crafty turncoat was very careful to not give any clues to his or her identity. Your progress as you gained additional talents was impressive. I quickly realized the only way I could survive your attack was to force you into a position where you had to choose between your life and those who had followed you. My dear, that is your pitiful weakness. You value all life and would give your life to save another. Such an idiotic waste of an extraordinary power, just to save someone beneath you. You could never rule while holding onto this childish ideology. It's just as well though - it will make all this much easier for me."

"I would rather die with my beliefs, then be a vessel for the evil inside you!" My voice reverberated, Beasty and I speaking as one. Unease skittered across Draven's face, and he stepped back.

"So be it," he said. "This is what will happen now. You will kneel on that altar, and I will perform a ceremony that will send your power into me. I have spent hours reading the forbidden scrolls to ensure nothing goes wrong. You need to be willing for the energy to transfer to me."

"I will not kneel, and I sure as heck will never willingly give you my power!"

My skin crawled as he laughed; there was nothing pleasant in the sound.

"Let's stop beating around the bush," he said with a smile. "You will allow yourself to be sacrificed and the wizards will be allowed to go free, completely unharmed. I understand that, unfortunately, your vampire mate will not survive your death, but the wolves and your faux wizard mate will live. As he will become the next in line for the blood driven throne upon your mate's death, Damien will be required to form an alliance with me. He too will be returned to his kingdom unharmed. Refuse this generous offer, and my men will attack immediately; everyone will die, and I will still take whatever power I can from your dying body as you watch those you love be slaughtered. I have ten men to each of your men, you cannot win today. Their blood will be on your hands."

I thought I watched a lot of TV, but apparently Draven watched a lot more. He had me confused with idiot women who can't see two minutes into the future and fall for the lies fed to them, believing their loved one will be spared. Idiots. If I agreed, he would take my power, and not only kill my mates and team, but then use my power to destroy countless other lives. It would be the beginning of an apocalypse. I loved my mates more than life itself but attempting to save them now would just cause them infinitely more pain in the future.

I snorted in derision.

My magic swirled, and I felt my stature change; my limbs grew longer, my hair and nails lengthened and glinted like the sun on a blade's edge. My vision shifted, my pupils turning to slits and causing the world around me to explode in color and detail. Blue light radiated around me as at last my wings burst free. I spoke into the mental bond, likely my last private moment with my mates.

If I die today to save your lives, it will only mean your death later at his hands, and the deaths of many innocents. My time with you all was far too short, but it was also more than I had ever dreamed I would have. I love you all, and I hope we end up snuggling in bed later, trying to forget how bad today has sucked.

I mentally cradled the luminous ball of energy in my chest. I had learned over the past few weeks how to pull from it to perform some neat battle tricks and pranks. A smile tugged at my lips as I recalled throwing energy balls at Damien's butt and burning the rear out of several pairs of his pants. His vampire speed had proved no match for my butt-seeking missiles.

I gently separated the energy into six sections, and mentally sent that magic into our bond. They would not be able to wield it as a weapon, but it would enhance their supernatural gifts. I prayed that it would be enough to ensure their survival today.

Twisting around, I became a blur as I rushed toward Draven, my swords poised in front of me, ready to destroy him or die trying. Draven roared in frustration, apparently not happy to see his perfect plan crumbling. The clang of sword slamming into sword, screams of fury, and howls surrounded me.

Deja vu. I had already been here. Horror froze the blood in my veins as realization stole the breath from my lungs. This was the battle from my nightmare weeks ago. I clung desperately to the hope that my nightmare was just a dream, and not a vision of what was to come.

CHAPTER THIRTEEN

Tia

My magic warned me seconds before a soldier tried to tackle me from my left side. Without slowing my run, I ducked, sending the assailant sailing over my head. I thrust my blade upwards, slicing across the top of his thighs to sever his tendons. He screamed in agony, but he would live.

I sprang back to my feet, only to have another attacker rush me from the right, his sword drawn and raised as he prepared to bring it down on my neck. Tucking my wings against me, I rolled and slammed my body into his knees. He tumbled to the ground, trying to keep his grip on his weapon; a wasted attempt since moments later I slammed the hilt of my sword into the back of his head. He went limp under me as I shoved his body off me and blurred toward Draven again.

He wasn't trying to get away; he wanted me to reach him, but he wanted me tired and weakened. I didn't want to admit how drained I was feeling after dividing my energy. I was keeping my magic trip-wires around me as a warning system, but I could only spare enough to alert me about the few feet around me. Hopefully, it gave me enough of an edge to survive this day.

I braced myself as two men tried to tackle me at the same time. Ducking and dodging, I managed to avoid the bulk of their impact, but the force still sent us all hurtling into the ground. I had lost a sword in the collision, but I still clung to the other. I rolled to the side, trying to get myself out from under the soldiers' crushing weight. Flinging out my hand, the hilt of my sword connected with a sickening thud against the one man's temple, and he dropped like a box of rocks.

The second man wrapped his hands around my neck, cutting off my air supply. I thrashed under him, trying to kick his family jewels, and when that didn't work, I clawed at his hands with my pointed nails. His face tightened in pain, but he didn't let up. Out of options, I stabbed him with my sword, it's thin edge cutting through him like jello. His hands left my neck, and he groaned as he clutched at his side. Warm blood flowed across my hand and my stomach heaved. I hadn't wanted to kill Draven's followers; I wanted to hand them over to their leaders for trial.

Stop being an idiot. The fantasy world you have created in your mind doesn't exist. These men made their choice; they're not innocent. Your mission is to defeat Draven before his evil spreads, at whatever cost necessary. Stop wasting energy trying to disable these goons with non-lethal injuries.

I staggered back to my feet, stumbling for a moment as my ankle wobbled again with my weight. Darting my gaze around, I realized that twelve men were circling me, while Draven moved toward me, no doubt waiting to jump me once I was subdued by his mercenaries.

Not today, Satan. Not today.

A blade sang as it flew through the air. Spinning, I kicked out with my boot, sending it hurtling into one of the men. Two more blades were thrown at me in rapid succession. I whirled, spinning as I jumped again, slamming my boot into the blades and lodging them in my attackers. I winced as I landed, but thankfully my bone was healing and the pain had dulled.

One of the mercenaries rushed forward, throwing punches with his meaty fists. I was surprised at his speed given his size, and he managed to catch me in the ribs and my shoulder as I dodged and kicked. I gasped for air as he knocked the wind from my burning lungs. A second man used that moment of distraction to rush forward, grabbing my wing. My stomach churned in disgust. No one touched my wings except my mates.

I roared in outrage, trying to yank it free, but he held on and moved to grip the bones above and below the last joint. A sickening crack was followed by pure agony ricocheting through me.

I had been trying to conserve as much of my energy as possible for my showdown with Draven, but at this rate, I would be too weak to fight him. We had worked so hard, and it had been for nothing. I was strong, and I could easily take down several highly-trained supernaturals in a fight. But these odds would have been impossible for any supernatural, male or female, and especially one who wasn't at full power.

It was time to put out or shut up. My parents had helped me escape the night this monster murdered them, but I would not run or cower this time. Never again. I was a goddess - a baby one with very little control of her powers, but a freaking goddess nonetheless.

I screamed out every bit of fury, feeling the ground quake under my boots, and the dragon fire in my chest began to spread through me. My tattoos began to pulse, the sapphire color changing to the colors of fire. Heat began to swirl around me, creating a spinning vortex that kept me in its eye as I moved.

The surrounding men had frozen, either in fear or awe. Draven's lust-filled eyes locked with mine. It wasn't a lust for me; it was a lust for the power he craved. I released my hold on my energy, and allowed it to merge with me, knowing I had precious little time to finish this before it was expended completely. It would replenish with rest and time, but that wasn't going to help in the middle of a battle. This was basically the equivalent of powering up in a video game and rushing to finish the level before the extra ability's time ran out... except this was real life, and the fate of the world was kinda hanging in the balance. No pressure.

I lifted my fists into the air, and then quickly brought them down to my side as though smashing a table. The men around me found themselves tossed onto the ground like rag dolls, the force creating craters around their bodies. Not a single man groaned or moved; I wasn't sure if they were alive or dead, but I couldn't allow myself to care about that right now.

Draven remained standing, apparently the only supernatural besides me to be able to use magic right now. I focused solely on him. Moving my palm, I held it between us in the universal sign to halt, quickly slamming my other palm against the back of the first. Energy shot from my palm, striking Draven with a force that flung him to the ground. A smile made its way to my lips as I heard the crunch of bones.

Staggering back to his feet, his lips moved as he spoke under his breath. The ground beneath my boots shook and shifted, swiftly turning from parched dirt to quicksand. Ignoring this impressive trick, I continued walking toward him, my vortex lifting me up with care and setting me down smoothly on solid ground. Draven's eyes widened in shock for a moment, and then he began whispering again.

Wind ripped across the clearing, gathering dust and debris into the air as it circled like a predator. I knew the instant it found me; the wind changed from a dust cloud to a spear as it shot toward my chest.

My fingertips slid along the side of my personal tornado, petting it like a beloved dog. It danced between my fingers and I let my energy begin to flow out into the vortex, the two swirling around me like playful dolphins. The spear impacted against the side of my windy cocoon. My energy sizzled along the length of the spear, my vortex whipping it around before hurling it with the accuracy of a sniper. All this happened in the blink of an eye. Draven was expecting me to fall; he didn't even realize the spear had been redirected until it pierced his chest.

This time, he did not get back up. His hate-filled eyes glared up at me as I accessed his injuries. The spear had dissipated, but the gaping hole in his chest remained. Blood pumped out at a rate that even I knew spelled certain death. He struggled to breathe, each breath making a wet suction sound.

"I may die today, but so will you." He began choking, his blood soaking into the ground.

Lightning crackled and time seemed to slow as the bolt shot toward me. When I was fully powered, nearly everything seemed slow to my dragon, but weakened as I was in that moment, the lightning had already grazed my skin by the time I reached out and grabbed it. The last remaining dregs of my power wrapped themselves around my organs, protecting me as much as possible as the electricity sizzled through my body. It singed a path through me and then bounced around like a pinball in a machine, damaging everything that wasn't encased in my waning energy.

When the smoke cleared (actually, it didn't clear since I was literally still smoking) Draven was staring at me in absolute shock. I was still standing, and I was holding a lightning bolt. The latter happened more by accident, rather than being a conscious decision..

"Such power is a waste on you," Draven mumbled. "I could have done great things with such a gift."

I snorted. "You would have released more evil upon the

world, and destroyed the humans and the supernaturals."
Leaning closer to him, I whispered: "My heart is not my weakness, it is my strength. You will not kill me today."

I felt myself growing weaker, my body struggling to repair the damage - a challenging task without my magic to assist. This had to be finished. Slowly, I shifted my grip on the lightning rod and then brought it down. Draven still managed to garble out a last few words before the rod pierced him.

"You may not die, but it is too late for your mates."

The rod slammed into his heart and electricity jolted through him, not stopping until the ground beneath his body was charred and black. I fell to my knees, unable to stand any longer. It should have been a moment of elation; Draven was no more, the evil was defeated. Instead, I was frantically searching the clearing for my mates.

For a moment, relief welled up inside me. They were still alive, scattered around the clearing and covered in blood, but alive. Only three or four of Gregor's men still stood, and my heart ached at the losses the wizards had been dealt.

A cruel voice echoed across the clearing to where I was slumped on the ground: "Finish this and then burn their bodies!"

A bloodcurdling scream tore from my raw throat as the soldiers lifted their weapons.

CHAPTER FOURTEEN

Tia

The scent of blood was thick in the smoky haze of the battleground. Casualties of both sides lay broken on the ground, their lives over far too soon— all because of Draven's greed. This battle had been fast yet devastating. Incredibly, my team had managed to take out half of Draven's men, even though they were drastically outnumbered.

Levi and Luke's wolves lunged and snapped at the men who were circled around them. Patches of their beautiful furs were missing or burned. Levi's back leg was twisted and dangled uselessly, and the skin that hung open at Luke's throat revealed the mangled muscles beneath. Could his wolf heal that? Would he be able to speak? Would he be able to join the wolves as they howled their beautiful, melancholy song to the full moon? I furiously blinked back tears as I turned to search out my other mates scattered through the massive clearing.

Mithraheal stood on a pile of corpses. His eyes were feral and blood red; long white fangs dripped blood as he dropped into a fight stance - clearly preparing for a final attack. His enraged hiss sent chills over my body. I knew that few who heard that sound survived to describe it. But even this powerful vampire showed signs of struggling after the vicious battle, his speed barely more than that of a human. Dark blood oozed from lacerations that should have already healed; how had they weakened such a powerful blood driven?

Leo and Damien stood back-to-back, swords drawn and pointed at the men raising their weapons. Damien's clothes hung in shreds, his skin oozed maroon blood. A dagger was embedded in his leg, another in his back at the base of his spine, and a third in his chest mere inches from his heart. It was clear he had protected Leo as best he could during a savage attack. Sobs tore from me at the devotion he had showed me in protecting someone I loved; someone still so new to our family. He was prepared to die fighting beside Leo.

Leo's arm hung limp at his side. An inch wide gash traveled from his scalp to his jawbone, the skin gaping in some sections to show the bone beneath. Blood trickled in a steady stream down his leg from a knife wound in his thigh.

The few wizards from my team that still remained standing were in far worse shape than my guys. As the mercenaries closed in on them, they couldn't even find the strength to lift their weapons or teleport themselves elsewhere.

I wanted to stand to my feet and rush to protect my men. I begged my exhausted power to return and give me a final burst of energy to stop this before more good men were lost. It made no difference. My body was desperately trying to heal the damage I had suffered, but the internal trauma was extensive. They had shattered my ribs with the savage punches I hadn't dodged fast enough. A piece of rib had pierced my right lung leaving me struggling to draw in a breath. My beautiful wing lay broken across the ground beside me, rather than tight against my back like the other, the unnatural angle forcing me to look away.

In choked anguish I watched the mercenaries prepare to slaughter the last of my team, and my mates. I had failed them.

Beasty! Help me! Misery filled my words, my heart breaking. *Please. You are powerful, do something. Save them.*

My dragon stirred, fully awake for the first time in the past few weeks. A tiny bit of hope fluttered in my chest. Surely she could do something.

Tia, it isn't me that has the power, that is all you. I have simply been guiding you as you while you adjusted to the changes. Ideally, your father could have helped guide you into controlling your power; as an ancient dragon he could have helped to siphon off the excess power until you were able to hold it without risking harm to yourself and to others. I have been holding it back as best I could, trickling out what your body could handle. Your power has been building in strength the past few weeks and it has taken most of my concentration to keep you in control. I don't even know if you will be able to handle your full power when it is unleashed. Her voice trembled, and for the first time since the day she started speaking to me, I heard real fear in her tone.

If I die trying to control it, then so be it. I have to try! Hurry!

For a moment it was quiet, and when she spoke again her voice was soft and sad.

Tia, there is one thing that might help you with control. When I open the floodgates of your power, we need to join.

Fine! Whatever! Just open it, now! My voice was shrill; we were running out of time.

Tia, the type of merge I am talking about is a complete one. Permanent. You will gain my memories of my time as a dragon and my skills in battle; this may be just enough to give you the ability to handle the magic and control the energy. But to do that we need to be one, no lags or delays while I try to guide you. This type of merge between the human and dragon natures hasn't been done in thousands of years. It will make you stronger, but it will also mean your beast nature is always right at the surface, regardless of which form you take. There will be no separation between the forms.

Her words were rushed, our time running out. But I suddenly understood her sorrow and the full weight of what she was telling me. I was going to lose Beasty. There would be no more sarcastic quips, no more words of wisdom, no more hilarious and horny commentary. I was going to lose someone I loved no matter what decision I made today. But I would have a chance to save the men who were still alive.

Do. It. I broke into sobs.

For the first time ever I felt her begin to unfurl completely inside me, tension coiled in me. I pushed back my tears and braced myself for what was coming.

Thank you for everything, Beasty. I will miss you more than you could ever know.

Her breath caught and her sorrow nearly overwhelmed me.

I will miss you, too. Now brace yourself, Cupcake!

I knew the instant she released her hold, allowing the full weight of my power to crash into my like a tsunami.

And Tia...

I waited for the last words I would hear from the voice that had been my rock as I floundered my way through this crazy paranormal world - words that I would replay over and over for the rest of my life.

Don't be afraid to collect more sexy mates, and be sure to keep your kitty well fed!

I spluttered in shock and then shrieked as our two halves collided and my body went supernova.

CHAPTER FIFTEEN

Luke

The enemy's finger tightened on the trigger of his gun. These hired guns had honored the ancient supernatural laws regarding battles between supernaturals, fighting with the gifts of their species, and handcrafted blades. But now it seemed that they were less concerned with honor, and more focused on ensuring we were put down quickly. I guess they weren't too pleased at how fast their numbers had diminished.

Something had caused Draven's spell to crumble and the wizards now used their magic to hold us in place. Our few remaining wizards no longer had the strength to fight.

Levi?

Yeah?

I'm proud I got to fight by your side.

Same. We had a good run, bro.

I stared my killer in the eyes, forcing him to meet my gaze as he aimed toward my head. Tia's sudden scream blew through the clearing, crashing into everything in its path. The wizards stumbled, losing their focus for long enough that their spell broke. I lunged forward, jumping on my would-be killer and sinking my long canines into the tender flesh of his neck. Beside me, Levi did the same with another wizard. It was unlikely we could kill them all before they took us down, but that wasn't going to stop me from trying.

As soon as the man beneath me stopped struggling, I stole a quick glance toward my beautiful mate, terrified of what I would see. My mouth dropped open, releasing the man as I stared transfixed at Tia, not believing what I was seeing.

Her body was pure light, and I don't mean like it was glowing around her, I mean she was a freaking ball of blinding light. The light began to blur and bend, the gorgeous shape of her body becoming less clear. My heart ceased beating. What had Draven done to her?

I expected the light to explode and disappear, taking the light out of my life with it. What I didn't expect was for the light to bend and stretch, the shape constantly changing until it stood several stories high. The clearing was completely still; time seemed to have stopped as everyone watched the light sculpt itself into a dragon.

A freaking dragon.

Uh. Do you see a dragon too? Levi's shaking voice interrupted my thoughts as I tried to process my bewilderment.

Yeah. I think it's Tia.

Did we know she turned into a giant lizard like something out of those movies you like to binge watch?

I don't think even she knew that she could shift into a full dragon.

The shape solidified and the light began to fade, leaving a white dragon the size of a house in its wake. It took a step forward, wobbling unsteadily like a newborn filly. I wanted to laugh; it wasn't every day you got to watch a mythological creature learning how to walk. I opened my mouth to bark a laugh, but it came out garbled, excruciating pain tearing through my throat and making me lightheaded.

The dragon's intelligent eyes narrowed on me, the color shifting from sky blue to cobalt as she studied me. Her wings flapped in agitation, sending debris scattering around us. Throwing back her massive head, she opened her mouth and bellowed her outrage into the sky.

That brought the wizards out of their stupor and they rushed to finish off our team so they could figure out what to do with the giant elephant—I mean dragon—in the room.

They moved fast, but it turns out dragons are shockingly fast.

Dude.... are you seeing this? I thought hippos running thirty miles per hour was shocking, but this should be impossible!

Why did he know such random trivia? Tia was going to whoop his butt when she found out he had compared her dragon to a hippo.

One moment she was at the far side of the large clearing, the next minute she was between my brother and myself.

Several mercenaries lay crushed beneath her talons. Her chest expanded, separating the scales slightly to show the skin glowing between them. Crackling echoed inside her and I immediately knew what was coming. She opened her mouth and blue fire poured from her chest.

The world around me was consumed by fire, men screamed and the noxious odor of burned flesh stung my sensitive nose. I waited for the pain, but it never came. Instead, a warm stream of air ruffled my fur. It was like having a giant blow dryer aimed at you.

When the fire died out, most of Draven's soldiers were nothing but a pile of ashes. The ground was no longer the red tones of earth, now it was completely blackened. Wispy curls of smoke added to the strange, almost apocalyptic, scene. Turning toward Levi, I let out another strangled laugh; my eyes stung from the laughter and the pain it caused. His fur stood on end, looking like a lap dog after being groomed. I would have given anything to have a picture of my werewolf twin puffed up like some pampered pooch. I must have looked the same because his chest rumbled in amusement.

We will never speak of this moment, agreed?

I agreed instantly. *Never again.*

I was knocked to the ground as the furious dragon roared and headed toward Damien and Leo. The last three wizards were charging at them, firing wildly. Why didn't the idiots just try to make a run for it? Gregor, Elani and three other wizards attempted to throw up shields to protect themselves, Leo and Damien, but they were struggling just like the rest of us. The outraged dragoness again stepped between her team and the enemy, their shots ricocheting off her glinting scales. She snorted in derision and then slammed her claws down onto the men. The crackling of her fire began again and her chest expanded once more. Her jaw dropped open, allowing the fire to flow freely and incinerate the men.

I watched her liquid blue flames and overwhelming relief rushed through me. It was over. The battle was truly over. Our little circle had survived. Sure, we were not in great shape, but we were alive.

Leo had an arm wrapped around Damien, holding him up as they hobbled toward Tia - a bold move since we had no way of knowing how much of our human mate was aware inside the mammoth beast. Gregor and Elani stepped under the protection of her body, likely attempting to avoid the scorching heat of her fire.

Those intelligent eyes once again searched the clearing, searching out each of us. A stinging pain in my mind was quickly followed by an awareness that I wasn't alone in my head. My wolf was overjoyed; Tia had created a pack bond between her mates, Damien and herself. Being without a pack was hard on a wolf; we craved the connection with our loved ones, something that my wolf had been mourning since leaving Cage's pack. Tia didn't speak in the bond, she simply brushed our minds to reassure herself that we were okay.

Leo's sharp cry brought my focus back to the world around me. Gregor had shoved a strange blade into the underside of Tia's chest. She shrieked in pain, jerking as she attempted to dislodge the blade.

"I am sorry, Dragoness," said Gregor. "It was an honor to

fight by your side, and we thank you for your service in cleansing the world of Draven and his evil. Sadly, it was decided long before we met that you were too powerful to be allowed to live. If you allowed that power to corrupt you after you gained full control of your abilities, nothing on earth would be able to stop you. I hope you will find comfort in knowing that Leo did not know of the decision to end your life. He did not betray you."

Gregor raised his palms and sent a blast of magic toward the blade, the force slamming the blade in deeper. A sound like shattering glass came from Tia's chest. A mournful call ripped from her throat, a sound that sent chills through my body.

Leo threw Damien to the ground, raising his hands and sending a blast of purple magic toward Gregor and his team. The wizards weren't expecting a magical attack, and had no time to defend themselves. His magic went straight through them, and for a moment I thought his magic had been harmless. But then their confused expressions contorted into agony and they disintegrated, until no sign of them remained. Leo dropped to his knees, breathing heavily.

Tia collapsed on the ground, her iridescent scales shimmering like they were made of nacre. Blinding light consumed her body, forcing me to look away. When the light suddenly blinked out, I found my mate's naked human body lying curled on her side, unnaturally still. I strained my supernatural hearing, trying to find the reassuring sound of her heartbeat, all I heard was silence.

Mithraheal's cry of sorrow was cut short, his body going

slack before falling face first on the ground. He didn't get back up.

Everything in me was numb. I didn't think I would ever feel anything again. My mate was dead. She had put an end to Draven's evil soul and those he had infected, only to die a senseless death by those she had fought to protect.

I curled against her body and closed my eyes. I had no intention of ever rising again.

Chapter Sixteen

Leo

This had to be a dream; nothing that had happened in the last fifteen minutes made sense. Damien and I had nearly been killed. Tia had transformed into a dragon, and I don't mean her partial shift; I am talking about an actual fire-breathing, mansion-sized reptile typically featured in action films and children's stories. And oh yeah, I had suddenly gained magic that I used to dissolve Gregor and friends. Using magic to dissolve people into thin air isn't normal, not even for wizards. Purple magic doesn't exist in the wizard community, so this had to be a dream. I would wake up any moment and this nightmare would be over.

Tears blurred my vision as I watched Luke's disfigured body curl against Tia. She couldn't be dead. She had turned into a mythological creature, kicked butts and taken names, saving us all and erasing all signs of Draven and his corrupted men. A puny sword couldn't kill her.

Once I met Tia, I had researched everything I could find about dragons. The ancients had written tales of massive dragons on earth, but they were all believed to be fiction. It was a shock to find out dragon shifters weren't myths and even more astounding to find out she was my fated mate.

I loved the blonde bombshell, regardless of her form, but I had wanted to explore her partial shift since the moment I laid eyes on her. I spent all my free time studying. I loved science and enjoyed understanding how things worked. Dragons were an unknown, and my excitement at the opportunity to learn more about her species knew no bounds. I had looked forward to spending the rest of my life adoring my dragoness and giving careful attention to every inch of both her forms.

Her last sorrowful dragon cry was echoing in my ears. How had it all gone so terribly wrong? How had I not noticed signs of the wizards' planned betrayal? They claimed to be an enlightened race, yet it took Tia's ultimatum to bring about change for the nadir. And now they had acted as judge and jury, deciding to kill her while she was still young enough to be vulnerable... all because, in their "superior" wisdom, they determined she was too great a risk to be allowed to live.

They would pay for their actions today. Tingling spread through me, and I realized that purple energy was crackling across my skin. It reminded me of the plasma balls I played with as a child. I remember watching with fascination as the electricity followed my hand as I moved it around the globe and laughing as it caused my hair to stand on end. This was so not a wizard thing.

I shook my arms, trying to see if I could get the magic to go away. It didn't work. I then tried frantically rubbing my arms, which created more purple magic that swirled up my limbs, giving me little static shocks. I was nearing a full-blown panic when a roar tore through the clouds above. I shaded my eyes as I looked into the sky, trying to spot the source.

A black dragon broke through the clouds, his massive wings blocking the sun for a moment before he tucked them against his body and dove toward the earth.

This had to be a dream. There is no way I had seen not one, but two, dragons in the same day.

He flung out his wings at the last moment, slowing his descent as he landed over Tia, careful not to crush her tiny body with his monstrous one. He roared again, and I didn't have to speak dragon to know it was a scream of rage. It was the same rage that was trying to consume my insides, while the purple magic was taking over my outsides. The dragon pressed his snout against Tia's chest, still careful not to crush her. He released a low keening sound, and again, I didn't need to speak dragon to understand.

He had lost his mate.

At least I had the memories of her laughter, her unconventional ninja moves as she beat up Damien, her sparkling eyes, her righteous indignation as she stood up for the nadir, her sexy body as it moved with mine, and her beautiful, white dragon form covered in iridescent scales breathing blue fire that incinerated evil, while at the same time it gently caressed her mates. He would never experience any of those things. My time with her was far too short, but at least I had been gifted those precious days. His only memory would be this one.

The black dragon's skin begins to waver, his body turning to smoke and shadows. I rubbed my across my eyes as the dragon slowly turned to shadows and then into a man. His skin was darker than Tia's other mates, reminding me of exotic deserts and warm beaches. His sleek black hair was long, nearly reaching his hips. He sat on the ground and drew Tia into his arms. Luke blinked and opened his dull eyes to study the man. He gave a short whine and then closed his eyes again; his will to live had died with Tia.

The man pressed his hands to Tia's chest, covering the area over her heart. He chanted something quietly, shadowy tendrils flowing around her body. The unfamiliar words of the chant were hauntingly beautiful, rolling off his tongue. His chest and hands began to glow red from the inside. It must have been painful because his expression grew strained and sweat beaded his brow.

Slowly, he leaned down and sealed his lips against hers. His eyes were closed and his forehead remained creased with concentration. The glow from his chest flowed out from his mouth and into Tia, the light from his hands doing the same thing. The shadows moved frantically across her motionless body.

He stopped abruptly and pulled his mouth back from hers. His face was exhausted and his hands trembled slightly. Whatever he had just done was clearly not easy. His finger stroked her face softly. I sensed he was waiting for something, but I couldn't understand what it could be.

The unnerving silence was broken by a sharp inhale. My heart missed a bit. Luke's eyes opened warily, and Levi staggered to his feet, bewildered. A soft feminine moan was the next sound to fill the hushed air. It couldn't be.

Damien's joyful exclamation drew my attention away from the dragon shifter. Mithraheal was trying to sit up while Damien crushed him in a hug. If Mithraheal was alive ...

I turned back toward the dragon shifter and stopped breathing. Tia's eyes were open and she was studying the man holding her with wonder. She reached out a shaking hand and pressed it against his cheek. He nuzzled into her hand, breathing out heavily, the action more dragon than man. She pulled his face down to meet hers and slowly captured his lips in a kiss.

It was a kiss that went from sweet to sensual in three seconds flat. She had just died, and now he was kissing her like he was going to devour her. Maybe dragons didn't do gentle? Her chest began to pulse with a blue glow, and his chest mirrored the action with the red glow from his chanted song. Realization dawned on me; this was their dragon fire. Their kiss had turned steamy, and by that I mean that literal steam came out with each exhale.

I wondered if we were supposed to do something, like get her medical attention and nourishment. I looked to the other mates, but Luke and Levi were thumping their tails into the dirt joyfully, clearly reveling in the fact Tia was alive. Mithraheal seemed a bit steadier and seemed content to gather his strength and give Tia time to greet her new mate.

Tia tilted her head to the side, and the stranger kissed and nipped the length of it. Her eyes moved to each of us, catching our gaze for a moment, assessing our injuries. Overwhelming love poured into the mental bond from my mate. Then I noticed her eyes. Her pupils were reptilian slits that somehow managed to simultaneously unnerve me and turn me on. The mate bond was still strong; I could feel her love washing over me, but something was different.

I didn't recognize her voice when she finally spoke; it was husky with a sultry tone that made a man think of long nights in bed.

"Hello, my drakon mate." She purred the words, shifting her head so she could nuzzle his neck. Her movements were odd, as if they were slightly feral and not quite human.

His pupils turned to slits and he responded with a whisper: "Mine."

I really wish the ancients had kept better records, because I don't think anyone knew how dragons claimed each other and mated. Because based on my observations, that was what these two were about to do. I didn't know if we needed to run for cover or remain still, avoiding the attention of the powerful predators currently at the top of the food chain.

I clung to the fact that Tia had recognized us even while in the dragon's arms, and he had not burned us to a crisp when he first arrived. That had to mean something, right?

This was without a doubt the weirdest day of my life.

CHAPTER SEVENTEEN

Ivo

I had a mate.

My mate was a dragoness, which was shocking as females were rare among our kind. But the fact that she was also a royal made this completely impossible. The royals had been slaughtered. That had been a dark day for all dragons, and it was on that day that I had decided I no longer wished to be part of this world full of monsters who walked on two legs.

I was the last of the fire-kissed dragons. While every dragon could breathe fire, only the fire-kissed could command the fire in the sky and on the earth around us. My grief had sent me to the place I knew I would never be found: the heart of a simmering volcano. I sank my body into the molten lava and allowed it to wrap around my body.

Outwardly, a dragon never aged beyond the appearance of a human in their second decade, but even among dragons, I was considered ancient. My age gave me strength and a control over my magic that few others possessed. I had begged my dragon nature to just let me sleep; I'd wished to never wake up. My powers had hummed across my scales before settling inside me, and I had fallen into a long deep sleep, my mind blessedly blank.

Until I heard the mourning death-cry of my mate.

This sound was one that a dragon always feared, and one that a mate could hear no matter how far apart they may be from their soulmate. It was like a flashing beacon. I soared into the air, lava exploding up out of the volcano behind me. I flapped my wings, adjusting to the sensation of flying again after so long.

A large metal bird nearly slammed into my side, forcing me to move out of its path. I didn't have time to ponder this new species, or to hunt it - I had always enjoyed tasting a variety of foods that my fellow dragons refused to touch. My mate needed me. I bellowed my rage and began teleporting to her location as quickly as possible, the distance so great I had to pop in and out several times before reaching her.

As I burst through the clouds, I spotted her crumpled form in the dirt. A gravely injured werewolf curled against her side. I searched for enemies, but only found grieving faces. A second wolf lay on the ground. He too was injured, but not as badly as the first. A blood driven was bent over the fallen form of another blood driven. I inhaled deeply. The motionless man was a child compared to my age, but for the rest of the supernaturals he was considered old and powerful. Interesting.

A flash of purple caught my attention and I watched a newborn warlock frantically trying to shake off his powers. Yet another rarity among supernaturals. Here I was seeing a warlock being "born". His power was unfurling, exploring its vessel and making adjustments as needed. What type of world had I awakened to? A warlock was coming into his powers, clearly having no idea what was happening and trying to rid himself of it. Warlocks were secretive about this experience, and few outsiders had ever been allowed to observe. I had been close friends with a great warlock many centuries past, and our friendship had granted me access to observe this twice. Someone was going to need to guide this young man.

I inhaled deeply, once more searching for the scent of enemies, but the scent was that of smoke and ash. The ashes of wizards.

I bellowed and dove for the ground. Now that I had accessed the situation and made sure there were no active threats, I could focus on my mate.

I covered her with my body, carefully touching my nose to her chest. My beautiful mate, so perfectly still. I merged my mind with hers and searched for the fatal injury. My heart ceased to beat when I found it.

This little female carried the dragon heart: a crystal heart that was now shattered in her chest. What had the fates been doing? Being a dragon was a challenge; the beast was exceedingly intelligent, but it's were instincts still that of an animal. However, by comparison, our natures were that of a house cat, while a royal dragon was like a tiger. It took much longer for them to gain control, and at times, some young royals had even allowed themselves to be caged until they gained control. Their instincts were too strong.

My mate was a royal dragoness carrying the weight of the dragon heart—more power than a dragon shifter had been asked to carry since the beginning of our species. Pride swelled in my chest; my mate was stronger than the world knew to be controlling such power. She should have been in an exhausted heap from the constant strain. Yet the sweet scent of dragon fire lingered in the ash around me, a sign she had been in the midst of this battle. I would have given a wing to have witnessed that glorious sight.

I knew what had to be done. I released my hold on the dragon's form, allowing the smoke and shadows to twist and manipulate until I was in my human body. I wasted no time gathering her into my arms, my actions feeling stiff and awkward as I tried to adjust to the form I barely remembered.

I chanted the song of dragon mates, the one that called the soul to stay for the love of their mate. The fire in my chest smoldered, while embers crackled up my throat as I chanted. There was no guarantee that what I planned to attempt would work, but there was no other alternative. My shadows swept through her, gathering the tiny crystal pieces and fitting them back in place.

The warmth in my hands began to heat her chest as I worked with my energy to hold the crystal pieces. Then, I pressed my lips to hers. I wanted to savor the first taste of her lips, but I had to remain focused as I finished my task. I poured my fire into her, the heat intense as I worked with my element to meld together what had been destroyed. When the pieces were once again whole, albeit with delicate lines running between them, I sat back. I was exhausted.

The silence around me was deafening, which made her first inhale that much more shocking. Her chest jerked as she sucked in another breath and moaned. I heard the dead vampire as he awoke behind me, the bits of this puzzle starting to take shape. I inhaled again, tasting the air with my magic. Other than the younger blood driven male, these men were her circle; they had been claimed. The dragoness had made unusual choices. I became more intrigued each moment I spent around her.

Her soft trembling hand brushed against my cheek, stirring the beast who shoved forward in my mind to study her, rubbing against her hand. The delicious scent of our mate called to us both. I had never had a fated mate, and I had chosen not to claim someone who wasn't my soulmate. The need that flooded my body stole my breath, my control slipping for the first time in centuries. Before I could regain it, the female had my lips against hers. My concentration was lost, and the beast took advantage and lunged through the opening. I was an ancient; losing control of my dragon was unheard of, but my exhaustion combined with the call toward my mate was proving more than I could handle.

I could not remember when I had last kissed a woman. One thousand years ago, maybe two? Time blurred when you had lived as long as I had walked the earth. But without a doubt, I had never experienced a kiss like this one. I could live for ten thousand more years and I would never forget the sensations that rocked my body as her mouth moved against mine.

I was still dividing my attention between soaking in my mate's love and my internal struggle with my dragon. That battle was lost the instant I felt the heat from her chest, the blue of her fire calling the crimson fire in me. Sharing fire was the prelude to bonding in our species.

When I had poured my fire into her to mend her heart, it had started a countdown inside my head. I had known that attempting to resist that feral instinct was going to be more challenging than anything I had dealt with in my lifetime. I hadn't counted on how fatigued I was going to be, or that my breathtaking mate was going to cause me such distraction. I felt like a dragon lad who hadn't yet learned to control his instincts or urges... something I hadn't been in a very long time.

She tilted her head to the side, giving me access to her throat. The gesture was that of trust and submission. Blood began pumping harder in my body, the sound pounding in my ears and rushing to forgotten parts of my human anatomy.

"Hello, my drakon mate." She purred into my neck, the vibration pouring fuel onto my already raging fire.

"Mine." The word rumbled from my chest. I yanked her tighter against me and captured her lips again. Our kiss became heavy with desire, our ragged breathing loud in the clearing around us.

She worries.

My dragon spoke, his words stilted as he tried out human

language. My brain was slow as it tried to think through the haze of lust. He never spoke. We communicated through the magic and emotion, not words.

The injured men distract her. She wants them whole. Fix them.

Her mates. Our circle. Yes, I couldn't let them die or remain in pain. And I really wanted my mate's attention.

Agreed. The beast purred.

Not letting the dragoness move off my lap, I reached my hand out and rested it on the most injured mate. He injuries were too severe for his wolf to heal, and even with my magic I wasn't sure his throat would ever be the same. I poured magic into him. My mate stirred on my lap and I groaned at the overwhelming pleasure. The second wolf had moved closer to watch me warily while I healed the first. When I'd done all I could do, I rested my hand on the second wolf and healed his wounds as well.

Each healing added to my fatigue, continuing to weaken my control. The strange warlock locked eyes with me; his were filled with curiosity and anxiety. Why was he anxious?

The child loves dragons. He wants to see how we breed. My beast chuffed in what I took as laughter. *He grows concerned we might eat him.*

I was both confused and amused by the warlock. It would be enjoyable to speak with him. But not now. Right now, I needed to hurry. I couldn't even allow myself time to wonder what had made my beast start speaking. The warlock's playful magic had already healed his injuries so I turned to the blood driven men.

Unwilling to let the female go, I stood with her in my arms. Her legs wrapped around my waist and her arms curved around my neck. I walked toward the vampires, trying to ignore the parts of my body that poked her rounded bottom as I moved. It had not gone unnoticed by her, and a mewling came from her hot wet mouth that was licking and sucking my neck. I almost tripped when her teeth nipped my neck. I swallowed past the desire clogging my throat. Were her fangs already out? Sun and moon! That wasn't supposed to happen until we had almost fully claimed each other. Bonding between dragons was rough, and things like fangs could lead to a lot of damage.

My dragon purred at the thought.

I rested my hand against the shoulder of the blood driven that was clearly a part of our family, but not a bonded mate. He had already partially healed himself, so my energy finished quickly with him.

I sat next to the old vampire, settling my mate on my lap and biting back a moan as she wiggled to make herself comfortable. My organ of penetration throbbed as it pressed firmly along her most sensitive skin. I rested my hand on the vampire's arm and allowed the energy to flow. He had few injuries so it did not take long to heal him, but he was dangerously depleted of blood.

"Drink." My word was an order not a request. It was an honor to be offered blood from a dragon, and it was not something we allowed often, outside of our mate. Dragons didn't need to drink blood to live, but it was often shared as part of bonding. The vampire hesitated for a moment before his instincts took over. His fangs sunk into my arm. I no longer had enough energy to leash my dragon, a dragon intent on making her his. I hoped that my mate would understand when this day was over.

Please don't hurt her, I pleaded.

The vampire lifted his head, eyes blood red as he watched me. One predator accessing another. He tilted his head in a silent thank you. My little dragoness shifted in my lap, leaning until she was able to kiss her blood driven mate. His kiss was gentle, surprising me as vampires were not known for having particularly kind natures. She licked a bit of my blood from the corner of his mouth and then turned back to me.

Her pupils flashed from human to dragon so quickly I thought I might have imagined it. "Thank you, dragon," she whispered.

Beautiful wings unfurled from her back. She stretched languidly on my lap like a cat, cerulean eyes sparkling, and then began to beat her wings. Ash and burned earth whirled around us like a dust storm from my home country. This was not a dragon behavior I was familiar with. What was she doing?

The scent of fire and battle, tears and blood, death and victory, hit me with the force of a falling star. My dragon purred and lunged for our mate, primal instinct overruling all other thoughts.

I hoped this little wildcat understood exactly what she had just done.

CHAPTER EIGHTEEN

Ivo

M y body was still that of a human, but my nature was now fully dragon. The beast in me no longer spoke with words; it wasn't needed now that my facade of humanity had crumbled.

The dragoness had stirred the ground, forcing my lungs to fill with the scent. I hadn't experienced this before, but now I understood the old tales. Dragons preferred their solitude in the mountains, avoiding humans and their messy affairs until it threatened the peace between species. Battles stirred the cold blood of our kind, setting it ablaze as we battled. Once the fight was over, this white hot intensity needed to be released. She had stirred the ground to incite my dragon, to show him her prowess. Now she sat preening on my lap, waiting for me to make the first move, to claim her where she had fought, died, and survived. For a human, this would be considered freakish, but this was a dragon's nature. A reminder we were not human. I hoped her other mates weren't squeamish.

I let my wings unfurl, beating with hers for a moment before I leaped up and into the air. Her legs wrapped around my waist and her wings tucked tight against her back. The wind snatched away her laughter and I soaked in the beauty of this perfect moment in time. Bursting through the clouds, I tossed her above me, before tucking my own wings and beginning to freefall at a dizzying rate toward the ground.

I kept myself turned to the sky and watched as she spun and dove toward me. She landed lightly on my chest, again tucking her wings as she leaned forward, planting soft kisses on my shoulder. She sat on my chest, casually swinging her leg completely unfazed as we both plummeted to earth. A lilting laugh burst from her lips and she leaned down again, but instead of a kiss, she sank her tiny fangs into me.

I let out a startled laugh, my dragon immensely pleased with his mate. I flipped us over and unfurled my wings, slowing our descent. Wrapping my wings around her I flipped again and allowed my body to slam into the ground. As I moved my wings, the billowing cloud of blackened earth and ash we had created fell around us. The apocalyptic beauty of the scene heated the fire in my chest and sent it surging through my body.

My mate's body was stretched against mine, skin to skin, heat radiating between our naked forms. Rolling her under me, I claimed her lips with a hunger, my tongue demanding entrance. The female rushed, playfulness dancing in her eyes. Instinct surged. My mate would not refuse me, just as I would not refuse her. I slid my hand up her hip, teasing my way across her ribs before squeezing her breast. This elicited a moan and her mouth opened involuntarily, granting me access.

Her tongue danced with mine, her lips sweeter than anything I had tasted in my long life. I continued to knead her breast, her pink peak growing hard from my attention. Her nails lengthened and I felt them scrape against my back. I rumbled encouragement and felt her nails sink a little deeper, tiny pricks of pain that stoked the fire building within me.

Reluctantly, I leaned away from her mouth, nibbling my way down her squirming body. I growled a warning for her to hold still, and she growled back. My own fangs dropped in response to her challenge, and my playful nibble turned to a bite as I sunk my teeth into her thigh. I snarled, and felt it vibrate through her body. She stilled instantly, obeying my order.

I released her thigh, inhaling a deep breath that brought with it the honeyed aroma of my mate's arousal. There were no more slow kisses down her body. I went straight for the nectar of her desire. I delved my tongue deep inside her tight channel. My fingers sank into her lush bottom lifting her slightly to give me better access.

Her eyes fluttered and she moaned. I greedily licked up her cream, her body vibrating from my purrs. My human tongue couldn't reach everywhere I wanted to lick, and annoyance flashed through me. I had not used this form for pleasure in such a long time, and I had forgotten its limitations, many of which were not issues in my other forms. My dragon quickly resolved this issue by partially shifting my tongue, and I eagerly thrust it in deeper, seeking the treat that had eluded me previously. The female cried out in pleasure as my long forked tongue stroked, its rough surface creating friction that had the female's body creating more of the addicting nectar.

My mate struggled to get away, the sensations more than she could handle. This was unacceptable. Huffing a warning, I tightened my grip and pried her legs apart. She purred, clearly turned on by the play of dominance between dragons. I thrust my tongue faster and deeper, allowing the ends to swirl inside her. The beautiful noises coming from her were driving me out of my mind. My fire rose unbidden up my throat and poured into her. She couldn't be harmed by the fire of her mate, but the sudden flowing warmth combined with my tongue was more than she could handle. She came undone, her scream inciting my dragon as he held her body and felt the aftershocks of her pleasure.

I bellowed, warning her of what was to come. She needed no warning; her eyes met mine, the lust in their depths assuring me she wanted this as much as I did. My mate launched herself at me. I held her to my chest, rubbing my body against hers, marking her skin with my scent. Her fangs sunk into the skin above my heart, the twinge of pain sending blood rushing into my already painful manhood. Grabbing her hips, I began to rock her back and forth across my throbbing organ.

Her mouth moved again, frantically alternating between

licking and biting. The dragoness sank her fangs deep in my neck and began sucking, pulling my life blood into herself. I nearly lost my seed from the sensuality of it.

I lifted her hips and slammed inside her. She gasped in surprise, her fangs coming free from my neck. I lifted her and brought her back down, hard. My vision blurred. Perhaps not everything about this male form was terrible; the sensations coursing through my body were vastly different than what I had felt when seeking release with females centuries ago.

I didn't need to lift her hips a third time, she lifted herself and came down hard. She gyrated, creating the maximum amount of pleasure for both of us as my stiff organ rubbed against her tight walls.

It wasn't enough. More.

I roared and yanked her off my lap. I positioned her in front of me on all fours and kneeled behind her. With a single thrust I penetrated her from behind. Arching her back, she pressed her bottom back into me. My claws sank into her hips, eliciting a purr from the little dragon.

Mine. Mine. Mine. The most primal urge of a dragon surged within me, the need to claim my soulmate. I increased my speed, pushing us toward the bonding. Releasing her hips, I took hold of the top of her wings, rhythmically rubbing my thumbs along the skin just under the bones. This was an erogenous spot for dragons, and she climaxed instantly, her body becoming boneless.

Using her wings to bring her body upright, I sank my fangs into her neck and held her still as my dragon again shifted my body, lengthening my manhood as I buried myself deep in her one last time. A dragon only did this with a female he was claiming as his own. Instinct caused the shift of our manhood to ensure our seed was released deep in our mate. Her delicate neck would bear the marks left by my fangs, forever marking her as mine. My mate jerked and screamed as she found her release a third time. This time I joined her, and pleasure consumed me. It stole all thoughts, except the incredible heat of my mate's body around me. I pressed my hand against her mouth and she bit down hard, leaving her own claiming mark. A mark that I was proud to have.

I opened my mouth and breathed crimson fire into the sky. My beautiful mate lifted her head and released a stream of blue fire that blended into mine until our fire turned a deep violet.

Contentment washed over me and I turned her in my arms, the overpowering instincts of my beast sated... for the moment. I pressed my forehead against hers as the brush of the bond formed between our minds.

My heart stopped beating as I tried to understand the emotions in the bond. I should feel both my mate and her beast. But her thoughts were jumbled and were more dragon than human. Apparently, it was taking her longer to come out of the mating lust.

My dragon spoke up, his words laced with shock.

There is no beast, nor human. She is dragon.

Impossible.

Chapter Nineteen
Mithraheal

"**I**s it just me, or is this unusual?" I asked, not really expecting an answer. The twins, Leo, and I all sat huddled together, trying to wrap our minds around the strange turn this day had taken. Levi had shifted back to his human form, while Luke remained in wolf form. Damien had teleported out of here as soon as things heated up between the dragons. He wanted to ensure our kingdom was safe and not under attack. The rest of us stayed because we just couldn't bear being away from Tia, or each other, while our emotions were so raw.

"Which part?" Levi asked. "Do you mean Draven's knowledge of our attack and his counterattack, the wizards' betrayal, Leo's increased weirdness, Tia's shift into a creature of legend that destroyed our enemies like it was child's play, your death when she died, her new mate who happens to be another horrifyingly massive dragon which isn't supposed to exist, his kiss bringing Tia back to life like a ridiculous fairy-tale, and then you coming back to life?"

Levi's tone was full of sarcasm. I started to respond, only to be cut off when he started again. "Or were you referring to the part where he healed everyone, gave you blood, and then started breeding with our little mate like they were wild animals? In the ashes of the battle?" His voice became higher and higher as he spoke. Panic.

"I think it must be some type of dragon ritual." Leo spoke absently, his eyes focused on everything Tia and the male were doing. "It's clear they're more dragon than human right now. Tia tried to spend time with each of us, wanting to ensure we wished to be claimed. She would've done the same with this new mate, had her human form been in control. I think battle must incite their beasts. This is fascinating."

He was an odd guy. Sure, we all sported a hard-on right now; we were guys and our little mate was hot. But while the wolves and I had watched, slightly freaked out, Leo had watched like he was on a safari, witnessing the breeding behavior of the wildlife. I bet he would have taken notes if he had access to a notebook.

An ancient curse word I hadn't thought I would hear again rang across the clearing. We all jerked our gazes back to Tia and the stranger. He was in a full blown panic as he met our eyes.

"We need to go. Now!" he cried. "Do you have a safe

place? A place that is not so important to you, in case it is destroyed?"

What was it with dragons and their penchant for demolishing my homes? I snorted and thought about how many homes Tia was likely to destroy in our lifetime, the thought amusing me.

"Nevermind! Lock hands!" The stranger grabbed Tia, her legs automatically wrapping around his waist, and then he firmly clasped my arm. We had obeyed his order, Levi sinking his hands into Luke's wolf coat to complete the chain. The familiar sensation of teleporting rushed over me and when our impromptu journey was complete, we stood in the middle of a large stone cavern.

"This is one of my cave homes," the stranger explained. "There are many rooms within this mountain, and an underground lake for bathing. I'm not sure how much society has changed since I last walked the earth, it's likely things have changed, but it will suffice."

"I am Mithraheal; I wanted to welcome you to our circle," I said, stepping forward. "Thank you for your assistance today." I held my arm out in greeting and he grasped it firmly.

"I am Ivo. There is no cause for you to thank me. We are family."

"Why are we here, Ivo?" I asked.

"Our mate, she is dragon."

Leo was peering around the cave in wonderment, the twins were both in wolf form and sniffing around the cavern, but at Ivo's words they all met my eyes behind his back. Their expressions clearly showed that they doubted his sanity.

"You didn't realize that until after you mated?" I asked him hesitantly.

Now he looked at me as though he doubted my sanity. "Of course I knew she was a dragon shifter," Ivo replied. "You misunderstand my meaning. She is dragon; there is no distinction between beast and human."

All our gazes swung to where Tia was stretched out, purring on the piles of furs. I walked to her and slowly laid down next to her. Her eyelids fluttered open, revealing cerulean blue eyes, the pupils thin slits as she observed me.

"Tia, my love. I thought I'd lost you today." My voice shook, the day's emotions catching up with me.

"I love you, mate." It was my mate's voice, but also not.

I reached out to touch her mind in the bond, and my stomach sank. Where was Tia? Where was Beasty?

Grief slammed into me like a freight train from the mind link. Her grief.

Darling, what happened?

For a moment, her eyes flashed between the human and dragon, her voice barely more than a whisper. "I couldn't lose you all."

Her face wrinkled in concentration, eyes flashing back and forth.

"This shouldn't be possible," said Ivo. He had seated himself on the furs, reaching out a hand to stroke her thigh. "Being a dragon shifter means a life of constantly trying to control your nature: the beast. We dragons are powerful, with many gifts and abilities, but it comes at a great cost."

The male dragon went on to explain the difficulties of

controlling the dragon instincts, and how young dragons are assisted by ancient dragons who siphon off their power. He also explained that Tia should not have shown the level of control she had done these past months, that she should have been curled up in bed from the constant internal battle, not training and planning an attack.

We told him how she struggled to not claim Leo immediately, and how she had tried to delay all the claimings until we managed to convince her we wanted it. His face was slack in shock.

"She resisted the bond? The instinct is always too strong for an ancient dragon to resist. Without having another dragon to assist her in controlling her power, she would've needed to claim several mates quickly to help her release that excess energy."

"She did resist. It was hard on her, but she wanted to do things right," I said. "Tia is still struggling to let go of the human way of thinking. We would've claimed her the moment we laid eyes on her if it had been our choice."

"I don't think that will be an issue now," Ivo said. "I don't understand how it happened, but she merged completely with her beast. This cannot be undone. Now our little mate will need to fight her dragon instincts and learn control."

"Are you saying we are essentially living with a full dragon at this moment?" Leo chimed in.

"It is a little more complicated than that, but the short answer is, yes. She has her human intellect, but she also has the dragon's nature... and right now, those instincts are going to rule until her body adjusts to the changes and she can pull it back."

"Cool!" Leo seemed excited, clearly not grasping the severity of the situation.

"Warlock, I think you haven't been listening," said Ivo. He must have been thinking the same thing as I.

"Yes, I heard everything," Leo replied. "You've made it very clear that this shouldn't be possible, even for a dragon shifter. Once again, Tia has shown herself to be full of surprises. She will gain control, she's awesome like that. But right now, I get to experience having a complete dragoness as a mate, something that, according to you, should be impossible. This is a once-in-a-lifetime opportunity and I'm going to enjoy every minute of it!"

Leo turned from our stunned faces back to Tia, who was watching us all with amusement.

"I am the luckiest guy in the world!" he said with a beaming smile. "You were incredible during the battle today, regardless of which form you fought in. I am so proud of you, gorgeous!"

Levi and Luke had shifted and moved onto the pile of furs as well.

"Leo is correct," added Levi. "Being your mate is an honor; it's a blessing to have more time with you."

Tia rose to her knees and crawled toward the men, clearly pleased with their words.

Ivo groaned and rubbed his face.

Seer on a staff! These men have no clue! They are encouraging her wild instincts.

His words were spoken directly in my mind, his tone exasperated.

I watched her lips move lower and lower down Leo's chest, while her hands began sliding up the twins' thighs... and I started to think they might be onto something.

There is no need to rush to join in. Her body is going to need food and sleep to adjust to the changes happening inside. She will need the mating to release the excess energy and power that will build up. It is a shame there are only five of us; a powerful dragoness would have at least ten men, and that's for a female that is not fully merged.

It may kill us, but we would die happy.

CHAPTER TWENTY

Luke

"Tia, honey, calm down." My brother's tone was soothing, but his word choice was idiotic. The other guys groaned and I pinched the bridge of my nose.

None of us were even sure what had set her on edge, but it was stressful watching her battle for internal control. Levi's words were like a match tossed on gasoline. Light imploded around us, the outline of her body bending until the house-sized pearl dragon stood in front of us. She roared and her wings fluttered behind her, taking out half the cave wall. Mithraheal flashed around the falling debris, grabbing each of us and hauling everyone outside.

Tia followed, her gorgeous white scales glinted in bright sunshine. The effect reminded me of opals, a rainbow of pastel colors shimmering as she moved. Her eyes tracked Levi; apparently, she still had a bone to pick with him. She leaned down and bellowed in his face, her warm fire engulfing him. When the fire died out, he was unharmed, but his hair had been blown back and stood on end.

She huffed out a startled breath and swung her head around to see who had touched her. Leo, either unnaturally brave or completely stupid, was stroking the scales on her tail.

"These are amazing, Tia!" he said, beaming. "I wonder what they're made of! It feels almost like a fingernail, but stronger. I bet there are few things that could penetrate this armor. Is it heavy?"

He was babbling on like a kid in a candy store. He was petting an out of control dragoness and talking to her as though she would answer him. We all adored our mate, but over the past week it had been a challenge not to lose sight of the fact that she was still the woman we loved, and not just a young dragon that was being controlled by instinct. Ivo had told us that this could go on for months or even years; it all depended on her strength and how quickly she gained control. Yet, Leo talked to her constantly as though she hadn't been changed in the battle. It was a good reminder for all of us.

Tia garbled a sound deep in her throat. She huffed and tried again.

"They are light." The words were spoken slowly.

Leo squealed, yes, he freaking squealed. "You can speak in this form? How? I learn something new about dragons every day!" he cried.

"Fascinating. That is yet another skill which takes years to master, and yet she accomplished it only days after her first full shift," said Ivo, as he strode toward her, grinning broadly. "Tia, I have never heard of a dragon with your color. You are a stunning dragoness! Would you like to fly?"

Her eyes swirled excitedly and she did a cute little bunny hop that shook the ground beneath our feet.

"Can I come? Please, Tia?" asked Leo.

"Yes." The word was garbled, but clearer than before.

"Learning to fly is challenging, it would be safer for him to remain here," said Ivo. His voice was firm.

"I would never harm him! He is mine!" Tia snatched Leo in her taloned claw, careful not to scratch or squish him. She used her large, muscled thighs to launch herself in the air.

Mithraheal's laughter rang out. "If this is what strong-willed teenagers are like, I am not sure I would survive fatherhood," he said with a laugh.

Ivo shifted into his black dragon in the blink of an eye, each scale tipped in glowing reds and golds. He bellowed his frustration as he followed Tia into the sky. The powerful beats of his wings stirred the dust and forced us to shield our eyes.

Leo's shouts floated down to us on the ground.

"Did he just say yeehaw?" Levi barked out a laugh.

Mithraheal was all logic and weighed down with responsibilities. My brother and I were loyal, but always on guard. Ivo was stuffed full of ancient wisdom, but his beast was always just under the surface. Our group needed Leo. His unbridled curiosity and open nature drew us all closer. The road we were traveling had been challenging, and we lost sight of our joy sometimes from the stress of it, but Leo would lighten everything up with his silliness. We made for such an odd circle, but I wouldn't have changed it for the world.

We watched as Tia and Ivo swirled and danced through the clouds, their dragons creating a beautiful contrast of light and dark. Occasionally we would see Leo fly through the air as Tia tossed him playfully, rushing to catch him as he laughed. Once she let him free fall toward the ground. He made no effort to slow his descent and his face showed no concern that she wouldn't get to him on time. They were both crazy.

The sun was setting as the two large dragons landed gracefully. Leo slid down Tia's wing, obviously planning to make a cool dismount, but as he went to stand, he tripped and landed on his butt. Tia chortled a laugh and even Ivo shook his massive head in amusement.

The dragons shifted back to their human forms, and we moved inside to eat the deer that had been roasting over a fire. Ivo's cave didn't have modern amenities like a kitchen, so we had been managing as best we could using a fire pit. I had some mean skills with a grill, and I'd quickly ended up being in charge of all our meals.

"I need to go to the castle to handle some business," said Mithraheal. "I'll be back in the morning." He nodded goodbye, kissed Tia gently on the lips, and then teleported himself away.

I stretched out on the furs, stuffed full and ready to sleep. My eyes closed and I started drifting off immediately. I jerked when I felt someone jostle my body. I cracked open one eye and watched as Tia settled herself along the length of my side.

I turned my head and pressed a kiss to her nose. I closed my eyes and began to doze again, enjoying the feel of my mate snuggled against me.

"Luke." Her soft voice had me opening my eyes again.

I looked at her with a raised brow, only then realizing that her pupils were round as she studied my face. Hope fluttered in my heart. Was she back in control?

"I never hear you speak, not since the battle," she said. "Are you able to speak?" There was a quiver in her voice, a gentleness that I had missed.

I hesitated. Finally, I shook my head.

"Oh, Luke!" She clutched me tightly as she began to sob. I shifted her so she was laying on top of my chest. Her tears soaked my chest as she continued to cry.

I felt for the mental bond in an attempt to speak with her telepathically. I hadn't been able to connect with her since she merged with Beasty. This time, however, I felt her mind and the connection glowed.

Darling, I've missed you.

Her sobs turned to hiccups. "I am sorry I failed you."

Don't let me hear you say that again! You did not fail me. You were magnificent! We were set up, the odds were terrible and we should all be dead right now. Are you able to tell me what happened that day?

She nodded against my chest and then slowly told the full story; how she had defeated Draven, and how terrified she was when she realized that she wasn't going to be able to save us. My eyes watered as she explained what Beasty had been trying to do for her, and then how they had merged, even though they didn't know if it would work. She was still grieving for her best friend, and my heart throbbed painfully for her.

You were both so brave.

"I'm not. I'd never been so scared. And then, once we merged, the power was so overwhelming. It burned like someone had poured acid inside me. My insides melted and reformed. It hurt worse than catching the lightning bolt—"

You did what?

"I grabbed the lightning that Draven called down to strike me."

Nothing had been normal since the day I had met my fiery little mate, but I was still dumbstruck at the visual of her snatching lightning like it was no biggie. And she thought she was weak? Ivo had taught us enough over the past week for us to realize that, while she was still young and just coming into her true power, she was going to bring the world to its knees when she learned to master her abilities. I was thrilled to get a front row seat to watch her transformation.

You take my breath away.

She huffed, her fingertips drawing invisible lines on my skin. "I'm tired, Luke." She sighed. "I have to fight to control my instincts every minute I'm awake. My instincts are so strong, and combined with the frantic energy of my power, it makes everything inside me volatile. I want to make love to you, not be driven to mate you by my instincts."

You seem to be in control now.

"I don't know for how long." She sighed again, her warm breath tickling across my chest.

Ivo sat at the foot of the furs, shifting Tia's legs so that her feet lay in his lap. "You have to learn to leash the dragon instincts," he said. "You must be stronger."

She was so still I thought she must have fallen asleep. But then she spoke. "I'm not sure. I think I have to learn to work with these instincts, not try to force them into a box. This is me, not a separate entity. When I merged with Beasty, I was gained her memories from her life long ago, as well as the abilities she possessed and the knowledge of how to use them. That is the only reason my full, unleashed power didn't destroy me. She is gone, but even now, her knowledge is guiding me as I learn how to handle my energy."

"I have never personally known a dragon shifter who merged fully with their beast, so perhaps I am incorrect regarding the best way to learn control," admitted Ivo. He was thoughtful, mulling over her words, his hands massaging Tia's feet.

Levi crawled onto the bed and took Tia's hand. Her smile was sleepy; her eyes began to droop. I was so proud; this was the first real conversation we had shared with Tia since the battle, and it had happened much sooner than Ivo had estimated. She was adapting and changing, whilst taking it all in stride, just like she did with everything else that came her way.

I slept like a rock that night.

Chapter Twenty-One

Tia

I woke slowly, blinking the sleep from my eyes. I was in one of my favorite places, smooshed between the twins. I felt the energy surge up within me, my instincts telling me I needed to be like an archaeologist and start searching for large bones!

My brain was clearly thinking too loud in the bond, because the twins choked, Ivo chuckled, and Leo burst into hysterical laughter.

Shnookerdookies! Had Beasty merged her dirty mind with mine too? I didn't know if that made me want to laugh or cry.

My cheeks burned with embarrassment. Thankfully, the embarrassment helped to ease my horny side. But it was quickly followed by the next rush of instinctual needs... food. I wanted lots and *lots* of food. My stomach growled and I crawled over Luke, scrambling to find some leftover jerky and stuffing it in my cheeks like a hamster. What? I managed to control one of the overpowering urges this morning, there was no way I could resist two. Baby steps.

Ivo reached to take some jerky for himself, and I growled. I would have liked to blame my new psychotic instincts, but the truth was I had always been protective of my food, dragon or not.

He playfully growled back before snatching a piece right out of my hand and popping it in his mouth. Oh no he didn't!

I sprang to my feet and launched myself on the large man's back. I fisted my hand in his long hair and yanked his head to the side. My gums tingled as my fangs dropped and I sunk them into his neck.

"You ate my food, so now I will just eat you instead!" I cried.

I would've sounded a lot more threatening if my words hadn't been muffled against his skin.

Mithraheal chose that moment to teleport himself into the room. He looked to my mates still lounging on the bed. "Have things escalated to the point that she's attacking her mates now?" he asked. "Why aren't you guys trying to calm her?"

Ivo began laughing so hard that I was nearly dislodged, and I scrambled like a monkey to cling on tighter.

"Our little mate is feeling a bit more focused this morning." Ivo snorted a laugh. "Why did no one warn me of her murderous tendencies regarding food? Has she not been fed enough?"

I snorted in amusement. He made me sound like a misbe-having pet. The twins and Leo shook with laughter, falling into a heap and wiping at their eyes. Mithraheal relaxed, but he still watched me warily. You jump a man's bones eight times a day for a week, and apparently it scares them. I snick-ered and pulled my fangs free.

I teleported myself into Mithraheal's arms, my hands snaked around his neck and my legs wrapped around his tapered waist. Without giving him time to react, I sank my fangs into his neck. So much tastier than that dried jerky. I pulled my fangs out after a few minutes, licking the two dots of blood from his neck.

Pushing myself up, I pressed my lips against his, gently.

"My love, is that really you?" He breathed against my mouth.

"It was always me, it's just a more impulsive version of me."

"That has to be the understatement of the year," he replied. His arms wrapped around me, holding me in a tight embrace.

"I would love to continue this, but we have a problem that needs our attention." Mithraheal sighed, his words heavy.

I slid off his body and stood, my good spirits dampened immediately. "What happened?"

Reaching into his perfectly tailored coat pocket, he pulled out a gold envelop with a red wax seal. "This arrived at the castle today. It's an invitation to the Harmony Ball."

I had no idea why a party invite was such a big deal, but

all around me, my mates sucked in a harsh breath and grew tense.

"Why do you guys look so worried about a party?" I asked. "If you guys hate parties, we can just not go, right?"

"No one is allowed to refuse an invite to the Harmony Ball," Mithraheal said solemnly. "This ball was first held centuries ago during a time of peace. All leaders and individuals of importance from all species are required to attend each year. It symbolizes our coming together in peace and harmony. Not attending is considered no less than a sign of war. Rumors about you have begun circulating and people are both curious and fearful. Your presence will help to reassure people that you want peace."

"Okay, so we can't get out of it." I sighed. "How long until the ball?"

"Four days." Mithraheal looked positively green, while the rest of my mates stood frozen in horror.

That wasn't much time. My panic began to surge and with it my dragon instincts. My eyes flickered back and forth as I tried to find balance between my natures. It was a losing battle, and my anxiety made my fight or flight instinct kick in.

Mithraheal stepped forward and wrapped his arms around me. "Shhh, it will be okay. Damien lives for parties! He will *love* making all the arrangements for us, and we'll all be there at your side. You won't be alone. My love, breathe."

My breathing calmed, but I was too far gone. Levi scooped me up and headed for the bed. "Mithraheal, you should strip quickly and join us," he said. "Time to help our dragoness release some of this chaotic energy."

Mithraheal was naked on the bed before Levi had even lowered me onto it. I gave in, letting myself enjoying the tender caresses of my mates and the feeling of their bodies moving against mine. Their kisses made me forget my panic, and I let myself enjoy this time with my circle.

AROUND NOON, THE MEN DECIDED THAT I WAS AS IN AN okay state of control, and we teleported ourselves to the castle. We did it secretly, all of us still worried that people might try to swarm us to get a peek, and accidentally get hurt if I went full dragon and started destroying things. What if my instincts took over at the ball?

"Stop thinking, little one," said Ivo. "We are working on a possible solution to help make it easier for you during the ball."

His words calmed the bats slamming into the sides of my stomach. No sweet fluttering butterflies for this girl.

"There's my BFF!" Damien's voice made me wince; it seemed far too loud for this secret visit. He twirled me in his arms and kissed my cheek with a loud pop. He didn't even let me catch my breath before he started dragging me toward a rack of dresses.

"Come on! I have some pieces from the top designers in our kingdom," he said with glee. "I always wanted a sister I could dress up! This is going to be *so* much fun!" He was stacking gown after gown in my arms, the rising pile of fluffy fabrics making it hard to see him. I felt his hands guide me behind a folding screen to start changing. I really wished he had to breathe, that way he would at least stop to take a breath.

I was buttoned, tied, crushed, and squished into more gowns than I could count. Damien clearly had a specific vision in his mind because I barely had the chance to catch sight of my reflection in the mirror before he was yanking the beautiful fabrics back off me.

Ivo and Mithraheal sat and clapped politely with each dress, but the twins and Leo were far less mature. After the second dress, I came out to find them holding pieces of papers with numbers written on them. They were scoring each dress like it was a sporting event. I rolled my eyes, but their silliness helped keep my instincts distracted. My mates were amusing and I was enjoying this game.

Damien slid another gown over my head, the fabric so soft it reminded me of water trickling over my skin. He said this dress was an A-line gown with a plunging neckline. He added that the fabric had been hand-dyed by one of his favorite designers, Anca. I tuned him out as stroked the rippling fabric. The bodice was a deep royal blue, and as it shifted down my body the blues shifted and changed like the aquatic teals of the sea. It was an incredible trick of the light and spoke volumes about Anca's artistic talent. This was the dress.

"Yes, this is the dress," Damien whispered.

"Stop reading my mind!" I cried.

"Stop being so entertaining!" he fired back.

I had always wanted a brother, now I questioned the

wisdom of that wish as I glared at him through narrowed eyelids.

He stuck out his tongue and gave me an exaggerated bow. I slipped around him and made my way carefully to the ornate gold mirrors that rose from the floor and up to the grand ceilings.

"You are the most beautiful woman I've ever seen." Mithraheal's voice sounded raw with emotion.

"The vampire is correct," said Ivo. "I have lived a lot longer than the rest of your mates, and you truly are the most exquisite creation to walk this earth."

"Dang. You guys make it hard for the rest of us to compliment her!" Leo grumbled.

Levi blew me kisses, and Luke brushed lovingly against my mind.

"Okay! Take it off, T!" Damien said. "We can't have you accidentally ripping the dress to shreds while you guys try to do some monster mashing." He winked and I groaned.

I slipped back behind the curtain and carefully removed the dress. I couldn't believe I was going to be wearing something so incredibly beautiful. I handed it over the screen to Damien, leaned down and picked up my T-shirt, slipping the worn grey fabric over my head. I picked up my jeans, but before I could step into them, I felt a warm wet trickle down my leg.

Glancing down I saw blood. Seriously? I had never had a cycle in my life, and my body decided that today was the perfect time to suddenly give me one? This week sucked donkey balls.

"Um, guys?" I was trying to figure out how to ask for the necessary girly items.

I shrieked as the screen was ripped aside and slammed into the wall. Mithraheal stood there panting, his eyes blood red. Gone was my well-mannered aristocrat, in his place was a vampire that had just smelled his most favorite thing on earth.

"Did you hurt yourself?" he asked. His fangs flashed as he searched my face for any sign of pain.

"Chill buddy," I said, raising my hands in defense. "I'm the one that is supposed to go all feral at the drop of a hat, not you. It's no biggie, I apparently just started my menstrual cycle—"

Ivo roared. "No, no, no!" he cried. "This shouldn't be possible! The timing is all wrong! Why have the fates cursed us?"

I've heard cycles were less than fun, but this seemed a bit of an overreaction.

"Ivo, it will be okay," I said. "This is normal for women, we'll get through this." His panic was making me panic, and two panicking dragons inside a castle was a very bad idea.

"It's normal for *human* females, but not for *dragon shifter* females!" Ivo snapped back. "A dragoness will have only one bleed each year, and they don't have their first bleed until they are at least three hundred years old."

Huh. And here I thought I was a late bloomer - turns out I was *way* early.

"Merging with your Beasty must have accelerated not only your magic abilities, but also your physical development," continued Ivo. He sounded like he had just lost his best friend.

"So, I'm weird, that's not exactly unexpected in my life." I shrugged.

"You will only bleed for one day, Tia. Then you will go into heat."

I gave an awkward laugh. "You mean like a dog or a cat?"

"I mean like a dragon. If we thought last week was difficult, it's going to be nothing compared to what's coming."

I wasn't exactly sure what was coming, but I had a good idea who would be coming ...

CHAPTER TWENTY-TWO

Tia

I spent the next day in bed. It felt like my body was trying to turn itself inside out. I would rather grab a lightning bolt than experience another cycle. The men had teleported several large mattresses into the cave, trying to make me as comfortable as possible. I was proud of myself for not giving in to my dragon instincts since the previous morning, but also I didn't feel confident enough in my control to stay near people yet. So, it was back to the cave for me.

The bed dipped as Leo sat next to me. He cheerfully held out a tub of ice cream as though offering food to his loving mate, and not a predator who might take his arm off along with the treat.

"Thank you, Leo," I said politely, before snatching the tub and spoon from his hand and guarding it in the crook of my arm. His laughter eased my tension and I began to eat, still keeping an eye out for anyone who might dare to steal my food.

"I would ask how you are feeling, but I am pretty sure that's on the list of top five things not to ask a woman."

I narrowed my eyes at him.

"So, instead I was going to ask what you'd been thinking about. Your expression for the past several hours has been a mix of pain and concentration. Is there something else going on? Anything I can help you with?"

How had I gotten such a sweet mate? I knew my five mates loved me completely and unconditionally, but I had also picked up on their unease after the battle. They weren't sure if I could find balance, or if my instincts would always rule my mind and my body. In some ways it was as if they were living with a bratty two year old, or an out-of-control teenager. I had to sort through my emotions and instincts; I had to learn to control them enough to ensure that others could be safe around me.

Leo had treated me the same after the battle as he had before it. Even when I felt the most out of control and my other mates were working hard to soothe me, he would casually throw an arm around me and start chatting away. It was endearing and slightly worrisome that he seemed to lack self-preservation.

There wasn't a box I could lock my dragon side away in, keeping it under lock and key until I needed to call on that power. Beasty was no longer there, helping me to control the energy that heated my blood and made everything so much worse. Ivo thought I needed to find a way to rein in my dragon instincts, but there was no distinction. There was only me and I had to learn self-control all over again.

"The ice cream helps, thank you," I said.

Leo smiled as I scooted up against him.

"I was trying to process the information in my mind," I added. "There's just so much, and it is overwhelming trying to sift through it."

"What do you mean? What information?"

"When Beasty and I merged, I received all her memories."

My other mates had settled themselves around me on the mattress. My heart was so full. These were my mates, my circle. We had defeated Draven and his army of mercenaries. Leo had taken out the wizards who'd betrayed us. We still needed to speak with the wizard council about what had happened, and we had to attend this ball to assure the para-normal community that we were allies. But the evil had been destroyed, and once I was ready, we could move into a home and start our lives together. That gave the greatest incentive to get my act together.

"I'm confused," Leo replied. "My understanding was that a shifter's beast didn't have memories of their own? They're born a new person, just like the human side, right?"

"I don't know the answer to that," I said. "I just know what Beasty told me, and what I am learning now. Beasty lived before, a long time ago. The fates used me as a vessel, and instead of being born with a brand spanking new dragon, I was given Beasty. I'm trying to piece it all together, but I think it has something to do with the whole goddess thing."

Leo, Mithraheal and the twins nodded thoughtfully. Ivo let out a strangled sound. "Goddess? Is this another word that means something different in modern speech?" he asked.

"The word can be used in other contexts, but I am referring to the original meaning of the word. You know, the whole 'dragon of the sea' thing?"

I watched as he paled, quite a feat for a man with such beautiful tan skin. Why was he so freaked out? Hadn't this come up in conversation already? Judging by his expression, apparently not.

"What's your name?" Ivo asked.

He was getting weirder by the moment. "Tia, but you know that," I replied. "You've been calling me by my name for a week now."

He waved off my answer, "Yes, but is that your full name? Or a pet name from your parents? Dragoness, what is your name?"

My power surged up within me in response, my chin lifting into the air. My tattoos glowed and energy crackled in the air around me.

"I am goddess Tiamat, Dragoness of the Sea."

The walls of the cave cracked ominously, and wind swirled around me.

Yep, I still had it.

Leo burst out laughing. Clearly, I had projected my thoughts in the bond.

Ivo wasn't laughing. He stood to his feet in shock, his hands trembling, his breathing fast and uneven.

"Ivo, babe, are you okay?" I handed Levi the empty ice cream container and moved to stand in front of my handsome dragon. My fingertips grazed his stubbled jaw.

He suddenly dropped to the ground, kneeling in front of me. I backed away, really not okay with the whole kneeling thing. The last time someone did this, they stabbed a knife through my heart a few weeks later. I guess kneeling didn't carry the same weight as it did back in the day?

"I am honored to be in your presence, my queen," Ivo whispered, his voice intense. "I pledge my loyalty to you for as long as I draw in breath."

I looked between Ivo and my other mates. They were just as confused as me.

"Um. I haven't gotten to Beasty's extensive library of sexual escapades, so I am still a bit new to the whole sex thing," I replied. "Is this some type of kink? What am I supposed to do?" My voice was a panicked stage whisper.

Levi and Leo burst into raucous laughter, and Luke made the roughened huffing sound that was his laughter. Mithraheal took pity on me.

Love, you are a goddess. This is one of those times that you should let your instincts lead you. We are all unfamiliar with dragon customs and have to muddle our way through as we learn. Do what feels right to you.

I looked back down at my dragon mate. I wasn't a short woman, yet even kneeling his bowed form was higher than my waist. Boy, could we pick 'em or what? I dropped to my knees in front of him, throwing my arms around him and pressing my body against his tense muscled chest.

"Ivo, thank you for your respect, but we are mates," I said. "You've seen me naked, this is silly."

He finally met my gaze, searching my eyes, looking for something. His voice was soft when he spoke. "You really don't know who you are, do you?"

I didn't answer him. Beasty had made references to our title, and now I was slowly trying to sort through memories of a life lived thousands of years before.

"You were the original dragon," Ivo continued. "You created beauty all around you. Later, you suffered at the hands of cruel people who were full of greed. I understand why you are the one spoken about in the prophecy. This is a chance to rewrite history and push back the evil that destroyed your life."

A deluge of pain and sorrow threatened to bury me. I may not yet remember all the details, but my mind clearly recalled the heart-wrenching emotions of those long ago losses and lies.

"The weight of your power is an even heavier burden than I had imagined. I am astounded at the strength you possess to even remain standing during your transition."

"Yeah, yeah." I sighed. "Everyone keeps talking about how powerful I was, but instead I keep getting knocked on my butt."

"Says the chick who literally grabbed a lightning bolt!" Levi laughed.

"I am still salty about not getting to bring it with me. It

made a wicked cool weapon, definitely more effective than a blade."

"You grabbed the lightning rod and then wielded it as a weapon?" Leo gasped. "The world isn't ready for your awesomeness!"

I smiled. Right now, I had to focus on resting while my body grew accustomed to the sudden onslaught of power. Then I could show these boys some really nifty tricks!

Another spasm wracked my abdomen and I groaned. Ivo scooped me up in his arms and moved me onto the bed again. "Let me help you, my queen."

I was about to protest the ridiculous title, but then he stretched me against his body. His chest clicked, growing warmer under my skin. He was a living, breathing, heating pad! I moaned in delight and pressed against him even tighter, relishing the warmth and how it eased the incessant cramping.

"Sleep now. Tomorrow will arrive far too soon."

CHAPTER TWENTY-THREE

Mithraheal

I teleported myself back to the cave. I was eager to tell everyone I had managed to secure the herb we needed.

I was attacked and thrown to the ground the moment I materialized. I tried to use my vampire strength to fling my attacker off, but instead I was pressed harder into the stone floor. My fangs descended and I sank them deep into the assailant.

My attacker purred. I froze.

"Tia?"

"Mmm," she purred. "Now do it again."

As my shock wore away, I was assaulted by a scent that made mouth water and another part of my anatomy snap to attention. What was that smell? I sniffed like a bloodhound. It was Tia, my mate.

I caught a glimpse of her eyes as she moved her body against mine, kissing and sucking every inch of skin she could find. Her pupils were completely blown. I glanced around the room. Where were the guys?

My stomach sank as I spotted a limp arm hanging off the side of the bed, a set of legs poking out from behind the bed, and a body slumped, unmoving against the wall. The last body was splayed across the floor next to me, the eyes glazed over. The lifeless bodies of my circle one of the most horrific things I had seen in my long life.

Had she lost control? How would she handle the shock when she realized what had happened?

I looked back at the body next to mine. I couldn't believe Leo was gone. Suddenly, he blinked. I screamed.

"Save yourself," he whispered, and his eyes fluttered closed.

"It's the heat," Ivo said, moaning. His body didn't so much as twitch.

I had only been gone a few hours, there was no way they could be this worn out. I snorted at their weakness and yanked my heavenly-smelling mate tighter against me. My lips captured hers in a kiss that had my toes curling. She rocked her hips against my pelvis, the heat of her body radiating through my pants. My hands roamed her body, eliciting moans of pleasure everywhere I touched. When I reached her slick folds, her body quivered. I sank my fingers deep inside her, stroking until she was frantic.

She ground down hard against my pelvis, her intoxicating scent making it hard to even think. Slowly, she pulled her lips away from my mouth. She licked my neck, her tiny fangs sinking into my skin with twin pricks of pain. She purred, the sound vibrating through my body and sending me over the edge of a climax with no warning whatsoever. My body convulsed with pleasure. I had never experienced anything like this in my life.

Leo's voice was a croak as he answered my unasked question. "Pretty sure there's something in her salvia and her scent right now. Instinct's way of ensuring her mates can't get enough of her, and that they enjoy the heat just as much as she does."

"Ivo, how long?" I asked. "How long will the heat last?" I was worried about his answer.

"A week if she is kept sated. Longer if she is denied," he replied.

Levi and Luke were still lifeless and silent. "Are you two okay?" I asked in the direction of the bed.

Dude! Shut up! You are going to blow our cover, Levi growled into my mind.

He clearly forgot that Tia was the one who created the mental bond. Her eyes snapped toward the bed, eyeing the shifters as they played dead.

Leo let out a wheezing laugh. "Ha, ha. Wolves playing dead. Good one, Rah."

"Rah?" I asked.

"Your name is a pain in the butt to pronounce and spell, it's gotta go. I'm trying out nicknames to see what fits."

I growled in annoyance at the nerve of the imp, and Tia's eyes snapped back to mine. Apparently, growls were a major turn on to the dragoness. She unbuckled my belt and slid my pants over my hips. My erection was back and it sprung free. Clearly it was time for round two.

FOUR HOURS LATER, SHE WAS CURLED AGAINST LUKE'S chest, smiling dreamily. Damien had popped in and was handing out ice packs and electrolyte drinks. He kept up a running commentary of jokes, enjoying our misery way too much. I had never been so content, but I was thanking our lucky stars that the female dragons only did this once per year. I was going to need a month to recover.

"Did you tell them about the herb?" Damien asked.

"No, I didn't exactly get a chance to discuss anything," I replied.

He snickered and settled himself on the couch, shoving Ivo's legs off one end to make room. "Mithraheal called in a favor and managed to get Ivleek," he said. "That should hopefully relax Tia enough that her instincts will be dulled. She will get to spend the evening at the ball, enjoying her handsome men and interacting with the supernaturals who are very eager to meet her. I've already bumped up our blood driven security detail as much as I can without raising suspicion. With her magic and senses dulled, you guys are going to have to stick to her like glue. She will be vulnerable. I really hate this whole plan."

"We don't have a choice," Tia said with a sigh. "My men will keep me safe. I don't love it, but I have to attend the ball or risk creating new enemies. I was just gaining some self-control, but this heat is making it nearly impossible. Could you imagine the scandal it would create if I stripped off my dress, grabbed my mates and started shifting into the beast with two backs right in the middle of the ball? Or would that be a beast with six backs?"

Tia slapped her hand over her mouth when she realized what she had said. Her eyes widened in horror. Damien and Leo cackled in delight. I hid a smile behind my hand. Ivo was completely confused; the poor guy had a lot of modern euphemisms to learn. Tia tried to get the conversation back on track.

"How long will the Ivleek last?" she asked.

"We aren't sure how long it will last in a dragon," I replied. "In werewolf shifters it lasts about twelve hours. We assume it will only last about half that amount of time with you. But that is plenty of time to eat dinner, make introductions, and reassure people that you want peace among all the species."

I tried to sound confident, but I had major reservations about using the Ivleek. It was a powerful plant; it made supers almost as weak as a human. The idea of Tia in a room full of the most powerful shifters in the world, while she had willfully weakened herself made me want to vomit.

"Same, bro," Leo murmured.

"Stop worrying, you guys," said Tia. "It'll be fine. I can simply be the pretty girl going to her first party, instead of an avenging dragon goddess." She had started wiggling, getting uncomfortable again but desperately trying to hide it. Her mesmerizing scent wafted across the cavern.

"And on that note, I'm out of here!" said Damien. "I'll see you a couple hours before the ball to help you get ready." He winked and teleported out of our nest.

The werewolves were up and had Tia tucked between them, a tangled mess of limbs. I was enjoying the sight, but I also needed a nap. Badly. It was just a matter of time until she turned her attention on me, and I wanted to make sure I was at my best. I closed my eyes and drifted off to the alluring purrs of my mate.

CHAPTER TWENTY-FOUR

Luke

I winced as I slid into my tuxedo jacket. Even with werewolf healing, every muscle in my body was sore. I had lost count of how many times my horny little mate had needed to ease the discomfort of her heat. Don't get me wrong, I loved every minute of Tia's needy body against mine, but I was beat. Werewolf recovery time lagged quite a bit compared to a dragon's, and I was dreaming of getting to sleep through a full night. Ivo groaned as he bent to slip on his shoes. I smirked. It appeared that even his stamina has limits. I understood now why he was worried that there were only five males for her. We were all struggling.

Tia had been given the herb, relaxing her so we could dress without her trying to undress us. Damien had poked and prodded her wavy blonde locks into elegant curls that framed her face and gave her face an angelic look. After the things I had seen her do in the last few hours, I knew she was no angel... and I loved it.

I watched as he finished lacing her up in the blue gown that managed to be elegant and sexy at the same time. I would have sworn that the designer was a witch; the various shades of blue seemed to shift in the light, the fabric creating the illusion of ocean waves. If I were a wealthy man, I would hire that designer to create every piece of clothing that Tia would wear from this day forward.

"We are in agreement," said Mithraheal. "I have engaged her services full-time to handle Tia's wardrobe, as well as ours. I have a feeling tonight is just the beginning of our social engagements with the supernatural world." I grinned, looking forward to seeing our mate in more of the designer's gowns. I enjoyed watching Tia get spoiled by Mithraheal.

I stepped forward to hold Tia's hand as she balanced and stepped into her crystal-studded heels. Mithraheal stepped forward and held out a slim box.

She smiled and opened it, pulling out a beautiful hair pin. One end had a diamond-encrusted dragon sitting on a half moon. Delicate silver chains hung from the moon and glittering gems dangled from the chains. It was an incredible piece of jewelry that likely cost more than a house. Our stunning little dragon immediately dropped it in her hand and tested the weight of it, and I suddenly understood the real reason behind the gift.

"I know you would have preferred a blade, but that would be considered a sign of aggression at this gathering," said

Mithraheal. "This is a way for you to carry something pointy in case you need to get all stabby."

"You know me so well!" She leaned up and kissed his lips. I started to panic, worried that the Ivleek was already out of her system. But she kept the kiss chaste. We all breathed out a loud sigh of relief, earning a giggle from Tia.

"I am still relaxed you guys, no crazy urges to start riding the bony express. ugh!" She pinched the bridge of her nose. "Why Beasty? Why?"

We weren't about to tell her, but we loved the weird sexual innuendos and euphemisms that Beasty had included during the merge. They were always unexpected, and seeing Tia flustered was adorable.

Damien glanced at his large gold watch. "Okay, people! Time to get this show on the road!" he said.

Taking a deep breath, we stepped forward, linking arms or dropping a casual hand on each other. We materialized in a large room that was empty aside from the blood driven security team, who stood in stark contrast to the walls in their crimson suits.

"Do you think they wear red so if they spill their drink, the blood won't show?" Leo whispered, although since everyone in the room had supernatural hearing, I don't know why he bothered.

I swallowed back a laugh at the disgruntled faces of the guards. I wondered if they heard that joke often.

Mithraheal had already explained that each species was given private chambers within this castle. Long ago, the castle was abandoned, and no one was quite sure who had originally built it. It sat on neutral land, meaning it was not on territory belonging to werewolves, wizards, or vampires. Eventually, the leaders decided it would be the best place to host events between the species. It was cleaned and brought back to its former glory. I glanced around at the opulent chamber. The walls were twelve-feet tall, and ornate scrollwork covered the thick natural wood trim. I touched the wallpaper, surprised to find it felt like fabric under my palm. I loved the dark green décor; it reminded me of the forests where I grew up.

"Let's go enjoy this party!" said Tia. "I can't wait for the world to see my handsome mates." She straightened her spine and lifted her chin. She linked arms with Levi and I, and walked toward the doors. Ivo and Leo followed behind us, while Mithraheal and Damien walked in front of us. We made such an odd group, and I totally loved it.

As the imposing golden doors opened, I was astounded at the beauty of the scene in front of us. The sounds hit my ears first. Instruments from around the world weaved notes together in perfect harmony, while delicate crystal glasses clinked, and musical laughter wrapped around us in an almost hypnotic effect. Women in brightly-colored gowns twirled around the golden dance floor in a rainbow of hues. Windows surrounded the entire ballroom, and the twinkling stars of the night sky could be seen through them, making it seem as though the party was being held outside. Glowing gold dust fell through the air, like confetti in slow motion; a final magical touch that completed the otherworldly beauty of the party.

We had reached the top of the grand staircase, the white

marble sparkling as the light touched the strands of gold that spun in elegant lines within the stone. Even knowing what was coming, I still wasn't prepared for the emotions that crashed into my body as our arrival was announced.

"I am pleased to introduce Luke and Levi Blackwood of the Werewolves. Mates of the Dragoness."

Levi and I released Tia's hands and made our way down the staircase. Interested eyes swept over us, curious as to who we were and how we had made the guestlist. I wanted to laugh. Damien had planned every word of what the servant was to announce, and the shock value was about to climb drastically.

"Leopold Tartal, Warlock. Mate of the Dragoness."

Confused murmurs rippled through the guests. Leo seemed to have that effect on people. After settling us into his cave, Ivo had asked in shock how we'd managed to adopt a newborn warlock. In bewilderment, we had asked him what a warlock was. Mithraheal and Damien had been searching the archives to understand more about Warlocks and why they had disappeared.

"Prince Damien Conlier of the Blood Driven. Best Friend of the Dragoness." Tia giggled in surprise as Damien strutted down the staircase like a model on the runway, winking flirtatiously at the women. I rolled my eyes, could the man be any more full of himself?

"King Mithraheal Conlier of the Blood Driven. Mate of the Dragoness." The guests didn't even attempt to hide their shock, the whispered murmurs were no longer hushed. The rumors that the King of Vampires had claimed a mate had just been confirmed and it left everyone in shock.

"Ivo, Dragon of Fyre. Mate of the Dragoness." At this, all sound in the room ceased; you could've heard the blink of eyelashes in the silence. Everyone watched as the giant man made his way down the stairs, his tanned skin a stunning contrast with the white fabric of his elegantly-cut suit. Damien had convinced him to braid his long black hair for the evening. Everything about Ivo screamed power and raw passion. My nose twitched as the scent of the women's desire wafted through the room.

This isn't good. I repeat, this is not good! Levi was panicking.

We just have to hope she is relaxed enough to not react.

I only have eyes for her, but even I can see that Ivo is hot as sin and I would be wetting my panties if I were a girl. What if she loses control of her emotions? Levi started darting his eyes around, probably counting how many bodies Tia would crush if she decided to shift into her dragon.

Our mate moved forward to the top of the staircase and gazed at the faces in the ballroom with serene confidence.

"Goddess Tiamat, Dragoness of the Sea."

The servant had barely spoken these words before purple fireworks began to sparkle behind Tia. Blue light flowed up her arms, lighting up her scale like tattoos. Her hair blew gently and she tucked it behind her ear on one side, displaying Leo's intricate claiming mark. Sneaky little minx. She moved down the stairs unhurried, creating the illusion she was floating.

Wait a second.

She *was* floating.

Our warlock had been practicing, and now the whispering between Damien, Tia and Leo made sense. They had been planning an entrance that would leave people slack jawed. Looking at the faces in the crowd, it was a success. There would never be a dull moment in my life again.

I grinned like a lovesick pup as my queen made her way toward us.

CHAPTER TWENTY-FIVE

Tia

I hadn't been too keen on Leo and Damien's plans for my entrance, but they talked me into it by telling me it would be good to show off a bit, and hopefully make people think I was at full power. I knew that Leo just wanted to try out what he had been practicing, and Damien wanted to make an entrance that no one would ever forget, but I caved and let them have their fun.

However, when I saw the women undressing my mates' with their eyes, and the smell of their arousal slapped me in the face, I was extremely happy I had agreed. I wanted to make it clear that these men were mine, and that you didn't want to test me. My instincts brushed uncomfortably against my skin. I shouldn't even be able to feel them while on Ivleek. It just needed to last a few more hours.

The next two hours were a mind-numbing blur of meaningless conversations. The women would find reasons to stand near my mates, accidently bumping into them and petting them. My teeth ached from grinding them together. I had learned enough about the supernatural world to know that this was extreme disrespect. Soulmates were considered sacred and touching another's claimed mate in desire was unacceptable. My instincts wanted me to take my mates on the floor in front of everyone, but the logical part of my brain knew I needed to keep my cool. I wanted to be respected, not thought of as a feral animal.

I spotted a familiar face coming my way and I squealed excitedly. I threw my arms around his neck. "Ernie!"

"Well, hello to you too, precious one." Ernie laughed into my hair and patted my back. "I've been seeing some interesting things in my dreams - you have certainly been busy."

"That's putting it mildly." Turning, I motioned toward Leo and Ivo. "Ernie, you've already met my wolves and vampire; meet my dragon and warlock."

Ernie eyed Ivo with wonder. "Is it truly you old friend?"

Ivo let out a rumbling laugh. "You were a newborn warlock when I last saw you!" he said with a smile. "I see you have grown back your hair and eyebrows."

"Laugh it up - the hair grew back and I learned to control my magic."

Ivo clapped him on the back. Ernie turned toward Leo, his face freezing.

"Hi, I'm Leo! I've been looking forward to meeting you!" Leo eagerly held out his hand.

Ernie still didn't move. Leo glanced back at me. "Is this normal for him?"

"How should I know? I've only met him once!"

Ernie held out a trembling hand. Leo reached out and grasped it. His purple magic crackled and popped like electricity as it circled around their clasped hands. Ernie watched it with amazement and slowly lifted his watery eyes to Leo's face.

"My son."

I choked on my champagne - Luke thumped me on the back. Leo tried to pull back his hand, but Ernie hung onto him. "I thought you were dead. That I would never see you again. Yet here you are, a grown man."

"I, uh, really don't know what to say," stammered Leo. Ever a sweetheart, he was trying to be polite but he was clearly uncomfortable.

"Please, can we speak privately?" Ernie asked. "I never attend these events, but my visions kept pushing me to come. I was sure I needed to be here. And now I understand! Please, let me explain things."

Leo, darling. Ernie is eccentric, but he isn't crazy. Maybe he can help answer some of the questions I know you've been obsessing over since the battle.

Leo nodded his head, and then looked around.

"Where should we go?" he asked.

"Come, the gardens are well lit, we can speak privately there," replied Ernie. "Plus I need fresh air. Between your mate's heat, and the disgusting lust of the female guests panting after your circle, I can barely breathe in here."

My skin felt tight, my sluggish instincts trying to press forward at Ernie's words. But then he fake gagged and I gave a weak laugh, some of my tension easing. I watched as he and leo walked off. Ernie had a little bounce in his step, and I hoped they could figure out this unexpected relationship. I smiled at the thought of Leo having a dad, one that had the same wacky sense of humor.

The sound of a throat clearing had me snapping my head back around. Three men stood in front of me. I took a discrete sniff. Ah, werewolves.

"Good evening, Dragoness," said one. "It is our pleasure to meet you." They all bowed deeply. I studied their eyes, searching for a sign of insincerity or deceit. I was still raw over the betrayal by the wizards; I couldn't help thinking that I should have realized their intentions. The wolves straightened and smiled.

"We are beyond pleased that you have taken two wolves as your mates. It is a great honor," continued the werewolf. They all turned toward Luke and Levi. "You two have done our species proud."

Luke winked at me. "It was our pleasure," said Levi.

I gave an unladylike snort, and the werewolves smiled. "We're hoping to speak with you about the possibility of setting up an ambassador to relay messages between your mate and the werewolves. We are eager to have an alliance with the goddess."

I couldn't stop my grin. I didn't enjoy the attention, but I knew that my wolves had sometimes questioned their position in our circle. Leo and Ivo were both supernaturals that were nearly extinct and ones that possessed unique powers. Mithra-heal was the leader of the blood driven and had an absurd amount of wealth. My wolves gave the best cuddles, made me laugh, and had been with me from the moment I stumbled into this insane paranormal world. I loved my mates equally and wanted the twins to understand their value.

"I would be honored to have an official alliance with the packs," I said. "I trust my mates to work out the details." I leaned forward, catching Luke's lips in a passionate kiss. I pulled back as I felt the heat begin to brush against my burning skin. I turned and kissed Levi as well. I wanted it to be clear to all who watched that the twins were adored by me. Mine.

"Go. I am eager to hear more about the details once you two have worked out a suitable agreement," I said.

I saw their hesitation; they didn't want to leave my side. "Go, so you can hurry back," I added.

They must have recovered some of their stamina over the past few hours because their eyes glowed with lust. Nodding, they turned and motioned for the werewolves to follow them. Pride warmed my chest, and my heat warmed other parts of my anatomy.

I grabbed some snacks off a waiter's tray; my hunger was growing. I really hoped we didn't have to stay much longer. Another waiter walked by and this time I snatched the entire tray of tiny sandwiches. I cackled with glee and stuffed several into my mouth.

"Incoming," said Damien with a hiss.

I looked up, my cheeks packed with food, and I looked

straight into the eyes of the former reigning monarchs of the blood driven court, and the parents of my vampire mate. I swallowed as quickly as possible and stood straight to greet them. They were a handsome pair; elegant and tall, crystal blue eyes and creamy pale skin.

"Greetings, dear," said the woman. "I am Elise, and this grumpy male is my husband." She clasped my offered hand and then pulled me close and kissed my cheek.

"I wouldn't be so grumpy if there was decent food around this place," said the man. "They tease you with tiny bits of food. Look! She has the correct idea, just take the whole tray."

I blushed and looked at Mithraheal. He was tense but seemed happy to see them.

"Father, Mother, it is wonderful to see you," he said.

Mithraheal pulled me against him. I wanted to laugh as I realized my big scary vampire was nervous about seeing his mom and dad. I relaxed into his side, letting our bond calm him.

"Yo! Pops!" Damien tried to fist bump the former vampire king.

"Damien! Manners! You aren't too old for me to spank you!" Elise's tone was horrified.

Damien winked at me. The idiot was goading them for fun. His future mate was going to have her hands full.

My anxiety eased over the next half hour. I laughed at the stories Elise told about young Damien and Mithraheal. It was such a pleasure getting to know them.

"Tia, you must bring your mates and join us at our summer home in a few months!" Elise said. "It would be such fun and the scenery is beautiful!" She gushed on about their summer home, and I found myself longing to see the ocean. I was raised in the mountains; I had never dipped my toes in saltwater or listened to the thunderous waves as they crashed against the shore.

"I would love that! Mithraheal, do you think we could work it out?" I asked.

"If that would make you happy, we will certainly make time. Whatever pleases you, Dragostea mea," he replied.

I couldn't stop the little purr that escaped.

"Oh! She's adorable! I am so happy for you, Myth!" Elise smiled.

"Myth?" I asked.

"Yes, Damien struggled to pronounce 'Mithraheal', so he called him Myth," said Elise. "It was cute, and in our family that's what he was called."

"I hate to bother you, Mithraheal, but we have had a couple of the blood driven mayors come to us with issues," Mithraheal's father interjected. "I've told them that they need to speak with you, but I would like to relay the information they gave me. Do you and Damien have a moment?" The former king looked apologetic, and Elise gave an annoyed huff.

"I'm going to go visit with the other ladies, don't keep the boys long!" She kissed his cheek, wrapped me in a tight hug, and then walked into the sea of bodies.

"Fine, but it can only be for a few minutes," said Mithraheal. "It's getting late, and I want to get my mate well fed and cozied up in bed." He kissed the top of my head and led both

Damien and their father toward the private blood driven chambers.

I sat down on Ivo's lap and yawned.

"You have done so well, hang in there a bit longer, little one."

Chapter Twenty-Six

Tia

A scream had me jumping up from Ivo's lap. I may be weakened, but I still had my training as a human and I was ready to kick butts and take names if needed. Another scream rang through the air and my skin prickled. It was coming from outside. I dashed outside, completely forgetting the part where I was supposed to stay safely behind my mates and be protected. Oops.

I stumbled as the fabric of my skirt caught on my beautiful heels. I kicked them off, and then paused. I really liked these shoes. I waved my hand and teleported them to the cave. I lifted my skirt and took off running again, sliding to a stop on the slick marble floor to take in the scene in front of me.

Five guys dressed in all-black were attacking three of our blood driven guards. I watched as one of the masked guys grabbed a woman and shoved her into the beautiful lagoon-style pool. It was the deepest pool I had ever seen, and I was in love. I totally needed one of these! I bet my dragon would enjoy splashing around in it.

The woman's gown had a long train and it wrapped around her legs and she started sinking. No one else seemed to notice her desperate struggle. One of the vampire guards screamed and went down, and our uninvited guests took that as an opportunity to rush the remaining two guards. Another woman was shoved into the pool and sank like a rock. Everyone else either stood frozen in fear or ran, desperately tried to get out of the way of swinging blades.

I just wanted one night off. One night to be a girl, and not a goddess that had to protect the world. I sighed and dug deep within myself, reaching out to my magic. It curled in a ball and rolled over like a teenager on the weekend. I yanked it, forcefully bringing it up and through the relaxing happy fog. My heat immediately caused a sheen of sweat to coat my skin. I needed my mates. No. I needed to focus.

I dove into the water. The cool sensation was a relief as it flowed across my skin. My energy undulated around me, and throughout the pool. It was sluggish, but at least it had answered my call. Once it had grabbed the women, I shot to the surface of the water. I held the soaking wet women by two glowing blue water tentacles. Without pausing I shot out five more tentacles and grasped the masked attackers, holding them above the water as well.

I glanced around, quickly taking in the rest of the scene. One of the vampire guards was motionless against the patio floor, dark blood pooling around him. Another of the vampire guards had nearly had his head sliced off and was struggling to breathe as his body worked to heal itself. Vampires heal, but it's still painful for them when they're wounded. I sighed and reached out with two more watery tentacles and pressed them against their wounds. The entire pool began to glow as my energy poured into the water.

The men healed and I let the tentacles slip back into the water. While I had been focused on healing, one of the intruders decided that now was the perfect time to throw a knife toward my back. Seriously? Couldn't he see I was busy?

In one smooth motion, I caught the knife, twisted it around, and sent it sailing back into the idiot's shoulder. It wouldn't kill him, but it would hurt like a son of a rum puncher. A second guy thought that I was distracted and decided to slash at me with his sword. I looked down at my beautiful gown. His blade had slit my dress from the hip down. My eyes blurred with unshed tears. This was the most beautiful thing I had ever worn, and I had planned to wear it every day for the rest of my life, and then at my funeral too.

"That was so mean!" I dunked him beneath the water and held him there. I turned to the first woman I was carefully supporting and laid her down on the patio floor. She wasn't breathing. My magic slithered over her chest, and I could feel the water in her lungs. I slowly pulled the water up her throat. It danced like a cobra listening to a snake charmer. She began coughing and sucking in deep breaths.

I yanked the guy back up, and he joined her in coughing and spluttering. "Are you going to behave now?" I asked.

"Do you mind putting me down now?" the second woman asked in a timid voice.

"Oh! Of course! Here let me help you with that." I gently put her on her feet, and then, drawing a bit more of my quickly waning power, I pulled the water from her clothing and hair. Her makeup was ruined, but otherwise she was dry.

More guards rushed out of the house and surrounded the pool. It was about freaking time.

One by one I dropped the assailants, a little harder than necessary, onto the slick marble in front of the guards. My magic spun and danced around me, putting on a show for the crowd that was pressing in around the pool. Once the water of the pool had settled, I began to walk toward the edge as casually as I could walk across the floor. My dragon instincts were pushing me to preen as the gasps of the onlookers came from all around me. I didn't feel like preening, I felt like sleeping. My body was still fighting the effects of the Ivleek.

I walked onto the marble and people pressed in around me, wanting to ask questions. I didn't want them to see me weak, so I stiffened my trembling spine and smiled. Where were my mates? Surely they had heard the screams. I couldn't sense them near me. I finally made a laughing excuse about finding my men and pushed through the crowd and into the house. My skin was clammy, the heat shimmering just under the surface.

"That was amazing! You took out the entire fight and saved the two women without any effort!" A girl had followed me inside, her voice excited as she gushed about what had happened. "And you looked so regal! We couldn't even tell where your dress ended and the water began. It was like you were part of the water and it wanted to play with you." Her voice was dreamy by the time she finished and I attempted a smile.

"Thank you," I replied. "Too bad that jerk managed to rip my gown. I hope Myth can talk her into repairing it somehow, although I don't even know if that is possible with this type of material." I ran a finger across the frayed edges of the fabric.

"I bet she can!" the girl replied enthusiastically. "Come on, let me help you into something else. That way the fabric won't fray anymore and you can feel a bit more covered since that slit is sure to get some attention form the guys around here. Especially since everyone can't stop talking about how delicious you smell."

I followed behind her, happy to have a chance at saving my beautiful gown. I also loved the idea of not showing my pink clam to all the strangers. My men had conveniently forgotten to give me underwear, and I wasn't sure how much I was flashing as I moved.

She motioned for me to go behind a changing screen and start undressing, and said she would grab some clothes and be right back to help me. I was twisting my arms like a contortionist in an effort to reach the laces holding the dress up, when I smelled him. I would never forget his scent.

My heart seized in my chest and I forgot how to breathe. Had he been here all night? Why hadn't we seen or smelled him before this? My hands started shaking and I pressed them to my mouth. I didn't know if I could face him again.

The door eased shut and I heard the quiet click of the lock.

"Tia, I know you're in here," he said. "Sara brought you here for me."

I guess the nice girl's name was Sara, and she had been waiting for a chance to get me away from my mates and the other attendees.

My heart ached with the memories of pain, and tears slid down my cheeks.

He stepped around the corner of the screen. His body was lit from behind, creating a silhouette of his figure.

"Cage," I whispered.

CHAPTER TWENTY-SEVEN

Tia

I had dreamed of seeing him again, of having another chance to figure things out between us. Maybe the photos that Draven had shown me were photoshopped, maybe they were of a friend. Maybe, maybe, maybe.

"You have been quite a busy girl these past months!" said Cage. "You have blossomed so much. Come and sit down. I've been wanting to speak with you, but you've been rather elusive and your mates have been a little clingy tonight." His laugh was warm, but I bristled at the way he had said "mates".

"I know when we met, you were going through a rough time," Cage continued. "I shouldn't have tried to force the claim, and I shouldn't have tried to change who you were meant to be. I scared you with the mate bite, and I pushed you away with my stubbornness. You just needed time to process

419

everything and I was a selfish jerk. I had dreamed of meeting my mate and had envisioned us marking each other on the spot. I never dreamed I would have a soulmate that didn't even understand the pull. I wanted everything to be as I had imagined it, and I never even realized that I had something better, right in front of me."

I couldn't breathe. I just sat there in stunned silence. He reached out slowly, his thumb sliding along my jaw.

"You don't have to answer," he continued, "but I have to ask. If I hadn't ran that day - if I had stayed, instead of throwing a tantrum and leaving you, would you have claimed me?"

Tears rolled faster down my cheek. "Yes," was the only word I could get out.

He squeezed his eyes shut. His voice shook as he spoke again. "Would I have been the first mate you claimed?"

My response was hardly more than a wisp of air. "Yes."

I watched as a tear slid down the side of his face. "Do you still think about me? Do you ever miss me?" he asked.

"Yes." I choked on a sob.

"Do you still love me?" His tears slid faster down his face.

"Yes. I never stopped loving you."

"Oh Tia!" He swept me into his arms and I sobbed against him. "I have never stopped thinking about you either. I love you, Tia. You were meant to be mine. I was so stupid."

He rocked me as he held me tight. My emotions were a churning sea inside me; it was too much emotion to pear.

"Cage." I paused, not wanting to ask the question, but

knowing I had to. "I saw photos. You were with a woman. Did you two claim each other? Are you still with her?"

I wouldn't be the one to break up a family, regardless of how badly I had dreamed of this moment.

"No!" Cage cried. "I had no idea you were shown photos. I can't imagine the pain you must have gone through seeing those. I did date a wolf female. I am ashamed to admit it, but I was trying to forget you. I was mad at the world and thought I could make my childish fantasy real. But it was never right. She wasn't you. You are the one for me. I felt our tenuous bond break. Was that when you saw the photos?"

"Yes," I confessed. "I wanted you to be free to claim another mate and not bound to me because your wolf decided to bite me."

"Even then, you wanted me to be happy." His voice was full of regret.

"Cage, please stop. We were both at fault. I was a terrified girl when I stumbled onto your pack lands. I had no idea what I was, or that supernaturals even existed. Draven showed up and kidnapped me, and that sent me into even more of a tail-spin. I didn't know about mates, and I know it hurt you when I struggled to understand. I was a mess and needed time; I shouldn't have gotten my feelings hurt when you struggled to accept me as a shifter. We both needed time, and patience."

"And I ruined it by locking myself away from you, and then storming back home," Cage added. "Tia, please believe me. There is no other woman. I ended it with her right after the bond snapped. I didn't even realize what I wanted until it was gone."

My heart broke as I looked at his sorrowful face. I slipped my arms around his neck and clung to him. I tried to remember all the reasons I had for getting up and walking out of that room but surrounded by his incredible scent and held in his arms, I couldn't focus enough to remember anything. It didn't seem to matter anymore. He continued to rock me gently, his warm breath blowing through my hair. My desire stirred. I tried to keep a grip on my self-control but it was getting harder with every passing moment. I needed to get out of there, back to the safety of the cave before my dragon instincts pushed to the forefront again. The heat that had been simmering, was now beginning to boil. I had to go. I had to—

"Tia, is it too late for us? Can you forgive me for being a controlling idiot who forgot how a mate should be treated?"

I had dreamed of this moment, and now it was happening. I was going to get a second chance with Cage.

"Oh, Cage!" I cried and pressed my lips against his. He froze for a moment and then, slowly, his lips moved against mine. His hand slid into my hair, using it to hold me still so he could explore my mouth. I moaned and unbuttoned his shirt, eagerly slipping my hands inside to glide across his hot skin. His other hand worked at the laces I had loosened on my gown and I felt the fabric slip down from my breasts like a lover's touch before it puddled around my hips.

Cage's mouth left mine and I growled in protest, until I felt his hot, wet mouth kiss my breasts, sucking and teasing. I arched into him. This was the longest I had managed to go without sex since my heat started, and it was coming back with a vengeance. The smell of my arousal tickled my nose. My heat added a punch to the scent to ensure that my mates wouldn't be able to get enough of me, and Cage responded with a moan. Suddenly, he stood, lifting me with him and letting my beautiful gown flow down my body like water, leaving me naked in front of his dark lust filled eyes.

He laid me gently on the floor, the plush carpet teasing my sensitive skin. I watched through heavy eyelids as he slid his arms from the open dress shirt, and then slowly slid off his pants. He laid them carefully on the chair, and then turned back to me. I had always thought Cage was the most handsome man I had ever seen, and now he stood naked in front of me. A Greek god in the flesh.

My heat turned from pleasure to pain, instinct telling my body that I had resisted too long, and I needed to mate. This wasn't what I wanted for my first time with Cage. I tried to shove back against it, clear my head, remember all the things I still needed to talk about with Cage. I needed to make sure... what?

"Beautiful, stop thinking," he whispered. "I love you, now let me ease the discomfort."

All rational thought fled my mind. He loved me, he wanted all of me. I was getting a second chance with my first fated mate.

He joined me on the carpet, lowering his body against mine. My skin burned everywhere his skin touched my own. His lips caught mine again and he kissed me with wild abandon. I cried out when I felt his fingers brush against my most sensitive parts, every slight brush sending shock waves of desire through me. My hands ran down his chest, memorizing every curve and muscle. One day I would explore those with my lips and tongue.

Cage jerked against me as my hand wrapped around his throbbing erection. Primal need pounded in my head. Mate. Mate. Mate. I fought it, wanting this first time to be a loving one.

Cage's fingers sunk deep inside me. I gasped from the sudden intrusion, but my dragon was pleased. My pupils shifted to slits as I groaned his name. He moved to kiss my lips again and then startled when he saw my face. My insides turned to ice - he was going to reject me again.

Instead, he leaned down and kissed me, and the tension left my body. He hadn't been repulsed. I wanted to laugh with joy, but another wave of pain slammed into my body, the heat reminding me that it hadn't gone away.

Cage's hand suddenly pulled away from me. He lifted my hips and slammed into me. This was no gentle stroke; this was hard and fast. A new pain ripped through me, and I cried out in surprise.

"Oh, Tia. You feel so good." Cage moaned as he slammed into me. Hearing his satisfaction reassured me. If this was how he liked it, I could adjust, just like I had for my other mates.

As he angled himself deeper, he rubbed me just right and I could feel my body begin to tighten. His fingers gripped my hips tighter and he slammed me against him with each thrust. With two more hard pumps, the coil of desire in me sprung free and I climaxed, moaning his name in ecstasy. I was lost in bliss, when my back was suddenly slammed into the floor from the force of his thrust, knocking the wind out of me. I gasped in a panicky breath, but before I could draw in a second, he had buried himself inside me again, hard enough that I bit my tongue. I whimpered in pain, and his mouth covered mine. Tenderly, his tongue lapped up the bit of blood and caressed the tiny wound.

"I'm sorry, honey. I am having trouble controlling my wolf," he whispered. "We've both wanted this for so long." He was panting hard as he spoke, slowing his pace, and giving me time to catch my breath. I melted under his touch, and he began moving faster, his movements more frantic. I bounced as he pulled out and slammed back in, harder and harder each time. Pain ripped through me again, from the rough love making or my heat I couldn't say.

My shoulders hurt from the impact with the floor, but I ignored the discomfort. My mate was holding me, loving me; life was perfect. Again, my belly tightened, and pleasure washed over me in wave after wave. My walls tightened and gripped him tighter, and with a growl he followed me over the edge, his body jerking with the aftershocks of his pleasure.

"I love you," I whispered.

My fangs dropped and I leaned forward to mark my mate and finish the claiming. Instead, a rag was shoved in my mouth.

"No biting, dragoness. That isn't part of the plan."

CHAPTER TWENTY-EIGHT

Tia

I was so confused. His voice had gone from tender to frigid, and as I looked into his eyes, they no longer glimmered with love. Instead, all I saw was disgust. Fear clenched in my stomach. I should've moved faster. I should've reacted, but my heartbreak kept me frozen, as still as a statue.

He quickly brought out a pair of handcuffs and snapped them around my wrists.

"Don't even try to break these; they have been spelled by a wizard friend," Cage said. "You might have been able to break them if you had been at full strength, but while weak from Ivleek, you don't have a chance."

How did he know about the Ivleek? What else did he know?

I should never play poker, because he read my face easily.

"How did I know?" He laughed. "Come on! Surely you didn't think that Draven was the only corrupt leader in the supernatural world? I knew it was spreading, and I tried to keep my pack out of it. I left you once I realized that you weren't going to stop shifting into your unnatural beast. Once I got back to the pack, I found myself growing more and more bitter. And then I started to hear rumors. You were growing in power, and the community was taking notice. You demanded the wizards treat their magic-less losers like they mattered, and the council immediately bowed to your wishes. The different leaders began to draw up alliances, hoping you would agree to them. People were talking about you like you were a celebrity, and they were so eager to find favor with you."

His voice had grown angrier as he spoke. He dressed again, and now tossed my torn and crumpled dress toward me. "Put it back on."

I struggled to put it on, and he watched me, his gaze making me feel dirty. I tried to call out for my mates in the bond, but I hit a brick wall.

"If I had just sucked it up and played my cards correctly, I would have been your first mate." He sighed. "I would have been given a position of power within the community. I didn't get the mate I wanted. A sweet submissive woman whose only focus was to care for me and my children. Instead, I got a prophesied dragon goddess with more power than she knows what to do with. The fates wrecked my life, and now I am taking what I want."

I choked on a sob at his cruelty.

"Would you shut up?" He walked over and yanked me to my feet. I tried to hold my dress against me, but without being tied, it kept slipping.

"This way." He led me through a hidden door that was cleverly painted to look like a smooth wall. The door led to a stone tunnel. How original.

Apparently, he wanted me to feel the most pain possible because he continued talking. "I bribed a network of spies to gather information and send it back to me. I also made contact with other members of the supernatural community that are not pleased about your existence. We have put a lot of time into this plan. Once you went full lizard, we knew it was going to be more challenging to take you down. You have nearly unlimited power, but you are too young to know how to handle it. However, since you are unpredictable, we had to wait for the perfect moment. When we discovered that you had obtained Ivleek, we decided now was the time to act.

"Your little show of power outside was impressive, especially since you should barely be walking with Ivleek in your system, but it exhausted you. How did you like that little show with the guards? I am still amazed at how perfectly everything went tonight." He stopped to laugh. "That crazy old man showed up and distracted Leo, and the spineless werewolves distracted the twins. Ivo played the hero and chased the men who had been preparing to shoot arrows at you, and the vampires were happy to have a family get-together. We thought we would have to knock them out, but they wandered away willingly. Each distraction worked like a charm and you were left unguarded and alone. Once they were away from you, our wizards threw up a spell that kept them from hearing anything else. That's also what's blocking you from contacting them with telepathy."

My bare feet were raw from the debris cluttering the tunnel. I was shivering from cold and fatigue.

"We are almost there, hurry up." Cage yanked me forward and I tripped on my dress. Without my hands to balance me, my face smacked into the cold stone. Pain pounded in my head and my vision blurred. Cage roughly hauled me to my feet and walked me down the shaft, his fingers digging hard into my arm as he kept me upright.

"What none of us expected was for you to be in heat," he continued. "I didn't figure that one out until I got to the castle this evening and caught your scent. I hadn't thought I would still feel the pull of the mate bond, but it was there. The longer I watched you and your mates, the more my blood boiled. My wolf fought me all evening to go to you and beg for another chance. The scent of your heat was driving me insane and that is when I realized my good fortune. My sources had already told me that, even with how I treated you, you still missed me. Tonight, with your heat distracting you, I knew if I just said the right things, you would cave. I still can't believe how soft your silly little heart is, and how quick you were to forgive. I don't want you as my mate, but I really enjoyed using your hot little body."

I struggled to breathe. The gag was still in my mouth, and between my face impacting with the stone and my constant tears, I could barely breathe through my nose.

"Have you figured out the best part yet?" Cage grinned. "I emptied my seed inside you."

My brain was shutting down but I tried to concentrate on his words. I knew they were important, but shock was setting in and I couldn't connect the pieces.

"You're in heat. The whole purpose of your body going into heat, and driving you crazy with need, is so that you will get pregnant and your species won't die out," Cage explained. "My child may already be growing in your belly—a child I will be able to take and shape into a leader fit to rule the earth. Once the leaders are done experimenting with you, they will kill you. That will leave me as the father to the most powerful creature on earth, a creature that will be eager to do anything to please their dear old dad."

I had never felt anything as strong as the horror I felt at that moment. I yanked at my magic, desperately trying to call it forward, cursing the fact that I sucked as a dragon. I dove into my memories, ignoring the painful throbbing in my head. I needed Beasty's skills. I let go of all my self-control and let instincts take over. Around me, the walls trembled and reflected the eerie blue of my glowing tattoos. Hope soared in my chest. I might actually be able to save myself, even while weak and in shock.

"Oh no you don't, slut!"

Cage backhanded me with the force of a werewolf and I was knocked into the wall. My head hit the stone with a sickening crack and everything went black.

CHAPTER TWENTY-NINE

Tia

Laughter was the first sound I heard as I woke. It was so loud, clanging around in my head like Damien and his obnoxious morning wake-up calls.

"I can't believe it went off without a hitch!" a woman's voice said.

"You should see her mates. They are frantically searching for her, and she's right under their noses! I heard them talking this morning; they believe the kidnappers have already taken her somewhere else, so they are leaving shortly." The man speaking sounded positively giddy.

"I hope you're right, Cage. If she is pregnant, that will make all our lives a lot easier. We'll try some things over the next few weeks to transfer, or at least siphon, her power. If we can accomplish that, we'll be able to take the thrones and destroy any resistance we meet. If not, we can kill her and use her child to destroy our enemies in a few years. We're immortal, waiting a few decades for the child to grow isn't a big deal." How could a woman be so cruel?

A loud banging on the bars had me jerking to the fetal position, trying to protect myself. I opened my eyes. They felt like they were full of sand and I blinked repeatedly before I managed to focus on the faces in front of me.

It was the former king and queen of the blood driven. The faces that had been so loving and friendly the night before sneered down at me now. The inky black evil had spread like a disease through the paranormal community. I had thought that by taking out Draven, the evil would be stopped. It had already seeped into the hearts of others, corrupting them and twisting their minds. This was the prophecy I was born to fulfill.

"My son is a softhearted fool that is too weak to rule, and yet he is still far too good for you," Elise snapped. "The thought of him claiming you makes my skin crawl. You are a beast, an animal, and now you will be treated as one. This room has been spelled so your magic is null. You are at my mercy."

She threw her drink in my face before spinning on her heel and leaving the room, the men following her out.

I reached down inside me and called upon my magic. It tried to answer my call but was blocked by an invisible barrier. I smiled to myself; she said my magic was null, but it was still there. I just had to figure out how to get it out.

The sound of footsteps had me shoving myself back into

the far corner. I needed time to heal myself; a slow process without magic, and while the heat was still eating away at me.

I watched as a guard strode into the room. He eyed me through the bars, and then unlocked the door and walked in, carrying a large box with him. I shrank further against the wall, not sure what his intentions were.

"Be still, rabbit," he said. "You cannot get away, so your actions are pointless."

I bristled at being called "rabbit". I was a dragon. A fire-breathing, lightning-catching, sword-wielding, enemy roasting, dragon.

The guard barked a laugh. "You have a high opinion of yourself, little bunny."

Great, he was a mind reader. How was a girl supposed to hatch a diabolical escape plan with a guard reading her mind?

This was really not my day.

Or week.

Or month.

Or year.

The guard tilted his head like a dog and studied me. "You are unusual."

"Right back at you."

"Hmm." He turned and started pulling things out of the box. I watched him warily. "I'm not going to hurt you."

"I've heard that before."

He moved toward me with a bowl of soapy water and a rag. He slowly washed my face. I moaned in pain when he swiped gently over the massive bruise where my face had ate rock in the tunnel. His eyes were sympathetic, but he made no comment. Then, he started cleaning the blood from where my skull had cracked into the stone wall. The blood had dried on my scalp. Pain like a knife blade stabbed my brain and I ground my teeth together to hold in the scream.

He cleaned my arms next and moved to clean the bloodied bottoms of my feet next. At one point, the pain caused me to jerk my foot, and my skirt fell open from where the sword had ripped it. We both looked down and my stomach churned at the sight. My legs were bruised and cut, but what had bile rising in my throat was the blood that was dried to the insides of my legs. Evidence that the pain I had felt the night before hadn't been from the heat, it had been from Cage. He had used me, not caring if he damaged me, and then tossed me aside.

Don't cry, don't cry, don't cry. I repeated it like a mantra.

The guard let out a hiss, and then rinsed his rag and began wiping away as much of the blood as he could without completely violating my privacy. I wanted to tell him that I could wash myself, but I just sat there, swallowing back the sobs.

Something caught my attention as I watched him. "You have ears like I get when I shift!" I cried. "I call them my fairy ears. What are you?"

"I am a wizard," the man replied.

I breathed in his scent. "Nope. You aren't a wizard. Plus, wizards don't have fairy ears."

"My ears are normal, and please stop saying that. Such a silly word."

Okay, ixnay on the arseay.

"What does that phrase mean?" His tone was curious again.

"Uh...to not talk about ears. You are clearly self-conscious about yours, and I don't want to make you uncomfortable."

"What language was that? I speak all of the earth's languages, but that one I do not recognize."

So, he couldn't speak Pig-Latin? Now I just had to think my entire escape plan in Pig Latin.

"Pigs don't talk, and I assure you that is not Latin." He held out a pair of sweatpants and a baggy T-shirt. "I'll leave to give you privacy so you can change. I have left the bowl of water as well in case you have other areas you wish to clean."

I watched him leave the cell and close the door behind him. I was grateful for his thoughtfulness, but also confused. I was brought down here to die, so why was he treating me with respect?

It took me a while to wash; I scrubbed until I bled, and I still felt dirty. Would I ever feel clean again?

I dressed slowly, my body protesting the entire time. When I finished, I sank down heavily on the cot.

It was only a matter of time before the heat that simmered below my skin became unbearable. The dragon instinct to survive was strong, and my body didn't care if my mates were nowhere around and I was trapped in a cage. It wanted to ensure the survival of the species by whatever means necessary.

I also knew that Elise would be back as soon as she could get away without raising suspicion. She had been planning my torture for a while, and I think she was relishing the idea of ripping me apart... even if it meant killing her son in the process.

My hand rested over my flat stomach. The craziness of the heat hadn't exactly given me much time for rational thought. I could already have a baby growing in my stomach. I smiled as I thought of my mates, wondering how each of them would react if I were pregnant. Then Cage's words barged into my mind. I couldn't let him take my baby. My child would grow up caring for others. He or she would make the world a better place, simply by their presence.

The elf had moved back into my cell. He gathered up the supplies and placed them outside the door. Then he returned and sat on the ground near the cot. His eyes were level with my own as he studied me. He carefully placed his hand on my head, and instantly the headache that had been banging against my skull eased. Who was this man? And why did my magic grow a little stronger when he was beside me?

"You intrigue me, Bunny."

I groaned. I was pretty sure that living with that nickname would be worse than the torture Elise was planning for me.

I focused back on my memories, trying to ignore the comforting glow that strange guard was radiating.

I had spent so much time trying to contain my powers, now it was time to let loose. I closed my eyes and started at the beginning of my memories, the ones Beasty had given me during our merge. If I was going to be stuck here until I worked up enough strength for an escape, I would put the time to good use. Right now, the most important thing I could do was learn from the wisdom buried in those memories.

This was the last time I would ever be taken by surprise. The last time I would be weak. It was time to take the training wheels off this bicycle.

This dragoness was going to come back with a vengeance.

I was done with hiding.

I felt the beginning flicker of my dragon fire.

This queen is coming for her throne.

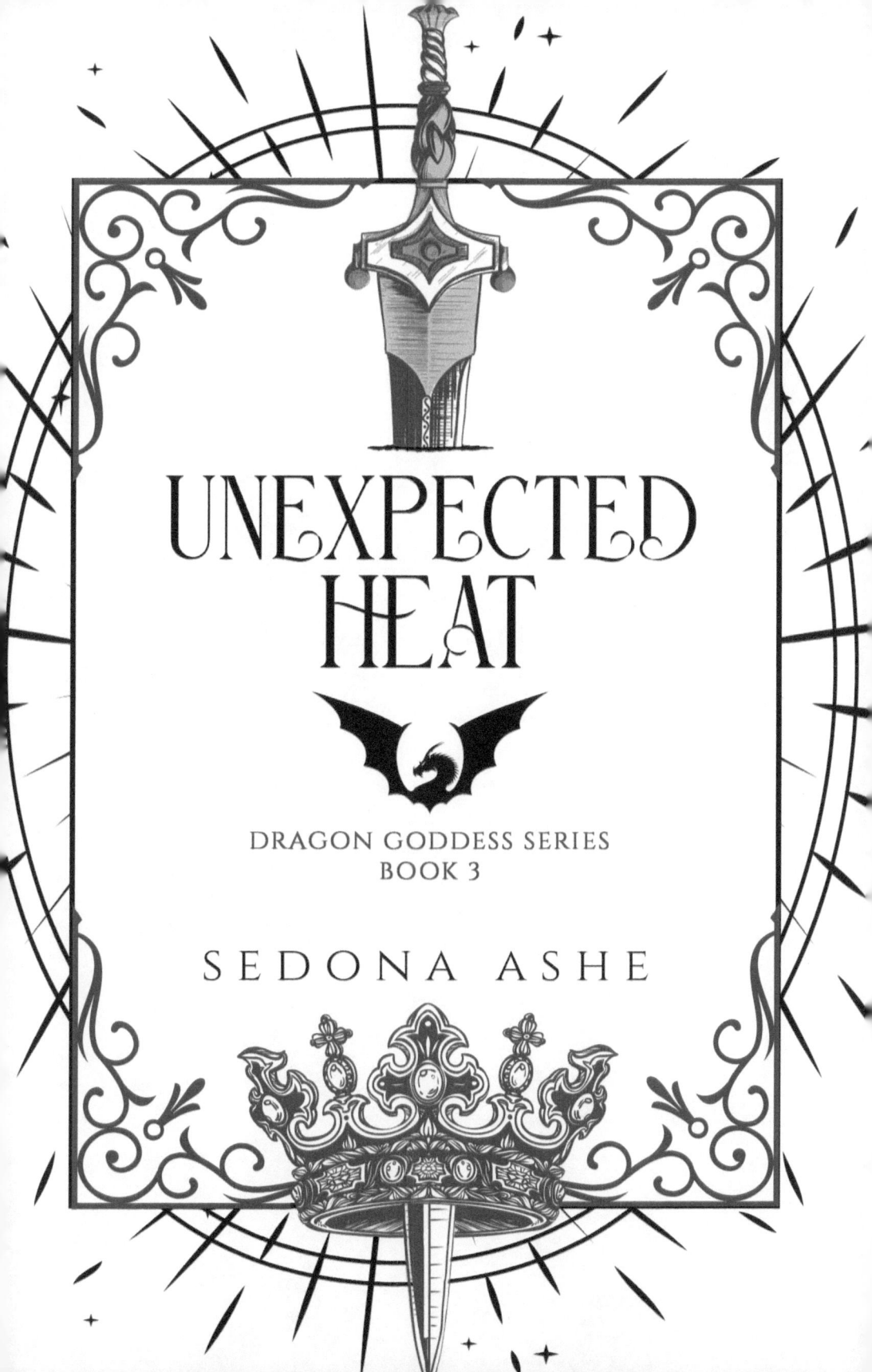

UNEXPECTED HEAT

DRAGON GODDESS SERIES
BOOK 3

SEDONA ASHE

CHAPTER ONE

Tia

"It all started when my mom met my dad, fell in love, and then had me." With a growl, I wiped at the sweat dripping from my brow.

"I am aware of how humans bond and procreate. You haven't answered my question. How did you come to be here?"

Fairy Man didn't look amused at my lame attempt at humor, although to be honest, he never looked amused at anything. I had yet to see the man truly smile. Who could blame him, though? There wasn't much to smile about down here.

His eyes bore into mine, searching for the answers to some great question that I was far too tired to care about.

"I'm a female dragon. A royal dragoness, and the last of my line."

He scooted a little closer, and I was almost flattered at his intensity. The man could be cold as ice, but then occasionally he would show a childlike curiosity.

"I fought and defeated Draven, a sick man with twisted dreams of making the world bow to him," I continued. "During the battle, my mates were injured. There was no way we were all going to walk away from that fight alive. To save them I had to merge with Beasty, my inner dragon. The upside was that I absolutely slayed the rest of the battle, but the downside is that I lost my best friend. She was annoying, and always horny, but I never felt alone with her constant rambling in my mind. After the merge, things got a bit messy. I died. My dragon mate came to my rescue, and we claimed each other in a freaky hot dragon way." The memory had me ready to purr, but I swallowed it back at the fairy's raised eyebrow.

"We hid while I healed and learned self-control. Then we got the invite to this stupid ball. 'Harmony,' what a joke! I'd hoped that after destroying Draven and his followers, we were finished fighting and could enjoy our lives together. Obviously, not. We played right into each individual trap that had been laid for us, all by enemies we never expected. How could we have been such idiots?"

He snorted. "You need to think like a soldier. Never let your guard down, and always remain suspicious."

There I was, sitting in a cell, hidden from my mates, burning with fever from my raging heat, and suffering from devastating blood loss. Between the vicious beatings and the dozens of vials of my blood they took each day, I was surprised I had any blood left. I doubted a mosquito would have given me a second glance at this point. Yet, I preferred to endure this agony than to never trust anyone again. That would be a lonely existence, which said a lot, considering my entire life had been one of isolation. Lifting the hem of my shirt, I moved to rub the sweat from my stinging eyes.

"Hm. Maybe, but it is also safe."

Great, he was back to reading my thoughts. He brushed away my hand that still held the tatters of my shirt. Reaching into his bucket of clean water, he pulled out a wet towel. Moving as though he had all the time in the world, he squeezed the excess water from the rag and gently washed my face, careful to not press against bruised and torn places on my skin. For someone determined to not care, he sure seemed to care. This man was a walking contradiction.

He rinsed the rag before washing off my grime-covered neck and shoulders. The cold towel was a stark contrast to my feverish skin, and I wasn't surprised in the least to see steam waft up from the cloth as it pressed against me. I closed my eyes, determined to relax and enjoy this kindness.

It had been impossible to keep track of time down here, but I knew it had been at least a week since I had been with my mates, perhaps two. My heat had gone from moderately uncomfortable, to painful, and finally, unbearable. I was struggling to remain conscious, and my personality was growing less stable by the hour. If I hadn't been separated from my mates, this wretched heat would have been over by now.

Instead, I was growing weaker by the day as it continued to burn me alive.

When I had been left alone in the relative privacy of my cell, I'd tried to ease the discomfort, only to discover that my instincts were not easily fooled. The heat had punished me by raging twice as hot for several hours. The only thing that had eased the pain had been when the fairy sat next to my bed. There was something about his comforting glow that calmed the inferno inside me. Not completely, but enough so that I could rest for a few hours.

"I'm not a fairy," he said firmly.

"Stop reading my thoughts, pixie." I shouldn't snap at him, but I was ready to take a bite out of anyone who dared annoy me.

Rinsing and setting aside the now dirty cloth, he gently lifted my shirt and began to wrap around the lacerations covering my chest and stomach.

"I can do that myself." The words came out in a sigh instead of the powerful command I had been aiming for. It felt so nice to have someone, even this odd guard, treat me with kindness, but I also hated showing weakness. That was in my past.

"You could, but there is no need. Turn around."

I did as he instructed and bit down hard on my lip as he cleaned the worst of my wounds. Dragon healing would've come in seriously handy right now, but my magic was still trapped.

"Sit."

If he didn't stop talking so much, I was going to need ear

plugs. Pixie narrowed his eyes and I stuck out my tongue. Ignoring me, he began washing my feet, moving slowly up my calves and then thighs. The higher he moved, the louder the pounding in my chest.

Take.

My body knew what it wanted, but my mind was confused. I was drawn to him, but not in the same way I had known instantly that Myth was my mate. Then again, I hadn't instantly known Luke and Levi were my mates, so how accurate was the instinct? Beasty had once said that I could choose my mates. Did that mean I could choose this man as my mate? Even if he hadn't been fated? That was assuming he would want a mate, and an unstable dragoness at that. How did fairies mate? Was it for life?

My anxiety rose. Could I take a new mate, one that might not even be a fated mate, without talking it over with my men?

Agony ripped through my stomach, doubling me over. I ground my teeth together and slammed my eyes closed tightly, determined to not scream or cry in front of this man. Elise and her twisted friends had yet to pull a scream from me. I'd die before I allowed myself to show even the smallest sign of weakness during my stay here.

I'd learned so much from Beasty's memories. It wasn't me who should be scared, it was those who were keeping me caged. The moment I would be able to release my magic, they would realize the sheer depth of their stupidity. There wouldn't be a place on earth they could hide from me, and I was long past mercy. Also, my mates should probably be scared, too. I had learned some interesting things from Beasty's mind that I couldn't wait to try in the bedroom.

"An interesting dream, Bunny."

My temper flared and I gave a half-hearted growl. He had done nothing to deserve death, so I couldn't in good conscience kill him. That didn't stop me from wanting to, though. But first, I wanted to feel his naked body dance against-

I froze. He froze.

"I will leave you to finish washing in private." He stood quickly and moved outside the cell.

Relief, regret, and pain fought inside me. I quickly washed my lady bits and rinsed out the cloth. I couldn't hide my wince when I stretched myself out on the cot. I tossed and turned several times before curling into the fetal position. I tried to meditate, working to drown out the sensation of knives slicing my insides, and focusing instead on Beasty's memories. I would use every minute I was conscious to learn and prepare.

CRACK!

The sound of the whip snapping against my bare back was followed by a searing pain as my flesh was sliced open.

CRACK! CRACK! CRACK!

It was as annoying as a dripping faucet. I had to hand it to Elise—she was definitely developing some upper body strength. The first few days she tired out before she managed to snap off more than ten cracks of the long, tapered whip; kind of lame for a vampire if you ask me. Today, I lost count at thirty lashes. I knew she would stop if I moaned or showed even the slightest sign of pain.

Never.

I was *the* queen, and I'd die before allowing this 'had-been' queen to feel like she'd won some type of victory over me. Sure, she was holding me captive, but that wasn't going to be the case much longer.

My magic was stirring. It was nearly time. The only question was whether I destroyed them with my human senses in control, or if the heat pushed me over the edge and I rained down judgement as a dragon in both mind and body. It wouldn't be pretty either way, but option number two would likely involve considerably more damage and bloodshed.

That last thought made me snicker, a sound that I quickly regretted.

"You think this is funny? Maybe I have been going too easy on you!" Elise's shrill voice pierced my eardrums in much the same way her whip had ripped open my skin.

Metal clanged as the whip handle clattered onto the stone floor. The chains holding me in place didn't allow me to turn and watch her, but the creaking hinges of the wood chest informed me that the vampire queen was digging in her toy box full of horrors. How did Mithraheal not notice the fact that his mom was a demented psychopath?

Elise moved so that she could look at my expression. "I saw your lips move! Do you have something to say?" She was taunting me. I knew I shouldn't, but I opened my mouth.

"Myth and I aren't inviting you to our wedding."

Her pale skin turned a splotchy red color. "I'll not have my reputation damaged by my son marrying trash!" Oh yes, I'd managed to tick her off. Now we were both having sucky days.

I nearly bit off my tongue when icy steel hit my back. From the glimpse I got as it slid to the ground, the whip was made of thin chain link with spikes on each link. I had never heard of a weapon like this one. Frankly, I'd have preferred to keep it that way. My skin frayed open when the claw-like whip lashed my back a second time.

Don't scream. Don't scream.

I repeated it over and over like a mantra in my head. In that moment I would have given anything to hear Beasty in my mind. Anything to distract me from the wet squelching sound of blood as barbs slashed across my lower back and thighs. My sweat and blood mixed, dripping from my skin onto the rocks beneath me.

"Are you insane? She could be carrying my baby!" Cage's outraged roar shook the walls.

Someone else was gagging. Fighting dizziness, I turned my head and caught sight of the newcomer.

Trixie.

My life sucks donkey balls. Black spots exploded in my vision and my body went slack.

Chapter Two

Tia

"Girl, you aren't supposed to be here yet."

The voice was familiar, but the words sounded wrong. I fought to open my heavy eyelids.

"Sleeping Beauty, you are far too early for this part of your journey. What on earth happened to you?"

Her voice was silky, and her words lilted in a sing-song way. Again, I was struck by the sense that I should know the voice. I struggled to pry open my eyes, but they had given up the good fight and stayed tightly closed.

"Mom?" The word was a barely intelligible croak.

"Dang, Cupcake!" the voice cried out. "I know time works differently here, but I haven't been gone long enough for you to have forgotten me already!" Her beautiful melodic laugh drifted around me. I knew instantly who she was.

My eyes spang open, the lead that had weighted them down disappearing in an instant. "Beasty?" The word came out strained and high pitched, like I had inhaled helium and then been punched in the stomach.

"Well duh, Sweet Cheeks." Exasperated, Beasty rolled her sparkling blue eyes. Eyes that were very much human in a very human body. I had seen both her forms while going through our shared memories, but it was still hard to adjust to the idea that she was also my inner dragon.

"Now, let's go somewhere a bit more private," she said. "We have a lot to discuss before you leave."

"Wha—"

I didn't even get the full word out before she snapped her fingers and the world around me flickered, like every lightbulb in every horror movie.

My stomach lurched, trying its hardest to leap from my body before slamming back into me with a force that left me gasping for air. "Ugh!"

"Someone would think you'd never teleported before." Beasty sniffed.

"That didn't feel like teleporting." I ground out the words through clenched teeth, afraid that if I unclenched them, I would lose what little there was in my stomach. Blinking furiously, I tried to get the world around me to stop spinning.

Beasty shrugged and gave me a little playful smile. "You have a point. Reality is a bit different here, and that makes teleporting a bit more jarring. Here, have a drink."

She shoved a delicate crystal glass into my trembling hand. A bubblegum pink liquid sloshed over the side, while a tiny paper umbrella spun crazily as though caught in a whirlpool. I stared stupidly at the drink for several long moments, my exhausted brain working overtime to process everything that had just happened. Finally, I looked up into the electric blue eyes that were both familiar and unfamiliar at this same time.

My dragon, my inner voice of not-so-good-and-usually-thirsty advice, gazed back at me. My heart ached with the remembered pain of losing her, of not really getting to say goodbye.

Beasty reclined on a dazzling golden chaise like a model in the middle of a photoshoot on a Greek beach. Her long, pale, and very human legs were crossed elegantly at the ankles. She wore delicate soft leather sandals with tiny braided straps that laced up her legs, making them appear even longer.

A gown so sheer it was nearly transparent draped over her willowy body. Light caught and glinted off tiny crystals dotting the gown like raindrops. It reminded me of being back home in the mountains; the rose gold sunrise would touch the dewy grass and the entire field would glimmer and sparkle.

Beasty's long silky hair fell nearly to her waist in flowing waves. Gold and pearl jewelry peeked from between the locks as she moved. An intricate woven band wound around her head, the precious metal curving and swirling like the waves of the ocean. Realization began to dawn on me. It was a crown. She looked like something from a Hercules movie. Like a...

"Goddess?" she finished. A long, tapered nail tapped at her chin, and she tilted her head playfully.

"Yes." My lungs constricted. This had to be a dream. It couldn't be real. I had been beaten to the point of passing out and now my brain had conjured up this lovely little scene. That made more sense. Or who knew? Maybe I had actually died, and this was heaven.

"Kinda, sorta." Beasty took a long sip of the rose-colored liquid in her glass before continuing. "Well, actually, you aren't truly dead. I take that back. But on the human plane they would consider you quite dead. Are you an organ donor? I would hate to think that they were beginning to harvest your organs right now."

I was an organ donor, although if they were chopping up my body, I highly doubted it was for a good cause. My throat squeezed shut, making it impossible to speak. All I could do was stare at my inner dragon in wide-eyed horror with my mouth hanging open.

"I would tell you to close your mouth so you don't swallow a bug, but they don't exist here. Those mean little creatures go straight to hell." She shuddered delicately before saying, "If your body was fully human and you'd attempted this stunt, there would be no going back. Thankfully, you aren't human, and after our nice little chat, you will return to your body. I think. I was still researching the finer details of how this works between realms. It wasn't supposed to happen yet, although I shouldn't be too surprised. Sweet girl, you seem to thrive on the unexpected and I am *loving* it!"

"So, you're real, not just a dream created by my fragmented mind?" I asked. There was no hiding the tremble in my voice. There was so much I wanted to say, a multitude of questions I wanted to ask, I just didn't know where to start.

Sitting up, she lowered her legs to the ground and reached out to grasp my hand. "Yes, Tia. I am real."

That was all I needed to hear. Dropping the delicate glass, I threw my arms around her and sobbed into her neck. She stiffened for a fraction of a second, but then her arms wrapped around me, squeezing me tight against her and stroking my hair. Never in a million years had I thought I would get the chance to speak with Beasty again, let alone hug her.

I wanted to ask her how this was possible, but every time I opened my mouth another sob escaped. I settled back into my chair, trying to regain my composure and wiping my face with the tissues she had conjured from who knows where.

"I'll explain as best I can, Sugar Plum," she said sweetly. "It's hard figuring out where to start. I had a grand speech prepared, but your early arrival messed up that plan. Speaking of early arrivals, I need to know what has happened since I left you. There was a nasty little spell in place that prevented me from seeing you or interacting with you. The only way to break it was for you to come to me. Man, they are going to be *so* mad that you already managed that! I can't wait to rub it in their faces."

If I had possessed any more doubts that this was indeed Beasty, the gleeful tone and the mischievous sparkle in her eye would have squashed them immediately.

"Okay, so you are in the realm of the gods," she continued.

"This is a place between places, a veil between dimensions, a space between worlds, a crack between butt cheeks."

I choked.

She ignored me and continued on, "The gods hang out here, pretending to be better than everyone else. It's a source of pride to them that only the gods and goddesses can enter here, like their own personal clubhouse with a secret password. Seriously, you would think they were eight years old with the way they act. They don't like each other and bicker constantly. I doubt they could make it any more boring here if they tried."

"How am I here?" I asked, my brain finally managing to string a few words together into a coherent sentence.

"Funny story about that!"

I doubted that. My life had been seriously lacking in the humor department lately. I raised an eyebrow.

"You're dead. No, don't look like that! It's not permanent, well, at least not yet. As long as we get you back into your body within the hour, you should be fine. Mostly."

My face felt frozen in a mask of horror. I had died? I wasn't going to ever see my mates again? Hot tears scorched my eyes. I never got to say goodbye.

"Don't start with the waterworks again!" Beasty cried. "We don't have much longer left together here, and I have zero desire to spend what's left with you in tears. You aren't truly dead, and there will be plenty of sex in your future with all those yummy mates." She flashed me a wicked grin before continuing, "Now, think of it like teleporting, except in this case, you left your physical body behind. Almost like astral projecting, but you aren't tethered to your body at all. You've managed to split yourself in two, a talent that is rare and essentially considered impossible. Very few beings manage this feat, and those that do are many centuries older than you. I was among the few that possessed the ability, and the fact that you have done it at such a young age is *really* going to tick off the other gods."

Her beautiful lips twisted into a gleeful grin that was eerily reminiscent of a creepy clown from an old horror movie. The cat-that-caught-the-canary expression on her face left no doubt in my mind that she couldn't wait to rub this in their faces.

"Beasty?" I whispered, but she didn't seem to hear me.

And because poking a dragon goddess while she was deep in thought about revenge was a horrible idea, that's exactly what I did. I gently touched her shoulder.

"AH!" She jumped like I had stabbed her and clutched at her chest.

Startled, I also stumbled back. "AHH!"

Bemused, her mouth snapped shut and her head tilted to the side. "Why are you screaming?"

"Because you screamed and scared me!" I'll admit it, I'd grown jumpy over the last few weeks. Without even realizing it, I'd grown accustomed to the reassurance of my magic as it swirled constantly around me. My ever-present alert system. Having that abruptly taken away had left me feeling vulnerable. Yep, I wasn't a fan.

Beasty began laughing. The joy-filled sound pulled me away from my inner ramblings. I had missed her and the annoying, yet endearing, way she forever kept me on my toes.

"When you were my inner dragon, you said we were Tiamat, Goddess of the Sea. How is that possible?" I asked. "You are clearly your own person. We can't both be the same person. Can we?" I was no longer sure what was or was not possible.

"Alright, Lollipop. Let me try to finish explaining before our time is up. This is hard to explain because the human and god realms play by different rules. Think of it like this, a human mother gives birth to a human child. Flesh of her flesh and all that. You are my very essence. In this realm, the gods and goddesses can choose to be corporeal or incorporeal. It is of little importance unless we are looking to take part in a bit of horizontal refreshment."

The wiggle of her eyebrows and the sly wink she gave me left no doubts as to what she was talking about.

"Please tell me that you aren't trying to tell me that you are my mom!" Hysteria bubbled up in my chest. She had been in my head while I had claimed my mates, while we had...

I was going to be sick.

"Calm your tits. I'm not your mom. That would have been creepy!" She shook her head violently. "Our kind are made of energy, time, and magic. If we are powerful enough, we can divide our essence and infuse it into a vessel. The challenge is that the god, or goddess, must have an insane amount of magic built up to perform this feat, and the vessel must be strong enough to survive the onslaught of raw power.

"It is risky for all involved, and throughout the history of our universe, it has only been done successfully three times. You are the third. A goddess or god only gets one chance to divide their essence. We are not allowed to change the past, but we are given that one opportunity to change things by giving of ourselves. Everything had to be in perfect alignment for it to work. Your bloodline, the prophecy, the peak of my power. The world needs you to set a balance, and I wanted a chance to right the wrongs done to me in the past."

I stayed quiet, but my unease must have shown on my face.

"I am not your mother!" Beasty emphasized. "Perhaps a clone would be the best word to describe it? There really isn't a human word to describe what we are. We are made of the same base ingredients, but in two bodies."

Her brow wrinkled in concentration, and her nail clicked as she absentmindedly tapped it against her teeth. After another minute, her eyes lit up.

"Identical twins!" she squealed. "Like I said, there isn't a human concept for what we are. Our spirit is one, but our minds and bodies are divided. Your mind and body are fully your own... At least they are now that I am back in this boring realm. I think identical twins is the closest we can come to an Earth term for our relationship. Identical twins are formed from the dividing of a single egg, and we are from the dividing of a single essence."

I listened to her with narrowed eyes, not sure I was following, but willing to accept any explanation that meant she wasn't my mom. Because, ew.

Suddenly, a sharp stab of pain sliced up my spine. I cried

out and my back arched reflexively. Beasty appeared in the empty space beside me and wrapped her arms around me.

"We are running out of time," she said. "The tiny invisible threads that will guide your spirit back to your body are beginning to break. Quickly, let me see what has happened since we were separated."

Her cool fingers slid to each side of my head, stopping once they rested on my temples. Faint sparkles danced in my vision, and the spots where her fingers pressed grew hot. I stared into her eyes and watched as one emotion after another danced across her face. Faster and faster. Sadness, joy, lust, horror, anger, love, curiosity, loss, fear, shock, outrage, pain.

She lurched away from me, agony twisting her features. The soft sound of her sobs hurt me far more than being whipped ever had.

Another stab of pain traveled up my spine, bringing more tears to my already damp eyes. My fingers turned white where I dug them into the seat in an attempt to stop from screaming.

There was no hiding it, we were still connected in a cosmic way that I didn't fully understand. Turning back toward me, Beasty clasped my hands in her own.

"I'm so proud of you, Tia. I knew your path would be difficult, but even I hadn't realized how quickly things were going to happen. Listen to me. The horrors you are going through right now will be over soon. You will survive this and come out swinging. The knowledge you have gleaned from my memories will help you with what is to come. If you can learn to control it, there is a possibility that this new ability of yours may allow us to communicate in the future."

Tears rolled down my cheeks. I didn't feel strong, I felt tired, and I didn't want to leave her. She brushed her knuckles against my cheek in a comforting gesture.

"You are going to have to stop fighting the heat. It doesn't care how strong-willed you are, and dang girl, you do have an iron will. I have never met a dragoness that was able to hold back her heat for more than a few hours, let alone days on end. Dragons are beasts that carry literal fire in their chests. We are primal in our passion and our ability to survive.

"Your body is doing what it is programmed to do, continue our species by whatever means necessary. Perhaps if you were a normal dragoness, you could be chained and the heat would eventually fade, leaving you weakened but alive. That isn't going to work for you though. You are the last royal dragon, and you possess the essence of the gods.

"When you fused fully with the dragoness's nature, it sent everything in your body into overdrive. That is why your heat came centuries too early, and why it hasn't abated. It is getting worse, Tia. You are growing weaker each day. The weakening of your body should have forced the heat to abate, but instead, instinct is causing the heat to intensify in an effort to ensure you produce an heir."

My mind was reeling. I had been clinging to the hope that I would wake up any day now and find that the fever of my heat had broken. If Beasty was correct, I wasn't going to have relief until I was with my mates again, or until I managed to free myself which would allow my magic to heal my battered body.

I didn't see how I would be able to do either option in my

463

current condition, and who knew what was being done to my body while I was taking a field trip to this realm. My mates were no doubt searching for me, but I wasn't keen on playing a damsel-in-distress who just sits around waiting to be saved. How could I take back my kingdom if I couldn't even take back my freedom?

"You can't. Not alone, at least not this time."

My gaze met hers.

"He has been kind to you, and for now that may have to be enough. There are many things I am not allowed to disclose to you at this point, and countless lives hang in the balance. You have been so busy fighting to control the heat that you've yet to realize the powers you've unlocked. You are ready, the world needs you now. Your mates need you."

I continued to stare into Beasty's shimmering eyes as she continued, "If you are both willing, stop resisting and give into your dragoness. The sooner you do, the sooner you can bust out of there and light 'em up! Stop fighting against the very fiber of your being. You aren't human, you are a butt-kicking, fire-breathing, blade-loving dragoness. It's time to own that crap! Take what is yours by birth right."

At her words I felt my skin begin to tingle, the warmth spreading across it. My tattoos, which I hadn't seen since being chained in the dungeon, flickered with blue light. I was a dragon, hear me roar!

Black spots danced in front of my eyes, and all the oxygen was sucked from my lungs. Beasty's eyes shimmered with unshed tears.

"It's time to go, Buttercup! Go back and show everyone what legends are made of!"

My vision went dark as the world around me swirled at a dizzying speed. I groaned as her parting words drifted to me moments before I was sucked into oblivion.

"Let's get this party started! Set stuff on fire, destroy a few cities, eat some bad guys, and don't forget to let those mates plunder your little pink fortress!"

CHAPTER THREE

Guard

I stood guard over the female's lifeless body, careful to position myself between her and the cell door. Some part of me knew that I was trying to shield her from the raving lunatics should they return, but I refused to acknowledge that truth.

Fae had been considered cold and calculating in the past, and to an extent that was entirely accurate. The truth is that logic was prized above all else in our world, and so we spent our lives making decisions without the burden of emotions. Fae did possess emotions, but with careful training, we were able to gain control over that weakness.

The strongest of our kind, those trained in battle and logic, joined the elite guards that protected the Fae realm from threats and potential threats. Nothing could distract a Fae soldier from his mission. So why on this fae-forsaken earth was my body reacting to a weak female?

Squinting my eyes, I took in every minute detail of her still form. She didn't have a heartbeat, nor did her chest rise and fall. Something ugly flickered inside me, and it took me a moment to recognize the emotion. Rage. How odd. The female had been treated despicably, but it was not a surprise to me. I hadn't expected much better from Earth's inhabitants. The greed and cruelty that ran rampant on the planet were the very reasons I had been sent here.

Whether the female lived or died was of no consequence to me. She was simply the captive I was guarding while working on my covert mission. Watching the queen's delight in inflicting torture emphasized the depths of evil that had consumed this world. I didn't approve of the unfair treatment Bunny received, but logic dictated I should remain uninvolved. I had my orders, and she was certainly not on that list.

I'd stood by as the vampire guards dragged their victim to the circular chamber the queen preferred for her playtime. This had been the routine every day of Tia's captivity. She would be forced to her knees before having thick chains wrapped around her wrists and ankles. The forced bow gave the sadistic queen a sense of power over her bedraggled prisoner.

Sometimes, the queen would further humiliate her victim by ripping off whatever scrap of fabric the female had managed to wrap herself in. Since her wounds were never fully given time to heal between these sessions, the blood-soaked fabric was almost glued to her skin. When the clothing was yanked from her body, it tore open her devastating wounds with a sound that would have made lesser men vomit.

Yet, no matter what new flesh-shredding toy the queen devised, she could never get her captive to scream. I'd nick-named the little female Bunny—a name she despised—for her skittish ways the first time we met. Her body had flinched away from every sound and movement, but her eyes had held strength. It turned out the name was ironic. She was no scared rabbit.

Beneath the dried blood and the dark bruises that covered nearly every inch of her flesh, she had the heart of a warrior. I had no doubt that if she'd been born Fae, she would have been a leader among our kind. She also would have had many Fae men seeking an heir agreement with her.

My stomach jerked at the last thought. Glancing at the clock I saw it was several hours before we were to eat again. Fae were not susceptible to the illnesses that plagued this realm. I could think of no logical reason for the twisting of my stomach, and it was not something I remembered experi-encing in the past. Strange. I would need to document this and discuss it with the Fae elders.

I had been on break when the sound of the queen's angry screeches and a bellowing man's voice had shaken the stone walls of the dungeon. Moving quickly into the queen's play-room, my eyes scanned the room and took in the pandemonium.

A small female dressed in training clothing emblazoned with the werewolves' emblem was pressed against the far wall. Her eyes were nearly white as she stared in wide-eyed horror at the crumpled body on the blood-covered stone floor. The new female was no threat; her emotions caused her body to freeze in place. I couldn't see the doctor and scientist that were always there to take Bunny's blood after each beating. Either they had already taken their samples, or today's session had been interrupted unexpectedly.

Cutting my eyes to the opposite side of the room, I studied the pair trying to out scream each other. They both needed to die. Among the Fae, crimes were met with a swift and absolute end. We did not find pleasure in torturing and maiming others. It was a waste of time. If you are convicted of a crime worthy of death, you pay the punishment instantly. These two should have ceased breathing long ago.

I debated for a moment on whether to separate the fighting duo or hold back in the hopes one would fatally wound the other. The queen's guards seemed to be thinking the same thing, moving slowly toward the pair. My decision was made when I turned to look at Bunny.

She hadn't moved from her position, the flow of blood that had soaked the floor had ceased. The temperature in the room seemed to drop.

Her blood wasn't pumping.

Calling on my Fae gifts, I strained to hear her heartbeat. Nothing.

Her heart wasn't beating.

My stomach jerked for the second time that day, but I didn't have time to be concerned about what contagion in this realm was affecting me. I needed to get the female back to her cage. The thick bars and lock kept her away from freedom, but in that moment, it offered her only hope of keeping these two monsters away from her. At least for a time.

My movements, sure and steady, unchained her limp body in only a few seconds. Scooping her in my arms, I found that she weighed far less than I'd guessed. Even as dead weight, she was little more than skin stretched on a skeleton. Fae were well-versed on human anatomy and the nourishment their bodies required. While the food had not been lavish, they had fed her enough to sustain her body. The alpha werewolf had made sure of that. He hoped she carried his child in her womb, and while he cared nothing about her, he did care about the status her child could give him. Hence the reason for his fight with the queen.

The queen had grown increasingly cruel with each session in this room, leaving wounds that even a supernatural at full strength couldn't heal. Bunny's continued defiance in the face of the queen's rage had added fuel to the queen's insanity. Had she finally gone too far and killed her captive today?

I shifted the rapidly cooling body in my arms and eyed the protruding bones that were on display due to her missing shirt. Could the 'heat' she kept worrying over in her thoughts be the cause of the drastic decline of her body?

The spell that dampened the magic in the dungeon had made it very hard for me to glean much about her species using my Fae senses. What little I knew had come from the thoughts of those around me, and frankly, it didn't seem like any of them knew much about what she was. Dragon. That was the word that bounced around in all their minds, a word that made no sense. What precisely was a *dragon*? It was a species that had not been mentioned by the elders.

"I am returning the prisoner to her cell," I said. My voice was clipped. I sank deep into the shadows and away from the others before anyone could argue with me.

She may have been dead, but until I was positive, I saw no reason to leave her to their whims. Especially the werewolf alpha. *Cage.* He'd been the one to toss her disheveled body into the cell that first night. His scent had clung to her skin. I had gathered enough from his thoughts, and hers, to piece together what had happened. Her joy in their reconciliation, hope for a new beginning, and then his ice-cold betrayal that had shattered her heart.

He'd come to the underground dungeon every day, and each day he'd left with a headache, confused as to why he was there. It had taken me significant focus to cloud his mind and bend his will. The migraine I suffered after each encounter was an acceptable price to pay for the knowledge that he had not laid a finger on her body. I was unable to change the past, but I did not wish her to experience further hurt from the dog.

She deserved to be treated with love and tenderness.

This concept was foreign to me. Where had it come from? Fae didn't do love or tenderness. Things like marriages and families didn't exist in our realm. On Earth, my kind would be considered wanton. We have a strong sex drive, and logically, it is an efficient way to burn off the excess energy that our bodies collect.

The phrase 'like a moth to a flame' is an apt description of the way energy seeks out the Fae, much like a homing beacon.

We are living energy conductors, taking it in, using what we need to accomplish our tasks, and then forcing the excess into nature. The problem is that when the energy builds to a dangerous level, our bodies become walking weapons of mass destruction. The most effective way we have found to funnel off rising energy levels is sex.

It is common to walk the streets and see a couple assisting each other with a necessary release. If you are on a mission, and the levels of energy are distracting or dangerous, it is easy to find a Fae willing to copulate. We do not feel shame or guilt over taking care of a primal need, and we don't feel envy over who partners with whom. Our couplings have none of the love or passion that humans seem to require.

The dungeon dampened the energy, which had spared me from having to deal with an energy buzz. Once I left this place, the energy was going to hit me like an angry bull.

That's not to say we don't find it enjoyable, quite the opposite. While we've chosen to control unnecessary emotions such as guilt, sadness, love, envy, and anger, we still have things we enjoy and things we dislike. Sex is a favorite pastime of the Fae, and since it serves a purpose for our species, it was only logical for us to study and practice it. I could say we excel at the sexual arts, but even that would be a massive understatement. We also excel at killing, which is what would have happened instantly to Cage had he been in the Fae realm. He was getting off far too easy.

For now.

Angry voices echoed down the hallway, before finally disappearing in the distance. This was followed by footsteps stomping away from the dungeon. Assured that we had some time before anyone would return, I moved to sit on the floor next to the cot where I had placed the battered body. She remained motionless, her lips taking on a pale blue hue. I laid my hand on her forehead to check the temperature of her skin. It was icy to the touch. Far too cool for a living human.

My mind, normally a well-oiled and organized machine, faltered. *She isn't dead.* That thought repeated over and over in my mind. But logically, I couldn't deny the concrete physical evidence of her death. Not when her lifeless body was mere inches from me. Had the heat weakened her to the point that her system gave out? Or had the queen lost control and pushed her traumatized body too far?

In the end, the result didn't matter. She was gone, and I had done nothing. A fire began a slow burn in my stomach, the heat spreading through my upper body. With a lurch, my intestines twisted and churned.

A loud pounding filled my ears, blocking out all other sounds - the chirping cricket that evaded capture with the skill of a Fae, and the soft drip of the water traveling down the moss-covered stone walls to plop into the stagnant, green-tinged puddles beneath them... Even with my Fae abilities I was unable to hear anything other than the drumbeat banging in my ears.

My brain flashed through logical possibilities to explain the sudden illness attacking my body. Had I eaten spoiled food? Perhaps I was affected by a spell? Poison?

Looking back at the beautiful dragon, realization dawned on me. This was grief. I was grieving for someone I had barely known. The flicker of emotion I was experiencing would have been faint for a human, but for me it was overwhelming.

The pounding drumbeat grew louder as it picked up speed. I clapped my hands over my ears to drown out the onslaught of noise, only to realize the skull-rattling sound was my own heartbeat.

Of all the things I had experienced that day, that was the one that shook me most. It was impossible because a Fae's heartbeat is unchanging. From our first beat until the last, the heart of a Fae drums a song that is as unique as the human fingerprint. Just as every snowflake in this realm was an original work of art, so was the unique composition of each Fae's heart-song. Our magnum opus. The tempo never accelerates nor does it slow, not until it plays its final notes.

As grief continued to spread pain through every fiber of my being, I gathered the woman with a warrior's heart into my arms. I was seeking comfort from another for the first time in my life. Logic dictated I should scoff at the futility of my actions, but for the first time in my life, I ignored logic. I allowed myself this one moment to truly feel.

A new emotion snaked its way up my spine to twist around my heart. Regret. I should have done something to help her escape, regardless of the risk to my own mission.

I had watched as her body had shaken with fever from her heat. She had shoved her dirty shirt into her mouth to muffle the sounds of her screams as pain from the beatings and her heat had tried to tear at her insides. I had watched the sparkle of mischief begin to fade as she had used the last of her reserves to stave off the demanding call of her heat.

Her sobs late at night had been so quiet that only my natural abilities had allowed me to hear them. She had only cried when she longed for her mates, the separation and loneliness too great to keep bottled inside. I had gathered enough from her thoughts to have a general idea of what her mates meant to her and what her heat was. What I couldn't understand was why she had spent every ounce of energy she had to fight it. It almost seemed like she'd feared her own nature more than she feared being held here and tortured.

She deserved so much more.

If I was given another chance, I would do things differently. I cradled her in my arms, unable to do anything else.

"Beautiful, broken rabbit." The rasp of my throat distorted the words.

A glow lit the dark cell. Its pale-yellow light emanated from me and enveloped us both in a soft light. Yet one more thing to add to the growing list of things I didn't understand. I stroked a finger against her cheek.

"My little Bunny."

CHAPTER FOUR

Tia

You know how hard you have to suck to free the chocolate candies that get stuck in the straw of your milkshake? Yep, being sucked back into my body was pretty much exactly like that. The suction of being vacuumed was jarring and my insides vibrated like a tuning fork. I would've seen double if my eyes hadn't been squeezed closed. I promised myself I would never go gallivanting between realms without a body again.

"*...Bunny.*"

The deep masculine voice penetrated the haze in my brain. I recognized the voice instantly. Pixie-Man better not be referring to me by that idiotic nickname. Once we got out of here, he was going to get the surprise of his life when I shifted into my dragon and sat on his annoying self. Gently, of course.

My lungs, that had just remembered how to breathe again, ceased moving. In my mind, I was assuming that once I gained my freedom, he would stay by my side. We were barely more than strangers to each other, though. What if he didn't want to go with me? That possible outcome sent a sick feeling straight to the pit of my stomach.

As my senses returned to my body, I realized several things at once: I was shivering from the cold, every joint in my body was stiff, and pain was zinging its way across my skin as my nervous system sluggishly came to life. The only parts of me not currently in horrific pain were the parts pressed against the warm stone wall I was propped against. I shifted, pressing every inch of skin I could manage against the delicious heat.

"Mmmm." My sound was half a groan of pain and half a moan of pleasure. No wonder women paid exorbitant amounts of money to have a hot stone massage. I knew what I was asking Myth to get me for my birthday.

The solid rock wall shifted.

Son-of-a-butt-munch. I survived vicious beatings from a vampire queen, and being vacuumed through realms, only to die from an earthquake. Beasty's pep talk had pumped me up, and now, just minutes after our last encounter, I would be landing on my back in front of her again.

"Bunny, stop panicking. Your body cannot handle any more stress."

I was sick of people telling me what to do. If I wanted to

panic, *I would panic* the house down. The thing was, he was wrong. I wasn't feeling panic, it was frustration that surged through me. I snapped open my eyes and locked gazes with the infuriating guard.

"I wish everyone would stop trying to control me!" I snapped. "I'm sick of everyone telling me what I should or should not do. It was so much easier when I stopped trying to cling to the human customs I grew up with and merged with the dragon. For a brief time, I made decisions without second guessing myself and worrying over the opinions of everyone around me."

White hot rage surged through my body, heating my blood, and eradicating the chill. There was no mistaking the slight widening of his eyes at my slitted pupils and glowing irises. Satisfaction bloomed in my chest at catching the emotionless man off-guard, even if only the tiniest bit. I'm a dragon, hear me roar and all that jazz.

"This shouldn't be possible. You were dead." His fingers brushed gently through my dirty hair, the gesture awkward, but strangely endearing.

I shrugged. "News of my death was greatly exaggerated."

Sadly, my snark went unappreciated. Maybe fairies lacked a real sense of humor, or maybe they were born with a stick up their butt. I would be happy to check out his fine butt and offer my assistance in helping him to loosen up. The thought came unbidden into my mind, and I prayed he hadn't heard.

That hope was quickly dashed when his nostrils flared, and his pupils dilated. The signs were nearly imperceptible, but I'd seen them. His ears twitched in the cutest way ever. It was the equivalent of a puppy tilting its head, or a bunny twitching its nose.

"Aww!" Reaching up, I traced the length of his pointed ear.

"You shouldn't be able to see—" But his words cut off as his eyes tried to roll into the back of his skull.

"Sweet wittle pixie wuvs his earsy-wearsies scratched!" I cooed the words in that tone reserved for adorable babies of the human and animal varieties.

The poor man's face had changed from a black mask to one that shifted between horror, outrage, confusion, annoyance, and...desire? My breath caught in my throat.

In the blink of an eye, his face once again became blank. For some irrational reason, the change sent a pang of hurt through me. I tried to push away from him, to put some distance between myself and the confusing man, but my body refused my command.

I tried again, managing to shift myself in his embrace, barely. Beasty's warning had come too late. The vicious attacks from the queen, the separation from my mates, and the energy required to keep my sanity while fighting back against the demands of the heat had all taken their toll on my body.

At that very moment, my stomach was contorting itself into a tight knot, and pain had begun creeping through my traumatized body. With my spirit back in my body, and my senses returning, the brief reprieve from heat was drawing to an end. I knew with certainty that I would not make it through another night of agony, fever, and vomiting.

I would not see my mates again on this Earth. Tears

sprang to my eyes. Unconsciously, my hand had moved to rest on my flat stomach. It would be a miracle if a baby was able to survive the nightmare that had become my life since the ball. But I'd never get the chance to know for sure.

Pixie cleared his throat, but I couldn't find the strength to lift my head.

"I have a proposition."

At my silence he continued, "We are both aware that you will be dead within a day, either from torture or by the vampire's hand. You cannot walk, and I cannot fight the other guards while also carrying you to freedom. I am still unsure of the specifications of a dragon, but from my observations, our kind are physically compatible. Your heat is weakening you more than the torture you have endured. If what I have gleaned from your thoughts is correct, you need to breed to satisfy the heat. Is this correct?"

Still, I didn't look up. I only nodded, the motion dislodging the tears in my eyes and sending the fat droplets splashing onto the blanket wrapped around my chest - a clean blanket and one I didn't recognize. I sniffed, breathing in the scent of allspice. The cold, unfeeling man had wrapped my filthy body in his own blanket.

"If we copulate, will your body be able to repair the damage?" he asked.

Each of my mates had wanted me with a burning passion, the exact opposite of the cool business arrangement Pixie seemed to be proposing.

"Yes." I knew without a doubt that my body could repair itself quickly. Once my body healed, I would be free to focus on turning this place into a fire pit. There would be nothing left when I finished. My magic rubbed faintly against my skin, a reminder that it lurked and waited to be freed.

"Then the answer is simple. I know from your thoughts you would not ask it of me, so I volunteer my services. There is no reason for you to die when there is a logical solution to save your life."

I finally lifted my head and studied his face. Those words coming from any other man would have been epitome of arrogance, but not from him. I had spent enough time with the pointy-eared giant to know this wasn't just a sick ploy to get into my pants. While the man was aloof and kept to himself, he had shown a gentleness toward me and had treated me with nothing but decency.

I was surprised to see the fine lines that wrinkled his brow and the corners of his eyes. He was worried - another emotion I hadn't thought he was capable of feeling. My instincts screamed that I should pounce on him and take the lifeline he had offered me. The golden ticket to my freedom.

I just couldn't do it. My loyalty to my mates meant more to me than my own life. We had shared many conversations discussing our family, my circle. They had all made it clear that, should I find another mate, they were in full support of him joining the family. Personally, I hadn't wanted to claim another mate. I adored my men, and they were my world.

I knew their insistence was partially due to the fact that they liked the idea of keeping me protected at all times. What better way to do that than to have several mates with me at all times? I hated knowing that they were likely blaming themselves for my disappearance. They hadn't failed me, my own trusting nature had.

I would not have a one-night stand with a man. If I was going to accept his offer, he was going to have to be willing to be claimed at the same time as my mate.

He must have been reading my muddled thoughts because he asked, "By claiming and mates, are you speaking of a bonding for life? Like that practiced by werewolves and vampires?"

"Yes. Humans call it marriage, although for me it is far more permanent. If I claim you, there is no way to sever that bond, at least not one that I know of."

His expression was a blank mask as he contemplated that information. He was a man of logic, and I knew that the logical course of action for him was to toss me away from him and walk—no, run—from this cell. There were exactly zero reasons for him to take on a world of problems by mating with me. I didn't know how much information he had gathered from my thoughts and the thoughts of those around him. Was he aware of who I was, or did he see me just as the current plaything of a sadistic vampire queen?

My heart rate began to increase, the strain of the coming heat flare pushing the tired organ to pump faster. Each beat was a lopsided thud that didn't bode well for my long-term survival. The pain had gone from hot fire to searing lava. I ground my teeth together and swallowed back a whimper, unwilling to risk my actions swaying him to make a decision he would regret.

"I have only experienced regret once in my life," he suddenly confessed.

I was surprised that he was giving me such a personal piece of information. With no small amount of effort, I shifted my hand until it rested atop his and I gave it a weak squeeze. "When did it happen?"

His eyes were riveted to our hands. When he finally answered, the words sent shock waves crashing through me. "It happened today."

When his eyes met mine, his face bore no signs of indecision or confusion. For better or for worse, his decision had been made.

"I accept your proposal. I am agreeable to being claimed as your mate."

In another situation, I would have found this hilarious. I might have even bent down on one knee to complete the reversed roles we were playing in this life-altering moment. But it was not a joke or something to be made light of. An emotionless man, with nothing to gain but a buttload of problems and a target on his back, had just agreed to tie himself to me for the rest of his life, all to save me from dying. He could walk out of this cell, get a good night's sleep while I breathed my last, and wake up tomorrow free of me.

Reading the hesitation in either my thoughts or my expression, he responded to my unanswered question, "I am Fae, and my species sees no value in emotions. They are a hindrance to be squashed. I have never felt anything for another human beyond appreciation for their skills, or a respect for their knowledge. You are different. I feel something for you, and I find myself wanting to be near you. I do not love you, and I am not even sure if I am capable of love. However, you will have my loyalty. I will honor our bond, and you have my vow that I will protect you for as long as I draw breath. That is all I have to offer you. If you wish to proceed, that will have to be enough."

I remembered Beasty's words from what felt like ages ago. A dragoness was given the ability to choose her mates; it ensured she was never forced into a bond and that she could pick the mates she needed most. The man cradling me against his chest was honorable and he was offering me his all. I couldn't say that I loved him, not yet. But there was something between us, and for now that would have to be enough.

I needed him.

"I would be proud to call you my mate."

With a sigh of relief, I relaxed. I dropped the tenuous hold I had on my crumbling human facade and stopped fighting to control the dragon's nature.

I stopped clinging to the idea of how I saw myself, and finally accepted who I was... And dang, but it felt good!

My fairy leaned down and nipped my lower lip before sucking it gently between his own.

I purred.

CHAPTER FIVE

Tia

I had expected sex with my soon-to-be-mate to be detached and clinical, or fast and rough. It was neither of those things. His every caress was designed to heighten my pleasure. He handled me with the same gentleness that you would handle a priceless work of art. There were no declarations of love, yet I still felt treasured.

"I take care of what belongs to me," he whispered into my ear, sending a shiver down my spine at the sensation of his tongue tracing the delicate curved edge.

I couldn't have stopped my embarrassing moan even if I had wanted to. I needed this, and I wanted him. Fighting to focus, I tried to find brain cells that still worked to help me string together a coherent sentence.

"What is your name, fairy boy?" My human voice was

gone and now my words reverberated with a seductive tone that promised wonderfully naughty things. I suddenly remembered how I had nearly killed my mates with the demands of my heat, and there were five of them. Weakly, I pushed away from him, anxiety washing over me at the thought of killing him by riding him until he died.

Instead of letting me go, he grasped my waist and turned me toward him until my legs straddled his lap. "My species does not shy away from death while serving the Fae kingdom," he said firmly. "It is considered an honorable death, and it is the preferred cause of death among my kind. However, I am finding that I am not opposed to the concept of dying with my rod inside you and you screaming your release."

HO-LY CRAP. Forget butterflies, my stomach danced an Irish jig and my ovaries swooned. My mouth went dry as my body gathered all the liquid it could find in this dehydrated form, only to send all of it to my needy core.

There was something important I needed to know, but for the life of me I couldn't imagine what could be more important than jumping the hot guy with pointed ears whose body I was pressed against ...

"You wished to know my name."

"Uh. Oh. Yeah," I stammered. "I think it would be kinda weird to mark you and then have to ask what your name is."

Not knowing his name had seemed like a big problem earlier. But with the thick lust-filled haze of the heat spreading across my vision, the only problem I could see was the fact that he still wore pants. Less talking, more thrusting. I licked my lips, eying him like he was my meal and I hadn't eaten in two weeks. Come to think of it, that wasn't too far from the reality of the situation.

"It is forbidden for me to speak my name outside of Fae," he continued. "Our names and language are only ever spoken within our home realm. I have used a false name for myself since arriving, but it carries no meaning. I find that I do not wish for you to call me by that name."

I was kissing my way up his neck, trying to focus on his words, but finding that challenging when exploring the curves of his muscles and slipping my fingers into his blonde hair that was nearly longer than my own. "I have to call you something," I murmured, "unless you prefer I just call you mine."

If I wasn't so unbelievably turned on, I'd have gagged on the amount of sex my voice had just promised. I rolled my eyes, but it wasn't out of annoyance with myself. Nope, it was caused by the man who had managed to rock his hips in a way that rubbed me in all the right places. I was surprised I didn't pass out and wake back up with Beasty standing over me.

"You have called me by the name Pixie. I believe this was meant to annoy me, much as the name Bunny annoys you. However, it is a name you and you alone have called me. I find I do not dislike the idea of keeping it. My body has a reaction to the name, which is unusual, and I wish to study it further."

He wanted to be called by the silly pet name I had given him? Unshed tears burned my eyes and tickled my nose. This man craved love, whether he realized it or not. "Pixie is my special name for you. To the rest of the world, you can be Pixel."

His shoulders relaxed a fraction. "We are in agreement. Now we mate."

My body responded like those words, spoken in a clipped emotionless voice, were the most romantic thing anyone had ever said to me. Was I starving for attention or what?

His lips pressed to the corner of my mouth for the briefest moment, teasing me with the promise of things to come. Curling my fingers in his hair, I tried to pull him tighter against me, but my weak efforts weren't enough to move him even an inch.

"Stop tiring yourself more, little rabbit. Use your strength to heal. Trust me to see to your needs."

I growled. My dragoness wanted to show her mate that she was no little bunny foo-foo. If I were at full strength, he would be the exhausted one needing to heal. I would have to be satisfied with the knowledge that if this worked, I had plenty of time to show this man the side of me that he had yet to see.

Hot lips brushed along mine with a featherlight touch. My instincts screamed for me to capture his lips and cling to him like a spider monkey, but I forced myself to relax. I would trust him.

The moment that thought crossed my mind, he sucked my bottom lip between his, before giving mine a gentle nip. Large hands grasped my hips and began to slowly rock my lower half, while at the same time, his pelvis did another of those sinful rolls. The firm contact, combined with his sexy undulation, very nearly melted my brain.

I groaned, and he was quick to seize that opportunity to

bump our kiss from sweet to spicy. My chest began to burn, not in the *I'm-having-a-panic-attack* way, but more in the *I-have-literal-fire-burning-in-my-chest* kind of way. My heat was returning with a vengeance, and my magic was testing the barrier blocking it.

"Is it normal for your skin to smoke during copulation?" he asked.

It took several seconds for his words to penetrate the fog in my mind. I was imagining him penetrating something else. "Huh?"

Then I glanced down. Sure enough, there were wispy tendrils of smoke coming from me. The evidence of the beatings still-marred my too pale skin, but there were no burns, only the curling puff of smoke. "I'm going to have to say no," I confessed. "This is new...and weird."

"Do you have a theory for the cause? Is this a sign of a shift? Should I step back to give you room? Or is this a sign of imminent death among your kind? A detonation?"

I snorted. For a logical man, he sure had a flair for the dramatic. Did he think I was going to burst into a pile of ash when I died? I bet he thought my ashes would sparkle too. I'm a dragon, not a vampire. The remark about standing back was cute, though. He thought my dragon body would fit in this room. I think the poor man was confused about the differences between lizards and dragons. But why had he jumped straight to detonation? We were supernaturals, not living bombs. I didn't know of any species that would just suddenly go, BOOM!

The sad thing was I didn't have a clue what the smoke

meant either. It might be a good omen, or a sign my day was going to get a whole lot worse.

"I think it could be the heat," I suggested. "It is escalating. My magic is restless too. Maybe that is the cause?"

We both tried to figure out what to do next as we watched the smoke twirl into the air around me.

"I think we should complete the bond without delay," Pixie said. "This smoke may be harmless to you, but it will not matter if your heat kills you tonight. I had planned to make this as pleasurable as possible for you, but that will take time I am no longer sure that you have. Are you agreeable with speeding up our mating?"

How could he be so sweet and so pragmatic at the same time? The thing was, my inner hussy was all about instant gratification. I had no interest in spending another night suffering through the agony of my heat.

"I agree. You can show off your skills another time, Pixie."

That was all the encouragement he needed. Tucking his forearms under my butt to create a seat for me, he stood in one fluid motion. Dizziness caused the world around me to tilt. I closed my eyes and wrapped my arms around his neck, attempting to steady myself.

I felt one of his arms move away from me. The only sound in the cell was the soft whoosh of cloth dropping to the floor. His pants. Heat exploded in my body, but this time it wasn't centered in my chest. Nope, this fire was far lower.

I had expected him to slam me against a wall, or even to toss me onto the tiny cot, but he just stood still. Hesitating.

"Um. Is everything okay?" *Did he change his mind?*

"Bunny, you have much to learn about me. Until I met you, I had never once changed my mind on a matter."

I wanted to ask him more, but now really wasn't the time. Sweat was beginning to coat my skin. Instead of delicate wisps of smoke, I was sizzling like a fajita plate in a Mexican restaurant. The main difference being the fajitas released a mouth-watering aroma, while I, assuredly, did not.

Could our bonding be any less romantic? I knew this was more of a 'bonding of necessity,' but we could have at least pretended. Pixie winced and my gaze darted to his face. His brow was coated in almost as much sweat as my own and his skin had turned red with strain. Surely I wasn't that heavy? Were his muscles just for show?

"It's not your weight. You are hot," he explained.

It was a weird time for him to compliment me, but a girl will take what she can get. "Um. Thank you..."

He grunted. "I mean, you are smoking hot."

Okay, that was pushing it. I had eyes and a nose. I certainly wasn't at my best these days.

"Flattery doesn't really seem like your thing?" It came out more of a question than a statement.

He winced again and began to shift my butt quickly from one arm to the other. So, this was what it felt like to be the potato in the anxiety-inducing hot potato game.

"Put me down before I burn you!" I struggled trying to get away from his skin. The world around me spun as dizziness made me lightheaded.

"No."

"Don't be a hero! This isn't going to work!"

"Be still." His body jerked and chains rattled, but I couldn't see what he was doing.

"Little cooked rabbit. Perhaps I will call you 'Hasenpfeffer' from now on," he said through a clenched jaw, all the while continuing whatever he was doing with the chains.

"You speak German?"

"Of course. I speak every tongue spoken in this realm. I appreciated the logic of the German's language."

He finished whatever he was doing and set me away from him. Not on the cot, which would probably have burned, and not on the floor. Nope, I was dangling several feet above the hard stone floor. He had fashioned a swing from the ancient chains that hung from the ceiling like macabre Halloween decorations. By shackling together three sets of the chains that hung side by side, he had created a makeshift seat.

It wasn't going to win awards as the most comfortable swing in the world, but it sure beat having a single chain digging into my bare tush. More importantly, the chains wouldn't burn which made them a safer option than the cot. I admired his ingenuity, but I still didn't understand why he didn't put me on the floor. That would have worked just as well. Right?

Never in my life had I been so happy about being proven wrong. *Never.*

"I did not want to risk the stone and filth on the floor doing further damage to your back," he said softly. "If you begin to feel weaker, let me know so I can steady you."

He leaned forward, capturing my lips in a toe-curling kiss that had stars sparkling behind my eyes. The sensation of long fingers brushing my knee and then sliding up along the inside of my thigh stole the last remnants of rational thought from my mind. Inch by torturous inch, he drew closer to the apex of my thighs. Squirming, I moved my legs apart to give him better access. My body ached to feel his touch.

His exploring fingers paused for the briefest of moments before I felt the brush of his cool skin against my lower lips. If he had decided to tease me at that moment, I probably would have exploded into a sparkling pile of ash. I shouldn't have worried; he was a man on a mission.

Me. I was *the* mission.

Without any further hesitation, his finger found my entrance and slipped inside. My body turned to jelly, and the chains rattled as I clutched them tighter to stay seated. His stroked me with purpose, neither gentle nor rough. But *boy howdy,* did he possess a lot of talent in that finger.

The need building inside me was turning ugly. The dragon's heat was determined to get what it wanted—or destroy me in the process.

"You are wet with your need, little dragon." His blunt observation only served to fan the flames scorching my insides.

He then gave a rumbling growl that vibrated my insides and had me purring in response. "Widen your legs," he ordered.

My body obeyed him embarrassingly fast. Glancing down, I saw the evidence of his own desire. His erection was not as large as my other men, but it was still larger than what I was guessing was considered 'normal.' Not like I had much experience with penises outside of my mates, though. My instinct surged forward, demanding I mount him and ride him until we didn't remember our own names. My body was so weak that the chains creaked in protest, and I wobbled.

"Good girl." Grabbing the chains, he steadied me. I didn't miss how careful he was not to touch my sizzling skin any more than was absolutely necessary.

"All I want you to do is to hold the chains," he instructed. "Let me do the work. You must focus on healing."

I nodded. I was far too exhausted to do anything more.

CHAPTER SIX

Tia

S lowly pulling me forward, he lined himself up and slowly pressed inside me. After fighting against my heat during this imprisonment, my body was hypersensitive. I moaned, the sound loud in the chamber. He hissed between his teeth and slid back out of me.

I opened my mouth to ask if he had been burned, but instead, I growled at him. And not a cute sexy growl, no, this was the growl of a starving dog whose bone had just been taken away. Come to think of it, that wasn't too far from the truth.

"I am fine," he said. "Stop worrying over what cannot be changed."

He had gone from cold as ice to a wise monk. All I wanted

was a bit more male stripper, like the movie about Mike with the magic body.

The swing rocked, and for a moment the pain from the heat eased as his body and mine became one...and then the swing rocked me away from him.

I growled, my vision going to that of a predator as I locked onto his face. There were no windows in the dungeon, but here and there pinpricks of light peeked through cracks in the stone ceiling. The sun must have gone down because the room was dark other than a soft yellow glow from a single torch on the wall. The blue glow of my eyes reflected on his skin and glinted in his eyes.

Mine.

While this might not have been our first choice, at that moment, it didn't matter. My dragoness had claimed him for her circle.

His change of pace had my insides curling tighter like a beast waiting to pounce. Our ragged breathing and the protesting chains were the only sound in the room. My temperature rose, causing the metal under my palms to heat. Pain and desire fought and blended together until I couldn't tell where one ended and the other began.

The ache in my gums told me that my fangs were struggling to descend. My magic had gone from rattling the door that confined it to full on body-slamming it.

Pain. Pleasure. Panic.

My ears itched and my heart fluttered, while the world around me darkened. The open wounds on my arms sealed themselves. I was healing, but other parts of my body grew weaker. It was racing against the clock to see if I could heal myself before succumbing to my injuries.

Shifting his hips, my Fae lover found my most sensitive spot. Swirling ridges around his erection rubbing ...

Wait.

My mind tried to focus through the heavy fog of exhaustion and heat. Men didn't have ridges, and I certainly would have noticed something like that when his thick member had stood fully erect in front of me earlier. He slid out and thrust in again, the ridges providing mind-shattering friction.

"It is magic, but now is not the time for this discussion."

I was being screwed. Literally. And with a magical dick, no less. Beasty was going to love this. I certainly was.

Twice more he pulled himself free, before filling me again. That's when all Hades broke loose. Actually, it was my magic that burst through the barrier, but it was pretty close to the same thing. You know what they say. Hell has no fury like a horny dragoness' magic scorned.

WHOOSH!

My wings burst from my still-healing back. The itch on my ears disappeared right along with my human ears, leaving my pointed ears twitching in their place. Cerulean blue light flickered faintly; my scales were back.

"AGH!" Pix shouted from surprise. Clearly, he hadn't seen that coming.

The problem was the moment he took a step away from me. When I had released control of my dragon instincts, I had been too weak to take him the way the heat demanded. At that moment, my magic was traveling through every inch of my body in search of damage to repair.

My chaotic magic was fanning the flames of the dragon heat. We were not finished, and he did not bear my mark. Pixie had taken a step back from a predator.

Oh, heck no.

I lunged for him. The chains clanged together as my wings smacked into them. I didn't care.

Mine.

Throwing my arms around his neck, I hung on like my life depended on it. There was a soft 'pshhh' sound as my skin pressed against his. He flinched, but to his credit, his arms circled me to steady me against him. Wrapping my legs around his waist, I enjoyed the feel of his cool flesh pressed up against my feverish skin. My wings circled around us in what probably looked like a protective gesture, but in reality, it was just one more way of ensuring he didn't escape me.

"Your sudden shift was unexpected," he stated firmly. His voice softened when he added, "I wasn't leaving you, Bunny. You have my word. I will never leave you."

He caught my lips in a kiss that held an awful lot of passion for a man who claimed to have issues with emotions. Our tongues danced, feeding my frenzy. I wanted to enjoy this moment; the heat wanted more.

Pulling away, I looked into his heavy-lidded eyes. We both wanted this. With the speed of a striking cobra, I sank my fangs into his neck. His body jerked in automatic shock from my attack. Then he moaned. Not in pain. Oh no. This was a moan of bliss so deep it vibrated through his body. Feeling those vibrations against my slick folds currently pressed against him, I gulped. His body shuddered.

My guys liked my bite, but it seemed that the Fae were extremely responsive to a dragon's bite. Wanting to test my theory, I retracted my fangs and sank them a second time. This time when his body jerked, he purposely loosened his arms from around my butt, letting me slip. Straight onto his rock-hard erection.

My fangs popped free of his skin as I gasped at the sudden fullness. Gripping my thighs, he lifted me and dropped me again. Fireworks exploded in my vision.

"Bite me, Bunny. Mark me so the world sees who I belong to." His tone had lost its former cultured edge and now oozed pure sexual tension. He was speaking my dragoness' language now.

My fangs sank a third time into his flesh. Mine.

"Yes. Yours." Each word was punctuated with a hard thrust of his hips.

Several more times he buried himself deep inside my slick heat. My belly knotted as it prepared for our tumble into pure bliss. He stopped. The head of his erection bumped against my entrance, and my need rushed back through me. Pulling my fangs from his neck, I turned and hissed at him like an angry cat. He didn't look away, instead he met my eyes.

"And you are mine." He slammed into me. I screamed my release and sank my teeth into his neck a final time. He pushed himself deeper inside me until our bodies ground against each other. His skin began to glow, enveloping us both in its light. He bellowed his release as his rod pulsed inside me.

My vision shifted and the world around me sharpened. With a roar, I sprung away from him even as he tried to catch hold of me.

A rubber band snapped into place in my mind, and in that same moment, I ran for the thick metal bars of my cell.

"Stop!" Pix cried out. You will hurt yourself! I have a key—"

Electricity rippled across my skin and my next roar shook the walls, sending small stones and dirt onto the ground. My body shifted as I hit the door, sending it flying into the far stone wall. I was trying to put enough distance between us so that I wouldn't squash him by accident.

Broken voices flitted through my mind.

I think the bond is back!

Leo. I would have cried tears of joy, but it would have to wait. I had business to take care of first. With a bellow that spoke of death and vengeance, I flung myself into the ceiling. Stone and debris exploded around me in a cloud of dust as I took flight.

It was time.

CHAPTER SEVEN

Myth

We shouldn't have gone to that idiotic ball. At the time it had seemed so important to play the political game and keep up appearances. It was the world I had grown up in, and one that I had trouble disconnecting myself from. Old habits die hard. Tia should have been snuggled in bed between all her mates, not stressing over a pointless party. Our mate had had her first heat, a milestone event among dragons, and we had found the farce of a party more important.

We were fools.

Glancing around the room, I took in the haggard faces of the men around me. None of us had managed to sleep for more than a few hours since that night and it was obvious in our dark circles, gaunt faces, and knotted hair. Nothing had mattered since that moment she had been yanked from our lives. She had simply ceased to exist. The leaders of the different species acted as though they hadn't heard of her, and our mental link with her had gone dark.

Our only hope that she was still alive was that I hadn't died, at least not permanently. Early today, I had died for a short time. When I had awakened and seen the heartbreaking devastation on each man's face around me, I was thankful to have been dead. For almost an hour they had known our mate was dead - all hope of finding her had been lost. She was truly gone.

I didn't know how much more our little family could take. Leo had worked tirelessly on one spell after another, trying to find anything that could help us locate her. Nearly all the experiments had exploded in his face.

Luke and Levi spent hours in their wolf forms. They ran miles every day searching in vain for the slightest hint of her scent. When they returned, they would sink to the floor and remain there until going out to hunt again.

Ivo was struggling to control his dragon form. The beacon that should have helped him to track our little dragoness was being blocked. Twice he had partially shifted and taken out part of the cottage's roof.

None of us were willing to go far from the castle where we had last seen her, but at the same time, we did not want it known that we had remained in the area. We took turns teleporting to other locations around the world, making sure we were seen, and then returning to this tiny home hidden by the towering mountains in this region.

There wasn't a man in this room that would admit it out loud, but we also hadn't wanted to be away from each other. Sure, we claimed it was best to stay together in case one of us found a lead, but the truth was that we were family. I'd always thought that without Tia as our center, we would have little to hold us together. We came from very different worlds. Instead, in her absence, we had grown closer. Disheveled sleeping bags and mattresses were scattered around the room, taking up most of the floor space.

Damien popped into the room, his face lined with exhaustion and worry. He sank into a chair and leaned his head back. I watched in bemusement as his hand found the top of Levi's head and began to stroke it like one would pet a dog. This type of easy-going friendship had never existed between the blood driven and the werewolves. Yet here I sat, watching two predators at the top of the food chain acting like a human man and his dog best friend. If my insides hadn't been hollow, I would have laughed. My eyes burned with unshed tears of loss and anger.

The sound of soft footsteps approaching the cottage was so shocking that none of us reacted. We all froze, our gazes riveted to the closed front door. The frantic knocking startled me from my stupor, and I flung open the door. A small female fell against me. Werewolf. I moved away from her, not wanting to be touched by anyone, accident or not.

"You have to hurry!" she cried. "They have her and that crazy vampire queen is going to kill her!"

"What are you talking about?" I asked. "And how did you know where to find us?" Hope fluttered in my heart, but my mind knew this might just be a trap.

The insolent pup rolled her eyes. "Seriously? Six of the most powerful and terrifying supernaturals on Earth are staying together in a small mountain town, and you think you wouldn't be noticed? The whole world knows you are here. You have to hurry! She isn't going to survive much longer in that dungeon!"

I needed to know more. "Come inside. I need to know everything you saw." Stepping to the side, I motioned her into the small room.

Levi's head snapped up and his howl of outrage raised every hair on my body. His muscles bunched as he prepared to attack. At the same moment, Damien's eyes locked on our guest's face.

"My heart." His voice was filled with wonder.

"Mate." Her voice was breathy.

With a savage growl, Levi lunged at her throat. He would have taken her down if my brother hadn't materialized between them. Shoving the shaking blonde behind him, Damien caught Levi by the throat and slung him into the wall. The cottage shook and the wall cracked at the impact, but it didn't even phase the near rabid werewolf. Luke stepped between the men, preparing for battle. Growling, he snapped at his brother. Levi was too far gone; his rage had unleashed his wolf and logic wasn't going to work.

Ivo materialized behind Levi and cracked him in the skull

with a sickening thud. The monstrous wolf dropped like a broken doll. Luke yelped in surprise but didn't move to attack. He sat down and stared at the werewolf female. While he didn't try to kill her, his raised hair and curled lips showing long white fangs was evidence enough that he wasn't a fan of her existence.

Ivo checked Levi's pulse. How hard had he hit the wolf? Satisfied with what he found, he turned calculating eyes toward the grey-eyed female. I wondered briefly if she realized that he posed more of a threat to her life than Levi had. "I seem to have missed part of this story. Who are you? What are you doing here? And why do my werewolf brothers wish to rip out your throat?"

Taking a deep breath, the female stepped out from behind her vampire shield.

"I'm Trixie," she began. "Your mate is being held hostage, and I am here to get help for her." Her eyes dropped. "I belonged to the same pack as Luke and Levi. They know my past treatment of Tia. I can't change what I've done, but I'm not that same person anymore."

"You are aware of how stupid it was to come barging into a home with five frantic mates, while smelling of terror and Tia's blood, all while admitting you know where she is being held. You should start speaking a little faster before someone loses patience."

Every eye in the room swung around in shock looking for the owner of the voice. All finally landed on Leo as he stood in the darkened door leading down the hallway. Purple magic flashed violently across his skin like lightning across the skies of a hot summer night, and his eyes swirled a deep violet. The oxygen in the room evaporated. Gone was the shy nerd that we all treated as the younger brother. In his place stood a battle ready, and likely unstable, warlock. This day just kept getting better.

"Agreed. Talk," I added. Every second we spent bickering was one too long.

"I learned yesterday that Cage knew where she was," Trixie continued. "He had been acting weird, but I didn't have any concrete proof that he was somehow involved until then." Her eyes dropped and her cheeks turned red. "I managed to convince him it would be fun to spend more time together. It worked and he wouldn't let me leave his side, even when he went to the dungeon."

"I'll kill him." Damien's arms snaked around Trixie and hauled her back against him.

"Take a number and get in line." Leo's new voice was downright creepy, and that's saying a lot from someone who sucked blood. I made sure to watch him from the corner of my eye. Hopefully, Tia could fix whatever had broken.

Ivo's voice was thick with emotion, "She's sick? How bad?"

Trixie's eyes filled with tears. "It's bad. Really bad. There was so much blood, and her entire body was covered with ragged wounds from the whip. They have a spell that blocks her magic, so she can't heal. Something else was wrong, too. Cage said she was in heat, but I've never seen heat that bad. Is it normal for a dragon's heat to try to kill them?"

"No. A dragon's heat is never easy, but her heat should have been over by now," Ivo replied. "We have to get to her! Maybe I will be able to help her." He sounded as though he carried the weight of the world on his shoulders.

Darkness had settled on the world outside the cabin. It didn't matter, we did our best work in the darkness.

"When did you last see her?" Ivo asked Trixie.

Trixie turned toward him and replied, "Cage and I walked into the torture ring during one of Elise's sessions with Tia. There was so much blood and she collapsed. Cage started screaming something about a baby and an agreement. Those two started trying to kill each other. In the middle of the conflict, a guard stepped into the room and took Tia away. I couldn't see if she was still alive."

If he touched her, I was going to kill him.

Suddenly, something brushed against my mind. "What—"

Static crackled, and again I felt a soft stroke against my mind. I rubbed at my temples. This was not the time to get a headache.

SNAP!

Blinding light exploded behind my eyes, the pain and surprise crushing my lungs and nearly stopping my heart.

Leo recovered first. *I think the bond is back!*

I heard him in my mind at the same time I heard a mountain-shattering roar. Tia's dragon. The sound was quickly followed by a man's voice, one I didn't recognize.

Bunny! I don't think he realized that his thoughts were somehow being transmitted to us because he continued, *This was not the plan. It was foolish to believe we would stay together once she escaped.*

Dang, this guy sounds sad.

Hearing Leo's voice and registering that it was in his mind, the man's demeanor changed abruptly. *Who's there?*

We didn't have time for this game. *We are Tia's mates, and you are in our mental bond. Who are you?*

I'm... There was a moment of hesitation. *Pixel. I've been claimed by the dragoness.*

Where is she? Is she alright? Ivo's anxiety mirrored how we all felt.

Leo's purple magic vibrated through the bond – alarming, considering his unstable mental state lately. Our link lit up like an old movie projector. We were watching what had happened from Pixel's point of view. We watched in awe as our feisty little mate got carried away and snacked on Pixel's neck, then it switched and we saw her magic break free, followed by her dramatic earth-shattering exit from the dungeon. Dirt swirled around her like a tornado while crushed stone fell around her. She looked like an avenging warrior.

"I know where she is," Ivo said and tapped his chest.

"Let's go," I said in immediate response. "We need to make a quick stop." No one questioned me, we all knew what needed to be done. Grabbing those who needed a ride, we teleported out of the misery-filled cottage.

We materialized in front of the guard, Pixel, the newest member of our circle. This was a story I couldn't wait to hear. Right now, I was just relieved that Tia's heat hadn't killed her. If she was on the hunt, we needed to get to her in case she needed backup. Once she calmed down, she would be devastated that Pixel had been left behind. She didn't need any more stress, so stopping for him was a no-brainer.

To his credit, the slight widening of his eyes was the only reaction he gave to our merry little band's appearance. Moonlight shone through the missing ceiling and down into the dungeon. The thought that my mate had spent even a minute in this disgusting place made me livid. I was seeing red, literally. The smell of her dried blood hit me, and I wanted to kill everyone who dared touch her.

"Would you like that list now, or later?" Pixel asked.

Surprised, my gaze darted to the guard. Scales that appeared to be etched in white ink circled his neck and moved over his shoulders.

"It's not ink," he explained. "Our mate had her arms around my neck during the worst of her heat. The high temperature of her body branded my skin with the imprint of her scales. I do not think she was aware."

His voice was even, not filled with emotion, but also not robotic. I studied his neck and the multiple marks she had left with her fangs. Why had she done it?

He must be a total snack. Levi's voice came through the bond, followed by his *oomph* when Ivo smacked him.

"I can sense her again. Let us go find our mate," Ivo said as his fist pounded his heart.

This is going to be fun!

I wanted to roll my eyes at Leo's enthusiasm, but this time I agreed with him. I couldn't wait to see our sexy, murderous dragoness.

CHAPTER EIGHT

Tia

Freedom tasted delicious. But the vampire soldier in my mouth? Not so much. But he had been one of those that helped hold me down, and today made the fatal mistake of standing between me and Elise.

Yeah, no.

I had places to go, people to see, and mates to...well, mate.

Tossing the limp body to the side, I lumbered up the grand tree-lined driveway. The queen had chosen to stay in a beautiful pale-green home with ornate woodwork, delicate spirals, and sparkling clean windows. A home with dead trees, cobwebs, broken windows, and dense fog would have been more fitting for the evil woman.

Another guard saw me coming, this one was far smarter and took off running. He hadn't been involved in my ordeal, so

I just gave him a gentle nip on his rear to ensure he maintained a healthy dose of fear. Plus, hearing him scream like a girl as he mooned the world was the most fun I'd had in a while.

Reaching the front door, I knocked it in. Leaning down, I roared into the tiny opening, enjoying the sound of glass decor crashing to the floor. My chest began to click, and my fire blazed into the entryway. The dragon's version of shouting, "Honey, I'm home!"

To her credit, Elise stomped into the entryway instead of trying to sneak out the backdoor. Her boldness made more sense when she stepped into the light with a gun. *Pfft. Pfft.* Nice, a double tap to my chest. Two darts were wedged between my opalescent scales.

"I do find myself impressed that you managed to escape, but I was prepared for this possibility," she began. "One vile of that poison is enough to drop a herd of elephants. It is a shame to lose you before we managed to utilize your powers, but I can't have you messing things up."

Soldiers rushed to surround me. Some were holding dart guns, and others held machine guns. The former king stepped out of the blackened doorway. His arm slid around his wife's waist, and he placed a gentle kiss on her temple. It would be touching, if they hadn't held me chained in a dungeon and planned to destroy Myth's and Damien's lives.

I stared at the pair, my expression one of boredom. They gazed back at me, their smiles dropping from their faces. The men around us fidgeted. It was awkward and I was loving it.

Gone was the insecure girl at the ball. I smiled a wide toothy dragon grin.

"Why isn't it working?" Elise whispered angrily at her husband.

"I don't know! I was assured it was the most potent toxin available."

Pfft.

The queen shot the soldier nearest her. He opened his mouth to yell but dropped to the ground before he could make a sound.

I could have told them it worked; I could feel the burn in my chest as my fire burned through the toxin. They didn't even have a clue who they were dealing with, which was going to make this even more fun. But first, I had business to attend to.

Energy crackled in the air, and my form shimmered before I was left standing in front of them in my human form. The queen gasped. I had learned a trick, or ten, from Beasty's memories. Instead of standing in front of them naked as the day I was born, I wore a gown made of dragon magic. The dress fit my body like the stiff plastic wrap they use on batteries to ensure the customer can never actually open the package, at least not until they have offered up a blood sacrifice on the sharp plastic edges.

My dress had just as many sharp corners. The fabric wasn't fabric at all. It was made of row after row of tiny razor-sharp dragon scales. As I moved, the light sparkled and danced across the gown, the colors shifting from pearl to pale blue, to the softest of pinks, and creamy yellow.

A long slit traveled the side of the gown from the ground to my hip and tiny scales draped like chains across my skin, holding the sides of the slit together. The top was made of a corset, the material was flexible and to the eye looked soft. In reality, it was more protective than the best military bullet proof vest. Scales covered most of my breasts, although managing to give the illusion that I might spill out of my top at any moment. Worst case scenario I could use that as a distraction, right?

Tiny scales dotted the skin of my neck and arms. My tattoos glowed brilliantly, no longer that pitiful weak flicker from the dungeon. I had bided my time, and now the day of reckoning was here. I couldn't wait.

Turning toward the soldiers, I spoke in a deceptively soft tone. "Today you must make a choice. Drop your weapons and vow loyalty to Mithraheal Conlier, King of the Blood Driven. You will also pledge your obedience to me, Tiamat of the House of Royal Dragons. If you do not, you will die."

You could have heard a pin drop around the well-manicured lawn. It was a shame it was moments away from looking like a war zone.

Four men dropped their weapons and crossed an arm across their chest.

"Are you all idiots? Kill her!" the queen cried.

But then she smirked, evidently pleased that out of nearly one hundred men, only four had been willing to risk her rage and drop their weapons. We were badly outnumbered, yet they moved forward to stand near me, spines stiff and heads held high. The way I saw it, the four bravest men here had just pledged themselves to my kingdom.

Guns were raised and fired in rapid succession. With a flick of my wrist, the four men dropped through the ground and disappeared. I needed to focus, and I couldn't if they were in the line of fire.

With a second flick of my wrist, the bullets around me froze. Twirling my finger, they spun around and headed right back to the soldiers who fired them. The lifeless bodies of every single soldier dropped to the ground around me. I felt no guilt. They had made their choices.

My hips swayed as I moved to the former queen and king. Leaning down, I picked up a dart, rolling it back and forth between my fingers as I continued to walk.

"My son deserved more—" the king began.

I cut him off. "Your son is claimed by a goddess, you old fool. He will rule the world at my side and will be honored in a way you will never understand."

He opened his mouth, but never had the chance to speak. The dart embedded itself into his throat. His eyes widened.

"Don't blink, don't even twitch so much as a finger, or I *will* push the plunger."

Then, I turned toward the royal pain in my butt.

"You are nothing more than a slut!" the queen screeched.

"Your time of insulting me is over. For a brief moment in time, I was at your mercy, you could have killed me. But you are a failure. You failed as a queen, and now you have failed as a villain. I will sit on the throne that once belonged to you, and

I will be such a fan-freaking-tastic queen, that your name will be wiped from the memories of all those on Earth."

Her hand shot out to slap me. She was fast, but I was faster. Catching her hand mid-air, I held on.

"Tia!" Myth's voice almost snapped me out of the blood-lust. *Almost.*

I turned to see my mate running towards me. His pace slowed and his eyes widened as he approached me. My stomach churned with disappointment when he stopped a few feet away. I wanted him to wrap his arms around me and tuck me against his body. Instead, he took in the scene in front of him.

"Darling! The dragoness is insane!" his mother cried. "She stalked us here, killed our men when they tried to protect us, and now she is going to kill us!" The queen tried to wrench her arm free, so I allowed my palm to heat. The stench of burning flesh filled my nostrils and my stomach recoiled. Clam-on-a-cracker, vomiting would ruin the vibe I was going for.

Myth's hard, golden gaze studied the queen's face, then his eyes shifted to me.

"It's not what it looks like—" I started but stopped as he arched one perfect eyebrow. "Fine, it is totally what it looks like. But she started it!" I wanted to facepalm. I had gone from an avenging goddess to a squabbling toddler embarrassingly fast.

I held my breath as his eyes moved across my face, inspecting every inch, and then searching for my own eyes. He must have found what he was looking for, because the next instant his arms slid around my waist, and I was tucked beneath his shoulder. I cuddled into him but refused to release my hold on Elise.

Myth didn't even acknowledge her, his eyes remaining locked with mine. "Hello, Dragostea Mea." Leaning down, he nuzzled my neck, sending delicious shivers down my spine. "I've missed you."

"Hi," I replied. I had spent days on end thinking of the grand speech I would give each of my mates when I saw them again, and now that Myth was in front of me, all I managed was that single breathless word. His lips brushed mine, a gentle reminder of his love, and a promise of things to come.

"How *dare* you take her side!" the queen cried. Clearly, she didn't appreciate being ignored, even if it meant she could stay alive a few extra minutes.

Sighing, Myth pulled away and straightened his spine, every inch the king of the vampires. He addressed his parents with ice in his voice. "You truly think you can lie to my face? I'm aware of the role you both played in the kidnapping and torture of my mate, and your queen. The lies you have spread among the blood driven and your plans to overthrow me have been discovered as well. Today, you will die traitors, and I will ensure that your reign is only remembered as a dark spot in our species' history."

He turned toward me, a playful smirk at the corner of his mouth. "The sooner you finish up with your business here, the sooner we can find more interesting things to do," he said to me. "I would offer to take care of this matter for you, but I sense your dragoness has already claimed this as her kill." The voice that had been full of sharp ice shards now dripped with sexuality that had me thinking of black silk sheets and breakfast in bed.

Heck yeah. Why were we still standing around?

Meeting her eyes, I called my fire. It jumped to obey me, already simmering inside me at the promises in Myth's eyes. Flames sizzled across my skin and sparked up her arm. In panic, her other hand grabbed for her husband. Just like with an electric current, my fire arced to his body as well. The royal pair's screams broke the quiet of the predawn hour. The last thing they saw was their son, and the king of their species, crushing my body against his and capturing my lips in a kiss that was hotter than my dragon fire. My flames swirled around him, teasing and caressing, but careful to not singe even a single hair on his head. It was wrong but felt so incredibly right.

The devouring flames died away only after the last of their ashes drifted to the ground. I blew gently and watched as a gust of wind scattered the dark flecks across the yard. Nothing remained of the royal duo that had terrorized and destroyed countless lives, all for their own enjoyment. We would clean up the dissension they had created and execute those who had taken pleasure in the previous monarchs' cruelty.

Ready or not, the world was about to change.

I took in the lawn strewn with dead vampires. Walking toward the bodies, I shifted mid step into my shimmering white dragoness. With a soft click, I opened my massive jaws and breathed blue fire as I spun in a slow circle, incinerating the traitorous soldiers. The green lawn blackened, and smoke rose around me like fog.

"Tia!" Turning, I blinked. Through the falling ash and smog, my mates, Damien, and Trixie walked toward me. They looked like action heroes from a movie...except they had shown up too late to help. I snorted in amusement. They were going to have to explain why Trixie was with them. Moving toward them, I shifted again. The change was effortless and within two steps I was back in my dragon gown, running toward my mates.

A werewolf lunged through the thick smoke, his muscles bunching as he propelled himself toward me. Not today, Satan.

I contorted my body to avoid the impact, wishing for a sexy black coat to add some drama to the moment. The soft brush of his fur tickled my skin as his momentum carried him past me. A month ago, my reflexes wouldn't have been fast enough to avoid the surprise attack.

The massive wolf hit the ground with a bone-jarring thud. Twisting to face me, the wolf's features shifted into those of a man. One I knew far too well. "Tia! You will stop this right now!" he cried out. "Yet again, you are being a selfish brat, messing up everything I have worked so hard for."

Well, at least this saved me the time of tracking him down. "Hello, Cage."

CHAPTER NINE

Ivo

A collective roar went up when Cage confronted our little mate. We were sick of being one step behind in protecting her. She was the most powerful supernatural creature on this planet, and I didn't believe the others had realized that something inside Tia had shifted. I hid my smile. This was child's play for her, and after her ordeal, the dragoness would need this. We were here for her, and that was all she required from us—for now.

"Tia! You will stop this right now! Yet again, you are being a selfish brat, messing up everything I have worked so hard for." Such brave words for a man lacking testicles.

Balls. The word you are looking for is balls, Leo whispered through the mind link. The young man had taken it upon himself to bring me up to date with modern language and customs. We stood together, out of Tia's way, but near enough to assist.

"Balls? How odd."

Damien snickered. "Anyone bring popcorn?"

"Hello, Cage." Tia popped her hip out and regarded the werewolf alpha with cold disdain.

I was still trying to piece together what had happened during her kidnapping. Obviously, we knew that Cage was involved, but we didn't know to what extent. We didn't have to wait long to find out.

Myth tossed his jacket to the werewolf. "Cover yourself up," he ordered. "You are in the presence of royalty, and she deserves to be treated with respect."

Cage snatched it midair and wrapped it around his waist. His lip curled as he addressed the vampire king. "It is nothing she hasn't seen before." He turned to Tia and addressed her again. "Isn't that right, Tia? You didn't seem to mind it when you were screaming out my name in pleasure."

"How dare you." The words were barely audible through her tightly clenched teeth.

My heart stopped when I took in her pale face. Every drop of blood had rushed from her face and her heart was beating painfully fast against her chest. Taking a deep breath, she steadied her trembling hands.

I fought with the urge to storm in and carry her away from the pain of this world. He needed to die. Now.

"I'm in agreement."

My head swiveled to the side. Through narrowed eyes, I

studied the newest addition to our circle. I had not spoken into the bond, so he must be able to read thoughts.

There was an imperceptible tilt of his head. I respected his honesty. Mind reading is a battle skill that works better when the enemy isn't aware of that ability. This man was a warrior and had shown great respect in revealing this talent to me.

"It's only fair that he knows something personal about you too, Ivo." I had forgotten that the younger Conlier practiced poor manners and ease dropped constantly. "Psst! New guy, the dragon likes to snuggle the bones of his enemies to go to sleep. Like a dog with a morbid stuffed toy."

"This is not the time, Damien. Also, the bones do not provide comfort. I sleep fine without them. They do, however, deter most people from visiting."

"That is logical."

I knew our mate would only claim the best of the best.

Damien groaned. "Great, just what we need. Two of you."

Our exchange, or 'bromance' as Leo would call it, ended when Cage began to laugh. It was a nasty sound that grated on every nerve in my body. My dragon *really* wanted to eat him. Why had no one told me of his instability? I was told he was focused on himself and his own wants, but I was never told he was delusional.

Cage wasn't always like this. He was focused on his own desires, but not usually cruel, Luke said, his sorrow pouring into the circle. Although he was no longer part of Cage's pack, it had been his home, his people.

Tia moved faster than the eye could track. Wings ripped

from her back, and her hand shot out and clutched Cage's throat. Thin trails of crimson blood trickled from where her nails sank into the soft flesh of his neck. "Today you will face judgment for plotting against the Blood Driven king, and for dishonoring your oath as an Alpha to protect your pack above all else. Finally, the ancient laws read that immediate execution is to be the punishment for any who dare risk the balance of the world to hold captive and plot to kill a royal dragon."

Her hand closed tighter around his throat, and thin tendrils of water came up from the ground. They curled around his feet like a living creature, slowly encasing his body in water.

His eyes grew wide, and he struggled against her hold. She was much smaller than him, but she was a dragon. "Have you forgotten? At this very moment, my pup is likely growing inside you. You cannot raise a fatherless—" He was cut off as water flowed into his mouth.

Startled, I glanced at Tia's stomach. It was flat, but that didn't mean anything. Dragonesses were obsessive in protecting and hiding their offspring. I knew females that waited until they were giving birth to even tell their mates of the pregnancy.

She could be pregnant. We'd been so worried over the heat and the toll it was taking on her body, then that farce of the ball, and lastly her kidnapping. How had we forgotten the entire purpose of the heat?

My dragon surged forward, my body shimmering as I fought to maintain the human form. Our mate might be pregnant, she needed to be in bed with a tub of ice-cream and having her feet rubbed. Every instinct in my body screamed to gather her in my arms and tuck her away amongst my treasures. The rational side of my mind told me that she held more power than all of us combined, and she could protect herself.

"If I am pregnant, it is not your child," Tia said. "My child will be raised by six loving fathers. Men of valor, strength, honor, fairness, and power you could never understand." Her voice was calm, and her arm didn't even wobble as she continued to hold the alpha werewolf still.

Gagging, he coughed up enough water to say, "Will you be able to look your son in the face and tell him you murdered his father—"

A sword sliced through his chest, bright blood spreading like a blooming flower. Cage slumped to the ground and Pixel yanked his sword free of the falling body.

"I will have no qualms about telling *her* child that you died on my sword." He wiped the blood from his sword and sheathed it with a casual ease.

We gaped at in open-mouthed horror. Leo recovered enough to hurry forward. Kneeling down, he checked Cage's pulse. "He's dead."

Shock rippled through the bond, followed by intense jealousy. Every single one of us would have loved to have been the one to remove the werewolf from her life...permanently. Leo's magic sparked. His hand still rested against Cage's neck. Purple electricity shot into Cage's body.

Cage groaned.

Leo scrambled away in shock. We watched as Cage stood

to his feet. He opened his mouth...and my dragon took control. The shift was smooth as silk. In the blink of an eye, my monstrous black dragon burst free with a roar that shattered several windows in the old house. Before Cage could so much as breathe out a single word, he was gone. My dragon licked my lips, pleased with himself.

"Bro! You just ate him raw!" Damien cried out. "Haven't you heard you should cook your meat first? Nasty! Who knows where he had been? You just ate a raw—"

Trixie slid her hands over his mouth, stopping his word vomit.

"Is he really dead this time?" Myth asked, hesitation in his voice. Vampires were like cockroaches, hard to kill and harder to keep dead, but the idea of a werewolf coming back made him uneasy? I huffed in amusement.

"Do you want Leo to stick his hand in there and double check?" Damien shot back.

"I think it is unfair that only Ivo and Pixel got a turn," Levi huffed.

I enjoyed the banter of our strange family, but there was one person who had remained quiet. Pixel and I stood side by side in front of her, like two boys caught with their hands in a cookie jar.

My dragon assured me that all would be well. He had a plan. But then, fear shot through me. My stomach churned, and it had nothing to do with my recent meal.

There was nothing predictable about a dragon.

CHAPTER TEN

Tia

Exhaustion, shock, and relief warred inside me. As a dragoness, I was beyond miffed that my 'kill' had been taken from me, but as a human, I was relieved that his death - er, deaths - hadn't been at my hand. Maybe I wasn't the strong avenging bringer-of-doom I thought I was.

Pixel finished wiping his blade and sheathed it before facing me. At his side, Ivo's obsidian black dragon licked his lips. Then he did *the thing*. He gave me an adorable smile, the same lizard smile that made happy gecko videos go viral, blinking first one eye, and then the other. His pupils were fully dilated, adding to the innocent puppy eyes. He had transformed from a man-eating monster to a 'furless pupper' wanting belly rubs in ten seconds flat.

"Is it just me, or does he look like that animated black

dragon you were obsessed with last year?" Myth whispered in Damien's general direction. I swallowed a snort. Myth wasn't wrong, Ivo's terrifying black dragon was doing a dang good impression, he just had a lot more teeth.

Trying to resist Ivo's dragon, I focused my attention on Pixie. He took the initiative and stepped forward. Cupping my face with his rough palm, he brushed his thumb across my lips. "I support your need to take back what they took from you, but I also admire your gentle spirit. This was the one death that should not have been by your hand."

I warred with the desire to show my strength, to show these men I was no longer the weak terrified girl who'd just found out supernaturals existed. The other part of me just wanted to go home and sleep for a week surrounded by my overprotective men.

Pixel, ever the pragmatic, spoke again, "This man's death had already been decided, now it has been carried out. Justice demanded it be done, but did not say by whom. He's no longer your problem. The only one who may yet have a problem with Cage is the dragon male. It would be unfortunate if he suffered from digestion issues."

Pixie eyed the dragon speculatively, as if the beast might start hurling all over us at any moment. Ivo huffed and blew smoke into Pixie's face.

I felt I should be annoyed, but I was growing accustomed to Pixie's blunt logic. He had done what he felt was right, and he made no apology for it. Yet, there was a tenseness in his posture that almost made me think he did care how I felt over the entire fiasco.

Meanwhile, Ivo's dragon had decided it was time to try a little harder to get his scaly butt out of the doghouse. The raven-colored beast tilted his massive head to the side like an inquisitive puppy, and his tongue lolled out the corner of his mouth. I would bet money that Ivo did not have full control right now, because I could not see him goofing off like this.

"Fine. Come here." I motioned for the beast to bend down.

With a weird little butt wiggle, Ivo complied. Grudgingly, I gave in and laughed. That was all the encouragement he needed to hop around me, begging to play. Each time he hopped, the ground shook and the trees threatened to uproot and topple over. When he finished his goofy display, he flopped on his back and dropped his head back onto the grass until he was looking at me, but upside down.

"This is so messed up. Do you think he has been poisoned?" Confusion laced Levi's words.

"I'm never going to be able to unsee this," added Leo. He was frozen in disbelief. The most revered creature on earth, and the magnificent beast of myth and legend, was currently wagging his tail happily at me.

I knew exactly why Ivo was acting this way. He was trying to distract me from dealing with what had happened, and from any anger I might be feeling toward him for eating the mate who rejected me. Ivo's pride was no doubt taking a huge hit from his over-the-top antics, and I loved him more for the ridiculous lengths he would go to make me smile.

There was still a stubborn part of me that wanted to cling to my annoyance, and his need to be my protector. My magic had returned once I'd broken through the binding spell. It was back and better than ever. I loved these men with every fiber of my being, but it was time they stopped trying to shield me. I had to fulfill the prophecy I hadn't asked to be part of, and the sooner the better. My mates would either have to learn to step back, or they were going to have to be left behind on the missions I had planned. But for today, I was relieved to have a small break. Soon my mates and I would need to have a long conversation about what all had happened since the night of the ball. I wasn't looking forward to revisiting those memories.

I spread my arms across Ivo's muzzle. It was far too wide for me to fully embrace, but I did my best to 'boop the snoot.' There isn't a human on earth that could have resisted that impulse. I stroked my fingers along the edges of his inky black scales, smiling when two sets of arms wrapped around my waist, sandwiching me between twin sexy-as-heck chests. I breathed in the comforting aroma of the deep forest. It smelled like home and tears sprang to my eyes.

We've missed you, darling. Next time you decide to go on a side mission, take us with you, Luke said as he nuzzled my neck playfully.

"Or maybe we should just stay at home in bed next time there is a ball," Levi added. His hands were brushing the scales on my gown, and to my surprise, they were as sensitive to his touch as my skin.

It was time to take our family home. I had another 'side mission' scheduled in a few days, but first we needed to rest. "Let's go back to the cabin where we trained with the wizards." It still felt the most like home. I leaned forward, preparing to give Ivo's snout a quick kiss.

"Gross! Are you going to kiss that mouth after what he has been eating?" Damien gagged.

"*Shhh!*" Trixie growled. "Now is not the time, Fangs!"

I smiled. She might fit in after all.

WE TELEPORTED OURSELVES HOME TO THE MOUNTAIN cabin overlooking the lake that I had grown to love so much. I breathed the clean mountain air deep into my lungs, it felt like it was the first breath I had taken in weeks. The soft gold and pinks of the morning sun glinted off the water's surface, bathing everything in a warm glow.

"Let's get you inside, darling," Levi said to me. "You have six mates anxious to pamper you." Levi's hand pressed against my back, guiding me toward the doorway.

Tossing a look over my shoulder, I saw he was correct. Five mates were trailing behind me like puppies, their faces creased in worry and relief. Except for Pixie, he appeared relaxed, although I didn't miss how his alert eyes assessed everything around us.

Trixie and Damien brought up the rear. They were holding hands and looking at each other with such love. I knew that look. Damien had found his mate. Remembering how the werewolves and vampires weren't too keen on each other, I couldn't help but smirk. This was going to be interesting.

We walked through the doorway and I moved toward the kitchen. Myth had arranged for a girl to come in and tidy the cabin and keep it well stocked, just in case we ever decided to pop in. It had seemed wasteful at the time, but he had assured me that the vampire female needed the funds this job would provide. As I opened the fully-stocked fridge, I had never been so grateful for his wealth.

People thought houses that looked like museums and flashy cars were the sign of being filthy rich. They were wrong. The true sign of wealth and opulence is having a refrigerator stocked with every conceivable food item you could possibly need to create a perfect sandwich. My stomach grumbled in appreciation and my mouth watered. Not wanting to waste another moment, I began pulling everything out and spreading it out on the counters. I was tempted to rip open the wrapped packages of meat and shove as much food into my stomach as possible. But after being unable to keep food down from the constant strain on my body, I was forcing myself to take this slow.

"Um, love?" Myth approached me. "Do you mind filling us in on what's going on?"

I spared Myth a brief glance before continuing to cover every inch of space on the counters with various packages, wrappers, and glass bottles. "I am making the biggest sandwich on earth," I informed him. "It feels like forever since I ate last. The soldier at the mansion doesn't count. He tasted nasty and I spat him out."

Luke and Levi howled in laughter, Myth looked shocked, Leo looked queasy, Ivo patted his stomach with a smirk, and

Pixie looked impressed. My heart swelled with love for my merry band of mates. Each man was so different, yet they all fit so perfectly into my weird life. Dang, I was a lucky girl.

Myth coughed a few times and tried again. "Yes. It is obvious you are making food, which one of us should be doing while you sit down and rest. My question was regarding them." I looked where he was motioning with his hand and felt a grin spread across my face.

At the rough-hewn dining table sat the four guards who had pledged their loyalty to me, even while severely outnumbered and facing what they believed to be certain death. They were eating thick slices of a fluffy chocolate mousse cake. Their eyes were wide with awe as they took in each of my mates. I was surprised by how easily I forgot that my guys were essentially living legends among the supers. They had earned respect, admiration, and in the case of a couple of my mates, they had also earned fear. The soldiers' spoons were frozen mid-air in front of their gaping mouths. They needed to get over their hero worship real quick if they were going to be part of my military team.

"Hey guys!" I said cheerfully. "Glad to see you made it here safely."

"Thanks," one of them replied. "The housekeeper was here when we, uh, arrived? She gave us the cake and wouldn't take no for an answer. We'll pay for it." They all started to get up.

"Sit back down," I insisted, gesturing for them to take their seats again. "Today was a weird day for all of us. I hope the trip wasn't too rough. Teleporting someone to a new location, while not actually going with them, is a bit more challenging than I had expected. I didn't have much choice today though, I couldn't risk you guys getting caught in the crossfire, and teleporting was the best option I had at that moment. You can use the guest quarters downstairs. For the time being, you will work in pairs, on alternating shifts to patrol the area around this cabin. Damien will show you the perimeter. Enjoy your cake!"

I gave a little wiggle of my fingertips and turned back to the meticulous work of building my sandwich, drawing up short when I found Damien and Luke had taken over the sub construction. I probably should have protested and threatened to stab them both. Instead, I allowed Ivo to lift me up in his arms and carry me down the hall and into the bathroom I loved so much.

Once Ivo had the water cascading into the swimming-pool-sized tub, he sat on the edge, holding me against his bare chest. I relaxed into him, enjoying the smokey smell of his skin. He needed to reassure himself that I was alive, that I had survived. I just wanted to bask in the warmth of his skin, and the love that poured through the bond.

Ivo's hands slid up my back, then his husky voice sent tingles through my body. "Little Dragon, I cannot figure out how to remove this beautiful gown."

In the blink of an eye, it vanished, and I was left very naked in the lap of a very shocked male dragon.

"That is not possible. I have never heard of a dragon shifter manipulating their scales into garments." His voice was so full of wonder that I couldn't stop my laugh.

"I'm not an ordinary dragon," I told him, "and I have a few new tricks up my sleeve." Seeing that he was about to ask for more details, I pressed my finger to his sexy-as-heck lips. "Not now. There is so much to do and discuss, but these next two days are just for us."

He sucked my finger into his mouth, swirling his tongue around it. My mind thought of all the other uses for that tongue and my belly clenched in anticipation. He winked and lowered us into the steaming water.

"You are still in your pants!"

"Yes, and they need to stay on if I am to see to your needs without being distracted by you."

Scrunching up my face, I growled at him.

"Stop it, minx. There is plenty of time for other needs to be attended to. First you must let us take care of your primary needs."

True to his word, he grabbed some shampoo and began to lather up my hair. His fingers gliding along my scalp felt heavenly and I couldn't help my moan.

He stiffened...

Then *he* stiffened.

I surreptitiously wiggled my butt, just checking that my memory had been accurate. It totally was.

Ivo grabbed my hips, presumably to hold me still, but I felt how he pulled me ever so slightly tighter against his lap. "Be still, dragoness. My dragon is fighting me enough for control as it is. I have not had this much trouble since I was a youngling."

I knew better than to ask what age that was. To dragon shifters, a teenager was probably three hundred years old.

Reaching for a rag, he began to wash me. I idly wondered if I would ever be allowed to wash myself again.

"I doubt it." Leo's voice surprised me, and I jerked. Ivo groaned. Leo snickered.

"Why would you ever wash again," Levi started, "when you have mates who are eager for their turn to pamper you?" He leaned down and captured my lips in a soft kiss. I tried to reach for him, to pull him in with me, but he danced away. "Ah, ah, ah. Not yet, kitty."

Luke leaned down and set an adorable floating tray in the water. A sandwich, that had to be at least a foot long, took up most of the tray. It had layers of thinly sliced meat, various cheeses, and crisp vegetables. My favorite sauce dripped from the sides like a television commercial. My eyes watered.

"It's too beautiful to eat," I whispered.

I expected them to tease me for my love affair with food. Instead, the room became so quiet you could have heard a pin drop. The bond was open between us, and it overflowed with a wide range of churning emotions. Guilt, anger, sadness, and my personal favorite—love.

"Guys, stop. I was fed," I insisted. "Sure, it wasn't the greatest food, but I didn't starve." It didn't take a rocket scientist to see the dubious expressions.

"She is correct," Pixie corroborated. "They fed her sufficient food." I nodded my appreciation at Pixie, but then he added, "However, due to the pain of the heat, the severity of the blood loss, and the extreme nature of the beatings, she was rarely able to keep down the food provided."

I scowled at my newest mate, but his expression remained

unconcerned. My sandwich had begun to float away. Snatching it up, I bit into it and enjoyed the explosion of flavors in my mouth. Chewing quickly, I took another bite and another. The entire tray was empty of food in five minutes.

Around the room my mates were snacking on their own plates of food. Myth stood against the wall, his legs crossed elegantly. Leo sat cross-legged on the floor near the edge of the tub. Luke sat up on the sink, one leg dangling while the other foot was propped up on the large vanity. Levi had rolled up his pant legs and sat with his legs soaking in the water.

Pixie stood against the door, the only entrance and exit from the room. All the windows were solid glass panels that did not open, so you either had to break the windows or use the door. It was weird, but knowing that he was continuing to watch over me made my heart flutter. I wondered if he would ever feel fully comfortable around us.

"Are you ready to get out, beautiful?" Leo asked me. Leaning forward, he snagged my empty tray and set it on the floor beside him.

"I don't ever want to get out. The water is amazing." I leaned back against Ivo's chest...and purred. Ivo's chest rumbled with deep laughter that vibrated deliciously through my body. "Mmm. How about you guys get in?" I suggested.

Luke choked on his food.

"All of us?" Leo's voice sounded strangled.

"It is efficient," Pix said. "We all stink, and the tub is big enough for us all to wash. It saves both time and water." He began to strip off his clothes. At least I knew that he was comfortable being naked around us. He caught my eye, and I would have sworn he gave me a wink.

My mates tried to avoid looking at the 'new guy,' instead they exchanged confused looks with each other. Pixie ignored them and strolled to the tub. Lowering himself in, he hissed at the temperature. What can I say? Dragons love it hot.

"Duly noted," he responded to my unspoken comment. Leaning toward me, he nuzzled my neck and then sucked my bottom lip between his teeth. Before I could react, he moved backwards in the water until he leaned against the far side.

"You can't just tease me and swim away!" I cried.

"I just did that very thing. Your mates need time with you, so I will sit back and wait." He glanced at the men who were still frozen. "Unless they continue to procrastinate, then I will certainly take care of any needs you have that are not being met."

I looked at my men. They were trying to pamper me and take things slow, but we all wanted and needed the bonding that came from making love.

Myth dropped his pants, the belt clanging against the floor. At our raised eyebrows, he responded, "If love making is what she needs, then I am going to show her every bit of my pent-up love."

The fact that he was reading my mind, when he was such a stickler for privacy, told more than words ever could how much he needed closeness with me. He couldn't bear any separation.

He removed his shirt and moved with silent steps toward the tub. Settling beneath the water, he pulled me to him. I straddled his lap, enjoying the brush of his cool skin against my heated skin. Shifting his hips, something hard and hot pressed tight along my slit. Smiling wickedly, he flashed beautiful gleaming white fangs at me.

Yummy.

I purred. "Are those fangs or are you just happy to see me?"

CHAPTER ELEVEN

Tia

Myth's lips molded to mine, just as skilled as I remembered. His hips rocked against me at an unhurried pace, while his tongue took the opportunity to deepen our kiss. My arms were around his neck, and I pressed more tightly to his chest, wanting to feel every inch of his bare skin against mine.

I absolutely wanted hot, passionate, neuron-frying sex, but I also wanted the closeness that came with intimacy. The pain of being separated from them had hurt, and my heart was still trying to mend from everything that had happened since I had last seen my mates. Call me needy, but I craved the reassurance and reminder of their love.

Don't ever doubt my love, Mea Dragostea.

My deadly vampire, my first lover and mate.

I must have been thinking inside the bond because my mates all responded. They each caught my gaze as they spoke in the bond.

You ain't ever getting rid of me, Darling.

Not a chance, Kitty. You are mine forever.

My loyal wolf protectors when I had been at my weakest, and my comforters when I'd been sad.

The wizard council loaned me to your team, but now you own me.

My shy wizard, and my playful mate who loved to find ways to keep our group laughing.

For the rest of eternity, not a day will go by where you worry about my love.

My dragon, who'd literally pieced me back together and would rain fire down on the Earth if I asked.

There was an awkward pause. Leo nudged Pixie, who just sent him a disgruntled look.

"Dude, you are supposed to tell her how much you love her," he said through coughs, a terrible attempt at covering up the prompt.

"She is aware I do not love her," Pixie responded curtly, "and I will not lie."

It was like a scene from a movie: time froze, no one twitched or breathed. All focus was on Pixie, who remained unconcerned. When the pause continued to the point of absurdity, Pix sighed and spoke out loud.

"Bunny, you are the only one for me until I draw my last breath. You're aware there are things I am unable to offer you, but I will give you everything that I am able."

My mates exchanged confused looks. We were going to have to talk this through.

Later.

My tears dropped into the water with echoing *plops*. I would never forget their words, nor their love...in whichever form it took.

"Oh!" My throat was too tight to say anything else. I threw my arms around Myth's neck and began to kiss the ever-loving-life out of him.

Hey! Luke cried in the link, *Save some sugar for me!* He shucked his pants and jumped into the water, sending waves splashing over the sides and onto the floor.

Pressing against my back, he began to suck at his mark on my neck. His hands moved around my waist and his calloused palms spread against my flat stomach. His erection bumped my back like a hot poker, causing me to clench my thighs in anticipation. Since I was still on Myth's lap, my clench had him groaning.

"I am not going to last long if you do that again," he growled and nipped my lip, not quite hard enough to draw blood.

That would've been bad, because then he would lose control—

Best. Idea. Ever.

I nicked my tongue on my own razor-sharp pearly whites. Playfully letting our tongues do a little tango, I waited.

Five, four, three, two——

His eyes shifted to crimson. He wanted to eat me. Yay!

With a hard bounce of his hips, I was nearly shoved off his

lap. Luke's hands grabbed my waist, and with a nod at Myth, he brought me down. Hard. I was impaled on Myth's rod in one smooth motion that hit all the right spots. I climaxed instantly and the world around me exploded in a shower of stunning fireworks.

My body was still shuddering as Luke lifted me and brought me down again. Myth's hips bucked up as Luke brought me down, providing wonderfully deep penetration. Luke was calm, although his ragged breathing against the nape of my neck showed he was affected as well.

What I hadn't expected was Myth's control. He was in 'monster mode' and yet he was holding himself back, allowing Luke to be in control. My sweet guys didn't want to hurt me. Their concern was sweet, but unnecessary.

My body had healed as much as it was going to. I would always have faint white scar lines from the many beatings I had taken. Most of those wounds had been forced to heal without dragon magic, and that meant my skin was left with scars. I was also thin from the stress of my imprisonment, but I planned to make up for lost time when it came to eating.

They know you are not a breakable doll, but they need time to deal with their emotions from your time away from them. Give them time, Bunny.

I glanced toward Pix, surprised to find that no one else seemed to have heard him. He hadn't spoken inside the bond.

I have superior telepathy skills. Everyone here needs training.

He should have sounded arrogant, but instead it came off as though he had stated a known fact.

I turned my attention back to my vampire lover, enjoying the warm water swirling around me as we rocked together. Smoky black mist swirled with the crimson of his irises, creating a mesmerizing combination. Leaning forward, I tried to get a closer look, only to have his fangs sink into my neck. That was a neat little trick; lure me in and bite me. Waves of pleasure rushed through me, followed by feverish chills of desire. Oh yeah, I would definitely be falling for that little trick again.

Myth's hands locked around my hips and took over control of our ever-increasing rhythm. Luke's hands slipped up my wet hips and stomach. His fingers traced along the curves of my waist, before brushing at the underside of my breasts.

"Oh, Luke." My words came out breathy and garbled.

Encouraged, he captured both of my breasts. His roughened palms against my sensitive skin had my muscles clenching painfully tightly around Myth's throbbing erection. Need was building fast, and my insides grew tighter with each thrust of my vampire's hips. Luke kneaded my breasts and then pinched both nipples. I screamed out my release, clawing at Myth as I felt myself get a bit lightheaded.

With my claws in his back, Myth's control broke and his desire burst through like water gushing from a dam. He yanked me away from Luke and slipped his own arm around my waist. Spinning us around, he slammed our bodies against the cool stone wall, his arm around my waist taking the brunt of the hit. I heard the wall crack, but my vampire lover had made sure I was unharmed.

Ever the protector, and unable to stop himself, Luke growled a rumbling warning. Myth was all too happy to respond with a hiss, while his blood-red eyes locked onto Luke. Luke refused to back down or look away, and Myth was too far gone to think rationally. We were about five freaking seconds away from a showdown. Why did that idea make me wetter? Was it possible to become wetter while still in the tub?

"Girls, you're both pretty and powerful," I said. "Now, let's all calm down." I'd always wanted to say that.

The tension filling the room must have sucked the humor right out of my mates, because only Leo burst out in raucous laughter over my ill-timed humor.

Peering around the spacious bathroom, I assessed the situation. I had two werewolves that were acting like alphas. A dragon who was blowing steam out of his nose, while the water around him bubbled and boiled. A wizard cackling like a stereotypical witch, thankfully unaffected by the shifter hormones filling the room. A Pixie with his hand on the hilt of his sword, ears twitching with the urge to jump into a battle at any moment. And a slightly crazy and very hissy blood-driven mate who made the mistake of pushing me behind him... implying I needed protection from Luke.

Needless to say, that went over like a lead balloon.

Luke's vicious growl sent tingles rushing along my spine. Myth responded with an angry hiss that had bats fluttering in my stomach. Luke lunged forward, and Myth grabbed me and flashed to the other side of the 'pool.' He sat me on the side and turned to face the angry wolf rushing toward him.

Levi took advantage of the situation and slid into the pool

next to me, in nothing but sweatpants. He lifted me to the edge and wrapped my legs around his waist. His hand sank into my hair, the fingers knotting in my damp silky strands. Angling my head to the side, he leaned down and licked the imprint of his mark. My belly grew heavy with desire. All the testosterone in the room was getting me hot and bothered, but it wasn't helping any of us find our release.

I knew I should be focusing on calming down my out-of-control mates, that is what a good human girl would do. But since I wasn't human, I was going to enjoy every minute of this primal show of power like any good dragoness would.

I sent my magic through the water, just to check the emotions of my amped up mates. It returned to me with a dreamy sigh. There were no intentions of murdering each other, so we could enjoy this little display without worrying.

I nibbled up Levi's neck, enjoying his involuntary shudder at my touch. Gripping him through his sweatpants, I stroked the thick length of his erection. One minute my other hand was moving for the waistband of his soaked sweats, and the next instant he was gone. Luke's roar reverberated through the room. I didn't know where Mithraheal was, but I didn't have time to contemplate it.

Luke pulled me back into the water, flipping me around so I faced away from him. His hand brushed my butt, then slid to the parts of me begging for attention. I thought he was going to tease me with his fingers, instead his finger was quickly replaced by the feel of him being buried inside me. Hard as steel and scorching hot.

I opened my mouth to cry out from the sheer pleasure, but

his hand gently covered my lips. Luke was careful to give me space to breathe around his hand, and I used that space to sink my fangs into his palm. Gently, of course. Kinda.

My bite excited the werewolf. Yanking his hand back, he hauled my hips tighter against him to sheath himself deeper. Shouts and splashing water sounded from the other side of the room, but I was too far gone to care. With each stroke, Luke was driving us both higher and faster toward the precipice.

"Oh. Luke. Yes." The words were spoken on a gasp. I was so close. A figure moved in front of me, and through my momentarily crossed eyes, I made out the figure of Ivo.

Yes, whisper his name now. In a few minutes I will have you screaming mine.

Every last brain cell I possessed fainted on the spot.

Ivo's lips met mine, in a kiss that was neither gentle nor demanding. It was confident. My body began to tremble. Luke responded by gripping me tighter. This guy must have been a genius at geometry, because boy-oh-boy did he know all about angles. With a tilt of his hips, he managed to hit all the right spots and my orgasm rocked my body and stars burst in my vision. He thrust twice more, and then his body stilled while he howled his release.

Levi's angry growl was the only warning I got before Luke was ripped away from me and tossed onto the bathroom floor. Levi leapt out of the water after his brother. Ivo steadied me against him as the two male wolves circled each other. The floor was submerged in three inches of water and their brawl had water spraying around them in a scene worthy of a movie.

Although, with both of them being naked, it wasn't the type of movie that would be playing in theaters anytime soon.

One moment Ivo was next to me, and in the next instant he was gone. Myth yanked him beneath the water, before surfacing across the pool with a bellow. Steam was rising from the water around Ivo, his temper flaring at being interrupted. Myth had changed from a polished man with elegant manners, to an animalistic male annoyed at anyone near me.

Having my guys show off their toned muscles and their body vibrating growls was a major turn on, but having them play hot potato with me wasn't my idea of a good time. I was growing frustrated, and with that feeling my heat began to flare. It must have been nearly over, because I had been able to control it since escaping the dungeon - at least until now. My anger was fanning those flames; I was just thankful it hadn't turned into the fiery inferno it had been yesterday. This was uncomfortable, that had been torture.

I stared wide-eyed at muscled men fighting for my attention. Water dripped down their naked bodies, and I thought I felt a little drool slide from the corner of my mouth. I was going to blame that on my heat.

Without a hint of a sound, Leo slid into the water beside me, a teasing smile and his finger pressed to his lips in the universal sign to be quiet. He dropped beneath the water and began to nibble up my leg.

Well, this whole fiasco was going way better than I had dared to hope.

CHAPTER TWELVE

Tia

Thwack! Splash!

Ivo and Myth had taken to tossing each other around, but I found myself unable to protest due to the magical things Leo was doing beneath the water. Purple magic swirled around my legs, a light brush against my hyper-sensitive skin.

Leo's lung capacity was impressive. He kissed up my leg, exploring every inch at a leisurely pace. My body was trembling from his attention to detail. When his head finally broke the surface, it was to press a tender kiss on my abdomen. Our eyes locked. I sucked in my breath at the love swimming in those dark depths. My stomach fluttered. Was that love for me? Could he possibly—

I cut that thought off.

I didn't get a chance to ask. Leo had opened his mouth but was cut off by the overgrown pup that launched himself from the side of the tub straight at him. And by overgrown pup, I mean the three-hundred-pound werewolf that was Levi. My other hunky werewolf was barking and preparing to dive in after the vampire and dragon duo.

I should probably put a stop to this.

Why? Your mates have been stressed, they need to burn off that pent up emotion. They haven't permanently maimed each other, no one has died, and the house still has walls. It appears your mates have found a healthy release—sex and sparring.

Pixie leaned against the wall, his posture now relaxed. His eyes tracked the brawl with the same intensity of men watching a football game.

Levi doggie-paddled around Leo and myself, pulling my attention away from the aloof Fae. Purple sparks began cracking along my wizard's skin with every lunge of the giant chocolate wolf, warning Levi to back off. Instead, I watched in horror as Levi snapped his powerful jaws and surged toward Leo's arm. I found myself choking on laughter when Leo calmly smacked him on the nose and shouted, "Bad dog!" The scolding did nothing to appease the angry agitated shifter, and a predatory glint was in the wolf's green eyes.

Amethyst light glowed around Leo's hands, the soft light pulsing in the water around him and me. A thin wall of water rose from around us to create a rippling dome over our heads. Levi lunged again, but rather than passing through the water, he slammed into it with a teeth-rattling force.

Reaching out a finger, I tentatively ran it down the wall of water, surprised to find it solid and several inches thick. It appeared to be made of water, but instead of feeling cold like ice, it was simply a solid clear pane like bulletproof glass. I had so many questions, but they would wait until later. There was no way I was wasting this chance to spend time with Leo.

A subtle flick of his hand made quick work of removing his clothes, and in the blink of an eye, he stood naked. Water covered most of his chest and everything below, but that didn't stop my gums from aching with the desire to bite his sweet derriere. When did I become so bitey? I was going to need to work on that impulse. Later.

His right hand traced the line of my jaw, his left moving to the small of my back to bring me closer. Even in a room that was drenched in testosterone, Leo remained my sweet lover. I wrapped my arms around his chest, enjoying the warmth of his body against mine and the steady rhythm of his heartbeat in my ear.

Long fingers brushed gently through my damp hair and massaged my scalp. My eyes crossed from how wonderful it felt. Knowing that there would be time for snuggling later, I trailed my hand lower. The slightest of tremors went through his body when my fingers brushed along the velvet length of his stiff erection. Enjoying his reaction, I curled my fingers around the base and massaged my way to the rounded head.

The water made everything deliciously slick, and with my next stroke I traveled the length of him faster. He groaned through clenched teeth and dropped his forehead to rest on my shoulder. I loved that he was letting me take control.

Wrapping my fingers tighter around his thick rod, I increased my pace and smiled as his hips gave small involuntary thrusts. His hot breath on my shoulder grew faster and his hand that still rested on my lower back shook.

"Beautiful, not this way tonight," he said. "I need to feel you wrapped around me."

It wasn't a command, rather, it was a request, and one I was happy to honor. I hooked my hands around his neck. Sliding both hands under the curve of my butt, he lifted me. Unhooking one hand, I aligned him with my secret channel. With a slowness that threatened to stop my heart, he lowered me onto him.

We moaned in unison when he could go no further. Neither of us moved as we enjoyed the moment.

"Ready?"

My response of "Mmhm" was as close to forming words as I could manage.

The dance began. Slow and steady. Did I mention slow? Leo was determined to enjoy every last moment of our time together as shown by the sweat beading his brow as he fought against his own instinct. I tried to wiggle and speed things up, the need growing so heavy I thought my insides might drop out. Leo's grip on my thighs tightened in warning. Afraid that he might stop altogether, I stopped trying to rush the moment.

My skin alternated between cold chills and hot flashes as every nerve in my body lit up like a Christmas tree. I wanted him to go slow and drive us mad, and I also wanted him to take me hard and fast.

A muffled growl came through our glassy dome and we

both jerked in shock having forgotten a world existed outside of this magical cocoon. Clearing the lust-filled haze from my eyes, I tried to focus on the direction the sound had emanated from. I found four sets of scowling eyes staring back at me. Desire and annoyance were stamped on their faces.

Well, this was awkward.

I lifted a hand and wiggled my fingers in greeting, hoping to lighten the mood. Spoiler alert, that didn't work. Myth's fist slammed into the watery dome, and for a moment, he wavered. Leo's brow wrinkled in concentration as he struggled to focus on doing me, and doing magic, at the same time.

The wall not only solidified, but he electrified the dang thing. When Ivo's entire body impacted with the wall, it set off purple lightning that flickered around the dome like a plasma globe from a science museum. The main difference being that plasma balls were safe to touch, and Leo's creation wasn't safe at all. Purple lightning surged into Ivo, frying his body like bacon in a hot pan.

Had Ivo not already been smoking hot and a creature whose favorite place to take naps was at the bottom of a volcano, he would have been killed instantly. Instead, Leo's magic tazed him and he sank like the Titanic. My heart surged into my throat.

Luke took pity on the dragon and ducked under the water, surfacing a second later with the band of Ivo's pants held in his mouth. It was no small amount of effort to drag the giant man up out of the pool. By the time Ivo was safely up out of the water, he was also sporting a wedgie of atomic proportions.

Leo snickered.

Laugh it up. Dragons possess long lives and a perfect memory. Your time will come.

Ivo's words were spoken in a genial tone, but I still caught the sound of Leo's heart skipping a few beats. It steadied almost instantly, and a mischievous smirk spread across his face.

"I had no idea the protection spell would work that well."

Okay, I get how that would make him happy, but the look on his face wasn't pride over his accomplishment. It was something else, something I couldn't quite put my finger on. I eyed him suspiciously. He tilted his head and kissed me.

It was a slow, movie-worthy kiss that I half expected to steam up the dome around us. Checking for steam, I caught onto the reason for the glint in Leo's eyes. He was watching my other mates, while they watched us.

We might as well have been an exhibit at an aquarium, and Leo had decided to put on a show. I felt him twitch inside me, and my body shivered in response. His breath was warm as he kissed and licked his way down my neck. Leo's hands moved from my thighs to rub the shape of my butt.

I couldn't see his face, but I would have bet money he was staring the others down the entire time. How was it that my almost-shy mate blossomed into an exhibitionist when we made love? And why did it turn me on so much? I doubted I'd ever been this wet in my life, and I wasn't talking about the tub water.

Leo's fingers dug into my rounded butt cheeks, not hard enough to bruise, but enough to get a good grip. Then he resumed our previous rhythm. A smooth stroke in, and a long slow pull out. This time when he buried himself in my slick channel, he added an extra little thrust at the end, making sure he was sheathed as far as possible, and making equally sure my circle knew it too. I couldn't have complained if I wanted to, because each time he added that bit of *razzle-dazzle* to this performance, his erection was rubbing against all the right places.

I was barely remembering to keep my lungs working as the ravenous hunger began to build inside me again. Leo's body was shuddering against mine; he wasn't going to last much longer either. This was going to be more of a halftime show versus a feature film.

"Would it be okay to turn to face them?" he asked me. His body language remained cocky and confident, but his whispered words were full of tender concern.

I nipped his bottom lip and then leaned back so I could look into his eyes. The purple ring around his pupil surprised me, although it shouldn't have, since we were all currently finding our powers shifting and changing on a weekly basis.

"I'm game for whatever you want to do in this little show of yours," I replied. Those were probably not the wisest words to say to a horny wizard, but hey, I wasn't thinking clearly.

Once I turned around, Leo's hand sank gently into my hair and pulled my head back slightly. My eyes connected with my five very ticked off and very turned on mates. If I had tugged even the slightest bit, my hair would have pulled free, but I remained still, enjoying this other side of Leo. And if I am being honest, it was hot as heck having them get to look, but not touch.

It took no more than a few more hard thrusts and it was over. I screamed his name as pleasure rushed through me. He stilled and followed me into bliss. With his concentration shattered, the dome turned to liquid and rained a glittering shower on us. I was relaxed and purring in contentment.

It would have been a stunning end to Leo's fun, except the moment the dome dissipated, Levi and Myth lunged for Leo. Growing up a nadir, Leo had learned to dodge bullies, and now he used some of those tricks to elude the vampire and werewolf as they shouted lame insults and growls at each other. It was the weirdest game of Marco Polo I had ever witnessed.

A low groan from the side of the tub had my head snapping that way. The sight that greeted me sent me into a fit of laughter. Ivo was still frozen on the floor, but his fingers had begun to twitch, and his mouth muscles had moved just enough for him to groan. Luke had sat his fat furry rump down on Ivo's head, much like a family dog might to a beloved human...except Luke was well aware of what he was doing. He was intentionally antagonizing the dragon shifter.

I'm protecting him from the others.

Sincerity filled Luke's voice. Between the voice and the giant puppy eyes he was giving me, I almost believed him. Almost.

Just wait, mutt. You will soon be a fur rug that I rest my feet on.

Luke just tilted his head to the side and let his tongue loll.

He could be the poster dog for man's loyal best friend. Maybe I should take a picture, he wasn't likely to live a long life once Ivo regained use of his limbs again.

Looking around the room, contentment filled me. This was my 'circus' and these were my 'monkeys.' It didn't look like wrestling, but we were meddling and becoming a family. My mates were among the deadliest supernaturals on earth, yet there wasn't so much as a scratch on any of the men. Even while fired up, they had been careful to pull their punches. Pixie had been right. They had just needed to blow off their stress and anxious energy.

I am rarely wrong, Bunny. Look around, this is a very good example of why Fae chose to extinguish their emotions. They cause unstable temperaments and create unnecessary messes.

I rolled my eyes and teleported in front of my fairy-eared mate. "Yes, but they can also be so much fun!" I replied.

Without giving him a chance to respond, I climbed his body like a monkey, soaking his clothes in the process. Wanting to make sure my prey didn't escape, I wrapped my thighs around his torso, and snaked my arms up his neck and into his long blonde hair. Using my grip to move his neck to the side, I felt the lazy stir of desire. I was beginning to understand why my mates kept tangling their fingers in my own pale locks. That desire would have to wait. First, I needed another sandwich, and then to sleep for the next twenty-four hours straight.

Popping us to the edge of the water, I shifted my weight, purposely throwing him off balance. We tumbled into the pool, water cascading all around us.

"Bunny!"

I only laughed in response to Pixie's shout. His voice lacked any anger, but it was dripping with disbelief.

"You are part of this crazy circus we call a family," I told him. "It's long past time that you learned to play." I kissed him lightly on the cheek.

His body remained motionless for a minute, then his arms encircled me and drew me closer to him. I purred harder when his talented fingers began to massage my back.

"I'll try, for you," was his reply.

My heart warmed at his almost hesitant response. My affection for this man hadn't stopped growing after leaving the dungeon. It wasn't yet love, but it was...more.

His fingers danced across my ribs, and I twitched and hoped he didn't notice.

I was fresh out of luck today. He noticed and then repeated the movement. I couldn't stop my slight twitch and I nearly bit off my tongue trying to keep from laughing and giving away my weakness. One perfect pale eyebrow lifted, and then it was on like a candy thong!

Pixie discovered he enjoyed participating in something other than sex and battle, while I discovered he was a sadistic fairy who loved to inflict the worst kind of torture on innocent people. He found every ticklish spot on my body, exploiting each discovery until I was sobbing with laughter.

I collapsed against my captor and begged for mercy through ragged breaths. His chest rumbled, and out of the corner of my eye I realized he had chuckled. I would melt this iceman one day. Just watch me. As my pants grew softer, I became aware that the room around us was silent. No sounds of a brawl or water splashing could be heard. Looking around, I found all my guys sitting calmly on the edge of the pool, and all looking completely human. A paranormal pool party had been just what we needed.

CHAPTER THIRTEEN

Myth

I watched as Tia twisted and twirled, the movements smooth and well-practiced. She could have been mistaken for a dancer if her hands had held fans instead of swords. This morning she had lightly scolded me when I 'd presented her with the box, but once she saw the pair of swords, she was smitten. I had many faults, but I knew what my girl liked best...shiny sharp things meant for stabbing. Could she be any more perfect?

Finishing the training session, she walked toward me, wiping at her face with a small towel. Her waist-length blonde hair was tied back in a ponytail that swished in time with her hips as she moved. She wore a tiny sports bra and shorts, neither garment leaving much to the imagination. I wanted to curse at the white scar lines that crisscrossed, not because they disgusted me, but because they were a sign of my failure as her mate.

"What's up, sourpuss?" she asked. "You have gone from looking at me like I am a snack, to looking like I am gum on the bottom of your shoe."

I barked a laugh. There was never any way to know what was going to come out of this woman's mouth. Snagging her hand, I pulled her off balance and she toppled onto my lap. She screamed in protest as I covered every inch I could find in kisses.

"Stop! I'm gross! At least let me take a shower!" She dissolved into giggles as I licked up her stomach and tickled her ribs. Then, her body stiffened and she sighed. "Incoming."

My brow wrinkled in confusion, not understanding what she meant until my lead court advisor popped into the grassy yard. I wondered if I would ever get used to that particular ability. There was no denying it was handy, though.

Tia wiggled, trying to get off my lap. Locking my arms around her, I cradled her squirming body to me.

"Myth! He's here to see his King, and this doesn't look proper," she hissed.

"Be still, my Queen. The kingdom will just have to get used to seeing you in my arms because I intend to have my hands on you every possible moment of the day."

I pressed a kiss to her lips before addressing our visitor. Anxiety rolled off him in waves, he shifted his weight from foot to foot in agitation. He was wise enough to not interrupt me.

"Markus," I began, "I assume if you are here, then a significant issue has arisen."

I was careful to keep my voice even, not wishing to worry Tia.

Markus had never left the vampire kingdom voluntarily. Not ever. I'd nearly had to drag him kicking and screaming when I brought him to this lakeside cabin one single time, and that had been back when the wizards were living with us. It had been necessary to make sure he'd teleported to this precise location to ensure he could teleport here in the future if the need arose. Needless to say, it wasn't a great sign that he had popped in for a visit, and now stood in front of me with a creased brow, wringing his hands.

"Your Majesty, there is an issue at the castle needing your attention immediately."

"You may speak freely in front of your queen, Markus," I said firmly. "What is truly going on right now?" I needed him to get to the point, so I could determine whether it required my immediate attention or not.

"There has been an uprising, your Majesty. When news of your parents' death reached the kingdom, your military commander, several hundred soldiers, and three of your advisors decided now was a good time to overthrow you. They want to restore the previous monarchy's feared reputation, and it is believed you are too soft to protect the blood driven."

Stunned silence was my only reaction. *Too soft.* They believed I was 'too soft'? I'd lost count many centuries ago of the number of humans and supernaturals that had been wiped from existence by my hand. Some had been more than deserving of death, but to my shame, many others had not. I did not enjoy remembering those times I lost control of my vampiric nature.

Unlike my father, I'd never found pleasure in maiming and murdering innocents while in full control of my mind. To the previous king, cruelty was an entertaining hobby. I had ended his reign and tried to repair the damage he'd done to our species. My people had come to respect me—or so I had believed.

"They are making their way to the throne room now, fully intent on claiming the right to rule," Markus continued. "There has already been much bloodshed, they are taking out everyone who gets in their path. I'm afraid you will have to be the one to stop them. The citizens know you have been gone more often than not lately, and rumors are being spread that you've abandoned your post for a woman who doesn't bear fangs."

"Mistaking my love of justice, and my generosity, for weakness is one thing," I began. "Insulting their queen is a whole different issue. That is something I will not tolerate, and it will be eliminated. Immediately."

I kissed the top of Tia's head and sat her gently in the seat beside me. I ignored the wide-eyed look on Markus' face at my show of affection. I was known as cold and detached, because that is exactly what I was until meeting Tia. My fiery little dragon had thawed my heart and warmed my soul, a change I was happy to embrace.

With reluctance, I rose to my feet. "Let's go sort out this mess."

Markus turned toward me, relief washing over his features when he realized that he wouldn't have to stay here any longer, and that I was returning with him without delay. He had always given me sound advice and was well respected among my people, but he had never been known for his bravery.

"Son of a motherless goat!" Tia's sudden roar of outrage had my heart lurching like it had been electrocuted. I watched wide-eyed as she leaped on Markus' back, holding a pair of knives that appeared out of thin air. She wrapped her arms around his neck and yanked them back faster than my vampire vision could track.

If he had been human, bright red blood would have sprayed in an arch as she decapitated him with that one blurring move. In stark contrast to her unnerving speed, his head toppled in ridiculously slow motion, falling to the ground with a thud. An ooze of dark maroon blood bubbled out like molasses from a tree.

I gaped at her, knowing manners dictated that I close my mouth, but unable to process anything that was going on around me.

"How stupid do they think we are?" Tia cried out. "I wanted one day. Just *one* freaking day to snuggle with my mates and discuss some things before dealing with the world! Is that too much to ask?" Finished with her rant, she wiped the bloody blades across her itty-bitty workout shorts...and teleported away.

My mouth was still hanging open.

"I am very interested in figuring out where she keeps

those blades, a closer inspection of her body might be in order."

Pixel. He stepped out of the tree line like a creepy stalker and moved to examine the fallen body of my advisor. He had only a few seconds to inspect it before the body disintegrated to dust, leaving behind only Markus' clothing. He had been a wonderful asset for the kingdom, and his death was a tragic loss.

"Don't be stupid, vampire," Pixel said, studying my face with narrowed eyes.

"You do know it is considered rude to read the mind of someone without their consent?" I replied.

"Perhaps it is rude in this realm, but among the Fae it is a powerful ability - one that has saved many lives. It would be idiotic not to use all of one's skills."

As a blood driven, I liked the Fae's stance on using all of your talents. But as someone who'd has spent time around human logic, I could respect the desire for privacy.

"We will need to finish this conversation later," Pixel added. "Right now, we should follow her."

"And where exactly are we following her?" I couldn't hide the sarcasm in my voice. Tia had a mind of her own and there was no telling where she had gone. Maybe she just wanted to go take a nap or grab a snack. Or maybe she had just freaked out, lost her marbles, and we had a serious mess on our hands.

"Tia went to deal with the trap that had been set for you."

"Everyone outside!" My shout was filled with the horror and seething anger that was now traveling through every atom in my body. It reverberated off the house, shaking the windows and echoing across the valley. I repeated the shout in the mind link.

Alarm bells rang in my mind, and our circle must have felt the urgency of my call, because the next sounds to ring in my ears were those of panicked shouting and thudding footsteps.

"Where is she?" Levi was the first to reach me, his green eyes glowing with a decidedly not-human glow.

"She's gone to the castle to stop a coup." My mind was racing. They needed to hurry, or I was leaving without them.

Luke and Leo rushed around the side of the house, Ivo hot on their heels.

"Your superhero 'call to arms' needs work, bro," said Damien as he approached us. "'*Everyone outside*' sucks as a catchphrase. Maybe something like 'Mates Unite!', 'Hurry Horny Heroes!' or maybe, 'Mates, Let's Mutilate!' No? How about—"

I grabbed Damien's arm, not sparing the time to acknowledge his stupidity, but wanting to make sure he came with us. Both of us being there would add a bit more terror in the hearts of those who had dared to plot against the throne. I then grabbed Pixel's bicep.

Ivo caught on fast, snatching Leo and Luke's arms so hard he nearly wrenched them off the ground. Pixel, calm as ever, rested his hand on Levi's shoulder, and placed the other on Ivo's shoulder. I didn't waste time explaining our destination, it was easier to just link everyone together. Without bothering to ask if they were ready, we teleported to the castle.

CHAPTER FOURTEEN

Myth

From the moment I realized where our angry mate had teleported to, one horrific situation after another had played through my head. I wasn't dead, so she wasn't either. That knowledge provided a tiny bit of comfort.

Of all my imagined scenarios, the scene we popped into was not on the list. She stood proudly, a queen in the throne room of the Blood Driven, a warrior surrounded by the bodies of her enemies. I stared in shock, trying desperately to comprehend the number of supernaturals she had just destroyed in the two minutes she had been here before our arrival.

"I think she has this under control. May I go back to my werewolf now?" Damien's expression was one of boredom, but I didn't miss the sparkle of amusement in his eyes. He thought this was funny.

"Our subjects lay slaughtered, our kingdom is threatened by traitors, and Tia has suddenly turned into the modern incarnation of Joan of Arc, except with supernatural abilities," I replied. "I think you should stay."

"Ahh, Joan. She was such a cool chick. I hated that we weren't able to turn her in time. Her death was such a waste."

"DAMIEN! Focus!" My patience was not just thin, it had snapped.

"Stop worrying, vampire," Ivo interjected. "Our mate is in control of the situation. You need to trust her judgment."

I knew Ivo was correct, and I trusted her with all my heart. But there had been so many changes recently in her life, and that worried me. I was also worried about the fact that nearly every dead body on the floor was an advisor to my court. Why had she executed them all? And how had she done it?

These men were powerful among the blood driven, some old and some young. I had watched her fight Draven and she did not have enough power to take on more than thirty elite supernaturals at the same time. Yet the bodies on the floor, and her blood-covered but uninjured body told a different story. I was becoming intensely curious about that talk she wanted to have with us.

Thud. Thud. Thud.

"Seriously?" Tia sighed. "This is *so* not the time for visitors." She blurred to the massive oak doors that lead outside, grabbed the handles—

"Tia, no!" Again, she moved faster than my eyes or brain

could process. My shout came too late, and she flung open the heavy wooden doors as if they were flimsy screens. Outside stood about fifty soldiers and a commander I had never liked.

"This is not a good time for a visit unless you are a cleaning crew, or you are selling cookies," Tia said sharply. "By the way, I like the flat cookies with chocolate and a hint of mint flavor."

Luke laughed a rough rumbling laugh, Levi and Leo joining in with loud guffaws.

It was like living with children.

"Did you just pull a sword on me? That thing is tiny! My sword is longer *and* thicker. Come on in, let's get this over with." Tia rambled on to the would-be assassins, even stepping to the side and waving them in with a flourish like they were honored guests.

I only barely resisted the urge to facepalm myself. My body was coming out of the fog that had held me immobile as I watched the insanity that was playing out in front of me. Moving forward, I prepared to get between her and my traitorous soldiers, but Ivo's arm shot out and stopped me.

"Her heart rate and breathing are relaxed," he said. "She believes they pose no threat to her. Let's stay back to see what our minx is up to. We can step in if she requires assistance, if not, it could be enlightening to see what trick she has up her sleeve." Ivo's voice all but shook with anticipation, and it caused a mix of alarm and interest to war inside me.

It went against my instincts, but in the end, my own curiosity won out and I hung back in the shadows along with the rest of the circle. A very impatient Damien huffed at my side. I could smell the she-wolf on him, but I had noticed earlier that they didn't bear each other's mark yet. It was interesting, but my curiosity would have to wait until I wasn't watching my mate invite highly trained paranormal soldiers into the grand throne room.

The cathedral ceilings were gold plated and designed to ensure the king's voice carried through the entire hall, and to enhance our musicians' instruments during parties. The sharp staccato of the soldiers' boots on the polished marble floor bounced around the room, the noise reverberating around us like a surround sound system. It gave the illusion that there were many more men than the number entering at that moment.

When the last man entered, Tia slammed the door like a petulant teenager. She strode through the armed men in her blood-splattered workout clothes. My heart squeezed painfully. Any one of those men could run a sword through her in an instant, but she moved through them like she owned the place. That was the moment it hit me.

She was acting like a queen. Not a new queen still learning the ropes, no, she carried herself with the confidence of a woman born, raised, and trained to rule. She was not the same woman that we had taken to the ball. I had thought her showdown with my parents had been adrenalin-fueled revenge, but looking back I realized she had carried herself with that same grace and confidence.

I fell in love with her all over again. My perfect queen.

CHAPTER FIFTEEN

Tia

I turned to face the soldiers. They all stood motionless, confusion and wariness etched on their faces. Who could blame them? It wasn't every day you decided to assassinate the King and those loyal to him, and then follow that up by taking over his kingdom.

I also doubted they had expected to be invited in by a blonde in dirty, blood-soaked workout clothes. My mates were trying to hide in the shadows of the hall, but I knew they were there, and I could feel worry and anger rolling off them in waves. Well, everyone except Pixie. I was still trying to learn how to read him, but I must not be doing it correctly because it seemed like he was just turned on.

Inviting the men inside was a tactical decision on my part. With the thick oak doors closed, it would make it difficult for any of them to escape. Unless they begged for repentance before the fighting started, there would be no mercy for them later. The old Tia would have been soft and given them another chance. The new Tia had more important things to do than waste her time on liars.

"Who's in charge of this group?" I let my firm voice shift to my huskier one, the one that promised things like death to my enemies, protection to those loyal to me, and rough, dirty sex to my mates.

"That would be me." Mister Tall, Dark and Butt Ugly stepped forward. Weren't all vampires supposed to be attractive? I felt a pang of pity for the man. I'd be angry too if I were surrounded by unnaturally attractive people but had to live eternally with a face that would make an onion cry.

"We are here to see the king, not you, *dragon*," he said and finished by spitting near my feet. The way he said 'dragon' implied I was lower than the vomit-colored scum on a pond. I didn't feel bad for him anymore; his face and personality were a perfect match. It took everything in me not to char him on the spot - I was struggling to continue maintaining this facade of being a polite 'human.'

"Let's drop the pretenses," I snapped back. "Your problem isn't with the king, it is with me and his relationship with me."

His reply proved that he was more than happy to tell me how he felt: "You are a dirty shifter, one that was hunted to extinction on purpose. The Blood Driven elders found the old scrolls and discovered that the dragons were judged by the supernatural council. It was decided they should be executed for interfering in our governments. You are defying our laws by the very act of breathing, and by mating with you, our king is living in defiance of the law as well. Today, you both will face execution."

My chest burned in rage. How dare he judge my species based on what some piece of crap Blood Driven had written in the scrolls so long ago? Dragons had died, not because we were trying to take over and control the world, but because we tried to maintain peace. My skin felt like a hot iron was pressed against it.

Click.

My internal organs felt as though they were being melted together by the heat of my fire, searing flames that wanted to come out to play. The soldiers were growing restless, and their commander's blatant disrespect excited them. The gleam of fangs made it pretty darn clear that they weren't here to protect Myth, or me. I hated to sound callous, but they had to die.

"You killed the previous king and queen, the true rulers of our people. Today, we will avenge—"

Thankfully, the ugly, angry vampire was interrupted by pounding at the oak doors on the opposite end of the long hall. Had someone hung out a welcome sign?

Sighing, I held a finger up to him. "Hold that thought for just a sec."

Temper flaring at yet another delay to getting home to my mates, I flashed to the far end of the hall, flinging open the doors with enough force to send them slamming into the walls and then bouncing back toward me.

"If I had known you were coming, I would have left!" I all but growled my fury at this latest interruption.

A new group of soldiers watched me with wide eyes. As it had been doing all day, my magic moved unseen through the men, seeking out their intentions toward Myth and the kingdom. As it flowed back inside me, I felt a bit of the tension leave my neck. They weren't here to harm my mate; they were here to defend Myth and those loyal to him.

"Fine, you might as well join the party," I said with a sigh. "But stay out of the way - I don't want you getting hurt." I begrudgingly let them move past me and into what was quickly becoming Grand Central Station. I slammed the doors and locked them.

I wove my way through the new soldiers, appreciating their show of respect to not jostle me, but also to not shy away from me like I was diseased. They deserved a raise. Myth needed to get on that, especially since his number of employees was about to be cut drastically. I hiccupped and tasted smoke in my mouth. That was new.

I motioned for the new troop to stop about twenty feet from the enemy troop. I didn't want them hurt, but I wanted them to witness what was about to happen so they could spread it around the kingdom. It would serve as a warning to those considering crossing me and mine.

"Since blood has yet to be drawn between us," I began, "I will extend this offer to you and your men." My eyes locked onto those belonging to the leader of the rebel troop. His were filled with malice and murder. I swallowed another smoky hiccup. Hmm.

I continued with my offer: "Drop your weapons, kneel, and pledge your loyalty to King Mithraheal Conlier and your life will be spared. Draw your sword from its sheath and you will die. Zero exceptions."

Ugly spoke first, big shocker. "You and what army? We are one of the three elite troops in this kingdom, feared by the supernatural and human worlds alike. The men behind you are cannon fodder; they are new soldiers that haven't seen combat. We will slaughter them with our eyes closed."

"Actually, you are mistaken. They are here as witnesses and will not be fighting."

He laughed. It wasn't a snicker or a chuckle either. No, he full-out belly rolled. His entire body shook with each roar of amusement and the men around him joined in the raucous laughter. I hiccupped again, this time burning the roof of my mouth.

Wiping at his eyes, he choked out, "You plan to defeat us alone? All at the same time? Look at you!" He looked at the men over his shoulder, many of whom were still laughing. "Do you hear that, boys? The blonde in her panties and bra plans to kill you all!"

Their laughs bounced around the room, like the taunts of a playground bully. Glancing at the large clock face hanging above the two-story fireplace, I was irritated to discover this jerk had wasted thirty minutes of my time. If he wanted a show, so be it. He wouldn't remember it because he would be dead. But it would give the young troop behind me that much more to gossip about.

There would be no more hiding. I wanted the news of my

power and my plans to spread like wildfire. Enough was enough. I swore to myself that within two weeks, the prophecy would be fulfilled...one way, or the other.

Summoning the skills I had practiced over and over in my mind during the time in the dungeon, I shifted the atoms around my body. It was like sculpting, except you started with nothing and pulled the elements you needed to you and arranged those atoms into the creation you visualized in your mind. Easier thought than done, though. Gasps came from all around me, and I hoped against hope that I had followed my own pattern, and hadn't just crafted the 'emperor's new suit.' And by that, I meant I hoped I wasn't naked.

I opened my eyes, taking a quick peek and then lifted my head with every ounce of self-satisfied arrogance my drag-oness could muster.

"Did you... Did she? That isn't possible. Is it?" Commander Butt-For-A-Face stammered over his words like a two-year-old who was just learning to put sentences together.

"Why yes, yes I did." I gave him a huge toothy smile.

His eyes dropped to the floor and took in my steel-toed boots with the strategically placed spikes. Moving up, he took in my double padded leather and dragon scale pants; they would protect me from all but the most vicious knife stabs. They hugged every inch of my long legs and rounded butt, sexy and functional just as I imagined them. His piercing gaze slid higher to take in my tight, moisture-wicking shirt and the thin dragon-scale-covered vest protecting my torso.

I had my blades strapped across my back, and my twin knives now rested in sheaths against my outer thighs. Could I have beaten him in my workout shorts? Absolutely. But seeing his shock and growing trepidation at my transformation was rewarding as well.

When at last his eyes met mine again, I let my smile shift into a snarl, lifting my lip and snapping my teeth together. I wanted to make sure my prey got an eyeful off my dragon fangs, which were now significantly longer than the fangs on any vampire I had met thus far.

The dilating of his pupils and his clenching jaw told me he wanted to kill me, and also wanted to wet his pants. He shifted his eyes between me and his men, the pace so rapid it made me nauseous. I focused on the rest of his men until his gaze landed solidly on my face. I swallowed discreetly, not wanting him to misinterpret the action as fear, but also trying to settle my queasy stomach.

I hiccupped for a fourth time, and this time, it wasn't polite or ladylike. Nope, this was the type of sound I imagined a bullfrog would make if it was being squished by an elephant. My lungs spasmed and I was confident I pulled a muscle in my chest. Tears filled my eyes, and my throat burned just like the beautiful floor to ceiling velvet drapes on the windows nearest me—

Friggin'-flippin'-shoot! I hiccupped fire? This wasn't in Beasty's memories, and it wasn't part of today's plan!

Panicking, I pulled air from around the room into a whirling dervish and tried to blow the curtains out like birthday candles, but instead the flames accelerated like the curtains were made of gasoline.

That one moment of my surprised alarm was all the

opening the men around me needed. With a shout, the commander rushed at me, sword raised and prepared to decapitate me. His men drew their weapons and moved to circle me. The less experienced troop decided I needed assistance and with their own battle cry, they too rushed toward me.

Meanwhile, the flames had reached the ceiling and the floor and were licking at both like a starving dog. I needed to concentrate; I should be able to control this fire before it got any more out of hand. The clanging of armor and the shouts of the men as they neared me and each other was just too much to deal with.

"STOP!" I released my own battle cry...one that was promptly ignored.

Batting away a sword that swiped near my face, I summoned my magic. I wanted to use just enough to lift the men around me several feet from the floor and keep them held there in suspended animation. However, my magic added a little extra oomph, and instead of being a few feet from the floor, my magic plastered every last man, including my mates, on the high arched ceiling. They were all spread eagle and reminded me of swatted flies.

I needed to get a grip on my jumpy magic before I hurt someone. What if someone prepared me a good meal and my burp instantly turned them into ash?

Focus, Tia.

Okay, I needed to put the fire out first. I also needed to keep enough focus on my swirling magic to ensure it didn't see a squirrel and go chasing after it, thereby letting at least some of the men fall to their death. I called the fire to me, and I was relieved when it came to me like an obedient puppy. The warmth of the fire enveloped me, and I focused on drawing it back inside myself.

Once the fire was out, I turned my focus back on the men. I lowered them until their feet touched the floor, but I didn't release my hold on them. They all stood frozen, unable to move.

A wave of exhaustion rolled through me, and I sat down cross-legged on the floor and took in a long, deep breath. I had planned to move through the traitors and run each through with my sword. I hadn't even tried my full speed out yet, but I knew it was many times faster than a vampire. They would all be dead before they had time to react.

My stomach roiled at the thought of the world blurring around me. I gagged and struggled to keep down my breakfast. *In and out.* I began to center myself. I needed to get home and figure out what was wrong. This needed to end quickly before I barfed in front of my mates and embarrassed myself.

In and out. My breathing slowed, my heartbeat slowed.

Focus.

Sickening snaps were heard around the room as each rebel's neck was broken. Hard thuds as their bodies hit the floor were the next sounds, followed quickly by the noise of fire popping and crackling as it incinerated the bodies of the treacherous council and soldiers. As the fire died, silence filled the room once more. My magic still swirled around the room like tentacles, exploring and searching. It was on the hunt.

Go.

Instead of calling my magic back inside me, I unleashed it to seek out every person in the kingdom with a dark heart and a plan to betray the king. My Mithraheal. Those with evil in their hearts would find themselves dispatched in the same manner as the soldiers. I needed to know we would be safe here, and I needed to finish with the blood driven kingdom quickly. This wasn't the only kingdom needing a good house cleaning.

I reluctantly released my hold on the men around the room, allowing that magic to hunt as well. I wanted to savor this last minute of peace.

Without my magic swirling inside, everything was perfectly quiet. Except for one sound. Tears spilled from my eyes and slid down my cheeks.

It was the most beautiful sound I had ever heard in my life.

CHAPTER SIXTEEN

Tia

I was scooped off the floor and into Myth's arms and I let my head drop back against him. It almost seemed like I was the one suspended in time as I tried to absorb my discovery.

Myth's chest rumbled as he spoke to my circle, "I am taking her to my bedroom. Damien will guide everyone there."

His eyes took in the awed and confused faces of his soldiers. "Damien, I want you to station these men in pairs in our personal wing of the house," he continued. "Until we can sort out who is on our side, and who helped plan our murders, we cannot let our guards down."

"Stop worrying so much," I said softly. "My magic is taking care of all that as we speak."

Every eye in the room turned toward me.

"What exactly does that mean?" Levi asked the question with growing alarm in his voice.

"It means that this is the beginning of the prophecy. The blood driven decided to accelerate my timeframe a couple of days, but what is done, is done." I shrugged, and then continued, "The time has come for the world to be balanced, otherwise life as we know it will come to an end in a couple years. The supernatural world chose to hunt the dragons so they could upset the balance without consequences, now they will pay the price. My magic is hunting every last person in the kingdom who harbors that evil in their hearts and is executing them on the spot. It is painful, but over in the blink of an eye, then the bodies are consumed by fire until nothing remains of them."

"I didn't know you could be so efficient," Pixie chimed in. "Well done, Bunny." I should've known he would be impressed.

"Are you positive that no innocents will be harmed?" Levi asked me. His question hurt, but I couldn't fault my soft-hearted wolf for asking.

"The innocents are safe. Levi, I was made for this task, to fulfill some ancient scribblings. You guys are going to have to trust me to do my job, otherwise I could fail the entire world." I couldn't help glancing at Myth, aware that he had believed that Markus was innocent, and I had murdered him in cold blood.

I was shielding my thoughts, but I guess he could read them on my face.

"I'm sorry for doubting you, my love," Myth said gently. "I don't know why I trusted him over you, even for a minute. You are the kindest person I know, giving chance after chance, and I know you would never murder someone for the fun of it." He dropped his head until our foreheads were pressed together.

"I heard his thoughts, Myth," I replied. "He had found a way to block them from you, but my abilities work differently, and I could hear everything in his mind. Markus was supposed to lure you back. Since everyone knows he doesn't leave the palace unless forced, they knew you would follow him without question. Once you teleported in, Markus was going to attack you from behind with a dagger coated in poison. As I felt your suffering, I would have followed and met the same fate. They were going to pick us off one at a time."

Myth looked stricken as the depth of Markus's betrayal sank in. His face then shifted to one of horror. I didn't need to ask what caused that expression; I'd heard his thoughts as Markus' body hit the ground. Myth had believed that his innocent friend had died unjustly at the hands of a crazy chick. For that one millisecond, he had given Markus the benefit of the doubt before me, his own mate.

Myth's arms quivered around me.

"Myth! Don't beat yourself up," I soothed. "I haven't exactly had an easy time of it lately, and it is a shock that I'm not absolutely bonkers. I wish you had trusted my judgement right away, but I also understand that there is not a single thing about our lives that has been 'normal.' If I had lost my mind and started killing innocents, I would expect that my mates would ensure I was stopped."

"I'm so sorry, Mea Dragostea," Myth replied weakly. He opened and closed his mouth several times, unable to say anything more, seemingly unable to find the words he wanted. Shaking his head, he flashed through the halls toward his chambers.

Compared to my new speed, Myth's speed was like a relaxing stroll in the park. Several hallways and doors later, we reached his room and he placed me gently on the edge of the bed. The shift from speed, even one I considered slow, had my stomach doing a backflip. Swallowing hard, I tried to focus on settling my insides, but my tummy rebelled. I jumped off the bed and rushed for the bathroom. Seconds later, I was kneeling in front of the 'porcelain throne' and losing everything in my stomach.

The door squeaked softly as Myth joined me in the bathroom. Shame and embarrassment sent a heated flush across my already damp skin. I didn't want anyone to see me like this. It was gross and humiliating.

"My love, you are sick. There is nothing for you to feel embarrassed about," Myth said in response to my unspoken thoughts while gently pulling locks of hair away from my face. I was relieved I could stop fighting to keep both my insides and my hair out of the toilet. A cold, damp cloth dabbed at my face, helping to cool me down.

"Can you shift back? Or do you take these clothes off like store-bought garments?"

His fingers slid along the seams of the clothing trying to locate a zipper, but I knew there wasn't one.

"I haven't mastered that yet." My voice was a rough croak. I began struggling to my feet, but then I felt his arm loop around my waist to pull me up.

"Do you have a toothbrush I can use?" I asked weakly. Like a fairy godmother, Myth opened a drawer in the sink and pulled out a new toothbrush still in its wrapper. I brushed my teeth three times before I felt clean.

Myth stepped up to the cabinet and brought out a bottle of sparkling water. Of course, he would have sparkling water in his bathroom. I tried to roll my eyes, but the movement caused a tiny ripple of nausea, so I stopped that real quick.

He handed me a small, beautifully cut crystal glass filled with bubbly water. I drank the glass, and then another. I wondered if I would ever know why I never managed to get my fill of the liquid. If it weren't for the whole prophecy thing, I wouldn't want to leave the tub at the lake house. Or maybe I would float around on the lake all day, and at night I'd go skinny dipping with my mates. That brought a smile to my lips.

Feeling a bit better, I pushed away from the sink. "Myth, can you make sure the others are able to find your room?" I asked. "I want to take a shower, and then we have a lot to discuss."

His hands wrung together, and he rolled his bottom lip between his teeth; the man was reluctant to leave me. It was likely about to get a whole lot worse, which is exactly why I wanted to take this shower alone.

"I'll be fine. Go on - maybe you could even find me some crackers?" That did the trick. With something to do, he left the room and shut the door behind himself. I flipped the lock, knowing that one of my mates was likely to find an excuse to let himself into the bathroom to check on me if I didn't.

My clothes fell into a tattered heap on the ground. I had literally sculpted the clothes to my body, there were no buttons or zippers. If I planned to continue making my own garments, I might need to take a basic sewing class or two.

I turned the water on hot, enjoying the heat on my skin and the steam in the shower. Did all dragons love water?

No, little dragon. Remember? Each dragon has an affinity for a certain element. Mine is fire.

Ivo.

Curiosity won, and I let my mate off the hook for disturbing my alone time. I asked, *What is my affinity?*

You are a royal dragon. You could be drawn to one, and exceedingly skilled in that single element. Or you could be drawn to all four, and still have fairly good control. We've seen you control more than one, so I think it is safe to assume you are capable in all the elements.

Hmmm, was my only response before I closed the connection. I needed to be alone with my thoughts; there were things better said in person. Somehow, facing them made me more nervous than I had felt facing Draven on that battlefield.

I stood motionless under the spray, losing all track of time as I thought about the past, and my future. Apparently, I had stayed long enough to worry my mates, and I screamed as the door cracked and fell to the side, crushing the beautiful little cabinet.

"Ivo!" Every man in the room yelled in unison as the heavily-muscled dragon ripped the remaining pieces of door from their hinges and tossed them on top of the collapsed shelf. Steam and dust swirled in the room, and I began to cough.

"See?!" Myth cried. "I told you she was sick!" Myth's brow was furrowed as he watched Ivo wrap a massive red towel around my body and lift me from the tub like a toddler. *He would be an amazing dad someday*, I thought dreamily.

I managed to say, "Not sick" between strangling coughs, but it didn't seem like anyone was listening.

Ivo carried me toward the massive bed with an intriguing design. There were at least two mattresses inset into a wide platform. Three large steps rose from the ground to the top of the platform. Dark velvet pillows and blankets were tossed haphazardly on the stairs, making the wide steps a nice seating area. All my mates could fit in the bed at the same time. I blushed, thinking of what we could be doing on the monstrous mattress if we didn't have a serious discussion looming over our heads.

I was still blocking my thoughts, so Myth must have seen my blush. "I had it created after Leo joined the family. I wanted there to be room for whomever you wished." He looked away and added, "We can make it bigger if other mates join our circle."

I rested my head on Ivo's warm shoulder and breathed in his smoky musk. "No. No more mates, this is our family," I said softly. "Our circle is complete."

My life was perfectly crazy and crazily perfect.

I just hoped that wouldn't change after I said what I needed to tell them. My stomach tied itself into a knot as I steeled myself for what I was about to say. The talk I had planned to have before Markus's untimely arrival had morphed into something far more complicated. A tremor rippled through my body, followed by a second and a third.

"She's shaking!" Ivo panicked. The giant of a man, a fire breathing dragon, the one who faced down entire armies, freaked out. Not knowing what to do with me, he tossed me—yes, *tossed* me—to Leo. I had gone from pampered mate to hot potato in the blink of an eye.

My face paled as my stomach churned, and another tremor shook my body. Leo lost it. He ran to Levi, shoving me into the werewolf's arms. With the additional jostling, my face changed from pale to green, and I shoved my fist over my mouth. Luke caught on first, and with a ragged growl, he yanked me from Levi's hold and rushed me to the toilet where I promptly threw up nothing but the no-longer-sparkling water.

"I told you she was sick!" Myth shouted, his voice loud, echoing through the chamber.

"I'm not—" I tried to speak but I started dry heaving instead.

"We need to get her a doctor!"

"She needs to be in bed!"

"A vampire doctor isn't going to know what's wrong with her!"

"I don't need a—" But the men were too busy bumping

into each other while searching cabinets for who knows what to actually listen to me. Except for Pixie. He stood against the wall, one leg crossed over the other and his hands in the pockets of the jeans that one of the guys had loaned him. I didn't miss the amused glimmer in his eye.

"Where is that doctor?"

"Do you have a thermometer?"

"Guys, I'm not sick. I'm—" My voice was exhausted, and they couldn't hear me over the racket they were making.

"Why would I have one of those?"

"Could the five of you shut up and give our mate a chance to speak?" Pix demanded, trying in vain to get my mates' attention for me. The men continued to argue over how to deal with my illness, and worked to create an hourly schedule of who was going to sit by the bedside until I was well.

"Idiots! She's pregnant, not sick!" Pixie's words slammed into every man in the room like a physical blow.

Six faces turned to where I slumped against the toilet.

Leo, Ivo, Luke, Myth, and Levi all wore the same expression. Shock.

But it was Pixie's expression that sent shock coursing through me. His normally emotionless face now showed regret and frustration.

CHAPTER SEVENTEEN

Luke

What the heck was the robot mate talking about? If Tia was pregnant, we would know. We would be able to hear—

Thump. Thump. Thump.

The baby's heartbeat. Breath catching in my throat, I listened to make sure it was fast and steady. My heart swelled with love for my unborn child. I didn't care who the biological dad was. All our children would grow up with five goofy, loving dads and one very intelligent, but emotionless, Fae. He could tutor them or something.

Pix stepped to the side as Tia moved from the bathroom and seated herself on the ledge of the bed. Her long blonde hair was smoothed back. She must have brushed it after Pix shoved us out of the bathroom. He had given Tia time to brush her teeth and gather her thoughts before we over-whelmed her with our questions. There were so many.

How had we missed the heartbeat? Supernaturals didn't need a pregnancy test to know when they were pregnant, we just listened. How far along was she? I opened my mouth to ask but closed it when I remembered my scarred vocal cords. I tried to cover it by wiping my mouth on my sleeve, but Tia's eyes had already locked on me, and her brows furrowed. My gut sank. I knew my girl needlessly blamed herself for my condition. I hated that she had the weight of the world on her shoulders.

Ignoring the others, she motioned for me to sit beside her.

I moved instantly to obey, not caring if my brother teased me with obedient dog jokes later.

"Kiss me," she murmured. Her throaty voice was the sexiest thing I had ever heard. I didn't have to be asked twice. Our lips met, her soft puffy lips an arousing contrast to my own. My hands sank into her damp hair, and in response, her hands wrapped around my throat and squeezed. That wasn't normally my thing, but when her tongue slid across my lower lip, I decided that this new experience might be worth it.

Burning hot desire clouded my mind, while liquid heat poured into my groin and throat. Wait. Throat?

The warming sensation turned painful, and fire felt like it was burning through my skin. I tried to pull away from her lips, but she held onto me.

Trust me, Luke. Relax.

Relax? Was I supposed to ignore the fact that my throat had tightened to the point I could no longer breathe?

Please.

That single word was my undoing. I stopped struggling. If my mate wanted to burn me alive, I was just crazy enough to go along with her... As long as I could share some of the pressure she put on herself, and she was smiling.

I'm going to barf. Leo spoke through the bond, but made gagging sounds out loud.

The pain increased to a white-hot intensity, and right when I was sure I was about to incinerate, it disappeared. There was no residual burning or aching skin. I was pain free.

Relieved that I didn't implode, I laughed. To the amazement of everyone in the room, the sound that came out wasn't the raw rumble that had become my voice since the battle with Draven. No, this laugh was normal. It was *my* laugh.

My chest squeezed tight for a whole new reason. Hardly able to breathe, I asked, "Did you heal me? Is my voice back?"

Tia's eyes shimmered with unshed tears, and she pressed a chaste kiss to my lips. "Yes. I learned a lot of things from Beasty's memories when I was sitting alone in the dungeon. Things about myself, things regarding abilities I didn't know I possessed. I'm sorry it took me a while to figure out how. I wanted us to have this discussion with everyone, when everybody was able to have their voice heard."

"Thank you," I croaked. My words were rough, not from damage, but from emotion trying to claw its way out.

She nodded, and with a small smile on her lips, she turned to face the room. She tucked her feet beneath her and interlaced her fingers, before motioning with her free hand that the questions were free to start.

Unable to hold my voice back, I spoke first, "I can hear the baby's heartbeat now - why couldn't we hear it before?"

"It's really good to hear your voice," she replied. She grinned, breathed out a quick breath and centered herself. "My magic has been in a state of constant flux since I broke through the spell in the jungle. It is stretching and growing with each passing hour. I believe it was shielding the baby from everything, in a protective cocoon of sorts. It was so strong and impenetrable that even I couldn't tell."

"Do you know when you got pregnant?" Leo asked. His question was spoken with unabashed eagerness. In fairness, we all wanted to know which magical night might have been *the* night.

Tia's breathing turned erratic, and her posture fell.

I grabbed her shaking hand. "It doesn't matter which one of us is the biological dad," I reassured her. "Though, house-breaking pups would be easy. Dealing with a little vampire whose hiccups might teleport him to another continent, not so much."

That was the wrong thing to say. Tears spilled down her cheeks in harsh, body-wrenching sobs. She dropped her head into her hands.

It was blatantly obvious that we were missing something, and it was something big. I moved forward to pull her into my lap, but I was too slow. Pixel sat down on the side of the bed. He gathered Tia into his arms, pressing her against his chest. Every mouth in the room dropped open as the 'man of ice' began to rock her and hum an unfamiliar song that was equal parts melancholy and reassuring.

Tia's sobs eventually quieted to hiccups, thankfully without any smoke or fire this time. Resting her head against Pixel's chest, she began to speak, starting her story at the Harmony Ball and what had transpired after we were all separated. She told of Cage's perfectly crafted apologies, and his subsequent betrayal that ripped out her heart.

My fingers itched with the need to grow into claws. Despite our best efforts, bloodlust overwhelmed our connection.

After hearing Cage's taunts to her about the possibility she was carrying his child, we had wondered among ourselves if something had transpired between them. We hadn't questioned her about it, since it didn't take a rocket scientist to realize things had gone downhill enough that she was prepared to end his life. Either that or he was just *that bad.* We also knew that she had longed for reconciliation, and he was a fated mate.

"He deserves to die again for what he has done!" Mithraheal cried, his voice breaking. Bloody tears ran down his face.

"I should have ripped each limb from him," hissed Ivo, "and then chewed slower to crush every last bone in his body." A mask of dark fury seemed to shroud his face as he spoke. Red lines of dragon fire glowed beneath his skin.

Leo leapt to his feet, eyes swirling purple, while magic of the same color crackled and popped around him. My stomach dropped and my breath caught as I watched the violet light show move angrily around him like a prowling creature without a target. It was exactly how all of us felt.

Leo screamed in outrage. The pain he felt for our mate's

suffering drew out our own cries of grief. The roar of the dragon, the hissing wail of the vampire, the eerie howls of Levi and me, and the otherworldly hum of the Fae filled the bedroom. Each relayed the depth of the sorrow we felt for the sobbing dragoness that held our hearts.

Leo's magic turned to streaks of electric purple lightning that ripped at his clothing, shredding the material but not injuring his skin. The magic storm slowly bent into a cylindrical shape around him. His hair whipped in the turbulent wind and his eyes turned a solid violet hue.

Leo's face shifted from a boyish nerd to what I imagined a male stripper dressed up like a wizard would look like. The angles in his face and his jawline had sharpened, dark stubble creating a five o'clock shadow that girls around the world would have swooned over. His hair framed his face in perfect waves. Whatever this new magic was, I wouldn't mind being hit with it. I was straight as a board, but even I recognized that the warlock had gone from geek to gorgeous.

The only problem was that his magic hadn't died down after the transformation. Oh, no. It was worse. The curtains ripped from the wall, rugs were tossed about, and the lights in the room flickered. Black smoke poured into the room from Leo-only-knew-where, blocking the light from the windows and casting the room into an ominous semi-darkness.

Most couples cried and laughed and planned baby names when they found out they were expecting. We screamed, sobbed, and filled our bedroom with doom and gloom. Normal, right?

I glanced over to check on Tia and was relieved to find she

was on the ground, Pixel covering her body with his own. If we didn't die in the next few minutes, several people in the room had a lot of explaining to do. No more secrets.

When Leo spoke, my neck cracked painfully as I jerked my face up to see him. Those glowing purple eyes looked at Tia with such sorrow, the sweet geek showing through the enraged warlock's features.

"He deserves to die again for what he did to you!" he screamed.

The plaintive note in his words sent gooseflesh running along my skin and my heart, leaping into my throat. Or maybe I was having that reaction due to the fact that someone stood beside Leo. Cage was slightly less solid, and a lot more dead than the last time I saw him.

Leo's eyes widened at the man standing in front of him, well, kind of standing and sort of floating. The mighty warlock that had terrorized the room for the last five minutes froze like a freaking deer in headlights. The smoke and light show worthy of any rock concert vanished, leaving two very confused men facing each other.

"*Psst!* Leo!" Levi hissed. "Now would be a great time to carry out your revenge and all that." Levi spoke from where he lay on the floor, covered in several rugs that had been tossed around by the mini tornado.

Levi's words jolted Leo from his shock. Purple eyes glowing, he stepped forward until he was nose-to-nose with the semi-translucent version of Cage. The grin on Leo's face bordered on insane. I didn't know what he had planned, but I doubted Cage was going to like it. I was pretty sure I was going to love it, though. A broad grin split my face and my stomach dipped in anticipation.

Cage looked around the room before his gaze settled on Tia. He smirked. The butt munch actually had the nerve to smirk. "Missed me so much you had to bring me back from the afterlife?" he asked.

The soft sound of shuffling to my left had me glancing that way. Tia rose to her feet, lifting her adorable, pointed chin into the air. She was every inch the regal queen even with her wind-tossed golden hair. She wore her beautiful gown of opalescent scales, a reminder of her rank not just as a drag-oness, but as the Royal Dragoness.

Everyone held their breath, except maybe Cage, as Tia strode toward him. There was an expression I couldn't quite read on her beautiful face. Stopping a few feet from him, she smiled sweetly, a smile that showed off the size of her dragon fangs. Cage's eyes grew white, from horror, shock, or from the knowledge that he was dead and about to die again, I couldn't say.

Then his head tilted while he listened to something, and his smirk grew. He'd heard the tiny heartbeat of Tia's unborn baby. His gaze landed on her stomach.

"So, that's why you brought me back," he said with a smirk. "You couldn't tell my child you killed his father?" He looked at Tia from under his brows. "We can still fix things, as long as you learn your place."

"Bringing him back was a good idea. Although, bringing him back with the ability to speak, not so much," Ivo grumbled.

Anger lit up Cage's features, and he swiveled to look at Ivo. "Do you have any idea what it feels like to be digested, dragon?"

Ivo's only response was a derisive snort.

Just then, it appeared that our little dragoness decided it was time to be done with this Cage crap. With a loud snap, she released her wings from her back. Cage took a step back, and this time I easily recognized his expression. It stank of fear, and I was loving it.

"Yasss, Queen!" Ivo shouted, voicing what everyone in the room, besides Cage, was thinking. I had to wonder what shows Leo and Damien had been using to teach Ivo modern English. The corner of Tia's lip twitched in a genuine smile.

"Go ahead, Leo. It's your turn," she said, nodding to Leo as she spoke.

"Don't eat me!" Cage cried, backing up, his show of bravado long gone.

"I could end your afterlife right now," Leo teased. "You wouldn't have to deal with the questionable hospitality of your current residency, nor could you be brought back like this again. You would just be nothing. Gone in the blink of an eye. *Poof.*" Leo snapped his fingers and Cage jumped like he had seen a ghost... Or himself. He really was better looking when he was fully alive.

I didn't miss the sliver of hope that passed across his face. The afterlife must not be very kind to Cage if he preferred the idea of a permanent death to continuing to exist in the realm of the dead.

Leo's smile promised things I knew I was going to appreciate. "I said to myself, '*Self? What could possibly make a life, that is literally living in hell, even worse?*' And do you know what I answered myself?"

Cage shook his head slowly, wary eyes glued to Leo's face. I gave him credit for being smart enough to stay silent for an entire five seconds.

"I remembered this nifty little fact my dad told me about the afterlife during one of our phone calls. You see, no one can really die there. If you do, you wake up the next morning to start the cycle all over again. I could drag you here every day for the rest of eternity, kill you, and then do it again tomorrow. How cool is that?"

I would have expected that level of demented genius from Myth or Ivo, but from innocent Leo it was impressively terrifying.

"But I have a life here to enjoy with my mate and our future child, and don't want to give you the pleasure of my company quite that often," Leo continued. "Don't look upset! I have a solution. I'm going to put a spell on you. If I spelled you while you were alive and in your human form, then the curse would have been rendered void at your death once you took your ghostly form. However, if I spell you in this form, you will stay cursed in this form. Death won't free you."

I wondered if warlocks tended to cackle like witches, because Leo was doing a banging impression of a witch's laugh. Purple magic danced hypnotically around Cage's shimmering form. I don't know what I expected Leo to say next, but it wasn't the words that came pouring from his smirking lips.

"Cage, you will spend your afterlife in the form that most pleases me," he said. "On Earth you were a shifter, comfortable in a body not your own. In the realm of the afterlife, you will be granted the same ability, although never allowed to shift back to the form you now hold."

Cage looked as confused as the rest of us felt. I was trying to figure out where Leo was going with this and how exactly it was a punishment.

"When you return to Hell, you will shift into the form of a worm. The lowest life form on earth, with the brain of what should be the highest life form. How genius is that? You will eat the dirt and crap left behind, and you will be fully aware of what you are doing. Each day will be spent trying to avoid predators, and when they eat you, which they will, you will find yourself back in the worm's body the next day."

Leo crossed his arms across his chest, his expression darkening to the color of Cage's soul. "I feel no pity for you," he hissed, "and I have no mercy for someone that could allow greed to destroy their soul and destroy the lives of those around them. Remember this, Cage. If I get bored, if I ever see Tia weep over your betrayals, I will call you back here. I will force you to shift into whatever despised creature tickles my fancy. You best hope I forget your name when you leave here today."

"Please, don't," Cage pleaded. He dropped to his knees as best he could, prepared to beg for mercy. Or so we thought. Suddenly, Cage pushed off the ground and shifted into his wolf in a flash. He lunged for Tia with his canines extended. Idiot. Knowing that Tia was going to appreciate the opportunity to wipe the floor with his hide, I leaned back to enjoy the show.

With a flick of her wrist, her magic caught the opaque wolf mid jump and held him suspended in front of her. In a voice laced with power and authority, Tia said, "You will *never* lay so much a finger or a fang on me again."

Her magic moved around his body until he was dangling by his scruff like a helpless wolf pup. Tia smirked, leaned closer to him and whispered, "I want you to remember this feeling of being powerless and completely at my mercy."

Cage growled, his jaws snapping at Tia. She laughed in his face, a beautiful, full, throaty laugh. Then she looked him in the eye and spoke two words.

"Eat dirt."

The room filled with laughter as she waved at Leo to get on with it. Even Pixel gave a chuckle, although his face was scrunched up in a way that made me think he was constipated instead of amused. Leo directed the flickering purple magic around him. With a poof of purple smoke, Cage disappeared. When the smoke cleared, all that remained was one thick, wiggling worm.

"I think I overdid it a bit." Leo scratched at the back of his neck. "Cage is going to be stuck in the solid form for a few hours before he fades back to the ethereal one. My bad."

"Dibs!" I shot to my feet while simultaneously trying to decide which shoe to squish worm Cage with.

"We could take him fishing!" Levi suggested, kicking Cage back in place with his shoe when he tried to inch away.

"We should vote who gets to kill him."

"You already got to eat him once!"

The room erupted into chaos as all of us argued about who deserved to kill Cage more. Tia stood with a hand over her mouth, shoulders shaking in silent laughter.

Then, a high-pitched scream pierced the air from the door, and it began to rain scrambled eggs.

"Damien, what is wrong with you?" Myth snapped as he flicked an egg off the shoulder of his suit.

Damien didn't even acknowledge his brother. Instead, he flashed through the room like a ninja and landed on the worm, I mean Cage. A gross squelching sound followed.

"Ew! Ew! Ew!" Damien's feet landed over and over on the squished worm. He shivered and peered around the floor with his now empty frying pan raised next to his head as if he thought worms were going to begin attacking him at any moment. "Are there more?"

We all stared at him in horror.

"Damien, what is going on? You better not have dropped my food!" Trixie marched into the room.

"Stay there!" he shouted back. "You aren't safe in here!"

"The only one that isn't safe is you." Trixie snatched the fry pan out of his hand. "I told you to ask the others if they wanted food. Not to throw it at them!"

"There was"—he lowered his voice to a whisper—"a worm."

Trixie motioned at the mess scattered on us and the floor. "All this for a worm? What happens if you find a centipede? Or, gasp, a spider?" She clutched her chest in mock horror.

Damien shrugged. "We burn the house down and start over."

"That wasn't just a worm!" I yelled. "That was Cage. Leo brought him back so we could kill him again and you just...just...*squished* him!" I hated that I sounded like a petulant toddler who had just had his favorite toy taken away.

"I left you guys alone for less than two hours and clearly a lot of things happened." Damien sighed and rubbed his forehead as if he had a migraine.

A tiny flicker of movement on the floor had Trixie snatching the pan out of Damien's hand. She slammed the pan over the squished worm until we were all backing away from her. "Why. Won't. You. Die?"

"Is she okay?" Ivo whispered to Damien between the percussive bangs of the pan.

"She's perfect." Damien grinned as the handle of the pan went one direction and the base another.

"Okay, that should do it." Trixie rubbed her hands together, perspiration rolling down her forehead.

Once Leo used some magic to whisk the remains of the worm away, thus 'killing' the douche for the third time this week—or three and a half, if you counted Trixie's beat down—the room felt lighter. Maybe the third time really was the charm.

Tia threw her arms around Leo's neck and kissed him soundly on the cheek. She didn't notice or didn't seem to care that his face wasn't the same as she remembered. I had a lot of questions for Leo and Pixel at this point.

We all turned to Tia as she sat down, folded her hands in

her lap and spoke with the poise of a queen, "The baby in my womb could be Cage's child. You each promised your devotion to me and the children born of our circle, but you did not promise to raise another man's child as your own. I will not hold it against any of you if you choose to leave." She looked at us with an expression of sincerity and strength. "If you cannot love this baby as if it were your own," she continued, "then I ask you to leave immediately. I will not raise a child in a home where any child is treated differently than his or her sibling."

Around the room everyone stared in stupefied horror. Did she really believe we would walk away? Or love the baby any less?

"That is my baby," Levi replied, "and you will not keep me from Levi Jr." He crossed his arms and scowled playfully at our mate.

"My love, the child belongs to you, and that means it belongs to us," Myth purred, moving to kneel in front of her.

"The child is dragon kin, that alone is enough to have my protection," said Ivo. "Knowing that a child is growing in my mate's womb makes me the happiest dragon on earth. The sire is of no interest to me; I shall be proud to bear the title of 'father' to your offspring."

I was impressed, the ancient dragon had a way with words.

"I grew up without a father, I would never allow your child to go through the same;" added Leo. He dropped down on the stair below Tia and rested his head in her lap. Idly, her hands stroked through his hair.

I slid onto the bed, wrapping my arms around our mate

and pulling her back against my chest. "Tia, I swore to protect you from the moment I laid eyes on you. We are going to be a family now, and I couldn't be a happier man. We are going to be parents!"

We all hugged and gave fist bumps, and then turned to the only member of our circle who hadn't spoken up. His emotionless mask was back in place.

"Well?" I prompted him.

"I do not understand the logic of repeating my oath to Tia again," Pixel said stoically. "I swore to protect her and be loyal to her. A family is still a strange concept to me, but any children she brings into this world will have my protection and care as well. But this whole exercise is illogical. Cage is not the father. Tia was already pregnant before he brought her into the dungeon."

His words caused tense silence to fall across the room before Tia cried out, "Why didn't you tell me, Pixie! I've been sick and stressed for no reason!"

"Because among the Fae, a male never speaks of a female's pregnancy until she announces it officially," the Fae replied calmly. "I should not have shouted out your womb status earlier, but I became...frustrated?" His brows drew together as he stumbled over the word like it was the first time he'd said it. Or maybe the first time he had ever felt it. "I apologize for my error in revealing the news before you had the chance to, and that I did not understand the peace that knowing Cage was not the father would have provided."

Pixel's voice softened further as he opened his arms to

Tia. "This realm is still odd to me, and family dynamics confuse me, but I am trying, Bunny."

Tia threw her arms around his neck and reassured him that he was forgiven. Meanwhile, the rest of us exchanged looks. Pixel had told us only the simplest of explanations for what a Fae was and why he was in that dungeon. He was trying to learn how to fit in with our family; it was time for us to do the same. And it was well past time to find out more about our Fae mate.

CHAPTER EIGHTEEN

Tia

My heart was overflowing with relief knowing that these men would love my baby no matter what. I couldn't deny that a weight had been lifted from me with the revelation that Cage couldn't be the father. No matter what, I would love my child. But the idea of a baby knowing that monstrosity was their father was something I was glad I was going to be able to avoid.

The emotional turmoil of this morning and afternoon had drained me, though. My body still pulsed with power, but my brain needed to rest, yet I also needed to finish discussing my future plans with my mates. Finding out I was pregnant had derailed our talks; killing Cage again had been a fun distraction, but I needed to get things back on track. I could do that from under the covers though, right?

I plucked a few chunks of scrambled egg from the comforter and popped them into my mouth. After emptying my stomach, a tiny bit of food helped settle the nausea. I scooted beneath the covers and shifted my scaled dress from my body. While I had crafted my armor from the atoms around me when I faced the vampire troops, this dress was special. It was a unique blending of my human and dragon DNA, with a touch of goddess magic thrown in for good measure. I could shift in and out of the elegant garment with the ease of shifting into my dragon.

I tucked my wings against my body, not yet ready to put them away. It felt nice to feel the soft blankets brush along the length of them, and I tried to remember why I rarely used this 'halfway' form, especially when it felt the most comfortable of my three forms. I always felt confined in my human form, while the monstrous dragon form felt heavy unless I was soaring in the air. This form, halfway between the two, felt just right. I huffed a laugh as I realized it sounded like nursery rhyme.

Pixel must have been reading my mind because he responded to my thoughts as he moved to lay with me on the bed. "Then you should stay in this form. Your circle finds you pleasing to the eye whether you are in human form, fully shifted, or partially shifted. Although your dragon form is far less kissable."

Had he just made a joke? Leaning forward, Pixie placed a sweet kiss on my surprised lips. I automatically lifted the comforter and invited him to join me beneath it. He hesitated only for a moment before shucking his jeans and shirt, leaving only his boxers to cover his well sculpted body. Then he slid in beside me. He may still be uncomfortable about belonging in a family, but he certainly didn't have any qualms about nudity, his or ours.

"Sex is natural among the Fae, and certainly nothing to be shy about," he explained, repeating what he had told me once before. It struck me just as odd this time.

As his skin brushed the length of my body, I trembled. My mind took a quick detour from planning a war to planning the ways my mates could plunder me.

"Behave, Bunny," Pixie scolded me, but his eyes twinkled. "First we need to talk, then we will see if you still have the energy to make love."

With a sigh, I pressed myself against his marble-like chest, wiggling a little to get comfy. Leo sat on the ledge next to my head and ran his long fingers through my hair, carefully combing it out.

Luke and Levi remained in their human forms, but curled on the mattress at the foot of the bed. Old habits were hard to break, it seemed. Myth scooted in behind me, maneuvering around my wings without so much as a complaint.

Ivo sat on the ledge at the bottom of the bed, positioning himself between the door and our circle. A perfect position to guard us. I blew him a kiss, which he caught and pressed to his lips. My dragon mate was such a romantic.

Pix's arm curved around my waist and pulled me even tighter against him. I focused my attention back on him. A pang of sadness traveled through me when I remembered our one time together had been when I was dirty, bloody and nearly dying. Followed by me nearly killing him. It wasn't exactly a dream honeymoon.

My fingers traced along the pale, white scars that circled from his collarbone to his back. They were the exact shape of my scales. I had burned him with my out-of-control dragon fire, and he had let me. Now he would forever bear these marks. He should hate me for all the trouble I'd caused him. Yet, here he was, holding me, protecting me.

"I am honored to wear these scales, do not feel sadness over something I would not change," Pix reassured me. "Fae appreciate the art of a beautiful tattoo." His finger brushed Leo's mark on my neck, causing a shiver to run down my spine. "Like this one. It is intricate and perfectly done. A masterpiece, like the woman that holds it."

I gave him a smile before reaching up to trace along the length of his long-pointed ear. "Do all Fae have pointed ears?"

"I cannot understand how you are able to see my ears. I am wearing a glamour, like a masking spell, to hide my ears in this realm."

"Because I am your mate, that's why," I replied, resisting the urge to add 'duh' or 'I'm a goddess' I thought that might be overkill.

"You were able to see my ears before we mated, and Fae do not have soulmates like the vampires and werewolves of this realm. At least not that I have been told," Pix said. The usually confident man sounded unsure. Shaking his head, he continued, "To answer your original question, yes. All Fae have pointed ears. The length of the ear varies. The longer the ear, the more powerful bloodline a Fae possesses. A short point denotes a Fae from the working class."

I ran my finger lazily around the edge of his ear, memorizing the shape and curves. "And you? Are your ears considered long or short among your peers?"

"That's what she said," Luke whispered.

Pixie didn't get the innuendo, but everyone else chuckled and Levi smacked his brother with a pillow. Catching my hand, Pix brought it to his mouth and kissed it. "Long enough, Bunny. We have plenty of time to discuss your questions about the Fae, but don't you think you should inform your mates about what you have planned for us this week?"

"Mind reader," I mumbled. But he was right. I had put it off as long as possible. It was time to get this over with and hope they didn't decide to lock me in a dungeon of their own to protect me.

I took a deep breath and then began speaking, "Tomorrow we are going to pay a visit to the wizards. I need to reassure myself that they kept to their agreement regarding the Nadir. Someone was working with Elise to try and find a way to steal my power. I want to know where all those vials of my blood went. I thought it was someone in the vampire kingdom, but my magic found no one that was involved in my captivity."

I exhaled. I had said everything in one breath, hoping they wouldn't realize that I planned to clean house there, just as I had with the blood driven kingdom. No dice. My men were q-u-i-c-k!

"Absolutely not," Myth interjected. "You are pregnant with our child, and that is not a risk we can take." His voice and expression were firm, and Ivo nodded his agreement. They both clearly felt the decision had been made.

Leo's mind was traveling a different path. "How are you going to know who is involved? I know your magic can sense intentions, but will that be enough among the wizards? And how were you able to read Markus's mind?"

"I spent every waking minute in that dank cell studying Beasty's memories, the ones I got when I merged with her," I explained. "Those memories showed the amazing abilities she developed through the centuries, and I paid attention to every little detail. There are still many things I haven't mastered yet, but some things came much easier." I wasn't going to mention the part where I traveled to visit Beasty; that might be a bit much for my guys to handle.

"Like minding? Are there other abilities that you have had success with?" Leo asked, sounding excited at the prospect of my new skills. I would bet money he was wishing for a note-book right now.

"Let's see." I tapped my chin. "Reading minds, blocking my own thoughts, shifting into my scale-covered gown, creating other garments, resistance to drugs, additional speed, teleporting others without needing to accompany them, and better control of the elements. I'm probably forgetting some, and I'm still working on others, but I am sure I will master them given time."

Myth pressed a loud popping kiss to the sensitive skin between my shoulder blades. "You are amazing, beautiful!"

Cold chills raced along my skin at the sensation of his hot breath on my neck.

Don't get side-tracked. Don't get side-tracked.

Too late. I was already sidetracked. I purred in contentment.

"Bad, Bunny," Pix scolded, but without any heat in his tone. How could he have heat in it, when every bit of heat in his body was pressed against my lower belly?

I blinked furiously, trying to remember what I needed to tell my mates before my brain caved to the growing lust.

"Fine! Tomorrow, the wizards, and the following day we deal with the wolves. Then we have a quick road trip this weekend."

How strange to think that this journey could be so close to the end. By next week, I could be planning my nursery, a prophecy no longer hanging over my head. Just a few more days.

Looks passed between the men, and finally they nodded agreement. We were in this together.

"We are going to leave and give you some privacy, my love," Leo whispered as he leaned over and kissed me.

Luke and Levi rose, a knowing smile flickering around their lips. They slipped soundlessly out the door, followed by Ivo and Leo.

I was alone with Pix and Myth. One man was pressed against my chest, the evidence of his desire hot against my belly, while the second man slid his hands down the length of my naked back, leaving a trail of sensitive skin everywhere his fingers touched. That was all it took to have my body dripping with need for them.

Pixie's hand moved to cup my surprisingly tender breast.

His thumb teased my nipple until it was taut and begging for his attention. Meanwhile, Myth's wandering hands had begun to explore my wings, his fingers probing and tickling my sensitive flesh. Unless a person has wings, they could never understand the sensations of having them touched. It was erotic with your mate, but felt like a violation of privacy from anyone else.

I moaned, unable to stop myself.

"There is no need to silence yourself," Pix murmured. "Enjoy this time to the fullest - do not be ashamed to express yourself."

Dumbfounded, I turned to look at him. Of all the people to tell me to express myself, I wouldn't have thought it would be him.

"I am finding that I rather like watching you express emotions. It is a beautiful thing and something I believe would be a loss if you stopped."

"And I feel the same about you, my Fae mate."

His eyes were considering as he pondered my words. "That is logical, I will give it some more thought."

My fingers ran along the velvet skin of his erection, smiling when it jerked eagerly in response. Wrapping my fingers around his thick member, I explored the length of him. I was surprised to find there wasn't so much as a single sign of the ridges I had felt inside me during our last hormone-crazed coupling.

"They are only present during penetration, when we are both nearing release," he whispered. He had read my mind and answered me. His tongue licked along the edge of my own ear, now pointed like his, just not nearly as long. The sensation of his warm tongue swirling around such an erogenous zone had my body vibrating with building need. He was a master with his fingers and tongue.

I slid my hand the length of him again, enjoying the feel of hard muscle and soft skin, the textures such extreme opposites. He groaned and jerked his hips. Our lips met in a kiss that was full of promises of things to come.

It was as if we were making love in slow motion, each touch offering the maximum amount of pleasure to the other. The movements were a type of pleasurable torture, both of us fighting the urge to give in to want and bang each other's brains out at the speed of light. It was painful in the best possible way.

His hand continued to knead my aching breasts while the other curled in my wild mane of hair. Myth caught on quickly and adjusted his own caresses to the same tempo as Pixie.

I moaned as Myth's hand brushed along my hip bone, then across my stomach, only stopping when his palm rested flat against my slick entrance. Taking his time, he traced a finger along my slit, before slowly slipping one finger inside me. He stroked my most sensitive pearl at a rate intended to make me pant, but not let me come.

Pixie took that moment to lean down and suck my pebbled nipple back into his mouth, then tease it between his teeth. My body trembled and I bit down on my tongue to hold back a cry. I could feel my brain as it melted into a pile of goo, and I no longer wanted to go slow. I wanted Pixie inside of me. Now. Yesterday. Forever. What day was it?

"Hold her, vampire." I barely registered Pixie's words before Myth's left hand slipped from my hot entrance and clamped down on my hip, his right snaking beneath me to hold onto my other hip. His fingers dug into my skin, but it wasn't painful. I tried to wiggle, seeking the friction I desperately wanted, but Myth's grip was unmoving.

"Are you okay with this? I need to know you consent," he asked,

I trusted these two men with my entire being. I wasn't keen on being denied my desire to urge things along, but another part of me was turned on even more by the show of control by my mates.

"Yes. I want this." I would like to say my voice was that of a silky siren, but in reality, it came out sounding like the croak of a hundred-year-old woman.

"Good girl," Myth whispered behind my ear.

I pressed myself back against him, wanting to savor every moment of this time with them. I tried to slip a hand between us and touch him, but I was stopped by Pixie's hand clamping around my wrist. Catching up my other wrist, he stretched them above my head until they rested on the pillow.

"Pull her hips back against you tighter so she cannot wiggle," he demanded.

Myth was quick to follow Pix's order and I found my butt wedged deliciously tightly against my vampire's throbbing erection.

"Now, tilt her hips forward just a bit." Pix's voice was basically a growl at this stage.

Myth again followed the directive without comment.

Keeping me pressed firmly against him, he used his hands to angle my hips a few inches, giving my Fae lover better access.

I barely resisted the urge to plead with him to hurry, and the only thing stopping me was the knowledge it would more than likely cause him to slow down instead of speeding up.

My stomach dropped from my body as Pixie scooted down the length of me to press his lips against my lower lips. My lungs must have given up the ghost and died on the spot, because I found myself unable to suck in any air. But I was distracted from my lack of oxygen by Pix's warm, slick tongue delving inside me. Have I mentioned his mind-altering skills with his tongue? He curved it just right and lapped like a cat licking up its favorite treat.

I could feel my release coming, but so was the darkness. I needed air. My vision flicked in time with the flicks of his tongue against my most sensitive spot. The world around me warped, stars glittering and then stretching in my vision.

Oh crap.

I thought when people talked about an orgasm sending them into outer space, or sex being 'out of this world,' they were just using figures of speech. But I was fairly confident I was about to experience it quite literally. I screamed my release as I was vacuum sucked by the universe into the grey between the realms.

I slammed hard into Beasty, who screamed in shock. "What are you doing back here?!" she cried.

"I don't know! It was an accident!" I cried back.

She snorted. "What? Did you 'accidentally' trip and fall into the grey?"

"Of course not! I was coming—"

"You were coming? That means you *planned* to make the trip..." She looked at me like I was stupid.

"No! Would you be quiet for half a second? Pixie, my fae mate with the magical peen, was doing things with his tongue that are probably illegal, and I forgot how to breathe, and I think I passed out right as I came."

Her expression was blank and then she squealed in delight. "You are being held down by two sexy mates who are having their way with you? Get back there now, girl!"

From what I pieced together later, three things happened at once. Pixie, in an effort to shock me into breathing again, bit down hard on my inner thigh. At the same time, Beasty gave me a magical shove that sent me toppling back into the vacuum. Oh, and Myth died.

Shocked from the sudden painful bite, and the over-the-top shove, I grabbed at anything I could to steady myself. The only thing near enough was Beasty, so I ended up yanking her into the darkness with me.

My spirit was sucked back into my body with an abruptness that had my teeth rattling in my skull. Dazed, I sucked in a beautiful lungful of air. Myth did the same behind me.

I breathed in several more deep breaths, trying to stop the room from spinning.

Scooting up the length of my body, Pix stared into my eyes. "You traveled again?" he asked.

"Just a quick trip this time," I wheezed. He must have gleaned from my thoughts what had happened in the dungeon.

"Are you hurt?" His knuckles brushed across my cheek.

"No, just lightheaded." I shakily took in another breath, this one only slightly less wheezy than the others.

Behind me, Myth groaned. "What happened? I feel like death warmed over," he croaked.

"You died," Pixie said dismissively, and then immediately focused his attention back on me again.

"I feel the love, man," Myth grumbled.

Pix only snorted in response.

I shifted in the bed, trying to make myself more comfortable. My body bumped up against Pixie's only slightly softer manhood. I rubbed purposely against him. His sharp intake of breath told me he was definitely still interested in a little boom-chicka-wow-wow.

Myth began coughing violently. "Please don't ever say, or even think, that again."

Pixie was finding himself too turned on to care what I called the 'parallel parking' we were about to do.

Myth whined something along the lines of wishing he could die, again. But I was already lost in Pix's kiss. I felt the head of his erection bump against me, and my mouth went dry. I wanted him now.

"As you wish, Bunny." His chest vibrated as he spoke. I loved his bedroom voice; it was sexy, deep, and reminded me of fine wine and dark chocolate. Absolute decadence.

He pressed into me in one long slow stroke, my walls stretching to accommodate him. I shifted my hips, wanting him to go deeper inside me. Once he bumped against my wall, he remained motionless, breathing hard as he fought the urge to move.

"You don't have to go slow," I whispered against his lips.

"I need to. It is the only way I have to show you—" he cut himself off.

"Show me what?" Color me curious, I wanted to see anything this sexy Fae wanted to show me.

"That I am feeling something...for you," he whispered. "I don't know the words, but I can show you."

Tears leaked from my eyes and caught in my throat. To anyone else on earth, his confession wouldn't have meant anything, but to me it meant more than I could ever describe.

"Show me what you feel," I whispered. "Show me that I belong to you."

And so, he did. Pix never lost control as he slid in and out, sheathing himself and then pulling out to rub my tight walls. His stamina was impressive, and his muscles never showed fatigue.

Myth pulled me back against his chest, holding my hips still as Pixie slowly increased his pace. Heat rushed to my channel at the sexiness of having one mate hold me still while the other thrust into me.

Mmmm...so hot.

My breathing grew shallow, and my heart rate accelerated. I was nearing my release. Pixie was too, if his growls and the hard staccato pump of his hips were anything to go by. I wanted him to speed up, but I also wanted to milk this moment for everything it was worth.

Milk it. Ha!

That's when I felt it, the pulsing heat of Pix's throbbing member. It was followed by the feeling of being massaged as he pulled out and slowly thrust back in. The ribbed ridges that twisted around his erection were the thing of wet dreams. Finally, the infuriating fae increased his speed, urging us toward our climax. Even in my foggy lust-filled mind, I saw the humor of the situation and a giggle escaped.

He was literally screwing me.

I'm just glad you stopped being a prude and let your freak flag fly after I left!

I froze, every muscle in my body seizing up in panic. It had an unexpected outcome as my body clamped down around Pix's magical tool. He sank deep one final time, and we gave ourselves to the waves of pleasure that washed over us. As he held my trembling body, I caught something flickering in his eyes. I would have sworn that while it might not be love, it was affection. I would take it!

Whew. Someone needs to turn on the AC because it is hot in here!

Dear goddess... Was that...*Beasty?*

CHAPTER NINETEEN

Tia

"**I**t can't be! Beasty? Is that you?" I asked the question out loud, even though she had only spoken in my head.

Myth pulled me onto his lap, slipping his arms around my waist. "Shh. Calm down, love," he murmured soothingly. "Why do you think Beasty is here?"

"Probably because there is a very wanton voice in her mind," Pix grumbled.

"You heard the voice?" Myth and I asked the question at the same time.

"Yes, I was listening to her thoughts while we... While we made love." Until my dying day, which was a very long time for an immortal, I would never forget the sight of the rosy blush as it spread across Pixie's face.

I leaned to the side and gave him a soft kiss on the lips. He smiled and brushed an unruly lock of hair from my face.

Twisting to look at Myth over my shoulder I said, "I know you heard it! The stupid comment about parking?"

His face paled, something I would have thought impossible. "Beasty's back?" Myth's voice cracked and I couldn't tell if he was asking a question or stating a fact.

"This is good news, correct?" Pix asked, looking somewhat confused. "Beasty helped guide you in the past on how to better use your powers. She can help protect you while we visit the wizards and the werewolves."

"She is also a sexual deviant with a one-track mind," Myth grumbled and nibbled at his lip.

"I fail to see how that is a problem?" Pixie's voice had gone back to its usual flat emotionless tone, and somehow that dry tone combined with his comment sent me into a fit of laughter.

I like this Fae mate! Beasty said gleefully. *The fae are strange creatures that avoid commitment, but they're excellent lovers. I'm impressed you managed to snag him as a mate. You go, girl!* She gave me a mental high five, which gave me a headache.

Yep. There was no doubt in my mind that Beasty was, indeed, back in my mind.

I decided to get straight to the point. *I am thrilled to have you back in my mind, I think, but aren't you supposed to be confined in the butt crack of the universe, or something?*

She sighed. *You've seen my memories. When I roamed the Earth as Tiamat, Dragoness of the Sea, the gods did me dirty. I wanted to be surrounded by my family and have fun with my life. They took that from me, and I let myself become consumed with revenge. It is always about balance, Cupcake. We threw that balance into chaos so many millennia ago, and it has never truly been stable since. More dragons were created to try and stabilize things, but everything we tried failed in the long term. You are my one and only chance to change my legacy. You will fix what we broke and set everything right. The other gods and I still don't see eye to eye on everything, but we can acknowledge our mistakes. So, to answer your question. I'm not in the butt crack because I can't let you fail, or everything I've done will have been for nothing.*

I wondered why nobody had told me before that I was just a pawn of the gods in their silly little game.

Because you aren't a pawn! Beasty insisted. *You know that we are of one essence, and you know that you are a royal dragoness. You carry the power of both a goddess and a royal shifter. The gods have also given you gifts. It was their way of showing they wished to right the wrongs of their past. I have not been allowed to interfere since you merged with your dragon, but I can interact with you as long as you come to me first. It's not just me who is rooting for you. Many of the other gods have found a way to pop in here and there to guide you or arrange an accidental meeting that would be beneficial for you. Tia, you aren't a pawn—you are our only hope.*

I thought over her words, trying to decide for myself if she was telling the truth. Memories began to pop into my mind. Running down the mountain straight into Luke and Levi's arms. Damien just happening to be in the middle of a forest. Ernie.

Beasty chuckled. *Yes, Ernie is more god than human, and has watched your growth with pride. His son Leo isn't just a rare warlock, nope! That shy hottie takes after his dad when it comes to genetics. Your kingdom will be ruled by the best of the best. A perfect example of fairness and equality.*

I saw the kingdom in the memories that you left behind. I was going to try to raise it, after I go visit the wizards and were-wolves— I was cut off before I could finish my thought.

Oh my! I got here just in time to act as your fairy godmother. No offence, Pixie.

None taken. His expression was back to its usual neutral position, but I felt all my mates in the mind link listening to Beasty as she jumped excitedly from one topic to the next. My heart ached as I realized how lonely she must have been.

Okay, so here's the thing, Lollipop, she continued. *You are queen, not just of a species, or a country. No, you are the freaking Queen of the World. Get that through your thick and adorably humble head. You don't go to them, they come to you. Give the supernatural and human leaders of the world coordi-nates and tell them their presence is expected tomorrow afternoon.*

"But that gives them just over twenty-four hours!" I didn't even realize I had spoken out loud until I saw Myth jump at my outburst.

So? Freaking Queen of the World. Politics is a manipula-tive game, and one that I advise you to avoid. However, in this case, a little show of power is in order.

Loud celebratory whoops drifted up the stairs from my guys who apparently loved her idea.

Please, Tia! Leo begged through the link. He'd missed the part about being a demi-god it seemed, or else he was just more interested in this new plan.

I took a deep breath and gathered up my courage. *Fine. Let's do this. We leave in three hours.*

My men scattered off to make calls and pack their bags for the road trip. Teleporting would be far easier, but since none of us had physically been to those exact coordinates before, it didn't seem safe to attempt it. Instead, we would teleport as close as possible and then travel by car.

The world as we knew it was going to change drastically in the next twenty-four hours.

Chapter Twenty

Tia

We reached the deserted stretch of shoreline before anyone else had arrived. This was the first time I had ever seen the ocean in person. The world around me faded away, the sound disappearing like someone had hit mute. All I heard was the playful roar of the sea as it called me home.

Home. My heart twisted painfully, and a knot formed in my throat. I had loved the small house high in the mountains where I grew up, and I was attached to the cabin by the mountain lake where I had shared so many incredible memories with my mates. Yet, I had never felt like I belonged in those places. I was comfortable and content, but that wasn't the same. This was where I belonged.

The salty spray splashed across my face, a playful touch

from a long-lost friend. I laughed in delight, spinning in a circle to embrace the sea. Water curled around my torso like a snake, while another tendril wove its way around my fingers in a mesmerizing pattern.

All my life I had craved water. I'd found joy in the lakes and streams and found comfort in long, hot baths. At the ball, it had felt natural to fight from the pool, the water an eager ally. But none of that compared to the saltwater of the sea.

"Guys! We've made it! We're home!" I squealed as I splashed toward them. My laughter was apparently contagious because Levi and Luke were quick to join me in the foamy white surf.

"I love seeing you happy," Myth whispered to me as he smiled and twirled me in the sand.

I kissed his nose and danced my way, albeit badly, back into the sea.

Beasty spoke. *It's almost time, Cupcake. This isn't going to be easy.*

I know, but I've got this! And you are here to guide me. I was antsy and eager to get this show on the road.

I will be watching, along with the other gods, but I won't be inside your mind. You pulled me to you, which means the rules changed and I can interact with you, but this is something you must do alone.

I understood why it had to be this way, but I didn't have to like it.

I'm proud of you, Tia. You have become more than I could have possibly dreamed. This is your moment to shine in front of the world. Now is not the time to be humble; presentation is everything and you need to blow their minds. Show them why there will never be anyone quite like you. Well, I imagine the twin dragonesses you carry will be a lot like you, but that takes away from the point I was trying to make...

I was having two daughters? Twins?

You didn't know? I thought you did. My bad. To her credit, she did sound repentant.

She had to be wrong though. There was only one heartbeat.

Your daughters share a bond so close that their hearts beat in sync. They are going to be amazing, Tia. But right now, you need to focus on changing the world. Think about the peace you want your children and the children around the globe to grow up with.

And with a soft pop, she was gone. I had a momentary pang of sadness over losing her so soon, but I shoved that into the corner of my mind to be dealt with later. I could see throngs of supernaturals and humans moving onto the beach. My mates were busy organizing the chaos, so I allowed myself this one moment.

Closing my eyes, I savored the soft breeze that teased my hair. I opened my mouth, allowing the salt to play across my taste buds. I breathed in the power of the sea, and I felt the waves beckoning.

I straightened my back and allowed all the insecurities to fall away. I was ready. This was what I had been born to do. The waves swirled around me, welcoming me home. I allowed myself to be sucked beneath the sparkling surface.

I'd thought I would struggle for air, or that I would automatically kick to the surface, but instead, my body shifted smoothly into my dragon form. My long tail easily propelled me through the water and toward the beacon that seemed to be calling me louder with my every heartbeat.

The ocean changed from one color to another the deeper I swam. The waters shifted from aquamarine to royal blue, and finally to a deep navy. My heart lurched in my chest as I spotted the silhouette of the castle from Beasty's memories. She had made so many wonderful memories in it, before the fight had broken out between the gods and they had sunk her home in retaliation. The world might have forgotten it ever existed, but that was about to change.

I swam to the highest balcony, the one that would have overlooked happy citizens as they bustled about their business. My body shimmered and shifted, all without conscious thought. The powerful dragon changed easily into my partially shifted form, the form I had decided would be my natural state. I focused my mind and went over every skill I had absorbed through practice and Beasty's plethora of memories.

I called upon the sea to obey me. My magic expanded slowly, enveloping me, then the balcony, and so on until it had become a glowing dome around the entire city. It was time. With every bit of mental strength and magic I possessed, I picked the city up off the sandy ocean floor and sent it, along with myself, hurtling toward the surface.

I didn't slow as the water shifted from the dark blue of the deep sea to the crystal blue of the surface. Water rushed along my body and across every inch of the long-lost city. With a mighty crash, we burst up out of the ocean, a gigantic wall of water exploding around us.

The wind smacked into my face hard enough to steal what was left of my breath. Then it tugged at my gown. I looked down as shock worked through me. I was wearing a beautiful gown I had never seen before. It rippled like waves, the light sparkling along its every delicate fold. Midnight blue, aquamarine, and cobalt blended together in a breathtaking ombre effect. Water splashed and rippled where the fabric should have been. I was wearing a gown made of water — one that was both inspired by the ocean and created by the ocean.

Once the entire city was above the surface, I called the earth and sand to obey my orders. When I was finished, my city sat perched on an island high enough above sea level to avoid flooding. A sandstone walkway led from the city gate to the beach 1500 feet away. With nothing more than a simple thought, I could sink the walkway beneath the sea and cut off visitors...or enemies.

I looked down at the faces that dotted the shoreline. Each one bore the exact same expression. Awe. Good, that should make this next part easier.

"You were all called here to make a decision," I said. "I know that everyone here has heard rumors about me. I can assure you, most of those stories were untrue. What is true is that I am bringing back the old way, the Dragon's way. This world is in constant unrest. Wars are fought daily, and innocent lives are lost. All because the balance was disrupted long before any of us were born."

Confused murmurs rippled through the gathered crowds, and I felt their unease growing. I needed to explain faster.

"Your governments will stand, but they will be overseen by me and my mates," I continued. "The werewolves will continue to run as individual packs within their territory, but they will be overseen by my mates, Luke and Levi." I teleported said twins to stand at my side.

"The wizards will keep their council, but they will report directly to my warlock mate, Leo."

One by one I brought my mates to the balcony and explained how things would work. It seemed either fate, the gods, or dumb luck had worked it so that I was mated to each of the paranormal species. Together, we could create equality and peace...if we were given the chance. The murmurs of the crowd grew louder. Now came the part I despised. Rallying my magic, I sent it racing along the ground.

"I will not tolerate cruelty at another's expense," I called out. "Nor will I tolerate greed or a willful disregard for another's life. I would prefer to be a sleepy godmother who never needs to dish out judgement. But if that is what I must do, so be it. The world is going to change; I will restore the balance and protect those who are weak. You will either stand by my side as an ally in protecting this world, or you will be my enemy. I hope you choose wisely."

My magic moved unseen through the audience, testing people's intentions, looking for a stain of darkness on their souls.

The pack leaders of the werewolves stepped forward first. I smiled when I recognized Trixie and an uncomfortable

Damien among them. I remembered the day I first met him when he complained that werewolves stank, yet that morning he had informed us that he would be moving to live among Trixie's pack.

She had taken over as Alpha of Cage's pack, a position I'd known she was made for since she fought to stand against my command at our very first meeting. Underneath the bimbo makeup, fake tan, and clingy attitude, there had been a strong woman with a loyal heart. She was the first female Alpha, and I was rooting for her.

"The werewolves stand with you," the leaders cried out. "Long live Tiamat, Dragoness of the Sea!" To my horror, they all bowed. My magic swirled around each person present but found only hearts that were eager to make changes.

Then, the wizards stepped forward, repeating verbatim the words of the wolves. But only a handful spoke with sincerity.

"I will not accept false promises and lies," I said with authority. "You have been judged."

Only a third of the wizards remained standing after my magic executed those who cared more about riches than about the needs of others. My heart ached at such a loss of life, and the visual evidence of how far gone so many of our leaders were.

The vampires and humans both pledged loyalty, and my magic enacted judgement where necessary. It was uplifting to see the number of leaders eager to roll up their sleeves and change the world. At the same time, every death, although warranted, weighed heavily on my heart. I reminded myself of the prophecy. Either we made changes, or the wars would escalate and the world as we knew it would be no more.

When it was all over, the sea breeze blew the smoke away from the beach. I sucked in my breath at the sight in front of me. Every single person was kneeling, an arm over their chest in a sign of loyalty. I crossed my own arm over my chest and released a victorious shout into the air. My shout was echoed by every voice on the beach, and soon, cheers broke out. This was the start of a new world.

At that moment, a figure strode from the arched hallway behind me. As I turned instinctively towards them, Pixie quickly moved to stand protectively in front of me. I peered over his broad shoulder to see a woman with long, pointy ears and piercing eyes walking toward us.

She stopped in front of Pixie. "Hello, brother."

"Your Majesty." Pixie tilted his head.

Shut. The. Front. Door.

"She's...she's your sister? And you...you're a—"

The woman shouldered her way past Pixie to stand in front of me. "Yes, and yes," she answered. She held out her hand to shake, and bracing my spine, I took it.

"I have come to congratulate you on what you have accomplished today," she said. "I must admit, I did not believe it was possible for a single female to shift the entire destiny of the world."

Turning to Pixie, she addressed him, "Does the Dragon Queen know of your mission in the Earth realm?"

"Unfortunately, we have been a bit busy, and I haven't had the opportunity to discuss it with her," Pixie replied. "I had hoped to locate you and work to create a plan with Tiamat on how to deal with everything."

"Then I will tell her." Yep, she definitely had the blunt Fae thing going on.

Turning back to face me, the Fae queen continued her explanation, "Earth had become an increasing threat to itself, and the realms connected to it. The Fae sent their best warriors to scout the Earth and decide whether it was logical to let it continue on its course, thereby risking other realms should the evil spread, or if we should cleanse this world of humans and paranormals and allow nature to reclaim this damaged planet."

My mouth dropped open.

"I was given a tip, from a mutual friend, that placing my brother as a guard during the Harmony Ball would prove a wise move. I am pleased to see that the gamble paid off, and now my people can go home far earlier than we had thought possible. My scouts have reported that one by one, the criminals and dirty leaders they were scouting are dropping dead, bursting into smoking ash. I assume that has something to do with you?"

I nodded. "Yes, I have sent my magic to circle the globe. This is a fresh start." In truth, the seek and destroy mission was draining my energy quickly. I needed to sit down, but refused to show even a hint of weakness.

"Judgement day has arrived, and just in the nick of time. I had already given the order to bring over our troops on the next full moon. It would have all been over in a matter of hours, and many innocent lives would have been sacrificed for the good of the realms. You have an open invitation to visit me in Fae." The Fae queen gave a polite, but firm, nod. "I look forward to seeing you again, ally."

Explanation concluded, the queen turned and began moving toward the arched hallway again. "Are you coming, brother?" she asked Pixie.

He shook his head. "No, I will be staying here, with my mate."

The Fae queen stumbled a half step, barely managing to mask her surprise. "You mated? A permanent bonding?"

"Yes, I am bound to her for eternity. I do not regret my decision." Pix looked at me and his eyes softened. "In fact, I would make the same decision again if the opportunity presented itself."

"But...but Fae do not bond for life! That hasn't been heard of in many centuries. We aren't even sure it is possible." The Fae queen studied both of our faces, searching for something. "Did you glow for her?" she asked her brother.

Pixie hesitated, seeming confused as to what she was referring to. So, I spoke up. "Yes, before we bonded, he glowed for me," I said. "It was comforting and eased my pain."

A smile ghosted across her beautiful face. "When I was a child, I heard the stories of Fae men who would fall in love with a woman, and he would glow as an outward sign of his love. I read everything I could on partners given by fate and the glow. But I could never prove if either had truly existed among the Fae. I would have continued my studies, but I was called to rule at a young age and there was no time to explore those silly tales. Now I find out that they were true all along."

"I never knew you wanted something different," Pixie said, sounding stunned.

"I did. But that doesn't matter now," the queen replied flippantly, trying to sound bored. She faced me again with a smile. "Tiamat, I am pleased to call you sister as well as ally. Welcome to the family."

Then she turned and seemed to disappear into thin air without the audible pop of teleporting. I had a lot to learn about Fae.

Exhaustion hit me and I yawned. In an instant, six men were at my side. "I'm fine, guys," I insisted, "just ready for a hot bath and a good night's sleep."

Then I paused, wondering if I should tell them.

I must have spoken inside the link because their eyes locked on me, and in unison they asked, "Tell us what?"

I sucked at keeping secrets, and this time was no different. "I'm...I'm pregnant with twin dragonesses."

I could have heard a crab fart. It was that quiet.

Ivo took a running leap off the side of the castle, and my heart plummeted until his sleek black dragon surged into the sky above us. He roared in joy and filled the darkening sky with red and orange flames. The embers rained down around us, a brilliant display of glowing confetti.

"We're having twins!" Leo cried out. He fist pumped the air and flashed me a wink. I really needed to tell him about the whole demi-god thing. It certainly explained his sudden transformation.

Luke and Levi shifted and howled the good news into the

night. Myth slapped Leo on the back and joined him in shouting the news to the sea life around us.

Pixie caught me up in his arms, and to my amazement, he glowed. It was much brighter than it had been those nights in the dungeon, but it was just as inviting, and I wanted to bask in it.

"Bunny?" His voice was soft.

I leaned back so I could see his face. "Hmm?"

"I love you."

My heart swelled. "I love you, too!" I cried out. I wrapped my arms around his neck and cried tears of joy. Around us, our circle whistled and clapped.

"It's about time you two owned up to it!" Leo said with a laugh, wrapping us both in a bear hug.

You did good, Cupcake. Just like I knew you would. Now, go let your mates do some cattle-prodding in your—

I cut her off, already knowing where her mind was heading. *Thanks, Beasty. For everything.*

My life had taken one unexpected turn after another, but it was absolutely perfect.

THE END

ACKNOWLEDGMENTS

I want to thank ...

My readers, for taking the time to read, rate and/or review my books, as well as those who messaged me with sweet comments and encouragement. I was a nervous wreck when I released the first book, not sure if readers would enjoy my voice as an author. I was an unknown author, but y'all gave me a chance! The overwhelming amount of love and support from my readers has truly taken my breath away. I am 100% confident I have the best readers on earth, and I can't ever thank you guys enough for pushing me ever closer to my dream!

Author Alana Ash (we aren't related, but I totally claim her as my sister) for being my own personal cheerleader and keeping me company while I stayed up all hours of the night to complete these books. I hope you are ready to do it all over again!

My amazing team of beta and ARC readers, editors, and my formatter for working with me around my crazy chaotic schedule! Y'all rock! And a big thanks to my family for feeding me when I turned into a grumpy old troll who never left her writing cave.

ABOUT SEDONA ASHE

Sedona Ashe doesn't reserve her sarcasm for her books; her poor husband can tell you that her wit, humor, and snarky attitude are just part of her daily life. While she loves writing paranormal shifter reverse harem novels, she's a sucker for true love, twisted situations, and wacky humor.

Sedona lives in a small town at the base of the Great Smoky Mountains in Tennessee. She and her husband share their home with their three children, adorable pup, five cats, two pet foxes, chickens, three crazy turkeys, two cows, and over a hundred reptiles.

When she isn't working, she enjoys getting away from the computer to hike, free dive, travel, study languages, and capture the essence of places and people in her photography. She has a crazy goal of writing a million words in a year and spending six months exploring Indonesia.

Hi beautiful readers!

If you are looking for something else to read while you wait for my next weird and kinda funny book to drop, please check out my other series!

But Did You Die?
Dragon Goddess
Royal Storm of Atlantis
Three of Me
Dino Magic

Or click HERE to see all my books!

www.ingramcontent.com/pod-product-compliance
Lightning Source LLC
Chambersburg PA
CBHW032250020726
47495CB00001B/40